SOME DIE ELOQUENT

"So determinedly traditional and classic . . . that almost everybody will be charmed . . . Miss Aird writes with insight and skill."
—*The New York Times Book Review*

"A tidily plotted and ends-knotted-neatly tale."
—*Publishers Weekly*

BY CATHERINE AIRD

"Aird's intelligence shines through every sentence."
—*The Washington Post*

BANTAM BOOKS offers the finest in classic and modern English murder mysteries. Ask your bookseller for the books you have missed.

Agatha Christie
DEATH ON THE NILE
A HOLIDAY FOR MURDER
THE MOUSETRAP AND
  OTHER PLAYS
THE MYSTERIOUS AFFAIR
  AT STYLES
POIROT INVESTIGATES
POSTERN OF FATE
THE SECRET ADVERSARY
THE SEVEN DIALS
  MYSTERY
SLEEPING MURDER

Carter Dickson
DEATH IN FIVE BOXES

Catherine Aird
HENRIETTA WHO?
HIS BURIAL TOO
A LATE PHOENIX
A MOST CONTAGIOUS
  GAME
PARTING BREATH
PASSING STRANGE
THE RELIGIOUS BODY
SLIGHT MOURNING
SOME DIE ELOQUENT
THE STATELY HOME
  MURDER

Patricia Wentworth
MISS SILVER COMES TO
  STAY
SHE CAME BACK

Elizabeth Lemarchand
BURIED IN THE PAST

Margaret Erskine
CASE WITH THREE
  HUSBANDS
THE FAMILY AT
  TAMMERTON
NO. 9 BELMONT SQUARE
THE WOMAN AT
  BELGUARDO

Margaret Yorke
CAST FOR DEATH
DEAD IN THE MORNING

Margery Allingham
BLACK PLUMES
TETHER'S END
TRAITOR'S PURSE

Elizabeth Daly
THE BOOK OF THE CRIME
EVIDENCE OF THINGS
  SEEN
THE WRONG WAY DOWN

SOME DIE ELOQUENT

BY CATHERINE AIRD

BANTAM BOOKS
TORONTO · NEW YORK · LONDON · SYDNEY

*All of the characters in this book are fictitious,
and any resemblance to actual persons, living or dead,
is purely coincidental.*

This low-priced Bantam Book
*has been completely reset in a type face
designed for easy reading, and was printed
from new plates. It contains the complete
text of the original hard-cover edition.*
NOT ONE WORD HAS BEEN OMITTED.

SOME DIE ELOQUENT

*A Bantam Book / published by arrangement with
Doubleday & Co., Inc.*

PRINTING HISTORY

*Doubleday edition published March 1980
A Detective Book Club Alternate Selection April 1980
Bantam edition / June 1981*

ISBN 0-553-14338-7

Published in the United States and Canada

*Bantam Books are published by Bantam Books, Inc. Its trade-
mark, consisting of the words "Bantam Books" and the portrayal of a bantam, is Registered in U.S. Patent and Trademark
Office and in other countries. Marca Registrada. Bantam
Books, Inc., 666 Fifth Avenue, New York, New York 10103.*

PRINTED IN THE UNITED STATES OF AMERICA

0 9 8 7 6 5 4

For Sylvia Cox and Norah Mallet—Scylla and Charybdis of my syntax—with love

Some die eloquent . . .
Some die wholly in half a breath
Some—give trouble for half a year.

A *Death-Bed*
by Rudyard Kipling

The chapter heads are taken from "The Canon's Yeoman's Tale" from *The Canterbury Tales* by Geoffrey Chaucer, translated into modern English by Nevill Coghill.

Chapter 1

For I imagine I have said enough
To raise the devil, be he never so rough.

It was a very long time indeed since Detective Inspector
C. D. Sloan of the Criminal Investigation Department
of the Berebury Division of the Calleshire County Police Force had felt such a fish out of water.

It was an unusual experience for him.

There are very few situations in daily and professional life which find your fully fledged police inspector
at a real disadvantage. In the nature of things, by the
time a man has reached that particular rank, working
experience alone has made him ready and confident for
the holding of rule, and life itself has taught him not
only his own place in the world, but that such niches
come in all sizes.

Actually it was his place in the world at this particular moment that was the whole trouble with Detective
Inspector Sloan. Whatever his rightful position in the
cosmos was on a normal Tuesday afternoon (on duty,
probably, and very much for preference) he didn't
really want to be where he happened to be now. Moreover, for a man whose collar had given up feeling tight
in tricky situations a long time ago, who knew what to
do with his hands, and who wasn't conspicuously large
for a policeman, he was feeling very uncomfortable.

He had known beforehand that he would and had
said as much.

It had done him no good at all.

"It's not a lot to ask, is it?" his wife, Margaret, had
said to that.

1

"No."

"One afternoon."

"I could make a start on the decorating," he had offered, "instead."

The corners of his wife's mouth had twitched at the very idea.

"The back bedroom's got to be done," he had said.

"It'll get done," Margaret Sloan had replied serenely.

"Before . . ."

"Before."

He had tried another tack.

"There's a villain . . ."

"Yes?"

"I've been keeping him under observation."

"Have you?"

"All the week."

"Well?"

"He might try something on Tuesday."

"In the middle of the afternoon?"

"He doesn't like night work."

"But"—her mouth twitched again—"he does like Tuesdays?"

"You never know."

"And now," his wife had pronounced sweetly, "you never will know, will you?"

He had given in meekly enough after that at the time but now that he was here he didn't feel any better about it. Accidents and incidents, charge room and court room, cottage and castle, had found the man unperturbed, his savoir-faire unshaken: but this was different.

"Of course," said Margaret Sloan, leading the way, "if you're afraid of hospitals . . ."

Sloan wasn't afraid of hospitals. He was even familiar with this one—the Berebury District General Hospital. Well, with certain parts of it, that is. All policemen got to know specialised corners of their local hospital over the years: the Casualty Department for a start, though they called that something else now. As they'd changed the name of so many other things these days, they'd changed the name of that lately too.

Accident and Emergency Department they called it

now: not that that fooled anyone. It was still where they took you if you smashed your car up or tried to cut your throat. And where you took the small children who stuffed beads up their noses or who had swallowed Mummy's pills. Or Pills. Or detergents. Safe as houses was an expression that never misled an ambulanceman.

Variety was the essence, of course. That was why Casualty sisters stayed so long on the job. Like station sergeants, they had some of the action, all of the interest, and very little of the routine which stultified lesser mortals. They took on all comers, in fact.

And when Sister Casualty—Sloan didn't suppose for a single moment that she thought of herself by any other name—had troublemakers in her patch she would ring down to the police station. There her soul mate in office so to speak—the Berebury station sergeant— very soon had someone around to sort out the drunk and the drugged. She had her own ways of dealing with the merely belligerent.

Detective Inspector Sloan knew her department well enough. It was this part of the hospital—where he was now—that he had never been in before today.

"Other husbands come," his wife had told him by way of encouragement.

That fact had not been a great deal of consolation at the time when she had said it and was absolutely none at all now. This was because as far as he could see there was only one other husband in sight.

"There," said Mrs. Sloan triumphantly, "I said you wouldn't be the only one."

"That," muttered Sloan, "is not the point."

"Isn't one other man enough?" asked his wife, settling down on a regulation hospital chair.

"Quite enough."

"Well, then . . ."

It wasn't that only one other husband wasn't enough either: policemen weren't shy.

"It's Larky Nolson," said Sloan distantly.

Being bracketed even in the same category group of husband with Larky Nolson was no cause for gratification in a self-respecting policeman. The kindest thing you could say about Larky was that he was an ethical cripple: and they didn't have a department which dealt with that sort of deformity at the Berebury District General Hospital.

Yet.

It would come, of course. In time. In a Brave New World. Born out of Science by Experiment or realised by Accidental Observation sired by Man Leaning on a Gate. Either way it would be called progress. And they didn't have it yet.

It was about the only department missing today, conceded Sloan. There were signposts within the hospital to all sorts of places—some as unfamiliar as Cotopaxi and Popocatepetl. In fact a truly bewildering maze of corridors confronted the new arrival. They led to an even more bewildering set of departments with strange-sounding names. He for one didn't care all that much for the sound of Haematology. If they meant "blood" they should say so: and wild horses wouldn't get him near anything called Nuclear Medicine.

There was one man, though, who would have been quite at home in the main entrance. That was Inspector Harpe of Traffic Division. And he wouldn't have felt so strange because hospitals, like roads, had suddenly gone symbolic too in their direction signs. And international. Words were out; logos were in.

You didn't move to numbers either these days. Not if you weren't in the Army. Cars and people in hospitals now took direction from a series of stereotyped pictures.

They hadn't all been an unqualified success, not the road ones anyway. "Uneven Surface Ahead" and "Men Working"—an exclamation mark—brought out the ribaldry, not unconnected with Miss Mae West, down at the police station, while "Stop Children" seemed to bring out the worst in everyone. Sloan had noticed that they had their counterpart in the hospital. Here, a tooth of prehistoric dimension pointed the way to the dental department while an eye with ancient Egyptian overtones indicated the general direction of the ophthalmic clinic.

Sloan fidgeted in his chair.

They did it all by symbols these days.

Not for those who couldn't read.

But for those who couldn't understand.

Neither thinking about something else nor the fidgeting saved him from having his own eye caught by Larky Nolson.

Sloan scowled.

The last time he had seen Larky had been strictly in the line of duty. Detective Inspector Sloan's duty. It had been in the Crown Court and that meeting was the natural consequence of an earlier confrontation over a little matter of safe-breaking at a greengrocer's shop.

Larky must be out again then.

He took a quick glance at the woman sitting beside Larky and revised this. Larky must have been "outside" for some time now. Or been on parole.

Larky saw him looking his way and jerked his head towards Sloan in open recognition.

Sloan scowled again.

At least, Sloan decided, one good thing was that it was Mrs. Nolson, his wife, whom Larky was with. He hadn't gone and got some girl into trouble.

"Someone you know?" Margaret Sloan asked him cautiously.

"In a manner of speaking," said Sloan.

"Ah . . ." If you were married to a policeman you had to get used to the fact that there were some people your husband introduced to you and some he didn't.

"The greengrocer's job on the corner of Pig Lane," he said.

"I remember." Margaret Sloan nodded.

"Good," said Sloan warmly. "A good memory's important. You need it on both sides of the family."

"It was the safe, wasn't it?" said Mrs. Sloan, ignoring this.

"It was." Sloan grinned. He hadn't forgotten the detail either. Larky Nolson, small-time burglar, and Detective Inspector Sloan, policeman, had both been surprised at the amount of money in the greengrocer's safe. Mrs. Sloan, housewife, hadn't. Nor presumably had Mrs. Nolson.

"Laying up for his old age," Superintendent Leeyes

had remarked when they had told him about it. "So my wife says."

Larky Nolson was doing more than just nod to Detective Inspector Sloan now. He was getting up from his seat beside Mrs. Nolson and coming over. Sloan, too, rose to his feet and then carefully made his way to a square of open space behind the clinic waiting area. Choosing your own ground was something you learned to do early on when you went on the beat. It was halfway towards winning.

Larky Nolson, however, had not come to do battle.

"Long time no see, Inspector," he began.

"That, Larky," responded Sloan easily, "is quite all right with me."

"Too long," said the little man meaningfully.

"I can bear it."

"Don't be like that."

"The longer the better," said Sloan firmly. That, in essence, had been the sentiment prevailing in the Crown Court too.

"That man . . ." Larky sucked his teeth.

"Which man?"

"Called hisself a judge."

"A good one."

"Him a judge!" said Larky richly. "He wouldn't even know which way was up."

"Black from white," declared Sloan. "That's all he needs to know."

Larky sniffed. "And the lawyers were no better."

"They're not in it for their health," said Sloan obliquely.

"You can say that again," said Larky indignantly. "And there wasn't much to choose between them if you ask me—mine or theirs."

"The legal profession's duty," recited Sloan piously, "is to the court."

"You'd have thought though," grumbled Nolson, ignoring this, "that mine could have got me less than he did."

"With your record?"

"If he was half as clever as he thought he was I'd have been a free man."

"I expect he knows a villain when he sees one."

"The other brief didn't help either. Your man."

"He isn't meant to," Sloan reminded him. "He's there to prosecute."

"Persecute, more like. Real nasty, I thought he was. Where did you get him from? The Kremlin or somewhere?"

"Too many short sentences about," said Sloan briskly.

"He made it all sound so much worse," persisted the burglar.

"Safes don't fall open on their own," observed the policeman.

The safe was a sore point with Larky. It had been difficult to open and that had been his undoing. He changed his ground.

"That your wife you're with over there?"

"It isn't anyone else's," said Sloan evenly.

"Your first?" enquired Nolson.

"Yes, as it happens it is."

"They're the worst," said Larky patronisingly.

"Are they?"

"Didn't think," sniffed Nolson, gaining strength, "that I'd ever see you here, Inspector."

"Say that again, Larky, and I'll hit you."

"Another little copper on the way." He rolled his eyes. "Give me strength."

"Causing an affray," said Sloan, moving forward irately. "That's what I'll get you for, Nolson. . . ."

The little man backed away. "It's as quiet as houses, Inspector. Honest . . ."

It wasn't as quiet as anything.

Hospitals were never quiet. And never still. At that moment the turgid procedure of the outpatient clinic produced a movement. A sister appeared and a woman disappeared through a door. Both men looked back towards their wives.

"I'm next," muttered Larky inappropriately.

Sloan started to make his way back to his own wife's side. He was diverted by the sight of another face he knew.

Dr. Dabbe was consultant pathologist to the Berebury District Hospital Management Committee. He was also police surgeon to the Berebury Division Police Force.

"Ah, Sloan, there you are."

"Good afternoon, Doctor."

The pathologist looked past Sloan and along the rows of heavily pregnant waiting patients, murmuring under his breath, *"Abou ben Adhem* [May His Tribe Increase]." He picked out Mrs. Sloan and waved to her.

"They said I'd find you here, Sloan."

"Did they?" said Sloan impassively.

"You're wanted," said Dr. Dabbe.

"Where?"

"Here."

"In the hospital?"

"Yes," said the pathologist.

"Oh, I am, am I?" began Sloan.

"Come along, man . . ."

"Who wants me?"

"I do, of course," said Dabbe impatiently.

"Where?"

"In the mortuary. Really, Sloan, I haven't got all afternoon to waste."

Neither had Sloan. He stood indecisively between his wife and the police surgeon. Margaret Sloan was giving him a look quite as enigmatic as that of the Mona Lisa. . . .

"There's no time to hang about," said the doctor. "Mortons are already on their way now."

Then Margaret Sloan raised her hand in an ironic gesture of absolution. Detective Inspector Sloan, a free man now, turned to the pathologist and said with alacrity, "Which way?"

* * *

The mortuary was on the ground floor of the hospital and admission from the outside world was by way of two sets of double doors. The outer set kept the curious at bay. The inner pair led to the mortuary itself.

By the time Dr. Dabbe and Detective Inspector Sloan reached the department a vehicle was already

neatly sandwiched between the two sets of doors—
looking for all the world like a barge trapped between
lock gates on a canal.

A plump young man clambered out of the driver's
seat as they approached. He nodded to the mortuary
attendant and then gave the engine bonnet an affectionate slap.

"Nice, isn't it?" he said to the world at large.

"Very, Fred," said Sloan.

And it was. As an undertaker's van it was a master-
piece of both strict convention and ambiguity.

"We've just taken delivery," said Fred Morton
proudly. "It's the latest thing."

It was white—like an ambulance—and indeed had
two red crosses on the smoked darkly opaque windows
of the rear double doors but there was also a precau-
tionary black stripe running round the white walls,
pointing a warning note. The neighbours would learn
nothing from a visit of a van like this. Only the cogno-
scenti—the police, the fire people, real ambulance-
men—would know what to make of it and its cargo.

"I said to Dad that we've got to move with the
times. . . ."

"I remember," remarked Dr. Dabbe, "your father
saying that to his father."

"We've still got that hearse," said young Morton reverently. "You can't touch Rolls-Royces. Fitted into the
stable a treat, of course, otherwise Grandad would
never have had it."

Morton and Son, Undertakers; Nethergate, Berebury, went back a long time.

Fred Morton moved around to open the rear doors.
"There's one thing Dad won't let go, though."

"What's that?" asked Sloan curiously. Undertaking
was a conservative trade and Morton and Son were
more conservative than most.

"The sign above the shop." He sighed. "I just can't
get Dad to change it for all that it doesn't make sense."

"What does it say?"

"Superior Funerals!" He groaned. "In black and
gold lettering with scrolls—I ask you." He opened both

the van doors as he spoke. "Here you are, Doctor. Beatrice Gwendoline Wansdyke."

"And what, exactly," enquired Sloan as he walked into the mortuary proper with the pathologist, "did Beatrice Gwendoline Wansdyke die from?"

"Diabetes," said Dr. Dabbe. "Or so I am told."

"And?"

"And nothing," said Dr. Dabbe blandly, "unless I find something else as well."

"So what's the problem?"

"The problem," said Dr. Dabbe, "is not so much what she died from as what she died with, if you see what I mean."

"No," said Sloan uncompromisingly, "I don't see what you mean. What did she die with?"

"A quarter of a million pounds," said the doctor.

Chapter 2

Sharp was the hope and hard the supposition.

"A quarter of a million pounds," said Superintendent Leeyes flatly. "That's what I told the doctor."

Sloan was in the mortuary office using the pathologist's secretary's telephone to ring the police station.

"Just sitting there," said Leeyes. "Doing nothing."

"Sitting where?" asked Sloan. As assorted bank and train robbers had found to their discomfiture, money of that order of magnitude took up a lot of space.

"In her bank account."

"Not under the bed or anything like that?"

"Nothing like that," said Leeyes firmly. "In her bank account. That's how we heard about it."

"From the bank?" said Sloan startled.

"No, no," said Leeyes. "Well, not exactly."

Sloan waited for enlightenment.

"Constable Blake's wife," said Leeyes, "overheard two young girls—bank clerks, actually—talking in the check-out queue at the supermarket yesterday dinnertime."

"Ah."

"Says one to the other, 'Fancy dying with a quarter of a million pounds in the bank.'" Leeyes grunted. "'Before you can enjoy it,' says the other. 'Shame, isn't it? Mind you, she was old. . . .' Those were their words, Sloan."

"Then what?"

"Mrs. Blake—smart woman, Mrs. Blake . . ."

"Used to be in the force. Before she married Ted."

"Ah, that explains it. Well, she tails the pair of them . . ."

"Back to the bank?"

"Precisely. And we set about finding out who died yesterday. Only Miss Wansdyke."

Sloan cleared his throat. "There's no word out about any job of that size unaccounted for, is there, sir?"

"Not that I know of," replied Leeyes. "I've got someone down here at the station going through the back numbers now to be on the safe side all the same."

"It's a lot of money," he said warily.

"Better than Brink's," said Leeyes.

"Quite so," said Sloan, acknowledging this.

Every policeman had his own choice crime that he mulled over in much the same way as a connoisseur swirled his wine around in a glass to get the best of the bouquet. The Brink's Incorporated job in Boston was the one that continued to fascinate Superintendent Leeyes. Done by small-time men, he never failed to remind them. And that hadn't stopped it being the most daring bank robbery in history.

"That was in dollars, of course," added Leeyes now.

Sloan coughed. "It's not exactly a crime—er—in itself, so to speak, sir, to have that much money in the bank."

"It may not be," said Leeyes robustly, "but you must admit, Sloan, it's a bit funny for someone who lives in Ridley Road."

"It's very respectable up there," conceded Sloan.

"Exactly," said Leeyes, who beyond a certain point did not equate money with respectability. Not new money, that is. In the superintendent's book His Grace the Duke of Calleshire could have as much as he liked. That was different.

"In fact," persisted Sloan, "my wife would like us to think of moving that way now that . . ." He felt a pang of unease when he remembered his wife. Was she still sitting in the clinic, he wondered, or had she moved forward on the ante-natal conveyor belt?

Leeyes grunted. "A nice quiet neighborhood."

"Decent houses."

"Trees on the footpath."

"No through traffic," said Sloan.

"Grass verges," said Leeyes.

"Just local vehicles." Policemen grew to dislike cars.

"Near the tennis club."

"Good gardens, too, sir." Sloan's own recreation was growing roses. It was about the only one that went with his sort of working hours. "Clay soil."

"No trouble up there either." The superintendent added the ultimate police accolade.

"Not even on Saturday nights," said Sloan, completing the sketch of suburban delight. A Town and Country Planning Conference on urban housing amenity would have taken two days to get as far.

"See what I mean?" demanded Leeyes illogically. "What would someone living up in Ridley Road be doing with that much money?"

Sloan let the vision of him and his wife taking possession of a house in Ridley Road fade and said he didn't know. "Though there's always the football pools, sir," he said. "She might have said 'No publicity' to them and meant it. Some people do."

"First thing we checked," grunted Leeyes. "I don't know about you, Sloan, but it's the only way I can think of of getting your hands on that much money straight."

"Sad but true . . ."

"It is a melancholy indictment of modern society," intoned the superintendent in his best Watch Committee manner, "that gambling seems to be the only honest path to financial glory."

"Inheritance?" put in Sloan quickly before the superintendent could hit his full oratorical style.

"Rich uncles, you mean?" Leeyes paused. "That's a thought. I could put someone onto checking on big wills."

"They would have had to have been very rich uncles indeed," pointed out Sloan, "to have left that sort of money net."

"Oil-rich uncles?" postulated Leeyes. That this was another melancholy indictment of modern society seemed—for the moment—to have escaped him.

"Sugar daddy?" suggested Sloan, seeing that they were exploring arcane relationships.

"She was a bit long in the tooth for that sort of thing," said Leeyes.

"Ah." Sloan pulled his notebook towards him. He had all the policeman's desire for positive fact in an uncertain world. "How old exactly?"

"Fifty-nine," said Leeyes promptly. "She was due to retire next year."

"What from?"

"Didn't I tell you?" said Leeyes. "She was the chemistry mistress at the girls' grammar school here in Berebury."

"Why?"

"Why what, Sloan?" he snapped testily.

"Why was she working?" said Sloan not unreasonably. "If I had a quarter of a million pounds in the bank I shouldn't be working. Would you, sir?"

"Another hundred and sometimes I think I'd stop," said Leeyes forcefully. "Today's been murder. Harpe's got himself tangled up with a pack of rabid conservationists—Malcolm Darnley's crowd—at a country planning enquiry over some trees on a bend in the Calleford Road. Haven't seen hair or hide of him all day and we've had three road traffic accidents already not to mention that Dr. McCavity's hit another bollard. That's his third this month."

"Chemistry mistress at . . ." began Sloan. Dr. McCavity was old Dr. Paston's new partner and visibly inclined to the bottle. His patients, however, liked him.

"Sergeant Gelven's over at Almstone looking at a break-in and if you ask me that's about all he's going to be able to do to it."

"Chemistry mistress at the grammar school," said Sloan resolutely.

"Kennedy's gone and got his foot trodden on by a bull down at the market." Leeyes believed in airing his grievances to his subordinates—it kept their ambition within bounds. "He's up at the hospital, too. And Constable King's on annual leave. He would be, just when he's wanted. . . ." Police Constable King routinely acted as coroner's officer in Berebury.

"Yes, sir. You . . ."

"You've taken half a day's leave."

Sloan drew breath, remembered that he hadn't got a quarter of a million pounds in the bank or anywhere else, and kept silent.

"And Crosby's underfoot here," said Leeyes, concluding his catalogue of woe by piling Pelion upon Ossa. Detective Constable Crosby was not the brightest of the bright and tended to still be at the police station when other members of the force were out on the job.

"So," said Sloan, "what you want to know is . . ."

"What I want to know," said Superintendent Leeyes, defining the problem neatly, "is exactly what a quarter of a million pounds is doing in the current account of Beatrice Wansdyke."

"Who died?"

"What's that, Sloan?" came his voice sharply over the line. "What's that?"

"The late Beatrice Wansdyke," observed Sloan pertinently.

"Exactly!" trumpeted Leeyes. "Dying must come into it somewhere."

"It usually does," said Sloan, putting down the telephone receiver.

*   *   *

Sloan put his head outside the pathologist's secretary's office door and said, "You can have your office back now. Thank you."

"Oh, there you are, Inspector." The secretary was standing in the corridor talking to a young girl in nurse's uniform.

"There was a message," the girl was saying breathlessly.

"You are . . ." began the secretary.

"Nurse Petforth." The girl looked anxiously first at her and then at Detective Inspector Sloan. "I came as quickly as I could."

"Miss Briony Petforth?" said the secretary.

She nodded, whey-faced. "Sister said to come straight round here but she didn't say why. . . . Is it

. . ." She halted in mid-sentence and made a visible effort to control herself. "It's not . . . who . . . ?"

"Would you by any chance be a relative of the late Miss Beatrice Wansdyke?"

"Oh, yes." A look of great relief passed over the girl's face. "She was my aunt."

"Then," said the pathologist's secretary briskly, "that's what the message will have been about."

An expression of puzzlement succeeded relief on Miss Petforth's countenance. "But she died on Sunday. At least we think it must have been on Sunday."

"Dr. Dabbe," said Dr. Dabbe's secretary, "wants to do a postmortem and we find that there's been no formal identification."

"A postmortem? But I thought . . ." She pushed back a lock of auburn hair that had somehow found its way past her nurse's cap. "Dr. Paston said . . ."

"Only if you don't mind," said the pathologist's secretary, "of course."

"I don't mind," said Briony Petforth in such a neutral way that Detective Inspector Sloan was quite unable to make up his mind whether she did or not. "It's just that my cousin's been seeing to everything."

"Yes, indeed." The pathologist's secretary conjured up some papers. "That would be Mr. Bertram George Wansdyke, wouldn't it?"

"He's her executor," responded the nurse obliquely.

"We did try to get in touch with him," said the secretary, "at his firm."

"Wansdyke and Darnley."

"But he's over in Calleford on business all day," said Dr. Dabbe's secretary, "that's why the doctor thought that as you were on the spot and as it would save so much time . . ."

"The funeral's been arranged," said the girl. A certain amount of colour had come back into her face now.

"Yes, indeed." If the pathologist's secretary was very well aware that postmortems took a certain precedence over funerals she did not say so. "For next Saturday, isn't it?"

"That was for the school," Briony Petforth said. "It's

to be on Saturday morning so that the girls themselves can choose whether they come or not. Not to have it thrust upon them compulsorily."

"How very thoughtful."

"That was my cousin's idea."

Once again Sloan was unable to decide what Briony Petforth herself thought of it.

The pathologist's secretary was gathering up her papers. "So, Miss Petforth, if you would just come this way . . ."

Briony Petforth did not move.

"Dr. Paston," she said instead, "gave us—the family, that is—a death certificate when . . . when . . . after she was found. . . ."

"Did he?" The pathologist's secretary turned to her file. "Then I may have it here."

"He put down hyperglycemia and diabetic keto-acidosis as the cause of death," said the girl. "I saw it."

"Oh, yes?" The pathologist's secretary might have been a member of the medical profession herself, so skilled was she in parrying questions.

"She was diabetic, you see." Briony Petforth had now succeeded in getting the stray tail of auburn hair back under her cap.

"Bad luck," said the pathologist's secretary sympathetically.

"Had been for years."

"Such a lot of it about, too, these days. Now, if you would just come this way please . . ."

"So why," asked Briony Petforth, "is there being a postmortem?"

* * *

Someone else in Berebury was at that minute asking the very same question of someone quite different.

"How should I know?" responded George Wansdyke at the other end of a telephone in Calleford, the county town of Calleshire. "All I had was that message to the office asking if I was available this afternoon and naturally they said I wasn't, because I was over here in Calleford. We've had this appointment with the director of United Mellemetics' Research and Development Department lined up for weeks now and with Malcolm being away until Thursday . . ."

"But," his wife cut him off short, "you told me that Dr. Paston gave you a death certificate." Mrs. Wansdyke never encouraged mention of business detail. In fact she spent quite a lot of time trying to pretend to herself and her circle of friends and relations that her husband wasn't actually in anything so commonplace as business at all. Messrs. Wansdyke and Darnley, she was wont to insist, were really more like scientific researchers than plastics manufacturers.

"So he did," said George Wansdyke. "Yesterday."

"Well, then . . ."

"And it said something which he told me meant that she'd gone into a diabetic coma."

"That's doctors for you all the time," said Mrs. Pauline Wansdyke, momentarily diverted. "Dressing everything up in words nobody can understand. Why couldn't he say what he meant?"

"He did," said her husband mildly.

"Your aunt died from her diabetes. . . ."

"And that's exactly what he put on the death certificate," said George Wansdyke.

"In Latin, though," his wife came back at him swiftly.

"They all do that." In Greek actually, but he did not say so.

"Showing off," pronounced Mrs. Pauline Wansdyke.

George did not argue.

Mrs. Wansdyke returned like a homing pigeon to her original point. "They can't do a post-mortem if they've got the death certificate."

"Can't they just!" responded George vigorously.

"Well, can they?"

"I don't suppose for one moment," declared George Wansdyke, businessman, "that they are doing anything at all that they haven't the authority to do." A working life spent—as a first priority—in satisfying an assortment of government departments, the Customs and Excise, the Inland Revenue, sundry local authorities, the Patents Office, and the Value Added Tax Commission-

ers had taught him only too well that there was invariably the power packed behind the punch. It was only in
the jungle of private enterprise that you had to make
sure first that you could see the colour of the other person's money, so to speak.

"But . . ." began Pauline Wansdyke.

"These sorts of people," he said ruefully, "don't need
to exceed their authority. They've got all they need and
plenty more where that came from. For all I know the
coroner can still clap people in the Tower."

"The coroner?" murmured Pauline Wansdyke.
"What's your aunt got to do with the coroner?"

"Nothing that I know about," said George grimly.
"Yet."

"Well then why should he want to put anyone in the
Tower?"

"What I meant was," explained George, immediately
regretting his flight into imagery, "that it seems to me
that the coroner in England can do pretty well what he
likes."

"Oh, I see, George. . . ." Pauline Wansdyke made
up in pertinacity what she lacked in comprehension.

"Yes?"

"Where does the coroner come in then?"

"Someone must have asked him for a post-mortem."

"Not you?"

"Not me," said George Wansdyke. "And I'm her sole
executor."

"Briony wouldn't have done, surely?"

"No, not without telling me. Anyway, she's a nurse
and she was sure that Beatrice had died of her diabetes."

"I know. She said so straightaway yesterday. So why
all the fuss if they know already?"

"You don't seem to have got the point yet," said
George tightly. "It isn't the medical people being in academic doubt about the cause of death and wanting to
find out so that everything's neat and tidy."

"No?"

"No," said George. "Otherwise they'd have asked
our permission for a post-mortem."

"Oh . . ."

"Someone's got the coroner to order one, which is a different kettle of fish altogether."

"Who would do that?"

"I don't know," said George Wansdyke, "but I'm certainly going to find out."

"Wait a minute," said Pauline.

"I know what you're going to say."

"Nicholas?"

"I wouldn't put it past him," said George Wansdyke.

"I wouldn't put anything past him," said Pauline spitefully. "Anything at all."

"No," said George.

"Nicholas Petforth," said Pauline, rolling the words around her tongue.

"Another name for trouble," he said ironically.

"No sense of family at all," said Mrs. Wansdyke, who had been a Miss Hartley-Powell before her marriage and never forgot it.

"He's not going to be buried in the family grave when his time comes," said George vigorously. "Not if I have any say in the matter."

"Oh," said Mrs. Wansdyke, whose attention span was not a long one, "that reminds me. Morton's rang to say that they were arranging to open the grave up as planned on Friday."

"Good," said George absently. "We'll see about bringing the stone up to date afterwards."

"I wonder if he'll come to the funeral on Saturday," said Pauline.

"Who?"

"Nicholas, of course. He always said he was fond of his aunt."

"Actions speak louder than words," said George Wansdyke. "We'll just have to wait and see, won't we?"

"He'll come," forecast Pauline Wansdyke with conviction. "For sure. You see if he doesn't."

"If he's still got a suit to his back."

Chapter 3

*Although the devil didn't show his face
I'm pretty sure he was about the place.*

The funeral of Beatrice Wansdyke was the last thing on the mind of Detective Inspector Sloan as he followed the pathologist through the mortuary doors into the dissecting room proper. In police measurement terms next Saturday and a funeral was a very long way away from this Tuesday and a post-mortem. A week was a long time in other things besides politics.

Dr. Dabbe was soon struggling into gown and rubber apron. He was helped in this exercise by his assistant, a perennially silent man called Burns.

"There's one thing, Sloan," said the pathologist, busily rolling up his sleeves.

"Yes?"

"The dibs don't show here, do they?"

"No, Doctor." Sloan was the first to agree with that. Nothing of this world's goods showed in the post-mortem room.

The pathologist, gowned now, moved over towards the dissecting table and ran his eyes over the body. "No external signs of violence immediately visible," he murmured. "I haven't missed any gunshot wounds, have I, Burns?"

"No, Doctor," said the assistant, adding, deadpan, "not yet."

This was evidently a private joke between master and man.

"Nor a stab in the back?"

21

"The back has not been stabbed," said Burns.

"That leaves the field clear to begin then," said Dabbe easily. He reached up and adjusted a small microphone hanging a little way above the post-mortem table. "Are you there, Rita? We're ready now."

The voice of the pathologist's secretary came back to them through some unobtrusive intercom. "I'm here, Doctor. Carry on."

"Body of an averagely nourished female," Dr. Dabbe began dictating, "whose age has been given to me as fifty-nine and whose name I am told is Beatrice Gwendoline Wansdyke."

The voice of the secretary broke in. "She's been positively identified, Doctor, now. By her niece."

The pathologist nodded and began peering forward at a wide area of thickened skin at the front of the dead woman's right thigh. He spoke into the hanging microphone again. "No external signs of violence except that there are indications that subcutaneous injections have been given over a long period."

"That's the diabetes, I suppose," said Sloan. What the police meant by violence was quite clearly something very different from that which the pathologist meant by violence.

"It's funny," mused the doctor, "how all the old diabetic hands find one site and use it all the time for their injections."

"Rather them than me," said Sloan.

"They've plenty of places to choose from," said Dabbe, "yet they usually find the one and stick to it."

"Does her choosing her right thigh mean she was right-handed?" asked Sloan. Anything that he could find out about Beatrice Wansdyke to add to his meagre store of information might be a help: you never knew with police work.

"I should think so," said Dabbe. He ran a professional eye over two biceps muscles. "You can take it from me that the deceased was right-handed anyway."

Sloan wrote that down. It was a beginning.

"Right, then," said the pathologist cheerfully, "shall we go in headfirst?"

Sloan stood well back. The hanging microphone

looked like the spider descending beside little Miss Muffet. . . .

"The deep end, you might say," murmured Dr. Dabbe as Burns busied himself with a stainless-steel knife.

"Beg pardon, Doctor?" In Detective Inspector Sloan's considered view this was neither the time nor the place to be playing with words.

"She was educated, wasn't she? Miss Wansdyke . . ."

"What . . . oh, yes. A science degree." That, too, had—like the quarter of a million pounds—been left behind outside the post-mortem room. This world's goods were not the only things that did not show up here. University degrees didn't carry any weight either. How right the ancients had been to drape what they were pleased to call achievements round the tomb instead. . . .

A wicked-looking bone saw had succeeded the knife in Burns' hand.

Sloan stirred. "What are you looking for, Doctor?"

"Cause of death, old chap. Nothing less, nothing more." He peered over his assistant's shoulder at the late Miss Wansdyke's head. "Looks all right to me."

"Yes, Doctor," said Burns.

The pathologist turned towards the hanging microphone and translated this for his secretary into medicolegal English for his report. "No macroscopic changes in brain tissue."

Presently: "Rita, are you still there?"

"Yes, Doctor, I'm here."

"No signs of strangulation. All the larynx bones are intact—hyoid and all."

Then: "Lungs normal. Got that?"

"Yes, Doctor."

A little later: "Some signs of myocardial degeneration. You'd expect that, of course."

And quite quickly after that: "Minimal diabetic changes in the pancreas. Bound to be with her history, I suppose. We'll have all the usual tissue sections, Burns, please. Rita, do a list, will you?"

"Yes, Doctor."

"And put the kettle on."

Detective Inspector Sloan had never relished post-mortems and he didn't enjoy this one now. Nevertheless, as always, there was something quite fascinating about watching a true expert at work. Gradually simple atavistic distaste fell away. It was succeeded by something much less primitive. The pathologist must have sensed his interest because he shot the policeman a shrewd glance and said: "You're quite right to take your shoes off, Sloan."

He started. "Beg pardon, Doctor?"

"Metaphorically, of course."

"I don't see . . ."

"You're in the Temple of Truth now," said the doctor drily. "As well as inside Nature's Temple."

"Oh?"

"The human body."

"Ah, I see what you mean."

"The greatest creation of them all," said the pathologist soberly. "Don't make any mistake about that, Sloan."

"No, Doctor."

"All alike and none exactly the same into the bargain."

"I hadn't thought about that."

"Mathematicians"—the pathologist waved a rubber-gloved hand—"contemplate infinity."

"Do they?"

"I contemplate human dissimilarity."

Detective Inspector Sloan looked first at the pathologist, then at Burns, and then at the body on the post-mortem table. "We're all one-off models, are we then? The long and the short and the tall."

"We're all the same and we're all different," said Dr. Dabbe the specialist. "Past, present, and future. That's the wonder of it, Sloan, the sheer wonder . . ."

There was a sudden clatter near the mortuary door. At the same time over the intercom came the hasty voice of the pathologist's secretary. "Rita, here, Doctor. You've got a visitor. He said he'd been sent."

The door opened and a very young policeman stepped into the mortuary. At once the atmosphere changed from the philosophic to the mundane. The newcomer addressed himself first to Sloan.

"Detective Constable Crosby, sir, reporting for duty."

Sloan sighed. "Come in, Crosby."

"The superintendent said to step round, sir."

"Did he?"

"There wasn't anyone else."

"No."

"And . . ."

"And?"

"And he'd got word that the assistant chief constable might be dropping in to the station this afternoon."

"Ah." That explained the superintendent's eagerness to get Crosby out of it. "Get your notebook out then."

"Yes, sir." The constable struggled with a recalcitrant pocket and gave a greeting to the pathologist the while. "Afternoon, Dr. Dabbe." He nodded amiably to Burns and then his eye fell upon the body on the postmortem table. He moved over politely as if she, too, was of the gathering. "Hullo," he said, "it's Miss Wansdyke, isn't it?"

"I didn't know," said Sloan with heavy irony, "that you two knew each other. How come, Crosby?"

*   *   *

A telephone bell rang.

Technical progress has done a lot for the telephone bell. In business offices unobtrusive warbles, discreet flashing lights, or quiet buzzers draw attention to the instrument. In the Berebury District General Hospital where a little extra peace and quiet would not have come amiss it rang with old-fashioned clarity.

"Ante-natal outpatients' clinic," said the young nurse who answered it.

"This is Fleming Ward," said a voice. "Can I speak to Dr. Roger Elspin, please?"

"Is it urgent?" enquired the nurse. "He's seeing a patient at the moment."

"Penny, is that you? It's Briony here."

"Briony! What on earth's the matter?"

"Penny, I simply must speak to Roger this very minute."

"But he's in the clinic with a patient. Truly."

"If I come straight down will you let me in for a minute to see him?"

"What if Sister Stork catches you here?"

"She need never even know that I've been in her precious clinic."

"She'll know," declared Penny feelingly. "She always knows everything. Don't ask me how, though."

"I expect she's a witch really," said Briony Petforth with surprising matter-of-factness. "All hospital sisters are. In disguise. Look here, are you going to let me in or aren't you?"

"Well . . ."

"Only for a minute, I promise."

"Oh, all right then. . . ."

"I can say that I've come down with a message from Fleming Ward."

"And exactly what sort of message," demanded Penny with some spirit, "would a men's surgical ward have got for an obstetrics outfit?"

"I'll think of something on the way down," promised Briony Petforth. "You see if I don't."

"Mind, you'll have to wait until Sister Fleming's back's turned."

This seemed to go without saying and Briony Petforth rang off and sped down to the ante-natal clinic. Her friend, Penny, gave her a conspiratorial look.

"Now's your chance. Sister Stork's on the other phone to the delivery ward."

"Bless you," said Briony. "I won't forget this."

"Sister Stork will kill me if she ever finds out," declared Penny dramatically.

"Sister Fleming will kill me if she finds out," returned Briony more tersely. "I should be doing dressings."

"It must be important," said Penny, wide-eyed. "He's in the first consulting room on the right."

Briony tapped on the door.

"Let's see, it's Mrs. . . . Mrs. . . . er . . . Sloan,

isn't it?" the obstetrics registrar was saying to his patient.

"It is." Margaret Sloan had at last worked her way to the top of the queue in the clinic and a moment ago had actually been ushered into the medical presence. Her husband—in the way of police husbands—had not returned to her side before she did so, but Larky Nolson had waved to her as he and his wife had departed from the ante-natal clinic ahead of her.

It had been poor consolation.

"Let me see now," said the doctor in the manner of all doctors, "the baby's due pretty soon, isn't it?"

The knock on the door was repeated.

"Come in," commanded Dr. Elspin.

"Dr. Elspin," said Briony Petforth formally, "could you spare a moment, please?"

"Certainly, nurse." The obstetrics registrar paused in the act of reading Mrs. Margaret Sloan's case notes and excused himself to her.

Mrs. Sloan murmured, "Of course."

Dr. Elspin stepped with alacrity into the adjoining examination cubicle and abandoned his professional manner. "Darling, what's the matter?"

"Oh, Roger . . ."

"You look as if you've seen a ghost."

She laughed shakily. "Only poor Aunt Beatrice."

"Now," he began briskly, something of his professional manner coming back, "you must start forgetting all about that. I know you found her and that you were fond of her but . . ."

"Not that."

"No?"

"You don't understand, Roger. Something else."

"What?"

"They're doing a post-mortem."

"Well, why not? After all, old Paston has every right to request . . ."

"No." She shook her head impatiently. "You don't understand. He gave us the death certificate all right. It was after that. Roger, what would make them change their minds?"

The young doctor frowned and paused for a moment before he spoke. "I don't really know."

"There you are then."

"But there's no harm done. You should know that, darling. . . ."

"How do you know?" she demanded tightly.

Dr. Roger Elspin made no audible answer to this. Instead there was a silence.

It was not broken for a long minute.

No one has ever pretended that those screens and partition walls in hospitals which do not reach the floor and are of less than ceiling height are meant to be soundproof. They exist solely to give an illusion of privacy to the patient—nothing more. And in any case that illusion was only ever meant to extend to visual privacy. Nobody, unless completely deceived by the token aloneness of being behind screens, could really believe that speech and sound were protected in any way.

Or could they?

Mrs. Margaret Sloan, no ugly duckling herself in her day, reckoned that she knew what a kiss sounded like as well as the next woman.

"No, Roger," she heard Briony protest, "not here!"

"Why not?" mumbled Roger Elspin indistinctly.

"Roger, mind my cap. . . ."

Mrs. Sloan was even more sure of the sound the second time she heard it. The partition was, after all, only an aid to dignity—the patient's dignity.

"Roger, stop it! Sister might come in."

"And she might not," said the obstetrics registrar promptly. "Then look what I'd have missed."

"Roger, be serious for a minute."

"I am serious," retorted the young man.

"Roger, you musn't. . . ."

"Give me another kiss and I'll prove it."

"Darling." The timbre of her voice changed noticeably.

"You know very well," said Roger Elspin gruffly, "that I am serious."

"And you realise what this means?" said Briony urgently.

"Your Aunt Beatrice dying?"

"Yes." Briony Petforth let out a sigh that Mrs. Margaret Sloan heard quite clearly. "It means that now there is nothing in the whole world stopping us getting married."

Chapter 4

I give fair warning you may search for ever;
A golden future lures one on to sever
Oneself from all one ever had, and trust
An art for which one cannot lose the lust . . .

"How is it, Crosby," repeated Detective Inspector Sloan evenly, "that you happen to know Miss Wansdyke?"

Constable Crosby did not—in any sense—live anywhere near Ridley Road.

"She's the lady who lost her little dog," said the detective constable. "Very upset about it at the time, sir, she was."

"And what time would that have been exactly?" asked Sloan. Someone down at the police station had been detailed to teach Crosby about the more precise reporting of fact but they evidently hadn't got very far yet.

"Saturday, sir." He turned back the pages of his notebook. "Saturday morning. Miss Wansdyke asked if anyone had brought her dog in to us."

"And had they?"

"No, sir. I looked in the book and all we had that day was a budgerigar, two umbrellas, a slide rule, four scarves, and a stone of plain flour."

"But no dog?" The esoteric wonder of lost property had palled on Sloan long before he had left the beat.

"No, sir. No dog."

"What sort of dog?"

"A lady dog, sir."

Sloan took a deep breath and then said very gently, "What kind of dog, Crosby?"

"She said it answered to the name of Isolde, sir." He sounded doubtful.

"What happy breed?" enquired the pathologist help-fully. He was engaged in poring over some wicked-looking instruments.

"An Airedale, Doctor."

"Ah, short hair and long legs." Dr. Dabbe picked out something slender in stainless steel from those arrayed on a tray. "Could have upset the diabetes, of course."

"What could?" said Sloan.

"Losing her dog. Anxiety and distress—worry—too much of that sort of thing can throw a diabetic quite off balance." He indicated Burns, who was busily putting specimens from the postmortem into labelled jars. "We'll be doing the blood-sugar level anyway. That'll be a good guide."

"When did she lose her dog?" asked Sloan.

The detective constable turned back his notebook. "It wasn't there when she got home from school the day before she came in to us."

"Friday afternoon?"

"That's right, sir. She thought it must have got out of the house somehow while she was at school but that it would come back all right for the night."

"And it didn't?"

"No, sir. She said that she went out to look for it herself but she hadn't been feeling very well so she didn't go far."

Policeman and pathologist both looked up at that.

Dr. Dabbe spoke first. Medically. "She wouldn't have been feeling very well anyway if she was already on her way to a diabetic coma."

"But she didn't know how it was that the dog got out?" said Sloan, thinking quickly along quite another tack. A law-enforcement one.

"No, sir," said Crosby.

The pathologist shot the detective inspector a shrewd glance. "Have we the same thing in mind, Sloan?"

"Ransom?" responded Sloan.

"It's a growth industry." Dabbe waved an instrument in the air. "First cousin to sky-jacking."

"Children in Italy . . ." It was something, he supposed, that there were national traditions in crime, and that Great Britain did not always lead the way.

"Dogs in England," said the pathologist, a cynic if ever there was one. "We're a nation of animal lovers."

"It might just have been an accident," said Sloan, "the dog getting out . . ."

"It is a truth universally acknowledged," said the doctor drily, "that a middle-aged woman in possession of a fortune will attract people anxious to part her from it."

Sloan coughed. "Would you say that an Airedale dog could be someone's—er—hostage to fortune?"

"Yes," said Dabbe simply.

"She was very upset," contributed Crosby, "especially when we told her that we hadn't got her—er—Isolde."

"We'll look for a note," conceded Sloan. "Just in case someone got ideas about ransom. Can't very well do more than that at this stage."

"No." The pathologist went back to his work and in a matter of moments was totally absorbed again in what he was doing. Detective Constable Crosby settled himself against a nearby bench while Sloan considered Miss Wansdyke and her curiously great wealth. It was some little time before Dr. Dabbe straightened up and began peeling off his rubber gloves. He continued, however, to address the microphone, which hovered—like Damocles' sword—above the neck of the post-mortem subject.

"Right, Rita. That's all. Get it typed out, will you, and I'll sign a copy for the coroner." He tossed his gloves into a linen basket. "It won't tell him much, Sloan."

"No?"

"I can't find anything except the diabetes." He turned his back on Sloan while his assistant, Burns, undid his gown from behind. "Of course she'd got the usual signs you'd expect to find going with that condition in a woman of her age."

"Change and decay?" Sloan's mother was a great churchgoer.

"Ever present, old chap, but no other cause of death

that I can see. Poison's always a problem though in forensic medicine."

"Yes, Doctor." And it was, too. That, as every policeman—and pathologist—knew, was where the undetected homicide lay. Nearly always.

"Naturally we'll take a look at the bits and pieces that Burns here has got in his jars," said Dabbe a trifle unscientifically, "but there are certainly no signs that lead me to suspect anything out of the ordinary in the way of what the lawyers call noxious substances."

Burns drew a white sheet up over the body of Beatrice Wansdyke.

"And no other natural causes," said Sloan, trying to keep his mind clear, "besides the diabetes."

"Just the diabetes," repeated the pathologist, tossing his gown into the linen basket after the gloves. "From my point of view there's no doubt at all what she died from even though someone somewhere may have smelt a rat."

"That's all right, Doctor," interrupted Detective Constable Crosby largely. He uncoiled himself from the bench against which he had been leaning. "After all, down at the station, we're in the rat-catching business, aren't we?"

* * *

Miss Simpson, headmistress of the Berebury Grammar School for Girls, picked up a piece of paper from her desk and studied it carefully. The deputy head of the school, Miss Walsh, had just brought it in to her study and laid it before her. The two women, seasoned schoolmistresses both, knew without discussion exactly how much burning of midnight oil the finished document represented.

It contained all the revisions in the school timetable made necessary by the sudden demise of the senior chemistry mistress.

Miss Simpson let it lie in her hands for a moment before she considered it, thinking instead of Beatrice Wansdyke. From now on someone else was going to have to persuade girls to think scientifically, to take a proper interest in those twins of fundamental discovery, Boyle and Charles and their laws, and to learn about elements and atoms and (as far as Miss Simpson was concerned—she was an English specialist herself) other things.

Anyway, from now on another teacher of chemistry was going to have to be categoric about nitric and nitrous and nitrate and somehow inculcate into her charges the intellectual reaches opened up by the study of organic chemistry.

Miss Wansdyke's syllabus would be up-to-date. There wouldn't be any worry there. The upper sixth's chances of university entrance would not be spoilt by her death. They would suffer only by loss of contact with a good mind. It had been a mind that had always been ready and prepared to stretch the thinking of the young. Girls who made sweeping statements once seldom made them a second time.

It had been much the same in the staff room. Colleagues who made unsupported assertions were apt to have them challenged pretty speedily. Miss Simpson sighed. Unfortunately staff-room politics seldom had anything to do with principles—scientific or even first.

Miss Simpson let her eye fall on the timetable. Had Miss Walsh . . . yes, she had. The head was not surprised to see that in her attempt to fill the gap in the timetable the deputy head had slipped in a couple of extra economics classes for the fifth form. Beatrice Wansdyke wouldn't have liked that. As a scientist she had always resented the intrusion of economics into the curriculum as a separate subject. Economics, she maintained, was not a proper teaching entity at all, but an ill-defined grey area, which knew no morality, somewhere between geography and history. And the proper study of history, she was wont to parody Alexander Pope, is power and if economics didn't come into that she didn't know what did. A science, she would insist, jealous of the purity of her own subject, it certainly was not.

The aggrandisement of economics as a study apart, though, thought Miss Simpson thankfully, Beatrice Wansdyke would not have minded the waters closing so quickly over the hole left by a departed chemistry mistress. The last thing she would have wanted was fuss. She would have thoroughly approved of the quiet rearrangement of the timetable and the stepping into her shoes of another teacher. The show, all dedicated pedagogues were agreed, must go on. Miss Collins would mind, of course. Hilda Collins and Beatrice Wansdyke had been good friends over the years—but then Hilda was a biologist and they were seldom sentimentalists.

The head paused in her thinking. She would have to decide herself whether to recommend to the governors that young Miss Peel should go up a rung in the academic ladder. A promising youngster, Miss Wansdyke had thought her. . . .

Mentally apologising to Beatrice's memory for meditating on her successor quite so soon, Miss Simpson was confronted by the thought that her late colleague had not been greatly looking forward to her retirement. Sitting back and resting was no fine ambition compared with the satisfaction of stretched elastic young minds. Better, too, to die while still searching for her own particular philosopher's stone.

Beatrice had been too much of a realist, too, she was sure, not to have observed the inevitable advances of old age, the decline in physical activity, the slow closing in of horizons that went with the passing years. Her manner had got more and more dry with the passage of time, though the girls whom she taught did not seem to mind. Miss Simpson smiled wryly to herself in the privacy of her study. There was no doubt that Beatrice Wansdyke had long ago reached that point in a schoolmistress's career when she was cherished by her pupils as much for her idiosyncrasy as her teaching.

The head laid the revised timetable back on her desk. No . . . Beatrice Wansdyke wouldn't have minded dying in harness, her duty done, her old friend Hilda Collins her chief mourner. She'd nursed her aged parents, kept her temper and her peace over the years with the silly snobbish brainless creature whom her brother's son had married, and done what she could for her dead sister's children. Nobody could have done more for the boy, Nicholas, than Beatrice, and who,

added Miss Simpson charitably, could say yet that she
had failed? He might improve and settle down in time.
Who could say?

Would he, though, she wondered, come to the funeral on Saturday?

* * *

The young man who was the subject of Miss Simpson's thoughts was at that particular moment by no
means as sure as Pauline Wansdyke had been that he
would be at his aunt's funeral. This uncertainty had
nothing to do with his wish to be there. It was to do
with the nature and conditions of his present employment.

"No," the foreman was saying flatly, "you can't have
next Saturday off."

"For a funeral," mumbled Nicholas Petforth.

The foreman, it transpired, had heard that one before. Many times.

"She was the only aunt I had," said Nicholas Petforth truthfully. That, though he didn't tell the foreman
so, was the whole trouble in the family. Aunts had been
a bit on the short side. His father had had no sisters and
his mother only one. This situation didn't usually matter but it had mattered in their family when it came to
the point. . . .

"And Saturday," said the foreman without emotion,
"is the only time this season that Luston Town will be
playing Newcastle United."

Nicholas Petforth's mobile face looked quite blank.

"Away," added the foreman meaningfully. "You'd
need the whole day to get there. And"—he was a
soured man—"and you'd be late back on Monday
morning into the bargain."

"Ah, football." Petforth rearranged his features upon
the instant to project a keen interest in the game. Negotiations about his going to the funeral had reached a
delicate stage and he didn't want them spoilt by an inju-
dicious reference on his part to spectator sport.

"Back late on Monday with a headache," added the
foreman for good measure.

Petforth dragged up a remark he'd overheard being made at a recent tea break. "The Town team haven't a chance without their usual centre forward."

The foreman nodded. "Unluckiest accident in the history of the club."

"And just before the big match," agreed Petforth solemnly. He became suitably deferential. "Do you think if he'd been fit to play . . . supposing he hadn't broken his leg . . ."

The foreman shook his head. "Not a hope, if you ask me."

"Ah . . ." Nicholas Petforth was careful not to make a specific comment. He had learnt a lot since he had come to work on the construction site. In his time there he had come to perfect an ideal response to almost all remarks thrown at him. Boiled down, it consisted of inviting the speaker to agree with his or her own last statement. It had proved a sure-fire way of winning friends and influencing people. Sometimes he threw in an additional "You've got a point there" for good measure.

He did now.

"I know I have," declared the foreman. "Stands to reason in a small club like Luston Town."

"True."

"This aunt of yours," said the foreman.

"More like a mother to me," said Petforth.

The foreman looked at him sharply.

The labourers he had under him these days weren't like the ones he used to have. University students were two-a-penny on the site nowadays, graduates almost as common. They'd be having women heaving earth about next, as the Russians did, and the Chinese—not that some of the men around didn't look like women. He'd got over thinking them all Maryannes though. There just wasn't anyone around any more with the clout to tell them to get their hair cut. And they weren't all fools either. There had been a law graduate wanting to make a quick penny to set himself up who had taught the foreman himself a thing or two about questioning the authority of those above him.

"Practically brought me up," offered the young man before him, whom the foreman knew only as Nick.

"No family?"

"Killed," said Petforth expressively, "in a pile-up on a motorway like this." He waved his hand to indicate the area they were working on. In fact at this early stage it bore no resemblance to a motorway at all. The three-lane landscaped tarmacadamed communications artery that was to come where they stood was little more than a twinkle in the planners' eye at this moment. In their minds' eye—and in the artist's impression—the well-intentioned road architects saw only the finished product—just as at Passchendaele the General Staff had visualised only victory. What the men on the ground saw in both cases was only mud.

"It happens," said the foreman.

"I was quite small at the time."

"Ah." That explained a lot to the foreman. Like why a well-spoken lad like this should be living in squalor and working with a road construction gang, though admittedly times had changed anyway. Time was when speech like his would have been aped up and down the site. Not any longer. The foreman reached for the last shot in his empty locker and said, "You'll lose your bonus, of course."

Nicholas Petforth shrugged his shoulders.

That didn't surprise the foreman. He couldn't get at any of his men that way any longer. The odd ones had minds above money and the others were earning so much that it didn't matter to them anyway.

In the end the foreman agreed to Nick having next Saturday off as he agreed to most requests these days. Partly because he didn't think for all his broken-down appearance and bizarre clothing that Nick Petforth was the sort of man to lie and partly because he calculated that he'd have the union after him if he didn't let him go. And then the consortium which was building the motorway and who would neither know nor care if he gave every manjack in the gang the whole week off, provided they didn't lose money, would be after his blood.

"You'll be back after the funeral, right?" he said,

conscious that if there was ever trouble on the site that he could be sure of just one thing: no one would ever uphold his authority.

"Not if she's left me a fortune, I won't," murmured the young man, picking up his donkey jacket and protective helmet. "That's for sure."

Chapter 5

If you would publish your infatuation
Come on and try your hand at transmutation.

"At least," murmured Mrs. Margaret Sloan, "I don't have to walk home."

"No," agreed Sloan warily. He'd gone straight back to the ante-natal outpatients' clinic from the mortuary and metaphorically thrown his hat in first.

There was a constrained silence.

"Everything—er—all right?" he asked.

"Yes," she said consideringly. "Yes, I think so."

"Good." He paused. "Er . . . good."

"If you're talking about the baby, that is."

"Yes . . . er . . . naturally."

"Then it is."

"Er . . . good."

"And me?"

"Of course," he said hastily. He'd fallen into that, headfirst.

There was another small silence.

"Is everything," Sloan capitulated, "all right with you too?"

"Yes, I think so," she said demurely.

"Good. Er . . . good. Here, let me take that."

Mrs. Sloan consented to having her shopping bag carried as they walked down the hospital corridor.

"The doctors are pleased then?" said her husband with unaccustomed heartiness and a wholesale avoidance of the equally germane matter of whether or not Mrs. Margaret Sloan was pleased at being abandoned in the ante-natal clinic.

"The doctor," said Margaret Sloan astringently, "was very pleased indeed."

"Good. I'm glad to hear it."

"But not with me."

Sloan looked up.

"He," said Margaret Sloan, matron, "was pleased with a young lady called Briony."

"Ah, he was, was he?"

"Exceedingly pleased. Mind you," she added, "Dr. Elspin is what I would call a very personable young man."

Somehow this statement contrived to put Sloan on the wrong foot.

"Would you?" he said.

"Very," said Margaret Sloan emphatically.

"Ah!"

"Nice manners."

"Has he?"

"For a doctor," she said.

"I see."

"And you," she said, "presumably were—er—caught up with someone called Beatrice?"

"I was," said Sloan carefully. The Ice Maiden was gradually—but ever so gradually—giving way to someone else—someone more like the woman he had married. He didn't want to say or to do anything that might halt the progression.

"Aunt to a nurse called Briony, I take it?" said his wife.

"That is so. The late Miss Beatrice Wansdyke. I understand that she has a niece on the staff at the hospital."

"If," said Mrs. Sloan, "what I overheard is anything to go by . . ."

"Yes?"

"She's going to have a nephew on the staff at the hospital too pretty soon."

"Ah."

"A nephew-in-law, actually."

"I see." He listened attentively to her recital of what she had overheard. "So now they can get married and before she died they couldn't?"

"That was what was implied certainly," said Mrs. Margaret Sloan.

"Well, well, well," said Sloan, "that is interesting."

"I rather thought," murmured his wife mischievously, "that you wouldn't think I'd been wasting my time."

"Margaret Sloan," he said gruffly, "I won't have that from you or anyone else." He took a quick look up and down the corridor. They seemed for the moment to be alone. He dropped the shopping basket and put both arms around her. He was delighted to find that the Ice Maiden had melted away completely.

"Larky Nolson waved to me," she said indistinctly.

"I'll have him for that," swore Sloan.

"It's not a crime."

"Incitement to violence," growled Margaret Sloan's husband, "that's what that was."

An Accident Unit porter wheeling a patient on a stretcher trolley around the corner at that moment rolled his eyes and said to his mate at tea-break time that the young doctors were bad enough these days but he really didn't know what the police force was coming to.

* * *

To say that Superintendent Leeyes was displeased by the news of the result of the post-mortem examination was an understatement.

Detective Inspector Sloan was sitting in the superintendent's office now. There had been a tacit—definitely unspoken—agreement between police husband and policeman's wife that he was going back on duty.

Leeyes was inveighing against all forensic scientists in general but medical ones in particular.

"It's always the same with pathologists," he complained. "When you don't want them to find something they go and do, and when you do want them to come up with the goods they don't."

Sloan maintained a prudent silence. Abstract truth was not a concept that appealed to the superintendent at the best of times. And this was not the best of times.

While it was not the worst of times either, it did not seem as if the superintendent considered it was the age of medical wisdom.

"So Miss Wansdyke died of her diabetes, did she?" he rumbled after a moment. Perhaps it was the epoch of incredulity.

"Dr. Dabbe couldn't find anything else, sir."

"He would if he could," conceded Leeyes illogically. "He's doing a drug screen, of course."

"Of course." That went without saying. Drug screens were routine in this day and age.

"They may discover something in some of the other specimens they've taken."

"Disappointing there being nothing to find at autopsy." Leeyes grunted. "I should have thought there was bound to be more to her dying than natural causes."

"Seems a pity to die with all that money," Sloan agreed with the unspoken sentiment and then added a witticism of his own. "All this and heaven too."

"Something doesn't fit, Sloan," said the superintendent severely.

"No, sir." Sloan was quick to agree.

"Doesn't feel right."

"No, sir," he said immediately. He didn't discount instinct. He never had. Hunch was halfway to detection. Always had been.

"Doesn't smell right either," pronounced Leeyes.

"No, sir." You used all your senses in police work.

"On the other hand I don't see that we can do a lot more about holding things up."

"No."

"So," said Leeyes generously, "you can just step round and tell the coroner we shan't be standing in his way at all any more over the burial order."

* * *

His office was not the only thing Dickensian about Mr. Robert Chestley. He was one of Her Majesty's coroners for the county of Calleshire and a practising solicitor. The man himself gave the impression of barely having left a hard butterfly-wing collar behind. A gold-rimmed pince-nez contributed to a general aura of the nineteenth century, which was reinforced by the decor of an office in which little had been changed since his grandfather's day.

Detective Inspector Sloan was not deceived.

Unseen legal scale fees kept pace with the rise in the cost of living practically of their own volition. There was no need for any other changes.

"You," said Mr. Chestley, notary public and nobody's fool, "have come about the late Miss Beatrice Wansdyke."

Sloan agreed that he had.

"Constable King's away," grumbled the coroner. Mr. Chestley himself never took holidays. "He usually sees to everything."

Sloan concurred with that too. They were all agreed that the coroner's officer was a useful man to have around at a death. He saved the beatman a lot of routine work, devilled for the coroner, and became—thank goodness—very skilled indeed at handling bereaved relatives.

"Your superintendent," said the coroner with emphasis, "prevailed upon me to order a post-mortem examination."

He and Superintendent Leeyes were old adversaries. They had had several notable clashes in the past—usually over the duties of the coroner's officer. This unfortunate policeman existed in a sort of leaderless no-man's-land. Hostilities had broken out over this more than once.

"Subject to my direction," the superintendent always insisted.

"Subject to my direction," the coroner would invariably counter.

"His office derives from the parish beadle," Mr. Chestley would reply, "and that's older. My pigeon, I think."

"Historical duties too obscure to be recorded," said Leeyes nastily on more than one occasion. The ancientness of the coroner's own office always rankled with him. Sir Robert Peel had been so unconscionably late on the scene.

"Jervis on Coroners . . ."

"The Police Act 1964 . . ." Superintendent Leeyes never gave up.

"Useful to have a police officer around in case a crime has been committed," would throw in the coroner.

"If you need a detective," Leeyes always came back smartly at that one, "we'll send one round."

"The job calls for a trained man." The coroner—a pillar of the legal profession—always had a riposte for every rebuttal.

"Waste of police manpower" had figured in Leeyes's broadside in response to that.

"If a job is worth doing," quoted Chestley, "then it's worth doing well."

"No man can serve two masters." Leeyes did not hesitate to fall back on primary sources when it suited him.

Then someone—the chief constable probably—had called "Pax" and a state of armed neutrality had been resumed.

"So," said Mr. Chestley to Detective Inspector Sloan now, "I ordered a post-mortem, the body being within my jurisdiction."

"Yes," said Sloan. It was the latter point that mattered with coroners, though he never knew why.

"That post-mortem examination confirms the cause of death as certified by the deceased's usual medical attendant."

"Yes," said Sloan again.

"Can you now give me any valid reason why I should not issue a Pink Form B?"

"No," said Sloan uneasily.

"I take it, Inspector, that Superintendent Leeyes had felt—er—a pricking of his thumbs."

"Information received," said Sloan tersely. Formal language was a refuge really, not an imposition: a cloak for that which was better not explained. "From persons about the deceased." The quaint archaism covered a multitude of hidden sources.

"Pink Form B," expounded the coroner pedantically, "is of course a superior category of medical certificate of the cause of death."

"Yes," said Sloan, surprised at the law's homely touch. Down at the police station forms had numbers, not colours and letters.

"Though," Mr. Chestley continued his lecture, "as it happens the result of the autopsy confirms the cause of death as certified by the registered medical practitioner who attended the deceased in her last illness."

"Dr. Paston," said Sloan for simplicity's sake.

"The fact of confirmation is irrelevant," continued the coroner, adjusting his pince-nez.

Not in Sloan's mind, it wasn't, though he did not say so. "Corroboration" was the word the police used for that and they could always use as much of it as they could get in the criminal investigation department of any force in the country.

". . . though," Mr. Chestley immediately added a rider, "no doubt a comfort to the member of the medical profession concerned."

"Dr. Paston," said Sloan again.

"But irrelevant." The coroner would not be gainsaid.

"Really, sir?"

"Post-mortems," declared the coroner, "do not always confirm the certified cause of death."

Sloan could well believe this. People could be ill with one thing and die from another. Easily. And doctors could be wrong. Even more easily.

"Mind you," said the coroner, unexpectedly reverting to his own profession, "counsel's opinion isn't always perfect either."

Sloan cleared his throat and made a valiant attempt to get back to the business in hand. "The superintendent says . . ."

"But the system's better than it was."

Sloan said he was glad to hear it.

"Not so simple, though."

"Nothing," said Sloan with unfeigned heartiness, "is as simple as it used to be."

The coroner adjusted his pince-nez again. "Before they had Dabbe and his fancy scientific outfit . . ."

"Yes?"

"They used to have a couple of old women."

"Did they, sir?" Sloan shifted his weight from one leg to the other. He hadn't come here on a busy day to be lectured on ancient customs. He was a police officer and he'd come about a sudden death.

"They called them searchers."

"Really, sir?" It was Sloan's invariable practise to allow other people to give him information—however recondite—without let or hindrance. Or interruption.

"Two of them," said the coroner gratuitously, "used to totter along to the graveside and view the dead before burial."

"Did they, sir?" He himself felt no necessity to bring the Bow Street runners into the conversation.

"They made up their minds what the cause of death was."

"It was one way of doing it, sir, I suppose."

"None of this stainless-steel nonsense," said the coroner, dismissing several thousand pounds' worth of highly sophisticated forensic pathology equipment with the wave of a hand.

"No." That would have saved the taxpayers a packet, though Sloan did not say so.

"Then they'd pop round and tell the parish clerk."

"No red tape," observed Sloan, aware that some remark was expected of him.

"He kept a stroke record," said the coroner.

"Saved a lot of paper work," agreed Sloan, entering into the spirit of the thing in spite of himself.

"And before you could say 'Jack Robinson,'" said the coroner, "you had your bill of mortality."

"Not," remarked Sloan, "quite as accurate as the registrar general's statistics but good enough."

The coroner readjusted his pince-nez and looked thoughtful. "No three-ring civil servant circus either, of course."

"And so," said Sloan, making a game attempt to get back to the matter in hand, "you'll just notify the registrar general that Miss Wansdyke died from the complications of diabetes?"

"I shall say," said the coroner cautiously, "that the

pathologist so advises me and that I deem an inquest not necessary in all the circumstances that have been presented to me. I may, of course," he added unconvincingly, "be in error."

* * *

Mr. Chestley might have considered this last possibility a little more seriously had he been present when Sloan got back to the police station.

Detective Constable Crosby rang in just after he reached his desk.

"You've done what, Crosby?" demanded Sloan martially. "Say that again!"

"Found her dog, sir."

"You're sure it's hers?"

"Long legs and short hair, sir, like you and Dr. Dabbe said. An Airedale."

"Answering to the name of Isolde?" said Sloan. It was not a name he for one would care to go around the streets of Berebury late at night calling out aloud, but even so . . .

"Not answering to any name, sir. Not now."

"What do you mean?"

"Dead," said Crosby lugubriously.

Chapter 6

No one can stop until there's nothing left.

At the Berebury District General Hospital, Nurse Briony Petforth came off duty from Fleming Ward with relief. She thankfully changed out of her uniform into a soft blue and brown mixture matching skirt and jerkin that went well with her auburn hair. After a moment or two's consideration she selected a rather more dressy blouse to go under her jerkin and slipped a couple of strings of contrasting beads into her handbag. They would do for later.

She debated with herself for a moment whether she should telephone the ante-natal clinic again but in the end she decided against it. Roger Elspin knew where she was going. He would come along as soon as he could get away from the clinic and the ward. She sighed. Obstetrics was no speciality for a clock watcher.

Dermatology, she decided, was what he could take up after they got married. Skin patients never needed their doctor urgently in the middle of a dinner party, or got him up in the small hours of the night either. They never died—and seldom got better for that matter—and yet were always profoundly grateful for whatever could be done for them that helped. Dermatology it would have to be.

Having thus mentally resolved the professional fate of one promising young obstetric surgeon, she slipped on a duffle coat and made her way across the town to North Berebury. Her cousin George Wansdyke and his wife, Pauline, lived in a detached house in Cullum Crescent. They received her with relief.

49

"Poor Briony," said Pauline Wansdyke with a shudder. "Come in and sit down. I couldn't have looked at Aunt Beatrice like you did. I really couldn't."

"I didn't mind." Briony brushed this to one side, marvelling, as she always did, at Pauline's capacity for striking just the wrong note.

"I couldn't have done it," repeated Pauline Wansdyke dramatically, "not if I'd been the last person on earth."

"We've all got to die," said Briony briefly. "There's nothing unnatural about that."

"That's the trouble with doctors and nurses," complained Pauline Wansdyke. "They get so unfeeling."

"No, they don't," countered Briony spiritedly.

"Dr. Paston wasn't in the least bit sympathetic about my bad back," said Mrs. Wansdyke, not listening. "Just rheumatism, he said, and nobody knew how painful it was."

"Doctors and nurses have feelings just like everyone else," insisted Briony Petforth, forbearing to remind her that everyone—but everyone—had known all about how painful Pauline's back had been. "More than some people, actually."

"Not Dr. Paston," said Pauline, always inclined to the personal. "He was quite unfeeling, I can assure you."

"But . . ."

"He gave me some white tablets that didn't begin to touch the pain and told me to go away."

"He did say to come back if you weren't any better though," put in her husband fairly.

"It's just," continued Briony Petforth more to herself than to the Wansdykes, "that doctors and nurses have to adjust to all the unhappiness around them all the time early on."

"Learn to live with it." George Wansdyke nodded.

"But I don't see why . . ." began Pauline.

"Otherwise," said Briony, between clenched teeth, "they'd go stark, raving mad, that's why!"

"Pauline was just going to make some tea," interposed George Wansdyke swiftly. He was adept now at smoothing over any hiatus created by his wife's approach to the world. "And the children are in bed, so sit down and tell me exactly what happened at the hospital."

Briony sank thankfully into a chair. "Nothing much, really, George. I identified Aunt Beatrice as Beatrice Gwendoline Wansdyke, that's all."

"Sorry I wasn't there," he said. "I would have come."

"I know you would," she said. "Couldn't be helped."

"I've been on to Mortons'," he said carefully. "They don't know what all the fuss was about either."

She shrugged her shoulders. "No harm done. In fact now we know for sure that it was the diabetes, don't we?"

"Yes, indeed," agreed George. "Not that there was ever any doubt in my mind."

"There was in someone's," pointed out Briony, "otherwise . . ."

"Quite," said George Wansdyke. "Anyway, everything should be plain sailing from now on, shouldn't it?"

"I hope so," said the girl fervently. "I hope so."

There was a pause and then she said more casually, "Roger's coming round to collect me as soon as he comes off duty."

Wansdyke nodded. "Right."

"We're going out somewhere to eat." She pushed back a stray lock of hair. "Not that I'm hungry."

"No," said Wansdyke, "but I daresay you'll have plans to make."

She looked at him curiously. "Perhaps."

"If you're not going to live in the house in Ridley Road you'll have to decide what to do about it pretty quickly, my dear. An empty house is just an open invitation to squatters these days. You can't just leave it."

"Don't rush me, George. Not yet. I'm . . . I'm not used to Aunt Beatrice not being there yet."

"Sorry. Take all the time you need, Briony." He pointed to a bureau in the corner. "I haven't really begun to look at her affairs anyway. I've been devilish busy at work. Malcolm's been on this export trip to the States. He'll be back on Thursday though for this product launching we've got laid on and then I'll be more my own man again, thank goodness."

Briony yawned. "Poor Aunt Beatrice never found her particular crock of gold at the end of the rainbow, did she?"

George Wansdyke shook his head. "Not that I know of. But she enjoyed looking for it."

"Perhaps that's all that matters."

"Travelling hopefully, you mean?" He gave her a quizzical look.

Briony wasn't really listening. "That's your front doorbell, isn't it? Roger's got away early if it's him."

It wasn't Dr. Roger Elspin at the front door. It was Detective Inspector Sloan and Detective Constable Crosby.

The superintendent never gave up. Bulldogs as a breed had nothing on Superintendent Leeyes when his jaws were locked firmly onto a problem. Nor was he one to accept a dead end. Immediately after writing off the post-mortem he had proceeded to turn his mind to other aspects of the death of Miss Beatrice Wansdyke.

It was therefore not very long before he came up with the question which came—like Death—late or soon to Everyman—or at any rate to every policeman.

"Who benefits, Sloan?" he demanded to know. "Tell me that."

Which was how it was that Dectective Inspector Sloan and Detective Constable Crosby came to be ringing the doorbell of a house called "The Laurels" in Cullum Crescent, Berebury, at this particular moment. George Wansdyke admitted them.

"Of course. Come in," he said, when Sloan had explained who they were. "We were expecting someone to come along to tell us what all the fuss was about."

Sloan decided that that line would serve as as good an introduction as he was ever likely to get.

"We're sorry to have bothered you, sir," he said, slipping easily into a semideferential manner, which, had they been privileged to witness it, would have at the same time both considerably startled Larky Nolson and vastly amused Mrs. Margaret Sloan. It was nicely done.

The tone implied apology without actually meaning it. "Some sort of mix-up somewhere along the line . . ."

"No trouble," said Wansdyke, equally magnanimous. "Briony . . . Inspector, this is my cousin, Miss Petforth."

"We have met," said Sloan. "At the hospital."

"Oh, really?" He looked up as his wife came back into the room. "Pauline, dear, these are police officers who have come to tell us about poor Aunt Beatrice."

"Poor Aunt Beatrice," echoed Pauline Wansdyke without noticeable conviction.

"Briony—Miss Petforth, here—stood in for me at the identification," said George to Sloan.

"You're her executor, though, sir, aren't you?"

"I am indeed." He shrugged his shoulders ruefully. "Not that I imagine that the duties are likely to be—er—exactly onerous."

"Oh?" said Sloan, utterly deadpan.

"Her pension rights die with her, of course, as she didn't reach sixty. . . ."

Like the mustard left on the plate, that was where the pension fund money was, thought Sloan to himself.

". . . and the house goes outright to Briony here," continued George.

Briony flushed but said nothing.

"I see," said Sloan mendaciously. "And the residue?"

"She wasn't a rich woman," said George Wansdyke.

"No?"

"My grandparents left her a little, naturally, including a small stake in the firm."

Sloan looked expectant. "She wasn't their only child though?"

"Of course not." George Wansdyke looked distinctly uncomfortable. "Otherwise she wouldn't have a niece, would she? But she had nursed them both, and my father—her brother—had built up the firm into something by then."

Sloan, who could count as well as the next man, said, "And Miss Petforth's mother?"

"Cut off with a shilling," said Briony, flushing again.

"She was not mentioned in the wills of either of my grandparents," said Wansdyke.

"I see."

"My mother, you might as well know, ran off with a no-good-boyo," said Briony Petforth, showing a working acquaintance with the works of the late Dylan Thomas as well as a sense of humour.

"My grandparents were very old-fashioned," said Wansdyke stiffly.

"When my great aunt married the coachman," said Pauline Wansdyke, "her parents went into black and never mentioned her name again. They were Hartley-Powells, of course."

"They turned my Auntie Nellie's picture to the wall," contributed Detective Constable Crosby chattily.

Everyone looked in his direction.

"She didn't marry anyone," said Crosby. "That was the trouble."

Pauline Wansdyke wasn't used to being upstaged.

"They drew the window blinds, too, on the day she married," she said firmly, "as if she'd died, and then they rubbed her name out of the family Bible."

"My parents did die, Inspector," said Briony softly. "In a car accident when we were little."

"We?" queried Sloan.

The interrogative hung unacknowledged for a moment.

"My brother and I," said Briony after a pause.

"Winding up Beatrice's estate," interposed George Wansdyke fussily, "won't be a difficult matter."

"Good," said Sloan warmly. If George Wansdyke believed that, then like somebody else, he could believe anything.

"She had a friend called Hilda Collins," said Wansdyke obliquely. "She gets a little. An eighth, actually. So does Dr. Paston."

"Her general practitioner?"

"He was an old friend as well as her doctor, Inspector. He'd been very good to her over the years over this chronic complaint of hers."

"Diabetes," said Briony Petforth rather crossly. "Why doesn't everyone say so and call it what it was?"

"Quite so," said Sloan. "And?"

"My children get a small sum between them," continued Wansdyke. "In trust, naturally, seeing that they're underage."

"Naturally," concurred Sloan. Trust laws might seem a contradiction in terms but they knew all about untrustworthy trustees down at the police station. The mediaevalists had done better still. They used to put the just judges on one side of a painting and the unjust ones on the other.

"It won't amount to much, of course," said Wansdyke. "Another eighth."

"Of course," echoed Sloan, reserving judgement on this.

"Briony gets the same as well as the house."

Detective Inspector Sloan did some mental arithmetic out loud. "Four eighths make a half, sir, don't they?"

"They do," said George Wansdyke reluctantly.

"That leaves a half," said Sloan.

Wansdyke coughed. "That goes to Briony's brother, Nicholas." He spread his hands open and apart in an age-old gesture. "If we can find him, that is."

Briony Petforth looked up. "The dog's missing too."

* * *

However Dickensian an impression the coroner's office gave to the casual visitor, it still sported a telephone. Mr. Chestley's personal secretary was middle-aged and competent. The calls she allowed to be put through to her employer were only those she knew he would want to take. To all other callers he was either "engaged with a client" or "in court."

"Mr. Chestley," she said now, "I have Dr. John Paston on the line."

"Put him through," he said immediately—as she had known he would. There was a pause. Then: "John . . ."

"That you, Chestley? Paston here. What's all this about my death certificate for Beatrice Wansdyke?"

"No problem," said the coroner.

"I've had the relatives round my neck and I can't get hold of Dabbe."

"No problem," repeated the coroner. "Your friend

and medical colleague, the pathologist, says she died of diabetes, too."

"That's a relief," said Paston frankly. "For a moment I thought . . ."

"Doctors have been known to differ," said the solicitor mildly. "Especially after death."

"I was afraid I might have missed something," said the general practitioner. "I'm not as young as I used to be and I've got a lot on my mind."

"If you have missed anything," the coroner said drily, "it wasn't anything that the pathologist could find."

"Shouldn't have wanted to slip up with her. The nephew's wife is a first-class menace. Besides, Beatrice was a decent sort."

Both men, professional realists, knew that the latter was very much a secondary consideration compared with the former.

"Of course," said Chestley, "Dabbe did a lot of hedging about in case anything shows up in his tissue testing."

"Pathologists," said the general practitioner, "are getting as bad as solicitors at that these days."

"Nothing's as certain as it used to be," countered Robert Chestley profoundly. "The law has always known it. Medicine's just catching on."

"The patient doesn't like his physician to share his uncertainty with him," responded Paston. "I've tried it and I know."

"Dabbe does let you have a copy of his report, doesn't he?"

"He does but I daresay it won't surprise me now. She was getting all sorts of signs and symptoms that indicated she needed more insulin. I saw her twice last week and told her to step up her dose each time."

"Ah."

"I should have thought it would have done the trick myself—surprising it didn't really—but you never can tell."

"No."

"And of course she lived alone. Then if you do go

over the edge of safety there's no one there to haul you back."

"She might not have acted upon your advice," pointed out the coroner, always able to find something to cavil at, and well used to doctors who wondered if they should have done more.

"I'll have you know, Chestley, that patients are usually more obedient than clients."

"Just as well," riposted the man of law neatly. "Clients who don't take our advice bring in a lot of work. Yours only die."

This response set up quite a different train of thought in the general practitioner. His tone changed completely. "Bob, I'm sending my junior partner round to see you."

"Peter McCavity?"

"I've persuaded him to consult you at last. Took a bit of doing."

"I can believe that."

"He's—er—got himself into a—er—little difficulty."

"Again?"

"Yes." The doctor sighed. "Yes. Again."

"The old problem?"

There was a pause. "I'm very much afraid so."

* * *

"The dog it was that died, eh, Sloan?" said the superintendent thoughtfully when the detective inspector got back to the police station.

"So Constable Crosby says, sir." Sloan toyed with the note he had made.

"And how did he find out?"

"Poking about in Ridley Road," said Sloan, looking out of the window.

"Poking about?"

"Digging," supplied Sloan uncomfortably.

"Where?"

"Miss Wansdyke's garden."

"He'll be the death of me, that boy, one day," breathed Leeyes.

"Of us all," said Sloan feelingly.

"Not so much as 'by your leave'?"

"No."

"Anyone's permission?"

"No."

"Search warrant?"

"Wouldn't know what that looked like, I daresay."

"Just went along with his spade?"

"Shouldn't be surprised."

"And his bucket," said Leeyes, "like he was at the seaside?"

"Probably."

"What will the neighbours say?"

Taking this literally, Sloan flipped his note over. "One of them gave him a cup of tea—a Mrs. Stroude. She confirms that Miss Wansdyke spent the whole of Friday evening looking for the dog. She heard her whistling and calling until quite late. And she saw her out and about early Saturday morning ditto."

"By which time the dog was dead and buried?"

"Presumably."

"Where?"

"Not far from a small compost heap at the bottom of the garden."

"Crosby knew where to look?" Leeyes sounded disbelieving.

Sloan cleared his throat and said carefully, "He tells me that in one of his training courses they had a lesson on how to identify disturbed ground."

"With pictures, I suppose," grunted Leeyes. "When I was a constable we were supposed to work that sort of thing out for ourselves."

"Yes, sir." Disturbed ground always meant something, all the same. The archaeologists knew that.

"Julius Caesar was here," said the superintendent, "and all that."

"Yes, sir."

"So he knew what to look for?"

"He found the dog," said Sloan elliptically.

"The dead don't bury the dead," said the superintendent.

"No." Sloan acknowledged this immediately. "From what he says there seems little doubt that someone . . ."

"Person or persons unknown . . ." intervened Leeyes.

"Er—quite, sir—buried the dog just after dark on Friday evening."

"How do we know that?"

"I gather Mrs. Stroude is the sort of neighbour who would have noticed—er—unusual activity in the next-door garden in daylight."

"I don't know where we'd get without inquisitive neighbours," said Leeyes frankly. "I reckon that's what keeps people on the straight and narrow—not morality at all."

"This one is positive nothing sinister went on in the garden in the early afternoon," said Sloan. He paused. "She went out a little later on though. That's when she noticed the car."

"What car?"

"A blue Allegro," said Sloan carefully. He paused. "A very battered one."

"Did she know it?" He grunted. "Women don't usually."

"Oh, yes."

"Do we know it?" enquired Leeyes heavily.

"Yes."

"Not the battered blue Allegro that we all know?"

"Dr. McCavity's," said Sloan, "from the sound of it."

"Hrrrrrmph," said Leeyes.

"Yes, sir," said Sloan. "Quite."

"How," enquired Leeyes pertinently, "did the dog get from house to garden?"

"How it got out of the house is what bothered Miss Wansdyke. She didn't know about it being dead in the garden, of course. She'd left it locked indoors when she went to school as usual. She was so upset about that fact that she told Mrs. Stroude she was putting the chain on her door that night."

"So someone opens the door with a key . . ." He paused. "Or do you think our promising young Sherlock Holmes was so busy digging up the dog that he wouldn't have noticed a break-in?"

"Miss Wansdyke would have done," said Sloan realistically.

Leeyes nodded. "Right. Then the door gets opened with a key, and someone kills Fido."

"Isolde," said Sloan distantly.

"You having me on, Sloan?" growled Leeyes.

"No, sir."

There was a pause, then: "I had forgotten we were in a superior part of the town."

"Quite, sir."

"Sloan . . ."

"Sir?"

"There's an old saying about dogs."

"Letting sleeping ones lie?" ventured Sloan.

"No," roared Leeyes. "Certainly not. We're police officers, man, not politicians."

"Sorry, sir." He coughed. "Another old saying, I think you said. . . ."

"Love me, love my dog," said Leeyes.

"Yes, sir. Of course, sir, but . . ."

"Have we got a case of 'Hate me, hate my dog' on our hands, Sloan? Tell me that. . . ."

"I hope not, sir."

"Sloan"—Leeyes had a second thought—"how do we know that Miss Wansdyke didn't find the dog dead herself later on the Saturday or Sunday and see that it was decently buried in her garden?"

"Because it had had its throat cut," said Sloan chillingly.

Chapter 7

Ah, no, let be! For the Philosopher's Stone,
Called the Elixir, never can be known.

Just as, in the immortal words of the poet, even the weariest river winds somewhere safe to the sea, so eventually every tired policeman finds his way at last to his own fireside. Lightly brushing a kiss onto his wife's cheeks, Detective Inspector Sloan dropped thankfully into an armchair.

"You'll miss me when I'm in the hospital," said Margaret Sloan. "When I'm not here to come home to . . ."

He did not attempt to answer this. "I'll know all about it, though, when you get back, won't I?" he insisted in mock despair. "A baby crying . . . nappies everywhere . . . another mouth to feed . . ."

"Talking of food . . ." she said, disappearing hastily in the direction of the kitchen.

When she came back he told her about the dog.

"Poor thing," she said, distressed. "Whoever would want to do a thing like that?"

"I don't know." He stuffed a cushion behind his head and said what was uppermost in his mind. "It's not a lot to go on—a dead dog."

"And a quarter of a million pounds," she reminded him.

"The family are all carrying on as if she's only left twopence ha'penny," said Sloan.

"Perhaps they really don't know."

"For my money," said Sloan with a fine disregard for metaphor, "someone somewhere does."

"And she did die naturally," said Margaret Sloan.

"The dog didn't," said her husband obliquely.

She shuddered a little. "Whose money will it be then?"

"You're as bad as the superintendent." Sloan stretched his legs out in front of the fire. "He keeps on asking that, too, only he doesn't put it quite so nicely."

"Gain usually comes into evil somewhere, doesn't it?" she said.

"Yes, my love." He was quite willing to go along with that: in fact he didn't know of any policeman who wouldn't be. If gain didn't come into evil then what you had instead wasn't crime at all but a suitable case for treatment—medical treatment.

"Immediate gain, that is," she said seriously, sitting down, too, by the fire. She stared into the flames for a moment and then said, "There's something sinister in one of the nursery rhymes about growing rich, isn't there?"

"Been doing your homework, have you?" he teased her, casting about in his mind for the allusion. "Ready for you-know-who?"

She smiled wanly and quoted, " 'When I grow rich . . . say the bells of Shoreditch.' "

" 'The bells of London Town,' " he said. Nursery rhymes were uncannily prescient. Then something stirred in his own childhood memory. "The Old Bailey comes into that, too, doesn't it?"

" 'When will you pay me?' " she sang softly.

" 'Say the bells at Old Bailey.' " He completed the couplet in a lower register.

"Trust a copper to remember that bit," she said, her turn to tease.

"Plenty of debts to society have been paid at the Old Bailey in its time."

"We shouldn't be joking about all this, should we?" she said quickly. "Not with Miss Wansdyke and her dog both lying dead . . ."

Somewhere in one of the books they had had handed out to them at the ante-natal clinic had been some advice about how a couple should comfort themselves during the wife's pregnancy. They shouldn't move house, for instance, or indulge in great arguments. Whims, however bizarre, should be indulged. Strange fancies for out-of-season strawberries or fresh oysters should be pandered to. Layettes should be prepared but—and the good books stressed this—pregnancy was no time for philosophical doubts. The profundities of life should be allowed to take second place to the most profound experience of all living.

He gave a huge yawn and deliberately steered the conversation towards more neutral ground. "There's one funny thing, though, Margaret. . . ."

"What's that?"

"The family have gone all quiet about the main beneficiary, Nicholas Petforth, Briony's brother. They say they don't know where he is."

"Perhaps," she said consideringly, "he'll come home again now that there's something to come back for."

"There! What did I say?" He gave her an affectionate grin. "You're really as bad as the superintendent after all. . . ."

"Me?" she said indignantly.

"All he does is concentrate on who gains." He stretched his legs out before the blaze in the hearth. "At least it means that I know what tomorrow's first job is going to be."

She looked up. "What's that?"

"Find Master Petforth."

"Not," she enquired ironically, "a search and destroy mission—destroy with great wealth, I mean."

"No." He shook his head. "We'll just put the word out. That's all."

His wife stared dreamily into the fire and quoted:

> " 'Instantly the under-
>   standing Seraphim
> Laid their fingers on their lips
>   And went to look for him.' "

"Jane Austen?" he hazarded. If they had a daughter she was going to have "Jane" among her given names. Margaret went on:

> *" 'Stole across the Zodiac,*
> *Harnessed Charles's Wain,*
> *And whispered round the Nebulae . . .'* "

He relaxed. "Nothing like that. Don't worry. Just a few questions here and there. If he's in Calleshire," said Sloan confidently, "we'll pick him up tomorrow. If we have to ask questions outside the county of course it'll take longer. . . . What is it?" His whole tone changed suddenly as he saw a spasm of pain crossing her face. "Margaret . . . Margaret, what is it? What's wrong? Is it . . ."

"I've just thought . . . that horrible nursery rhyme."

"Oranges and lemons?"

She stared at him. "I've remembered how it finishes."

"Don't look like that, my love," he pleaded. "You frightened me. For a moment I thought . . ."

" 'Here comes a candle to light you to bed,' " she intoned, " 'and here comes a chopper to chop off your head.' "

*   *   *

It wasn't the Seraphim who found out where Nicholas Petforth was in the end. Or, at least, not directly.

It was Detective Constable William Edward Crosby.

People who went native these days usually did so in one of two ways. They either took to the road or they joined a commune.

Putting the word out in the county had had the desired effect.

They learned down at the Berebury Police Station fairly early on that their man wasn't on the road in Calleshire. He was too young for that game for a start and those who were walking the countryside—that pathetic group whose worldly possessions were clutched to them, who tramped from somewhere to anywhere like a variety of land-locked Flying Dutchmen, without either anchor or rudder, answering to any wind or to no wind at

all—had not come across anyone sounding like Miss
Beatrice Wansdyke's nephew. There were fewer of such
travellers about these days, but those that there were
were conspicuous and—uphill and down dale—they
obligingly stopped long enough to tell the police that
Nicholas Petforth wasn't one of their number. Mind
you, stopping wasn't something they liked to do. If you
stopped, you had to think: and for them thinking was
the only unbearable activity.

Today's drop-outs didn't walk the countryside. When
they wanted to cast off society's links they squatted: especially the younger ones. If enough of them squatted
together somehow the community became a commune.

It had fallen to Detective Constable Crosby's lot to
call on the one in the town of Luston.

"You can't miss it, lad," the friendly station sergeant
at Luston had told him, adding, "I daresay there'll be a
bite left to eat in our canteen when you get back." He
chuckled. "If you still feel like eating, that is."

Any connection between what went on in this Calleshire commune and the dreams and the reality of the
days of the French Commune of an earlier age must
have been purely coincidental. Urban decay had
reached the old centre of the industrial town: urban re-
newal hadn't. Constable Crosby made his way to a
faded early nineteenth-century town house that in its
prime had had some considerable style to it. Now its
paintwork was peeling and some of its windows were
boarded up. Other windows sported blankets doing
duty as curtains. Somehow, though, the once-graceful
building had contrived to retain an air of decayed gen-
tility—distinction, even.

Detective Constable Crosby's pounding on the front
door shook it visibly but produced no answer from
within. Immediately, however, the door of the house
next door flew open and a raven-haired woman put her
head out.

"If you're the gas," she said, "you're wasting your
time. It's cut off."

Crosby said he wasn't the gas.

"They've found a way round the electricity meter for
sure," she said.

Crosby said he could well believe it.

"And if you're the Water Board," she grimaced, completing a trinity of public supply undertakings, "you needn't worry. They don't use it." She rolled her eyes. "The whole place stinks."

By now Crosby had been able to appreciate this fact for himself. Château Commune certainly had a bouquet all its own.

"I can tell you one thing for sure," she cackled. "They can't read bills in there."

"Some people have all the luck," said Crosby.

The neighbour's head, which seemed as disembodied behind its owner's front door as the Cheshire cat's on its wall, looked him up and down.

"Come to serve a summons, 'ave you?" she asked shrewdly.

In a way it was a tribute to his manner, if not his suit.

"I'm making enquiries," responded Crosby.

"You'll be lucky." She sniffed. She jerked her head towards the other house. "Not many of them get up in the mornings, I can tell you."

He looked up at the blind windows.

"Work's a dirty word with that lot," she said.

"Some of them must do some," protested the young policeman in spite of himself. They'd been very firm in his primary school about tying the male image to the work ethic. The boys hadn't learned knitting. They'd been taught instead that men must work. The corollary that women must weep ("Georgie Porgy kissed the girls and made them cry") they'd been left to find out for themselves in the playground afterwards. "You can't live without working," he said, though you couldn't be a policeman long without meeting a group who tried to do just that.

"Two or three of the fellers do go out to work," she conceded. "None of the girls." She raised her eyebrows heavenwards. "What they do all day long don't bear thinking about."

It was quite apparent though from her keen expression that she thought about it a lot.

Crosby kept silent.

She jerked her head towards the next-door building. "Beats me," she said, sucking her teeth, "how the police let them get away with squatting."

Crosby drew breath. "Civil law . . ."

"Take Fred Smith's boy down the road."

"Well?"

"They had him for breaking and entering last week."

"Did they?"

"Camera shop in Calleford High Street."

"Ah."

"Don't you go and say that that's different."

"I shan't."

"This lot next door," she said richly, "did their breaking and entering and they stayed."

"I can see that."

"And nobody's touched them for anything."

"No." It was funny how the word "touched" hung about the law.

"It's not right."

"No, madam." If anything, squatting offended the police even more than it did the public. "But the law is that . . ."

"You looking for anyone in particular?" she interrupted him off-handedly.

"Tall, youngish lad," said Crosby, also cutting the cackle and getting to the horses. "Auburn hair. Still a bit freckled."

"There's one or two of 'em in there," she said slyly, "that shouldn't be."

"I daresay. This chap . . ."

She jerked her head. "And not what you'd expect, either."

"Oh?"

"A couple of clever dicks and some girls who should know better."

"From good homes, you mean?" he said naïvely.

Her face assumed a curious expression.

"If that's what you'd call Calle Castle . . ."

"The duke's daughter?" Crosby took another look up at the dilapidated house.

"His youngest." She sniffed.

"Bit of a change, wasn't it?"

"I should think they had their hands full with her at home. She's a one, all right. Oh, her father came round and made noises."

"I'll bet."

"It didn't do any good. It was her mother that got her out."

"How?" asked Crosby in spite of himself.

"Sent the chauffeur round each week with a box of groceries and a brace of pheasants."

"How did that do it?"

The face grinned at his innocence. "The Lady Alicia was all for sending them back, snooty-like, unopened."

"Fair enough."

"Said it made her feel different."

"I'll bet it did," said Crosby warmly.

"But the others wouldn't let her," cackled the woman shrewishly. "They ate 'em."

"Too bad. Then she grew up or something?"

"After a bit," she crowed, "she got to see the others were making a fool of her."

"Sponging," pronounced Crosby.

"Enjoying what they said they despised," mimicked the woman in high lady-like tones. She grinned. "Give her another ten years and she'll be opening flower shows with the best of them."

"This fellow that I'm looking for . . ."

"Called Nick?" hazarded the woman.

"Could be."

"You're wasting your time."

"Not here?"

"One of the workers. Goes off early."

"Where?"

"Up the motorway site."

"Thanks." Crosby turned to go. Then he stopped. "You'd miss them now, wouldn't you?" he said.

She slammed the door.

*　*　*

"The bank," reported Sloan gloomily, "will surrender details of their late client's account if . . ."

"Yes?" said Superintendent Leeyes eagerly, leaning forward across his desk.

"If," repeated Sloan, "we get a court order."

"Bah!" said Leeyes, who never in any circumstances whatsoever himself divulged confidential police information to any unauthorised person or institution.

"And not without one," underlined Sloan.

"Obstructionists . . ."

"Any other assistance that we may require," repeated Sloan fluently, "they will, of course, be only too happy to give us."

"The source of the money," said Leeyes promptly.

"I asked them that," said Sloan.

"Well?"

"They said, 'What money?' as bland as butter."

"What about her life-style?" said Leeyes in a challenging fashion. "That didn't go with a quarter of a million pounds, did it?"

"That," admitted Sloan, "did seem to strike a chord with the bank manager."

"Well," said Leeyes tartly, "she wasn't exactly living it up, was she?"

"It's not," ventured Sloan cautiously, "quite the same down there at the bank as it is round here moneywise."

"I should hope not," retorted Leeyes speedily. There was a pause. Then he said, "Just exactly what are you getting at, Sloan?"

"Down there, sir, they're more used than we are here to folks without money spending it."

"Drinking whisky on a beer income," said Leeyes graphically.

"And to customers with it not spending it," added Sloan fairly.

"Orange juice on a brandy income."

"I understand," replied Sloan drily, "that they've got a fair number of those too."

Shaking his head at what he saw as a waste of natural resources, Leeyes said, "Anything else?"

"Every time I came up with a question they referred me to their client's executor."

"Bertram George Wansdyke," said the superintendent, who always did his homework.

"He doesn't use the Bertram," Sloan informed him. "They told me that at the bank."

"Don't blame him."

"He's always known as George."

"Never Bertram," noted Leeyes. "People can be funny about Christian names."

"Watch out for any man who calls his son Samson," said Sloan.

"You and your wife got all that sort of thing lined up all right, Sloan?" asked Leeyes gruffly.

"What? Oh, yes, sir. Thank you, sir." Potential names of babies were not in short supply in the Sloan ménage. On the contrary. And had they been, Sloan's mother had a reserve supply.

"Mind you," said the superintendent reminiscently, "our brigadier was called Cecil so it doesn't always signify."

"I was once attacked by a social misfit called Algernon," contributed Sloan. The superintendent had to be diverted from recounting his wartime experiences at all costs or the day was lost. "At least, his mother called him Algernon and the judge called him a social misfit and I . . ."

"This Bertram George Wansdyke . . ."

"A partner in Wansdyke and Darnley."

"The firm down by the bridge?"

"Them. Plastics manufacturers."

"Anything," enquired Leeyes, rolling his eyes, "to do with the celebrated Malcolm Darnley?"

"Everything."

"Good God! The agitator?"

"Conservationist," murmured Sloan mildly, "is what he calls himself."

"He's practically maniacal about it."

" 'Dedicated,' " said Sloan austerely, "is the word the newspapers use."

"Inspector Harpe can't get a roadway corner in the whole of Calleshire straightened," declared Leeyes. "Every time he wants a tree down it turns out to have a preservation order clapped on it."

"That's Malcolm Darnley," agreed Sloan. "He insists

that trees do not get up and hit passing motorists. He wins every time."

"And the Town Council can't widen the roads round by the cattle market either. Every building they want out of the way turns out to have had Queen Elizabeth sleeping in it or something."

"Listed," said Sloan more technically.

"And I have to have two good men and true down there every market day when they should be catching villains."

" 'His mission in life,' " Sloan quoted something he'd read in the local newspaper, " 'is the preservation of the environment.' "

"The man's a first-class nuisance."

"Public-spirited," murmured Sloan, "is the name of the game."

"Hrrrrrmph."

"Anyway, George Wansdyke seems able to cope."

"Firm all right"

"Appears to be flourishing," said Sloan. "They turn out the more rarefied plastic parts for industry and medicine and so forth. They do a lot of the research and development, too, I'm told. Take on promising young science graduates and all that sort of thing."

"No word of any money troubles?"

"None." He coughed. "Anyway, George Wansdyke doesn't get anything himself from his aunt's estate. His children get an eighth between them in trust, that's all."

"George Wansdyke," pronounced Superintendent Leeyes didactically, "is the sole executor of an estate that everyone believes to be small. . . ."

They were interrupted by the telephone.

"Who?" said Leeyes testily. "Well, put him through, of course." He looked at Sloan. "It's Dr. Dabbe." His tone changed. "Good morning, Doctor. About Beatrice Gwendoline Wansdyke . . . Yes . . . Yes, yes . . . I know all the background . . . Yes . . . Diabetes . . . Insulin . . . What's that?" His eyebrows disappeared upwards. "What did you say? . . . Yes, I've got that. . . . Insulin . . . No insulin? Do you mind repeating that? Yes, that's what I thought you said. I'll

send a man round for the report straightaway. . . .
Thank you." He made to put the telephone receiver
down, then changed his mind. "Doctor, are you still
there? . . . Look here, how are you on dogs? . . .
What? . . . No, not betting on them . . . doing post-
mortems on them. . . . On one, actually . . . We
may want one done . . . That's very kind of you . . .
Thank you." He did put the telephone down this time.
And then he turned back to Sloan, his face a study.
"The pathologist reports that there was no trace of insulin in Beatrice Wansdyke's blood. He reckons she's
been without it for several days."

Chapter 8

My face is wan and wears a leaden look;
If you try science you'll be brought to book.

The foreman on the motorway construction site was a much-tried man. He had, however, long ago reached that stage of controlled despair when he regarded each fresh burden with a certain masochistic satisfaction as providing further evidence of a malign fate's continued unkindness to him.

"Police?" he said to Detective Constable Crosby, rolling his eyes. "What is it this time? Something fallen off the back of a lorry again?"

"Not today," said Crosby cautiously. "So far."

"Or have you come to tell me that you've found that load of aggregate that got nicked on the Calleford Road?"

"Not yet," said Crosby, "but I daresay we shall."

"That's all very fine and large," said the foreman, "but it won't help me. I had to get onto the quarry sharp for another load."

"Perhaps next time," suggested the constable, "the driver will use another transport café."

The foreman gave him a shrewd look. "Mother Meg's again? I've always said it was a proper thieves' kitchen."

"Meals come a bit expensive there sometimes." Detective Constable Crosby surveyed the motorway site from the vantage point beside the foreman's hut. "Mucking Calleshire about a bit, aren't you?"

"Don't you start. . . ."

"Like being on the moon but dirtier."

The foreman twisted his lips. "You should have heard them at the enquiry."

Crosby grinned. "Our Mr. Malcolm Darnley from Berebury there?"

"It's a wonder he didn't get arrested."

"It's a free country."

"Stabbed in the back then," said the foreman.

The constable waved an arm. "Well, he did have something to complain about, didn't he?"

"Said he'd lie down under the first bulldozer."

"Someone nick that too?"

"Wish he had and all," grumbled the foreman.

"Saved a lot of trouble, would it?" said the constable, looking 'round.

"Someone," said the foreman with deep conviction, "will put that man Darnley in a wooden overcoat one day."

"A cement one, more likely," said Crosby, looking around at the desolate waste of concrete that surrounded them.

"What? Oh, yes. I daresay."

"It's been done before," said the constable seriously. "At least we think it's been done before. It's not easy to prove."

"I can see," said the foreman, casting his eyes in the general direction of an embryo fly-over, "that you'd likely be a bit short on evidence."

Detective Constable Crosby followed his gaze. "No more bother with that crane over there?" he enquired solicitously.

"Not that I've heard about." The foreman rolled his eyes. "Not that I get to hear everything, mind you."

"No," said Crosby consideringly, "you wouldn't, would you?"

"Not in my job," agreed the foreman. "Mark you, there's some things I don't want to know about, thank you very much."

"I can see that," said the constable.

The foreman indicated the crane. "We lock it up of nights now."

"Good," said Crosby pleasantly. "The inspector will be glad to hear it."

"Who would have thought," demanded the foreman of the world at large, "that anyone would have wanted to use a great thing like that for safe-breaking?"

"Someone thought of it," said Crosby. Larky Nolson hadn't been the only criminal to have had trouble with a safe in their manor.

The foreman shrugged his shoulders. "There are always more ways than one of killing the canary."

"It got it open all right," rejoined the constable. "By the time we got here there was money everywhere."

"If we were to drop you from that height onto a spot of hardstanding," said the foreman, "I daresay you'd break open too."

"Yes," said Crosby simply. The manifold highly unpleasant ways in which various members of the police force had died in the course of the execution of their duty was one of the many facts that they impressed on them at their training college. There was a book, too, where they turned over a page every day. . . . He pulled out his notebook. "I'm looking for a man. . . ."

"I didn't think you were just passing the time of day."

"Name of Nicholas Petforth. Tallish. Auburn hair."

"Nick? He was around." The foreman waved an arm. "Ask at the office."

"I did."

"Well?"

"They said he was this way."

"Doesn't look as if he is, does it?"

"No," said Crosby literally. "Can't say it does."

"Well, he was around then." The foreman pushed his cap to the back of his head. "Could he have heard that you were asking for him?"

"Might have done." Crosby coughed delicately. "The word does get around."

"Then," said the foreman, "he probably didn't stay to argue the toss and you've probably gone and lost me the only person who can drive that damned thing over there properly."

The constable followed his gaze towards an enormous earth-moving machine that looked like some grotesque mechanised caterpillar with extra, articulated jaws.

"Watch out," said Crosby solemnly, "that someone doesn't borrow that to dig up the Bank of England."

* * *

Smell is undoubtedly the most evocative of all the senses. At least, Detective Inspector Sloan would have been prepared to swear that it was the moment that he set foot inside the Berebury District General Hospital again. The hospital had that peculiar aroma compounded of as many ingredients as a witch's brew—and very nearly as unsavoury—that seemed to be common to all such institutions. It was one, he decided, that you forgot as you left it but remembered pretty speedily as you stepped over the threshold again.

He went in through the main entrance of the hospital and set about making his way to the pathologist's office. As he did so he lifted his head to take another look at the signs supposed to guide patients in the direction in which they wanted to go. He revised that sentiment almost immediately to "the direction in which they *needed* to go." He could not imagine anyone actually wanting to go to Isolation (a solid unbroken white ring with blankness inside).

He paused briefly under a symbol that represented a man leaning forward on one leg, the other thrust out behind him. The man could have stood for a ballet dancer or a skater. What he couldn't have represented was any medical or surgical speciality that Sloan could possibly think of. He moved on, hurrying past the sign that clearly indicated the nursery. This was three doll-like babies, side by side, wrapped papoose style. "Triplets," he thought in horror to himself, lowering his eyes and quickening his pace. It was a contingency he was not even prepared to begin to contemplate, and he turned off the main corridor as soon as he could.

His mind, though, stayed with the subject of hospital signs. The Mortuary didn't have one. The solitary giant tear-shaped symbol that could have fooled someone seeking that department (or tea and sympathy?) turned out to represent not a human tear but a drop of blood steering the way to the Blood Bank. Nothing representational marked out the Mortuary. He said as much to Dr. Dabbe as he entered his office.

"It's a nice thought," said that worthy. "The forensic equivalent of the good old barber's pole. What do you suggest?"

"Well . . ."

"Something simple?"

"Naturally."

"Skull and crossbones?"

"Too Captain Hook," objected Sloan.

"Ah, Sloan, you've been boning up on pantomime with the baby coming."

"There's the empty skull. What about that?" Sloan couldn't have said why it was that he suddenly felt so light-hearted: perhaps because the death of Beatrice Wansdyke had turned into a proper case after all.

"The 'Alas, poor Yorick' style?" said Dabbe. "Yes, that would do, Sloan, though I rather care for the French pattern myself."

"The French?"

"They have something rather discouraging in red enamel labelled 'Morte' halfway up their electricity pylons."

"Do they?" One day he would travel, of course. His child would need to be shown the world.

"The mediaevalists," Dabbe informed him, warming to the theme, "favoured a death's head as an emblem of mortality."

"Sounds appropriate."

"Especially if there was a moral attached."

"There was always a moral attached in those days."

"True. But if you want to be really modern . . ."

"Most people do," said Sloan inaccurately.

"Then I think I should recommend death ritualised twentieth-century style."

"How?" Sloan cast his mind around the possibilities. There were plenty of them.

"From the Wild West . . ."

Sloan had forgotten that the pathologist was an armchair cowboy.

"A smoking gun would do nicely," pronounced Dabbe. He stood up. "In the meantime, Sloan, we shall have to make do with what signs we've got, shan't we? Come through. . . ."

Sloan followed the pathologist from his office through a door marked quite clearly Medico-Legal Department.

"A nice touch for those of our subjects still able to read," remarked Dabbe. "This way—what we want is in the laboratory."

Seating the detective inspector on a stool in front of a bench, the pathologist reached for a series of little bottles. Less confidently, Sloan reached for his notebook.

"Beatrice Wansdyke died from the effects of diabetes," said the pathologist. "That still holds. She probably had all the symptoms—you'll be able to check on that. She certainly had all the signs, including dehydration. We got as far as that at the post-mortem yesterday."

"Yes."

"What I would have expected to find was some indication in the post-mortem blood-sugar levels that she'd had some insulin not so long before death."

"And you didn't?"

"I didn't." The pathologist pulled a sheet of paper along the bench and then started looking for a particular test tube in a long row in a rack. His hand hovered over them. "There's a fortune waiting for the man who can invent a foolproof way of keeping laboratory specimens attached to their pathological notes."

"And for the discoverer of a perfect jury system," said Sloan feelingly. "Every copper who's ever lived could have done with that."

"These two seem to match," said Dabbe, comparing two separate sets of numbers. "Anyway, this blood-sugar level is far too high for her to have been within shouting distance of a dose of insulin for days."

"Interesting," said Sloan cautiously.

"She also had heavy glycosuria."

"That'll have to keep for the expert witnesses," said Sloan, making a lay attempt at writing it down.

"And ketonuria."

Sloan wrote that down too. After a fashion.

"It all adds up to the same thing," said the pathologist.

"She didn't have her insulin when she should have done?"

"Exactly."

"So?"

"So either she stopped taking it," said the doctor.

"Or," said the policeman, "something or someone kept it from her."

"Medico . . ." began Sloan.

"Or legal," finished Dabbe.

"Difficult."

"Those are the only two inferences that I can draw, too," said the pathologist amiably. "And I shall be quite happy to say so in a court of law."

"Either way it didn't do her any good."

"Either way it killed her," said Dr. Dabbe unequivocably.

"She died of it," nodded Sloan.

"How it came about the way it did is your department, Sloan. Not mine. *Post hoc, ergo propter hoc* as we say in the post-mortem room."

Sloan stood up. Medical Latin was one thing. When the pathologist took to quoting classical tags it was time to go. "Thank you, Doctor."

"You know, Sloan," he said negligently as they crossed the room, "I think after all we only need the one notice here in our department."

Sloan followed the direction of the doctor's bony finger as it pointed to a sign above the door.

"Exit?" he said.

"It says it all," murmured Dr. Dabbe, "doesn't it?"

* * *

Miss Simpson sighed and pressed the bell for her secretary.

"Show them in," she sighed.

Once upon a time the headmistress of the Berebury Grammar School for Girls would have been seriously disturbed at the news that the police had arrived at the school and wished to see her. Not any more. The motor car had put an end to that. So many of the sixth form had their own cars these days that brushes with the law were commonplace.

And if it wasn't the motor car as often or not it was the lure of the great unknown. Time was when girls seldom left home alone. Nowadays even schools like hers had pupils who absconded. Improbable as it seemed, it was one of the drawbacks of the single-sex school.

Miss Simpson had her spiel on this theme practically word-perfect these days. The bolder spirits in a "girls only" school, she would insist to the school governors, were practically certain to find trouble. The quiet girl from a sheltered background in a little village, she would remind startled parents who were on their way to being overprotective, was almost always at even greater risk.

"And Gretna Green," she would say ominously to both groups, "is the only Scottish place name that they all know."

As always, Miss Walsh, the deputy head, agreed with her.

"There is nothing," ran Miss Simpson's favourite sermon to Miss Walsh, "like seeing spotty boys all day and every day for keeping a girl in touch with reality."

The deputy head, who cherished a secret passion for Omar Sharif and who read romantic novels in the privacy of her own bedroom, would nod sagely at this dictum too—but still call in at the library on her chaste way home.

"A gipsy caravan," she said wistfully to the head now. "That's what I set my heart on when I was young. Dear me, how we all do grow up."

"Really!" exclaimed Miss Simpson. "You should have known better than that even then." She looked at the door expectantly. "Let's hope it's not drugs this time, anyway. It will be one day, you know."

"The lure of another great unknown," said little Miss Walsh incorrigibly.

It soon transpired that it wasn't drugs or missing pupils or motor cars that the police wanted to see Miss Simpson about.

It wasn't even about a girl.

"Miss Collins?" said Miss Simpson, puzzled. "Miss Hilda Collins?"

"Miss Wansdyke's friend," said Detective Inspector Sloan.

"Our biologist," said Miss Simpson.

"In the lab," said Miss Walsh, consulting a timetable. "With the fourth form."

The fourth form at Berebury Grammar School for Girls clearly found the visit from an unknown male more exciting than the study of the life cycle of the dog fish upon which they were engaged when he arrived. Miss Hilda Collins, however, was equally the possessor of a lion tamer's eye. One swift look round the laboratory from her and the fourth form had turned its attention back to *Scyllium canicula*.

Detective Inspector Sloan said he was sorry about the death of her friend.

"You shouldn't ever feel sorry for anyone who dies suddenly," said Miss Collins gruffly, pulling herself up and straightening her white coat.

Sloan, who in his time had felt very sorry indeed for a number of people who had died with startling suddenness—mostly as victims—nevertheless knew exactly what she meant and did not argue.

"We don't let domestic and agricultural animals linger," said the biologist, "do we?"

"Not if we can help it," agreed Sloan, his mind turning unbidden to a dead Airedale.

"Then we shouldn't let humans," said Miss Collins trenchantly. She led him to a little office at one end of the laboratory that was above and apart from the class, and then turned and looked him squarely in the eye. "Now, what do you want from me?"

"When did you last see Beatrice Wansdyke?"

"Thursday afternoon," said Hilda Collins without hesitation. "We had a cup of tea together in the staff room after school finished. At least I had a cup. She had three. She said she seemed to be very thirsty all the time."

"Not Friday?"

"I didn't come in to school on Friday. I'd had a bit

of a cold and lost my voice." She twisted her lips wryly.
"It's the one faculty that you can't do without in this
job."

"And how was Miss Wansdyke on Thursday?" enquired Sloan, making a mental note.

"Not well," said Hilda Collins immediately. "She
hadn't been at all well lately. I—we'd—all begun to get
a bit worried about her. And so had she, I think. She
wondered if she might have picked up some disease
while she was in France."

If that noted xenophobe Superintendent Leeyes had
been present he, too, would have tried to blame the
French first.

"She went with a school party on a tour of the
châteaux of the Loire in the summer holidays, you
know, Inspector."

Detective Inspector Sloan, who had seen for himself
that "Calais" was not engraved on Miss Wansdyke's
heart—or anywhere else—and who knew about the
absence of insulin in her bloodstream, saw no occasion
for blaming the French.

"But the doctor said not," went on the biologist. "He
just told her to step up her dose of insulin."

"Quite," said Sloan, keeping silent on the highly germane fact that her friend had died without a trace of it
in her body.

"I'm glad she went quickly," said Miss Collins with
such fervour that Sloan looked up.

He hadn't, so far in his police working life, encountered a "mercy killing" but there was always a first
time.

"I'm a member of a euthanasia society," she said.

Sloan was not surprised.

"When my time comes," averred the schoolteacher,
"I shall take something."

Sloan nodded. A lot of people said that they weren't
prepared to wait for Death the Reaper. But they usually
did.

"Tell me a little about Miss Wansdyke," invited
Sloan. He needed to fill out the curiously empty picture
of a chemistry mistress that was all he had so far. "Had
she any hobbies, for instance?"

Miss Collins considered this. "Just the one."

"Ah."

"More of a passion than a hobby."

"People get like that," said Sloan. Other people, of course. Growing roses well was just a relaxation as far as he was concerned, naturally.

"Everyone has to have something."

"The dog?" he offered tentatively.

The biologist shook her head. "No, no. Not Isolde. No, Beatrice was looking for something."

Sloan waited.

"Everyone has their Holy Grail," she said.

"We're all seekers after something," he advanced in his turn. He was old enough now to know that. With some it was the Truth: but not with everyone. "What was Miss Wansdyke looking for, Miss Collins?"

"A way of using the nitrogen that's present in the air," said Hilda Collins unexpectedly. "She felt that it ought to be possible to convert it."

"Oh," said Sloan blankly.

Miss Collins took pity on him. "It would be a sort of latter-day turning of stone into gold. They tried that a lot in the Middle Ages."

"I see."

"Poor Beatrice," said Hilda Collins. "She never did find it."

"Where did she look?" he asked. "Or rather, where did she do the looking?" Air, after all, was free.

The biologist smiled. "She used to use the laboratories down at Wansdyke and Darnley. At weekends. They didn't mind. She'd done more than her bit for the family."

"So I'm told."

"Perhaps," added Miss Collins abruptly, "her nephew will come to his senses now."

"Nicholas Petforth?"

"Not a bad boy," pronounced the schoolteacher judiciously.

The phrase had long ago lost its meaning to anyone who had spent any time at all in a juvenile court.

"His trouble, Inspector, is that he spends all his time being afraid that he's taking after his father."

"It does happen," advanced Sloan cautiously. He had every intention of his son—if the baby should be a boy—taking after him. Or else.

"Nature not nurture?" murmured the biologist quizzically.

"Well . . ."

"Or nurture not nature?"

"A bit of both," comprised Sloan. He was going to see that that child of his—theirs—when it came was going to be brought up properly too.

"But then you're a policeman, aren't you?" She shot him an intelligent look.

"As the twig is bent," Sloan came back.

"It works with the right-handed thread clockwise honeysuckle," conceded the biologist with a glint of humour, "and the left-handed thread anti-clockwise bindweed."

"If you start it in the right way," said the policeman, who was also a gardener.

"Homo sapiens don't keep all the rules," observed Hilda Collins with profundity.

"There are those," proffered Sloan, "who say, 'Give me a boy until he's seven . . .' "

"And," responded Miss Collins, "those who say that the sins of the fathers are visited upon the sons."

"Even unto the third and fourth generation," finished Sloan. His mother had been most particular about his biblical education.

Miss Collins suddenly looked through the office window. "Turn the scalpel the other way, Veronica," she called out. "You'll never dissect anything with the blunt side. Go on, child! Cut! It won't bite you, you know. It's quite dead." She turned back to Sloan. "Where was I?"

"Heredity, I think, miss."

"Fathers," said Hilda Collins, looking Sloan up and down, "only amount to half the genetic programme."

Sloan had never considered paternity in quite that light before and said so.

"Though," remarked Miss Collins academically, "in some ways the rhesus monkey's father is of relatively little importance."

Detective Inspector Sloan said nothing. He had always in any case been on the side of the angels anyway. Apes were less appealing.

"The little woman," said the biologist, following a completely different line of thought, "does her share, too."

"Er—quite so," said Sloan, making up his mind there and then that Margaret, his wife, was not going to hear about this interview at all. Some aspects of police work were not for home consumption.

"There was nothing wrong with Nicholas Petforth's mother, I can assure you." Miss Collins plunged her hands deeply into the pockets of her white coat. "Young Briony's her living image."

"Nature not nurture," said Sloan neatly.

She acknowledged this with a quick jerk of her head. "And there'll be nothing wrong with the boy when he stops running away from himself."

"It would help," observed Sloan mildly, "if he stopped running away from us."

"Like that, is it?" She raised ungroomed eyebrows heavenwards: and then turned away from him again. "Deeper, Veronica! Cut deeper. . . ."

For his money, thought Sloan, Miss Hilda Collins could have slit the throats of a whole pack of dogs.

Chapter 9

My eyes are bleared with work on preparations,
That's all the good you get from transmutations.

"Just a few enquiries, Doctor," began Detective Inspector Sloan. The general practitioner's consulting room was a much less intimidating place than the hospital. There were no white coats about and precious few instruments visible. The chairs and the desk were more homely, too. Detective Constable Crosby was sitting in the chair that was slightly behind and to one side of the doctor's direct line of vision and was presumably the one intended for the patient's friend or relative. Sloan himself was occupying the patient's chair, facing the doctor.

Dr. John Paston regarded him straightly across the desk. "About what, Inspector?"

"The late Miss Beatrice Wansdyke."

"Ah, yes. Of course, Inspector." The general practitioner relaxed almost imperceptibly: but Sloan noticed. Few people realised to what extent body signs gave them away. And that those signs were the more revealing just because they were usually completely uncontrived. Even a professional straight-face like Dr. Paston was not able to conceal them completely. And the professional watcher of people across the desk from him duly took note.

"She was one of your patients, I believe," said Detective Inspector Sloan, realising, when he came to think about it, that this matter of understanding and portraying body language was one of the main ingredients of really first-class stage acting.

"Indeed, yes." The doctor pushed a stethoscope to one side. "For many years."

"We understand that she suffered from diabetes."

"That is so."

Sloan was as quick to notice the quality of the response as he had been to notice the body signs. Never to advance more information than was requested was the hallmark of the skilled interviewee. The doctor was the sort of witness who would stand up well to cross-examination in court. There was no spilling over of extraneous detail here: nothing to give an interrogator a handle.

"Long-standing?" said Sloan.

"Very."

"How did she cope?"

This at least elicited a slightly more expanded reply from the general practitioner.

"Very well, really. She was sensible—that's what matters most in caring for that condition."

Sloan nodded. "She didn't kick over the traces?" It was nice to know that there were other professions which also had to deal with kickers of traces. But if nobody in society ever did step out of line. . . . His wife had read extracts from *Brave New World* to him once. He didn't like the idea of programmed obedience either. He preferred the middle way. One way and another you usually came back to that.

"Let us say," said Dr. Paston, building a steeple with his fingers, "that she was an intelligent woman who understood her condition very well and acted accordingly."

"Not careless?"

"Certainly not."

"And not given to eating what was bad for her?"

"I would have thought, never." He frowned. "She would understand the consequences too well."

"Or missing out her insulin?"

"Out of the question."

"I see."

"She was most punctilious about that. In any case . . ." He paused.

"Yes?"

"In any case," the doctor said more slowly, "if she did forget she would begin to feel ill and that would remind her."

The doctor rearranged a prescription pad and a book of certificates on his desk top while Sloan said quietly, "That's what we thought."

"Besides," continued the general practitioner, "as it happens I had actually advised her to step up her dose the week before she died, not once but twice, so she would scarcely have forgotten. Quite the reverse, I should have said."

"Would it surprise you, Dr. Paston, to know that the pathologist could find no trace whatsoever of insulin at the post-mortem?"

"Very much," said the practitioner vigorously. "In fact, I would find it exceedingly difficult to credit."

"Moreover," continued Sloan, "he also found a number of signs that indicated quite positively that she had not had any insulin for some days before her death."

"I can tell you," countered the doctor immediately, "exactly when she had her last prescription." He flipped a switch and asked a secretary for Beatrice Wansdyke's medical case notes.

"She also had some symptoms indicative of shortage of insulin," went on Sloan firmly. "We have a witness of her being unusually thirsty, for instance, on Thursday."

The doctor's head came up most alertly at that but he did not speak, and there was a sort of silence while they waited for the notes to arrive. Detective Constable Crosby used it to turn over the pages of his notebook slowly and deliberately in such a manner as to emphasise that he was taking notes. Detective Inspector Sloan spent the time studying the general practitioner. He was grey-haired, sparely built, and not—at a guess—very far short of retirement. He gave every appearance at the moment of a puzzled man—but not a frightened one. Dr. Paston himself was clearly using the lead time for thinking hard.

When the patient's notes arrived the situation took a completely new turn.

"As I say," began the doctor, scanning them rapidly,

"Miss Wansdyke consulted me at Thursday evening's surgery last week and I advised extra units of insulin morning and evening. She had ample supplies. Her last prescription was . . ." His face changed. He looked suddenly older. "As it happens," he said carefully, "I didn't write her last prescription. It was given to her in September while I was on holiday."

"Oh?"

"My partner wrote it out for her, as I was away."

"Dr. McCavity?" said Sloan.

"Dr. Peter McCavity?" said Detective Constable Crosby from the patient's friend's chair in a manner which betokened prior acquaintance with the name.

"Perhaps, Dr. Paston," suggested Sloan, "if we might just check with him?" It would be interesting in any case to see the knocker down of so many items of what the town planners called "street furniture."

"By all means, Inspector," said the doctor without enthusiasm. "I'll ask him to step through."

There was an altogether different cut of jib about the man who came along in response to Dr. Paston's message. He was a much younger man but already his features had taken on the blur of self-indulgence. He positioned himself against the examination couch at the side of the room, a hand resting rather too heavily against it for normal support purposes.

"Police?" he said uncertainly. "If it's about that bollard in the Eastgate yesterday . . ."

"Our Inspector Harpe is dealing with that, Doctor."

"I meant to report it. No time, you know. Urgent medical work."

"You'll be hearing from him in due course," said Sloan formally.

"Oh . . . oh, yes. Thank you." Dr. McCavity managed an acknowledging nod. "Some fool cut in on me. . . ."

There was the accumulation of years of skill and experience in the totally expressionless way in which Sloan contrived to cast doubt on the driver's statement while doing and saying nothing provocative that an astute defence counsel could use in evidence.

"While we're talking about cars, Doctor . . ." began Sloan.

"Go on." Peter McCavity brought his gaze to bear upon the detective inspector but seemed to have some little difficulty in keeping it there.

"Can you tell me where your car was parked on Friday afternoon?"

"Friday?" Now he merely looked bewildered. "Last Friday?"

"Last Friday," said Sloan patiently. For the young doctor last Friday was clearly light-years away from this Wednesday morning.

An expression of genuine puzzlement came over his prematurely blunted features. "Friday? I should have to think about that. When on Friday?"

"Afternoon turning to evening."

"Friday was a long time ago."

"I daresay."

"With the weekend in between." He made the weekend sound as solid as the house but for which you could see to Hackney Marshes ("wiv a ladder and some glasses").

"It's easy to lose a weekend," agreed Sloan temperately. In fact "lost" weekends were quite a feature of a certain condition.

"My weekend off," said McCavity.

"I see, sir."

"Not on duty."

"I understand."

"Very tired."

"Quite."

"I didn't feel very well on Friday."

"I see, sir."

He looked around unsurely. "I may have had a little sleep in my car."

"Can you remember whereabouts, sir?"

The doctor roused himself to a modicum of belligerence. "Nothing wrong with that, is there, Inspector?"

"No, sir. Not in itself."

"Well?"

"Would you have been anywhere near Ridley Road?"

His aggression collapsed as speedily as a pricked balloon. His face changed pathetically. "Oh, my God, Inspector!" He clutched Sloan's sleeve in an alarmed manner. "I didn't . . . don't tell me that I"—his whole frame shuddered—"I haven't knocked anyone down, have I?"

His senior partner, Dr. John Paston, stirred at last behind his desk and said brusquely, "Oughtn't you to be cautioning him, Inspector?"

"I don't think so, Doctor," replied Sloan evenly. He knew his Judge's Rules as well as the next policeman and he didn't need any spectator—or even the referee, come to that—telling him he was off-side.

"What is all this anyway?" demanded Dr. McCavity. "This isn't a police state yet, you know."

"Just a few questions, sir, that's all."

"More like the third degree," complained the young doctor bitterly. His words would have carried more conviction without the fine tremor of his hands that shouldn't have been present in one so young.

"It's a wise man that knows his own movements," said Sloan prosaically. "Were you near Ridley Road on Friday afternoon?"

He hesitated. "I may have been."

Sloan turned back to Dr. Paston. "Perhaps we might ask Dr. McCavity instead if he can remember writing Miss Wansdyke's prescription for insulin while you were away."

The young doctor answered for himself. "That'll be down in black and white, Inspector. You'll be able to see that for yourself." He turned scornfully to a stony-faced Dr. Paston. "Wansdyke? That's the old bird who's left you some money, isn't it?"

* * *

"Well," demanded Superintendent Leeyes, "where are we now?"

Detective Inspector Sloan had reported to his superior's office as soon as he got back to the police station. If it hadn't been for the feminine overtones of the simile, he thought privately, you could have likened the superintendent to a queen bee placed firmly in the centre of her hive. What with worker bees reporting back all day honey-laden, other bees dancing attendance upon the queen bee (there was no shortage of lady clerical workers servicing the superintendent's out basket and telephone line), and sentry bees on guard duty at the mouth of the hive, the organisation of the police station at Berebury could have changed places with a beehive any day.

"How far have you got, Sloan?"

Except, of course, that there were no drones in the Calleshire Force.

"Sloan, are you listening?"

"Yes, sir," he said, pulling himself together quickly. Ants were known to be well organised, too. "We haven't made a lot of headway so far."

"You've had all morning."

"Yes, sir." There was no doubt either, thought Sloan confusedly to himself, about who was top dog in their hive, so to speak.

"Found the nephew yet?"

"No, sir."

"Got a general call out for him?"

"A whisper," replied Sloan, "has gone around the nebulae."

"What's that, Sloan?"

"Nothing, sir. Sorry, sir." He brought his mind back smartly to the here and now by getting out his notebook and opening it in front of him. "We're looking for Nicholas Petforth now."

Leeyes grunted. "You saw the pathologist . . ."

"He's quite certain, sir, that the deceased didn't have her insulin."

"And her general practitioner?"

"He's quite certain, sir, that she did." There was some elusive quotation hovering about in his mind about when doctors differ but he couldn't pin it down. "Or rather . . ."

"Yes?"

"He's quite sure that she wouldn't have stopped taking it."

Leeyes grunted again. "So?"

"So there remains the alternative that she thought she was taking it."

"You mean that when she gave herself an injection it wasn't insulin?"

"It figures," said Sloan cautiously.

"It didn't do her any good," agreed Leeyes grimly, "did it, whatever it was she had instead?"

"No. We know she wasn't feeling well on it. That's why the doctor told her to increase the dose."

"Compounding the error," pronounced the superintendent neatly.

"Er—quite, sir." The depths of the superintendent's knowledge and ignorance were equally unfathomable to his subordinates. They couldn't count on either. "Increasing the dose didn't help, you see."

"And it should have done, I take it?"

"Oh, yes. In theory, anyway. That's why Dr. Paston upped the dose again after that."

"Or said that he did, Sloan," warned the superintendent.

"Yes, sir. Naturally." That went without saying at this stage. There was always an unwritten and unspoken caveat in all police work acknowledging the difference between what was given in an untried statement and what was offered—tested—in evidence.

"Putting the dose up yet again didn't help either, of course," observed Leeyes.

"No, sir."

"Nothing and nothing is still nothing."

"It reinforces the theory that what she gave herself wasn't insulin." Sloan, who was no mathematician, shifted his ground slightly. "According to the medical men, her symptoms should have gone away on the bigger dose."

"Not got worse, like they did."

"No."

"Sloan, I don't like the sound of this."

"No, sir."

"Someone wanted that woman dead."

"There could have been an accident," pointed out Sloan, for form's sake as much as anything. "A duff supply or something like that."

Leeyes gave a Machiavellian smile. "Putting the whole thing down to bad luck, are you, Sloan?"

"No, sir, but . . ."

"And the quarter of a million pounds to good luck?"

"Never, sir . . ." He meant that. The one thing he didn't want any child of his to have was unlimited wealth on the grand scale. He didn't call that good luck.

"And," carried on the superintendent, pursuing his own line of thought, "as for having the bad luck to have a fatal accident at the same time as having the good luck to have come by a large sum of money . . ."

"Unlikely," agreed Sloan. The Furies usually went so far and no further. Not that you could count on that either.

"One in the eye for Yin and Yang."

"Beg pardon, sir?"

"The unity of opposites."

"Er—quite, sir." Sloan quickly racked his brains. The superintendent attended adult education classes in his spare time. Indiscriminately. One way and another they had all left their mark on the force.

"Equal and opposite, you might say."

"Indeed, yes, sir." Was that, Sloan wondered, a hangover from Mathematics for All and congruent triangles or Eastern Philosophies for Enquiring Minds?"

"Someone," repeated Leeyes forcefully, "wanted that woman dead."

"Yes, sir." He cleared his throat. "If we accept that then I rather think that we can go a little further than that."

"Come on then . . . don't just sit there, man! Tell me."

"I think someone wanted her dead sooner rather than later."

The superintendent shot Sloan a shrewd look from under his bushy eyebrows. "We've got a speedy Gonzales about, have we?"

"It would be possible to argue, sir," said Sloan, picking his words with care, "that withholding the insulin wasn't doing the trick quickly enough for someone."

"Would it, indeed," said Leeyes discouragingly.

"There's the dog, you see, sir."

"The dead dog," said Leeyes.

"The missing dog," Sloan corrected him. "I reckon that the missing dog was meant to be the last straw."

"On top of everything else. I see." He paused. "You think that even without insulin she was taking too long to die?"

"Too long for someone's comfort. Yes."

"What was the hurry?"

"I don't know," said Sloan uneasily.

"What had she got to be got out of the way in time for, then?" he said, putting it another way.

"I don't know that either, sir."

"Something that has already happened?" he mused.

"Or," said Sloan warily, "something that is going to happen?" That was always the policeman's especial nightmare: the spur that kept the officer on the job long after people in other occupations had gone home for the night.

Leeyes leant back in his chair, considering that. "Is there any hurry about the girl Briony Petforth's marriage to the registrar fellow?"

"Not that I know about."

"Times have changed," said the superintendent obscurely.

"Yes, sir." It was something that would have to be gone into, all the same.

"Your wife all right, by the way?" enquired Leeyes gruffly.

"Yes, thank you, sir." Sloan kept his voice even with an effort. The superintendent's patently obvious thought processes didn't need a Sigmund Freud on hand with explanation. They never had. "But," Sloan continued vigorously, "if there's anything suspicious about Dr. Roger Elspin I can tell you one thing, and that's that he's not going to have anything to do with my wife's confinement—obstetrical register or not— even if"—he searched wildly around in his mind for alternatives—"even if I have to deliver her myself."

"Don't tempt Providence," advised Leeyes soberly. "Remember that every policeman in his time . . ."

"Yes, sir. Of course, sir." Sloan let his pent-up feeling evaporate and came back to the case in hand. And the beehive. "Miss Wansdyke, sir . . . where shall we go for honey?"

"What's that, Sloan?"

"Ridley Road, sir. That's where I'm going now."

Chapter 10

The slippery science stripped me down so bare
That I'm worth nothing, here or anywhere.

"Mr. Wansdyke will see you now, Inspector." A young
secretary turned back from the telephone switchboard
at her reception desk. "It's the second door on the left."

The first door had Malcolm Darnley's name on it. It
was open and the room empty.

George Wansdyke's office was the next one to it.
Two men who had been in there talking to the business-
man slid unobtrusively towards the door as he and
Crosby approached.

"Our Mr. Carruthers," Wansdyke introduced them
briefly, "the head progress chaser . . ."

Detective Inspector Sloan acknowledged the introduction with interest. They weren't short of progress
chasers down at the station, though there they went under slightly different names. Like "the press" and "the
chief constable."

". . . and," went on Wansdyke, "Bill Benfleet, advertising and public relations executive."

The public relations man immediately gave Sloan a
hearty professional handshake. "We'll be straight back,
Mr. Wansdyke," he said over his shoulder. "That press
release has got to be done today whatever happens." He
waved another acknowledgement at Crosby and gave a
quick meaningless smile to George Wansdyke. "Time
and tide and newspapers wait for no man."

"Welcome, Inspector." Wansdyke motioned Sloan
and Crosby into chairs that were considerably more
comfortable than the ones in either the doctor's surgery

or the hospital. The man seemed more confident in his office than he had been at home. Sloan could understand this. Mrs. Pauline Wansdyke's propensity for not letting any time elapse between thought and speech must be unnerving.

"Thank you, sir."

"Sorry about the unfortunate aroma."

Detective Constable Crosby raised his head like a pointer and sniffed the air.

Sloan's mind went back to his childhood. "Carbolic?" he hazarded.

"We've just taken delivery of some phenol," Wansdyke explained. "It's one of the commonest components we use. That and the aldehydes."

Crosby lowered his nose again, like a bloodhound this time.

"The smell seems to get into everything." Wansdyke was apologetic.

"Plastic," said Sloan. "That's what you manufacture here, sir, isn't it?"

"It is," said Wansdyke, nodding assent. "We go in for the more rarefied varieties these days but"—he pointed across the room—"time was when we didn't."

The two policemen followed his gaze to an early set of crudely moulded red products in plastic laid out in a display cabinet. Crosby sniffed.

"That's what we made in my father's day. They're practically museum pieces now."

Crosby looked doubtful.

"We've come a long way since then technically and aesthetically," Wansdyke assured him.

"Plastic's never exactly beautiful, is it, sir?" interposed Sloan diplomatically before the constable could speak.

Wansdyke gave a short laugh. "I don't know about that but I do know the world would have a job to get by without it now."

"It did before," remarked Crosby mulishly.

"I suppose the end product is getting better all the time," said Sloan hastily, though surely he had read somewhere, hadn't he, that what really mattered was a better mousetrap.

"Research." Wansdyke nodded. "We do a lot of that here, Inspector."

"Your aunt was doing some, too, sir, wasn't she?" Sloan trawled the remark in front of Wansdyke.

He wasn't sure what it was that he had expected by way of response. Perhaps the half-deprecating indulgence that grown men usually showed to aunts. George Wansdyke's reaction to what Sloan had said however was totally serious.

"She was indeed. On a most interesting hypothesis, Inspector."

Sloan waited. Everyone had a different way of describing his own particular crock of gold that lay where the rainbow ended.

"Recovering nitrogen from the atmosphere was what she was aiming at—no less," said the businessman.

Sloan cleared his throat. "A worthy goal, sir."

"A great step forward for mankind. That's what my partner—Malcom Darnley—you may have heard of him, Inspector?"

Sloan nodded.

"He's devoted to conservation, you know."

Had Inspector Harpe been present he would no doubt have ground his teeth. Sloan contented himself with admitting that he knew Malcolm Darnley by reputation.

"Well, he feels so strongly about these things that he too was quite happy to let Beatrice use our laboratory facilities at the weekend."

"And had she found it—what she was looking for?"

"The sixty-four thousand dollar question, you might say," observed Crosby easily from the sidelines.

Sloan drew breath to speak. That was *lèse-majesté*, pure and simple.

"If she had," said Wansdyke lightly, "she hadn't told me."

"Your research . . ."

"Tied up with development," said the businessman. "Ours and other people's. There doesn't seem to be any danger of people not wanting synthetic resins for the rest of my lifetime, and my son's either."

Running out of crime was one thing they didn't have

to worry about down at the police station. There'd be plenty for his son to take care of, too. If he had a son.

Crosby started on another objection. "But . . ."

"At least," intervened Sloan hastily, "plastic lasts. Not like some things these days."

"Quite," said George Wansdyke briskly. He straightened the blotter on his desk. "Now what can I do for you two gentlemen?"

"What we'd really like, sir," said Sloan frankly, "is the key to your aunt's house."

"Oh?"

"Something's—er—turned up."

"What?"

"Her dog."

"How?" asked Wansdyke, startled.

"Dead."

"Good Lord."

"Dead and buried, actually."

"Beatrice must have found it herself then," said Wansdyke, relaxing.

"Must she, sir?"

"We looked for it everywhere after . . . when . . . after we found Beatrice."

"Did you, sir? It was in the garden."

"We thought it must have just run away."

"No," said Sloan thoughtfully, "I don't think that's what happened." His grandmother had been enough of a sentimentalist to have a copy of Sir Edwin Landseer's painting of a dog called "The Old Shepherd's Chief Mourner" in her front parlour. It had made a great impression on him as a small child.

"We were afraid it was hungry or frightened," said Wansdyke. "Briony was quite worried in case it was suffering."

"It didn't seem to have suffered a lot," replied Sloan tangently.

"Good. What with poor Beatrice herself . . ."

"Quite."

"It never rains but it pours, doesn't it?" observed Crosby chattily.

Wansdyke turned his gaze towards the detective constable. "That's true."

"So," said Sloan, rising to his feet, "we thought we would just check that everything was all in order round there, if that's all right with you, sir."

"Of course." The businessman felt in his pocket for the keys. "The electricity and water are off at the main but not the gas."

* * *

"Nurse! Nurse! Nurse Petforth . . ."

"Coming."

"Nurse!"

"What is it?"

"Sister wants you."

Briony Petforth straightened her cap in a purely reflex action before she looked round. "Where is she?"

One of Sister Fleming's most notable administrative qualities was that of always seeming able to materialise anywhere on the ward without warning.

"Her office."

Briony automatically smoothed her apron as she hurried there.

"A telephone call for you, Nurse," said Sister Fleming, oozing disapproval. "It should not be necessary for me to have to remind you that nurses on duty are not expected to receive telephone calls."

"No, Sister."

"Except of an urgent personal nature about family matters."

"Yes, Sister."

"The caller," she said, "insists on speaking to you."

"Thank you, Sister."

Sister Fleming gave her a curious look and handed over the telephone receiver.

"Briony?" said a man's voice. "Is that you? This is George Wansdyke."

"Yes?" she said cautiously. Sister Fleming was sitting at her desk only inches away.

"Look here, I've just had the police round at the office asking for the key of Ridley Road." Wansdyke lowered his voice. "I've given it to them naturally, but I'm worried about Nick."

"Yes," she said dully, "so am I."

"He's disappeared from his job on the motorway site. I checked."

"I know," she said miserably.

"And as far as I can make out from the layabouts there he's left that dreadful squat in Luston, too."

"I expect he's sleeping rough again," she said without thinking.

Sister Fleming lifted her head.

"Or else he's found somewhere else to stay," she added hastily.

"And," added Wansdyke, "they've found the dog."

"Isolde!" exclaimed Briony. "Where?"

"Buried in the garden," said George Wansdyke.

"Buried in the garden!" cried Briony. "Dead, you mean?"

Sister Fleming's eyebrows almost reached her starched cap.

"Dead, I do mean," said Wansdyke grimly.

"But who . . . how . . . why?"

Sister Fleming wasn't even troubling to conceal her interest now.

"I don't know," said Wansdyke, "and I don't want to start guessing."

* * *

Detective Inspector Sloan had not expected to be back at the hospital again quite so soon. This time he had Detective Constable Crosby with him.

"Which way, sir?"

"Ah," murmured Sloan, "you have a point there. Think of the place as a maze with a man in the middle—a man we want to talk to. His name is Elspin— Dr. Roger Elspin."

Miss Wansdyke's house in Ridley Road had been unrevealing. Neat and tidy but unyielding of clues to a quarter of a million pounds. And no ransom notes had been immediately visible—for the dog or anyone else. He was momentarily tempted to wonder if Ted Blake's wife had made a mistake in what she had overheard—

until he remembered the absent insulin. Dr. Dabbe didn't make mistakes.

"There's an enquiry desk over there, sir," said Crosby.

There was also an exceedingly attractive young receptionist sitting at it.

"No," said Sloan thoughtfully, "I think not."

Verbal enquiries for a doctor by members of the constabulary on duty seldom did that doctor's reputation any good. Besides, Sloan was as curious as the next man. He wanted to see where the symbolic direction signs got Crosby.

"We could have him called," suggested the detective constable, whose own personal radio was a perpetual anathema to him. "Let Big Brother find him for us."

"We'll find him ourselves," said Sloan decisively, "and then we'll have a nice quiet chat."

"Quiet, sir? Here?"

The constable had a point. The one thing the hospital wasn't was quiet.

"They could do with their 'Hospital—Quiet Please' sign inside here," remarked Crosby. "Not out on the road."

"It isn't there," remarked Sloan. "Not any more."

"Our Dr. McCavity been out for a drive then?" enquired Crosby.

"Friendly neighbourhood students, Inspector Harpe thought," replied Sloan absently. "Souvenir hunting." The ways of students remained obscure to him. "This way, I think."

The constable, though, seemed curiously reluctant to move away from the hospital's entrance concourse. "What, sir, if anyone asks us who we are?"

Sloan, who made a point of wearing clothes as unremarkable as those of the next man, looked Crosby up and down. The constable's wearing apparel tended to be influenced by the silver screen. Sloan drew a breath. "Representatives from a pharmaceutical company, I think." Then he caught sight of Crosby's trendy tie and added drily, "One of the lesser firms, I should say myself. Now, come on."

Crosby looked up at the daunting array of signs—

and perversely spotted a notice that Sloan had never seen at all.

"What do they do at the Gut Club, sir?"

"I have no idea," said Sloan icily.

"On Fridays at nine," added Crosby gratuitously.

"We are here on duty."

Crosby looked around. "Do we have to wait until the lights go down or can we start straightaway?"

"What we have to do," said Sloan with some acerbity, "is to find the obstetrical registrar."

Crosby said, "Lead on, MacDuff," but he said it to Sloan's back.

In the end they got to the right department—chiefly by following a pretty young nurse.

"She might have been going to radiotherapy," objected Sloan. It really was a most unfair world.

"Luck's better than judgement, sir," said Crosby laconically. "Now, where's our man?"

He—Sloan—was definitely not one of those policemen who went in for much reading about police work these days. In his book, practise had overtaken theory years ago. It had been different when he had been plain Police Constable Sloan and first feeling his way on the beat. Then he had read everything he could lay his hands on and one of the things that he had read then had stayed with him over the years. It had been advice on the easy identification of members of the medical profession.

A certain arrogance, his good book had said, went with the smell of antiseptic.

There was assuredly nothing tentative about Dr. Roger Elspin's manner.

"Yes?" he began peremptorily. Strange men did not often stray into his domain.

"I am Detective Inspector Sloan, Doctor, from Berebury Criminal Investigation Department."

"Well?"

"With a few enquiries."

"You'll have to make them short." Dr. Elspin was not noticeably apprehensive either.

"Yes, Doctor."

Elspin indicated the radio receiver clipped to the

pocket of his white coat. "I'm on call for the delivery ward."

"Big Brother is watching you, too," murmured Crosby almost under his breath.

"Big Sister actually," murmured Elspin wryly.

"I won't keep you long," said Sloan mendaciously. Dr. Elspin's sort of time-saving did not come into police work. Time was not money or anything else when law and order—let alone justice—were concerned.

"Good," said Elspin shortly.

"It's about Miss Wansdyke," said Sloan.

A frown crossed his forehead. "Well?"

"I understand that you and her niece, Miss Briony Petforth, are . . . want to . . ."

"We're not just good friends, Inspector," Elspin cut across his speech brusquely, "if that's what you want to know."

"No, sir?"

"Moreover, old-fashioned as it may seem, we're going to get married in the bargain."

"I see, Doctor." Elspin seemed determined enough to convince Sloan. He didn't know if Briony Petforth had taken any persuading.

"Her aunt tried to stop us," said the young man militantly. "That's the long and the short of that."

"Why?"

"Because Briony hadn't finished her precious training, that's why."

"Ah." Sloan nodded sagely. Training had been precious in the aunt's day and marriage a bar to finishing it. "The generation game."

"What . . . oh, yes, of course." Elspin relaxed slightly. "Beatrice said she should get her nursing registration first."

"I see."

"She was a schoolteacher, you see."

"They tend to think like that," said Sloan.

"The old brigade." Elspin endorsed that with feeling. "They think that every woman should have a career to fall back on."

"Those that haven't," observed Sloan moderately, "have sometimes regretted it."

Elspin wasn't listening. "What did Beatrice think I was going to do? Abandon Briony six months after I'd married her?"

Sloan forbore to answer that. There was no use reminding the impetuous young man that that too had been known to happen to new brides.

"There was something else she would keep harping on," said Elspin morosely.

"What was that?"

"That having a professional qualification," he snapped, "meant that a wife could always keep her independence."

"Ah, yes. Of course." He could see that the old schoolmistress would think like that.

"I shan't stop Briony working if she wants to."

"No, sir," said Sloan readily. "Naturally." He saw no point in exploring the narrow line of demarcation between being a working wife and being a woman with a career. Helping to bring home the bacon before cooking it was something quite different from being a career woman in one's own right. Roger Elspin would find that out soon enough.

"She'd only just started her third year," said Elspin, a note of grievance creeping into his voice.

"So that if the late Miss Wansdyke had had her way," observed Sloan, "you would have had to wait nearly another year from now?"

"And I didn't see why we should," said Elspin.

"Well . . ."

"Just because some old bird who was fifty years behind the times thought it wasn't a good idea."

"No," said Sloan, whose only real concern was whether the doctor had thought so strongly enough to take Draconian action in the matter; action outside the law.

"Beatrice was living in the past," he grumbled.

Sloan would have agreed with that straightaway. There had been nothing too modern about number fifty-nine Ridley Road. Furniture and decor both belonged to an earlier decade, and the Turkey carpet on the upstairs landing to an even older one still. There had been no sign of wealth either. That was what was so odd. Evidence of decent modest prosperity had abounded—and so had signs of care and attention to hearth and home but there had been no indicators that spelt money on a large scale.

"The time to marry," pronounced the young man in white coat sitting in front of him, "is when you feel like it."

"Ah," said Sloan, who was older, "that's as may be."

"So," responded Elspin smartly, "that's establishment heresy now, too, is it?"

"No, Doctor. That's practical politics, that is."

Detective Constable Crosby stirred. "Depends if she'll have you when you feel like marrying, doesn't it, Doctor?"

Sloan cleared his throat authoritatively. This was no time to be discussing *marriage à la mode*. "Dr. Elspin, exactly how much say did Miss Wansdyke have in the matter of her niece's marriage?"

"Taking Miss Petforth's consent for granted, of course," put in Crosby sedulously.

Elspin shot the constable an aggressive look but it was Sloan whom he answered. "None, Inspector." He twisted his lips in a wry smile. "She didn't carry any real clout. . . ."

"Well, then . . ."

"And yet she had the greatest pull of all."

"Which was?"

"An appeal to Briony's better nature."

"I see," said Sloan. And he did. In his experience people's better natures were only ever appealed to for causes that didn't respond to logic or common sense.

"Below the belt," commented Crosby insouciantly.

Sloan drew a savage breath. . . .

"All Beatrice said," remarked Elspin more calmly, "was that she was her aunt and had brought her up after her parents were killed. Naturally Briony didn't want to hurt her feelings. . . ." His irateness seemed to have evaporated now.

"Miss Wansdyke had nothing and everything, didn't she?" agreed Sloan. "Now, sir, if . . ."

That was the moment at which Dr. Elspin's radio receiver came to life.

"Dr. Roger Elspin," intoned in a nasal voice. "Calling Dr. Elspin. To go to room three . . . delivery ward . . . now . . ."

He stood up with a shrug. "By the way, Inspector . . ."

"Yes, Doctor."

"Your name's Sloan, isn't it?"

"It is."

"Got a wife?"

"Yes, Doctor."

"Called Margaret?"

Sloan nodded.

"That's what I thought," said Elspin. He essayed a formal smile. "Then we may meet again."

"Yes, Doctor," said Sloan heavily.

"Soon, perhaps." Elspin waved a hand and was gone.

"I think," said Sloan to Crosby, as they stood in the corridor, "that we could well use another chat with Nurse Briony Petforth."

"What I could use," said the constable, "is food and drink."

"If," said Sloan somewhat maliciously, "you can spot a sign made up of a knife and fork then I think you might be onto something—unless that means surgery."

Crosby pointed to a notice board. "They don't eat there, do they, sir, do you think?"

"Where?"

"The Gut Club."

"I hope not," said Sloan repressively. "This way."

Fleming Ward had not been reduced to a symbol. It proclaimed itself in alphabetical terms from afar and the two policemen had no difficulty in finding the right direction.

"They don't mention distances, though, sir, do they?" grumbled Crosby as one long white corridor belayed into another long white corridor.

"I think we're getting warmer," murmured Sloan. "Slow down a bit."

"Sir?"

"I may be wrong," said Sloan softly, "but I think we may not be the only ones making for Fleming Ward."

"Sir?"

"The man ahead, Crosby . . . the one in the donkey jacket."

"Auburn hair, five foot five, slight build . . ."

"Remind you of anyone?"

"Nicholas Petforth," breathed Crosby.

"Going to see his sister," concluded Sloan neatly.

"Hiding up in the hospital?"

"Nobody's asked us what we're up to yet," said Sloan reasonably.

The man ahead turned to the right and quickened his pace slightly. Sloan and Crosby lengthened their steps.

"One on either side," instructed Sloan quietly, "when I say the word."

They had reckoned though without that primordial sense given even to man to tell him when he is being watched or followed. No sooner had the two policemen started to draw close when the man looked around. As soon as he saw them he began to run.

"After him!" shouted Sloan, starting to give chase.

"He's got freckles," said Crosby.

"Never mind that now. Get him!"

Had that particular corridor been long and straight too the two policemen might have had a better chance of catching the man ahead. Instead their quarry ducked down the next turning and then took the next opening after that. Half a minute later he had put a stretcher case between himself and his pursuers.

Crosby dipped swiftly to one side of porters and patient and shot around the next corner after him shouting, "Hey, you there! Stop!"

If anything, the man put on an extra spurt.

Sloan pelted down the new corridor after him. This one at least was long and straight and Crosby appeared to be gaining on his man. Sloan summoned up his reserves for an extra spurt and prepared to fall upon the man in front when Crosby had caught up with him. His added weight would come in useful then.

And then—quite suddenly—the man they were chasing wasn't anywhere to be seen any more.

He had disappeared abruptly through a pair of swing doors.

To Sloan's surprise, Detective Constable Crosby did

not follow him through them. Instead the younger policeman skidded to a sudden halt.

"What the . . . Crosby!"

The constable straightened up and pointed.

Above the double doors were the unmistakable
words "Quarantine Area—Keep Out." And on either
side of the doorway there were equally unequivocal
signs proclaiming "Bio-activity—Do Not Enter."

Chapter 11

Our furnace too for calcifying action,
Our waters in a state of albefaction.

"What!" bellowed Leeyes. "Do you mean to just stand there and tell me you lost him?"

"We did," said Sloan. Sometimes with the superintendent a short answer stood one in better stead than a long one.

"And what were you afraid of?" snarled Superintendent Leeyes in a transport of rage. "Foot and mouth disease?"

"Quarantine," said Sloan, speaking for himself. Detective Constable Crosby had been muttering about the Black Death.

"He was within your reach. . . ." moaned Leeyes, taking a deep breath.

"But he slipped through our fingers," finished Sloan for him.

Unwisely, as it happened.

"Sloan, this isn't one of your fancy games of cricket. This is for real."

"So is the Bio-activity, sir."

"What does it mean?" asked Leeyes suspiciously.

Sloan, too, had had to ask. "It's the place in the hospital—in the whole of Calleshire, actually—where they keep the cultures of the stuff that they don't want to get out and about. Viruses, mostly."

That hadn't been quite how the administrators had put it to the two policemen but it had been what they had meant.

"Catching," said Leeyes, reducing the matter to its simplest.

"Highly," said Sloan. All the people working in the department there had had head-to-foot white gowns on and masks and there were lots of glass barriers everywhere. "You could see things, sir, but not touch them."

"Supermarkets should be like that," said Leeyes, momentarily diverted. "Save a lot of trouble."

"I gather," offered Sloan, "that there's quite a bit of medical research going on in there too."

"There always is," said Leeyes. "No one ever wants to get on with the actual job these days."

The administrator at the hospital and George Wansdyke of Messrs. Wansdyke and Darnley, plastics specialists, had both spoken more reverently about research but Sloan knew what Leeyes meant. The well-meaning and the academic had both been researching into crime since Cain killed Abel without coming up with a satisfactory solution.

"So," Sloan resumed his narrative, "we didn't go in. We rang the bell instead."

"And," snorted the superintendent truculently, "the footman said he would enquire if there were any wanted men roaming around waiting to give themselves up."

"And," said Sloan steadily, "we were told that even if Jack the Ripper were loose inside we wouldn't be allowed farther in."

"In the name of the law . . ." began Leeyes weightily.

"Furthermore," reported Sloan unemotionally, "we were also told that should we step inside as unauthorised persons we would be sent to an isolation hospital and kept in strict quarantine until such time as the medical authorities deemed us free of risk to the community."

It was this threat more than the nameless horrors of the Plague that had deterred them.

"And your man?" demanded Leeyes, who never for one moment lost sight of essentials.

"Disappeared."

"Carrying the Lord knows what in the way of germs all over the hospital?"

"We don't know how near the real stuff he got. They said that the next set of doors was locked but they promised to do a big search themselves and tell us if they came up with anything."

"Was there another way out?"

"Yes, sir." Sloan had been a policeman long enough to know that there was always another way out. That went for secure accommodation, too, as often as not. "There's a little staff door at the other end of the laboratories by their changing rooms and . . ." He paused.

"And?" prompted Leeyes urgently. "We haven't got all day, Sloan."

"And they have one of those small service-lift shafts so that—er—items can reach the laboratory without people having to go there in person from other floors."

"Big enough for a man?"

The administrator hadn't thought so for a moment but Sloan knew better. "At a pinch," he said.

"The hospital could be searched. . . ."

"Not without a handful of warrants and a couple of hundred men," said Sloan vigorously. "You should have heard them when I mentioned it. It was about the only thing the matron and the adminstrator agreed about. Except," he added, "that you haven't got to call her matron any more. She's some sort of a nursing officer."

"And as some sort of a police officer," said Leeyes without hesitation, "you shouldn't allow yourself to be bullied by her."

But he said it without his usual panache.

"No, sir."

"The house," said Leeyes. "What did you find there?"

"The insulin bottles," said Sloan. "Five unopened ones that looked all right. One half-empty one that could be all wrong. They've gone straight round to Dr. Dabbe's lab."

"Take out insulin and put in water?" mused Leeyes.

"Simple, when you come to think of it, sir, isn't it?"

"That reminds me, Sloan. What have you done with Crosby?"

*   *   *

Detective Inspector Sloan had only one thought in his mind when he left the superintendent's office and that was food and drink—well, a cup of tea anyway. The day was slipping by unpunctuated by refreshment for the inner man. There were, he knew, places of work where mealtimes were observed with military precision but the Berebury Police Station was not one of them. Fortunately their canteen staff were as resilient as the rest of them. If their customers wanted food and drink then food and drink would be there for the asking, irrespective of the clock.

And if by any chance a man thought he could eat and then found when faced with food that he couldn't—a common enough situation among men who had their ways among the sad end of society—then nothing was said on either side.

Inspector Harpe's plate was empty.

Sloan sat down beside him. "All quiet on the traffic front, Harry?"

"Just the usual foul-up round the market," he said, pushing his empty plate away. "I've got a friend of yours waiting to see me though."

"Policemen don't have friends," said Sloan. It was one of the things that worried him about his unborn son. Would he get roughed up at school because his father was a copper? He'd have to teach the boy how to handle that early on. . . .

"True." Harpe gave a short laugh. "You'll be pleased to know that Larky Nolson was heard to describe you as a working acquaintance in the pub down by the railway last night."

"So who's the friend?" Some bait Sloan rose to, some he didn't.

"A medico."

"Which particular pillar of the profession?"

"Peter McCavity." Harpe grimaced. "Hardly a pillar."

"More like an unsure foundation," agreed Sloan.

"Come in to confess about yesterday morning's bollard." Harpe jerked his head sourly. "I daresay he's forgotten about Friday's by this time."

"Friday's?" Sloan let his interest in Dr. McCavity's Friday activities show.

"He had the one on the corner of Cranmer Drive on Friday."

"That's leading into Ridley Road, isn't it?"

"There's just the church in between," said Inspector Harpe without conscious irony.

"How do we know?"

"Someone rang in to tell us he'd had it down."

"Who?"

"Ah, they turned shy when we asked them that."

"Pro bono publico?"

"Only up to a point," said Harpe realistically. "An anonymous telephone call isn't evidence."

"Disgusted, Tunbridge Wells, then."

"There was one thing though that was odd, come to think of it."

"Yes?" said Sloan. It was the odd things that made up police work.

"The caller was male."

"Now that is odd," agreed Sloan. Most men who were car drivers had a "There but for the Grace of God . . ." approach to minor motoring matters. Bollards weren't exactly punchballs—but they weren't people either. Not by a long chalk. Bothering to ring in with the driver's car number was usually women's work.

"Shouldn't think the good doctor knows what a no-claims bonus looks like," said Harpe, "so he'll probably . . ."

"When on Friday, Harry?"

Harpe looked up. "Late afternoon, I think. I could check."

"Please."

"Interested?"

"Very."

"Want to come along while he's in?"

"It might help."

It did. In a way. An unexpected way.

Dr. Peter McCavity didn't seem surprised to see Sloan. His lip curled. " 'Cry havoc,' " he declaimed, " 'and let slip the dogs of war.' "

Sloan paused. He didn't go to evening classes like the superintendent but sooner or later all boys' schools performed *Julius Caesar*—if only because it wasn't full of parts for boys who had to pretend to be girls pretending to be boys. Or worse: parts for boys who had to pretend they were girls.

For a moment he searched about in his memory for a suitable rejoinder but all that would come to his mind was something else from another school play. It was a picture of their third-form clown playing Stephano, the drunken butler in *The Tempest*—another play for schoolboys. Prospero's daughter was the only female called for: the competition, as he remembered, had been for the part of Caliban. Stephano had staggered on stage clutching a bottle and saying between hiccups, "Here's my comfort."

Sloan did not say that now.

There was a time and a place for everything.

When he came to think of it, it was the people who did things out of time and out of place who gave them half their trouble down at the police station. The preacher who had written that bit in the Bible about there being a time for everything wasn't wrong. And this wasn't the time for bandying quotations with the doctor. Even if he could think of the right one, which he couldn't.

Inspector Harpe wasn't even attempting to. He was taking down the details of the accident to yesterday's bollard.

"Corner of Eastgate," he said patiently.

" 'The moving finger writes,' " said Dr. McCavity, who had clearly recovered some of his spirits during the course of the morning.

"How about the one you had down on Friday afternoon," said Harpe impassively.

" 'And having writ, moves on,' " said Peter McCavity impenitently.

"Friday," said Harpe. "Junction of Latimer Avenue and Cranmer Drive."

"Another bollard?" said McCavity, faintly tentative.

"So we're told," said Harpe.

"So be it," said Dr. McCavity. Sobered, he was more presentable. He had a rather anxious air of willingness to please about him now.

Sloan stirred. "Near Miss Wansdyke's house."

"Really?" he said without apparent interest. "Yes, I suppose it would be that way. I don't know the house myself."

Sloan maintained silence.

"Dr. Paston always looked after her himself," said McCavity.

"Except when he was away," said Sloan.

McCavity shrugged his shoulders. "I couldn't even sign the cremation certificate, she being my partner's patient. He was ringing round on Monday to find someone outside the practise to complete the second part of the certificate."

"Cremation?" said Sloan. Mortons', the undertakers, had distinctly mentioned burial.

"Didn't you know? She was going to be cremated. It was all laid on. It was what she had wanted and apparently she'd always said so but in the end they didn't take any notice. Nothing's sacred these days, is it?"

* * *

Detective Constable Crosby was still at the Berebury District General Hospital.

His clothes, which lacked credence as a police officer, fitted his new role rather better. He was sitting in the corridor outside Fleming Ward disguised as an anxious relative. This meant that when necessary he was able to sink his head between his hands. Necessity arose only when a nurse who might be Briony Petforth passed.

From this vantage position he could at once observe the door of Sister Fleming's office and the swing doors that gave into the ward. There was another door beyond that of Sister Fleming's office that led he knew not where.

Yet.

Being young and as yet not in possession of any of Francis Bacon's hostages to Fortune, Crosby wasn't too familiar with anxiety and how it should be portrayed. Restlessness came into it, he knew, but too much of that might draw attention to himself and that was the last thing he wanted to do. He'd seen people pacing up and down in hospital corridors too but not with their heads sunk in their hands, whenever a certain third-year nurse passed.

So he had settled for an uninviting bench clearly placed just where it was for those waiting for news from Fleming Ward. As a situation it was not without interest. Someone came through the swing doors every other minute and twice they were held open for a patient on a stretcher coming back to the ward from the operating theatre. There was, however, no sign of a young man with auburn hair and freckles wearing a donkey jacket.

For some time he thought perhaps Briony Petforth wasn't on the ward, and then, soon after the second stretcher case had arrived, she came through the swing doors and made straight for Sister Fleming's office. Seconds later the sister sallied forth in person and went through into the ward with Nurse Petforth. Moments after that an invisible loudspeaker started paging the duty house officer.

Crosby was so wrapped up in this living charade that he didn't even notice at first when a large woman approached. He gave a genuine start when she suddenly plumped down on the bench beside him.

"Sorry, lad," she said, "but there's only one bus I can catch in from Cullingoak to be at the hospital when visiting starts and I might as well wait here as at the bus station."

He nodded and turned his attention back to the ward doors. As any television producer could have told him, it was compulsive viewing.

"Got someone in here, too, have you?" enquired the woman presently.

"Er—yes," he said, collecting himself.

A harassed-looking young man in a white coat with a stethoscope dangling from his pocket had just turned onto Fleming Ward. He would be the house surgeon.

"It's my husband," she said gratuitously. "Hasn't been well all summer and in the end they said they'd better operate."

"Bad luck," said Crosby.

"What's yours in with?"

Crsoby cast about swiftly in his mind. He had an aunt who had had to go into hospital once. "Gallstones," he said with conviction.

The fat woman patted his arm. For one awful moment Crosby was seized with sudden doubt, and he began to wonder if gallstones were a peculiarly feminine complaint. Then she said kindly, "That's not serious, dear, these days, is it?"

"With complications," said the detective constable a little coldly, his confidence restored. No hospital visitor likes to be demonstrated as visiting someone less ill than the next person's relative: even when it is not so much a case of *malade imaginaire* as of imaginary invalid.

"Ah, that's different," she said at once. The fat woman began to rearrange her parcels. "My hubby now—they said in the beginning that he wasn't going to be straightforward."

It was Detective Constable Crosby's turn to sound sympathetic. He hoped that it wasn't the stout woman's husband who was causing all the commotion on the ward. Yet another doctor had now appeared and a bottle of blood had been rushed through the swing doors by someone else. There was no sign though of anyone resembling Nicholas Petforth.

The fat woman was speaking again.

"Pardon?" he said.

"The person you've come to see," she said patiently.

"Yes?" Warily.

"Has he been in here long? Perhaps my hubby's in the next bed."

"Not long," said Crosby truthfully, adding even more accurately, "I'm not sure exactly where he is."

She nodded comfortably. "They do move them about so."

"Or even," said Crosby, artistically painting in a finer touch, "if he'll really want to see me."

This struck an immediate chord with his neighbour. "You never can tell how hospital will take people, can you?"

"No," he said. What he was actually doing was considering whether the door beyond Sister Fleming's office led to the sluice or not.

"Perhaps he'll have them to show you," she remarked.

"What?"

"In a bottle."

"Show me what in a bottle?" demanded Crosby wildly.

"His gallstones."

Crosby's aunt had spared him this.

"They give them to you sometimes," she said knowledgeably.

"Souvenirs?" said the constable weakly. After all they had a Black Museum at New Scotland Yard as incongruous, didn't they?

"They did my next-door neighbour," said the woman, "when she had hers done."

"Did they?" said Crosby, discovering like many another inventor before him that those who build Kafkaesque castles in the air run the risk of the whole tottering edifice that they have fabricated brick by unsteady brick crumbling at the first touch of reality.

"Seven as big as marbles," the fat woman said.

The swing doors of the ward opened suddenly and Sister Fleming appeared. She made for her own office. If she noticed those sitting on the corridor bench she gave no sign of it. Like the rest of the hospital staff, she seemed to have the gift of ignoring those who waited on benches—or perhaps it was a skill honed down to a fine art. Just to be on the safe side, though, Crosby tucked his feet well out of sight. It wasn't so much that they were large: just that they were a policeman's feet.

Then another loudspeaker call went out. The senior surgical registrar was wanted on Fleming Ward.

Now.

"If not sooner," muttered Crosby to himself. He reckoned he was as good as the next man at reading between those sorts of lines.

Sister surged back onto the ward.

The fat lady began to rearrange her parcels again.

Crosby decided that this was his moment.

"Just going along the corridor," he murmured with absolute truth.

All Sister Fleming's forces were deployed on the ward and no one even looked at him as he slipped past the door of her office. He could hear noises from a kitchen somewhere but it was the door beyond Sister Fleming's office that he was making for. If anyone had an eye on a rendezvous with Nurse Briony Petforth or was in search of a quiet place to hide, this was the ideal spot for it.

Crosby advanced cautiously. On closer examination he decided it wasn't the sluice. That he could now see—and hear—was beyond. He opened the door. He was in a linen storeroom of some description. Racks of sheets were faintly visible. He stepped forward and began to feel for the light switch.

It was the last thing he remembered.

Something very heavy came down behind his neck and hit him hard. A vicious reverberating explosion took place inside the confines of his skull. Detective Constable Crosby subsided in a kaleidoscope of mental colour and for a long time knew no more.

Chapter 12

Alkali, tartar, salt in preparation,
Matters combust or in coagulation.

Detective Inspector Sloan had had to take another constable with him from the Berebury Police Station instead of Detective Constable Crosby. He didn't want to interview Dr. John Paston alone. Actually he didn't really want to take the time to interview Dr. Paston at all at this particular moment. Not with Nicholas Petforth at large and the whole case a tangle of loose ends but there was in him ingrained an early training married to a dogged persistence which allowed no opening in an investigation to go unexplored.

The general practitioner's manner towards the two policemen could not have been described as inviting. He sat quite motionless behind his desk waiting for Sloan to speak.

"I have come," began that officer without preamble, "about the late Miss Beatrice Wansdyke."

"Again?" said the doctor.

"And," continued Sloan, "about your pecuniary interest in her death."

Dr. Paston gave a short laugh. "Oh, that!"

"That," said Sloan totally unimpressed. In his time he had heard a great many dubious actions dismissed with a short laugh by the people who had perpetrated them. The activities had ranged from minor peccadillo to major misdemeanour but long ago he had come to realise that the enormity of crime lay—like beauty—solely in the eye of the beholder. The eye of the person who had committed it was always firmly glued to the wrong end of a telescope. The victim's eye view was usually more accurate.

"Rather a grand way of describing a small legacy, isn't it?" remarked Dr. Paston.

"Were you or were you not," Sloan forged on with his inquisition, "aware of it at the time of her death?"

"No." He hesitated for a moment and then said, "No, as a matter of fact I wasn't."

"Let me go back to Monday when she was found."

"Yes?"

"You were informed of her death."

"Indeed I was."

"And visited the house."

"That is so."

"And began to prepare a cremation certificate."

"Yes." He looked puzzled.

"Why?"

"Beatrice had always told me that that was what she wanted."

"So," asked Sloan, "why are Mortons' now preparing for burial?"

"That was the family," said the general practitioner immediately. From his tone it was obvious that families were an everyday complication of general practise.

"Which part of the family?" enquired Sloan cautiously. One thing he had learned over the years was that families did not invariably present themselves as united groups.

"It was George Wansdyke who actually mentioned it to me," said Paston, "but knowing the set-up there I daresay it was Pauline Wansdyke who didn't like the idea."

"Ah."

"The Hartley-Powells," Dr. Paston informed him drily, "are all buried over in East Calleshire."

"I see."

"In the ancient village churchyard at Great Rooden."

"And always have been?"

"Since the Norman Conquest," said Paston gravely. "At least."

"Some people find ancestor worship easier with tombstones."

"I'd even begun to lay on a colleague," amplified the doctor, "to sign the second part of the cremation certificate when George Wansdyke told me the family wanted a burial instead."

"And when did you hear about the legacy?"

"In the same breath as the burial." He tightened his lips into the semblance of a smile. "Wansdyke's a businessman, not a sentimentalist, you know."

Sloan, no time waster himself, nodded.

"At least," said Paston, "he did read over the message that came with the bequest."

" 'In small recognition of his unfailing kindness over many years,' " quoted Sloan from his notes.

For the first time the general practitioner looked momentarily disconcerted. "She wasn't the sort of woman to leave everything to a home for lost dogs."

"No," said Sloan consideringly. Not for one moment had he forgotten a dead Airedale either. Late dog. Like late pig. Now that was from somewhere very far down in his subconscious. "You had no idea it was going to happen?"

"None," he said vigorously. "And if I may say so, Inspector, I should have signed a declaration to that effect on the cremation certificate without hesitation."

"Quite so," said Sloan quietly. "Were you surprised?"

"That, of course, is something quite different." He hesitated and considered this. "No, not inordinately."

"Have you any plans for using the money?" Suddenly Sloan felt self-conscious. He must sound as silly as a cub reporter talking to the winner of a football pool. The answer he got, though, wasn't exactly what he expected.

"The nuts," said the doctor astringently, "come when the teeth have gone."

"Pardon?"

"Let me put it like this, Inspector." The general practitioner drew breath. "I do not for one moment anticipate that exactly one sixteenth of Beatrice Wansdyke's estate is going to alter my entire way of life."

"I see, sir." Now who was it had drummed into Sloan's head that your income was the only thing you could anticipate: and that most of the other uses of the word were incorrect? His English master perhaps. He'd been taught mathematics too. . . . "You did say a sixteenth, Doctor, didn't you?"

"My partner is entitled to half of anything I inherit from a patient."

"I didn't know that," said Sloan quite spontaneously.

"Every contingency," said the general practitioner ironically, "is provided for in a medical partnership agreement."

"Even down to splitting legacies?"

"That is quite a normal feature," said Paston drily. "Even millionaires bleed."

"Quite so." Detective Inspector Sloan started to do a spot of quick calculating.

"Millionaires don't crop up often," said the doctor.

"But when they do . . ."

"There isn't an unseemly stampede in the practise to attend them." He coughed. "If you come to think about it, Inspector, I'm sure you'll see . . ."

Sloan did come to think about it.

Dr. Paston might be able to maintain a rather lofty attitude to money and riotous loving. His junior partner, though, was quite a different matter. It was quite obvious to all and sundry that young Dr. Peter McCavity had an instant use for every liquid asset that he could lay his hands on.

* * *

"I may only be a forensic pathologist," said a plaintive voice down Sloan's telephone, "but even I can distinguish margarine from butter."

"I beg your pardon, Doctor?"

The detective inspector had come back to his desk at the police station in Berebury to find a heap of messages piled on it. He had been riffling through them when the telephone had rung and Dr. Dabbe had been put through to him.

He turned the message sheets over with his free hand.

The superintendnt wanted a progress report.

He would.

Inspector Harpe of Traffic Division would like him to drop by his department. Happy Harry—he was always known as Happy Harry because he had never been seen to smile—was far too cautious to say why on paper.

Very well. He, Sloan, would drop by Traffic Division.

Soonest: as they said in telegrams.

Mrs. Margaret Sloan had telephoned to say that she was going out shopping during the afternoon. That was why there would be no reply if he should happen to ring home.

He looked at his watch and felt a stab of guilt. He was uneasy about the phrasing too. He didn't like the way the message had been put. "Should happen to ring" carried overtones. Of course he would have rung as soon as he could. . . .

The last message was from the duty officer in the control room. He wished Detective Inspector Sloan to know that there had been no answer to calls to Detective Constable Crosby on his personal radio. They had been trying to raise him over the air from the control room for the best part of half an hour. Would he have gone out of receiving range without notifying them?

And did Detective Inspector Sloan want anything done about it?

Sloan replaced the messages on his desk.

"Margarine from butter," repeated Dr. Dabbe into his ear over the telephone.

"What?" said Sloan blankly. Now he would have to down tools and find out what Crosby had got up to.

"And water from insulin," continued the pathologist. "Even I can spot the difference."

"Er—good," said Sloan.

"And it was water, old chap."

Sloan concentrated his mind on what the pathologist was saying, banishing with a great effort the possible import of each of the messages waiting for him.

"No doubt about it," said Dr. Dabbe.

"Someone had been at her insulin." All right, then. At least they knew where they were now.

"Someone," said Dabbe, "had removed it from the bottle and substituted water."

"So"—Sloan worked out his conclusions aloud as he went along—"she'd been having no insulin at all since she began to use that particular bottle. . . ."

"Correct."

"And she'd . . ." He stopped and gave their subject the dignity of a name. "Miss Wansdyke had been giving herself injections of water instead of insulin."

"That," agreed Dr. Dabbe with caution, "would account for her symptoms certainly." The pathologist spent a lot of his working life in the law courts and the long experience had made its mark.

"And . . ."

"There was something else that could be inferred as well."

"Was there?"

"So I checked."

"And?"

"I wasn't wrong."

"Well?"

"The water that was still left in the insulin bottle was quite sterile."

"Oh," said Sloan blankly.

"If it hadn't been," explained the doctor kindly, "she would probably have had a nasty abscess at the injection site by the time she died."

"Ah," said Sloan in quite a different tone. "And she'd have gone back to her general practitioner with that, wouldn't she?"

"She would. Painful things, abscesses."

"Someone might have put two and two together then."

"They might." The pathologist wasn't making any promises in that quarter.

"I see." Sloan nodded. "I should have thought of that, shouldn't I?" Time was when he'd never even seen that sort of thing—an abscess at an injection site. That was before the abuse of drugs became a feature of police life. Though there seemed a world of difference between youngsters dying in filthy holes and corners and a middle-aged schoolmistress meticulously treating her diabetes, presumably an unsterile injection had the same effect on all members of the human race. If you prick us, do we not bleed . . . no, that was something different.

"Someone took care," remarked the pathologist.

"The other bottles . . ."

"Right as rain," said Dabbe with singular inappropriateness.

"But there had been insulin in the one she was using though, hadn't there? Once, I mean."

"Oh, yes. It started off as the real stuff because there's still a very faint trace of it in the water left in the bottle."

"The bottle labelled insulin," said Sloan heavily, thinking of someone ill and failing, increasing her dose and not getting any better. "Nasty."

"Murder always is," said Dabbe. "And I should know."

"Doctor . . ."

"Yes?"

"Let me get this straight. Miss Wansdyke had been using this duff bottle up until the time she died. Agreed?"

"Agreed."

"And all the other bottles are perfectly all right?"

"Agreed."

"So," said Sloan, "if she had happened to pick on one of the other bottles in the batch she was using then she wouldn't have died when she did?"

"No."

Sloan paused. Then:

"Are you saying, Doctor," he asked, thinking aloud, "that someone must have tampered with the current one after she started using it? Not before?"

"Oh, yes," returned Dabbe promptly. "You see, Sloan, the only—er—nondestructive way into and out of that sort of bottle is by using a hypodermic syringe and pushing the needle through the rubber composition cap."

"Ah, I see . . ."

"The patient might very well have noticed a puncture hole in a new bottle that she hadn't used before."

"And would have suspected something then," concurred Sloan.

"The dirty deed," pronounced Dr. Dabbe in the manner of a pantomime king, "will turn out to have been done after she started using that particular bottle. You'll see."

"So," said Sloan, who had always been quick at school, "if we could work out how many doses she had out of it we could expect to find an extra hole in the rubber cap?"

"We could," said the pathologist. "It would be clever stuff all right but . . ."

"But?"

"Too clever for open court."

"Ah." They—policeman and pathologist both—knew the dangers that lay in that direction. The defence could be as clever as it liked. That pleased everyone except the police. The prosecution had to be more careful about the weight of evidence. Pitching the full resources of the establishment against the lonely figure in the dock had a counterproductive effect on some juries. Especially nowadays.

"Juries don't like it," said Dabbe.

"Juries," said Sloan shortly, "aren't what they used to be."

"Twelve good men and true."

"That's as may be," said Sloan. Since the property qualification had gone, juries were a random selection. Very. And it showed in the verdicts they brought in. "You don't know where you are with juries these days. Take obscenity, for instance."

"Anything to oblige," murmured Dabbe negligently.

"Often as not your new-style jury doesn't even know what the prosecution is going on about."

"Need French lessons, do they?"

"And when it is explained to them," said Sloan stiffly, "they won't convict. Can't see what all the fuss is about."

"I can tell you anyway," complained Dabbe, "that too clever by half prosecutions don't go down well either, and as for . . ."

"The trouble is"—Sloan rarely let himself be carried

away in this fashion—"that they can't be flattered into thinking they understand any more. They know there are a lot of things they can't grasp. People have been telling them so all their lives."

"They all know though," agreed Dabbe sagely, "when they're being buttered up."

"And they take against expert witnesses," said Sloan, not entirely inconsequentially.

"There's nothing new about that," said the pathologist sturdily. "A water-tight case isn't water-tight if the jury doesn't like it."

Sloan agreed. As he did so his eye was caught by the little heap of message sheets on his desk. He came back to the matter in hand.

"I think we can agree then," he said, "that it wasn't chance that Miss Wansdyke was using this doctored bottle now."

"If you're asking my opinion," said Dabbe, "I should say on the contrary. By the way, Sloan . . ."

"Yes?"

"Could you be a bit more careful with your adjectives? Gives the profession a bad name. Doctored, indeed! Whatever next?"

* * *

The very ill patient on Fleming Ward did die.

In spite of all that the doctors and modern medical science could do, the last enemy—death—supervened. Nature, as is her wont, won in the end. As it happened the patient wasn't the husband of the stout countrywoman to whom Detective Constable Crosby had been speaking earlier but he had been somebody's husband and Sister Fleming's first duty was to tell his wife that he had died. Where handkerchief work was involved, so to speak, she always felt the task to be hers. When she delegated it to the young house officers she usually had to see the relative herself all over again.

Once more with feeling, in fact.

On Fleming Ward itself a certain briskness set in as the man died. Death represented a new procession of tasks and another course of action. It was a clear-cut and speedy course. Porters were summoned, screens appeared. The house surgeon and a registrar, suddenly idle, were treated to a little oblique and educative propaganda from the ward sister *en passant*.

"I'll fight for a patient for all I'm worth," said Sister Fleming quite fiercely, "but once they've gone I forget them completely."

The two young doctors got the message and melted away, consoled, to other duties.

The ward sister always had been one to improve the shining hour. She turned her attention to the nurses.

"And when you've made up a fresh bed, Nurse Petforth," she said sharply, "be sure to check the drip on the hemicolectomy over there."

"Yes, Sister," said Briony obediently. In prison, in the army, in the police force, you might be a name and number: in a hospital it was quite different. If you were a patient on a medical ward you were known by the disease you had. If you were on a surgical ward it was by the name of the operation you had been admitted to have.

"That drip should have been attended to before," she said.

"Yes, Sister."

"And nurse . . ." She turned her baleful gaze towards the probationer who was helping Briony Petforth with her bedmaking and whose very first encounter with death this had been.

"Yes, Sister," said the young nurse tremulously.

"You should have noticed before now that the appendix has come round from his anaesthetic."

"Yes, Sister."

"See to him," she commanded, "as soon as you've finished the bed."

Rightly calculating that righteous indignation at this cavalier approach to the Pale Horseman of the Apocalypse would banish any backward thoughts about the patient thay had just lost, Sister Fleming swept off to see the ward clerk about the admissions waiting list.

Acknowledged tartar Sister Fleming might be, but there were times when she came into her own.

"The patient is dead, long live the patient," muttered

Briony rebelliously, attacking the bedmaking with a certain savagery. While the dirty linen was being swept into a bag by the other hurse she set off for the linen room to collect fresh sheets and pillow cases.

Something—she didn't know what—was stopping her opening the door properly. She gave it an extra push and stepped inside, feeling for the light switch. It was then that she saw the crumpled figure of a man lying supine on the floor.

Where another girl might have screamed, Briony Petforth reminded herself that she was a nurse. She bent down cautiously, noticing as she did so the blood coming from a wound on the back of the man's head.

She thought she recognised the man's face but it wasn't his name that she used.

"Oh, Nick . . ." she moaned. "Oh, Nick . . ."

Chapter 13

We seek and seek, and were it once discovered
We should be safe enough—expenses covered.

"What!" exploded Leeyes. "They've found who? Attacked? And injured, did you say?"

"Detective Constable Crosby."

"Where?" spluttered Leeyes. "Wait until I . . ."

"In the hospital, sir. On Fleming Ward."

"We should have searched it," declared Leeyes inevitably.

Sloan ploughed on with the meagre information at hand. The superintendent was a great one for being wise after the event. "Crosby was found lying on the floor in the linen room, sir."

"Assaulted in the execution of his duty," intoned Leeyes in tone suitable for a memorial service.

"He's unconscious," Sloan informed him hastily. "Not dead."

"One of my men," said Leeyes sonorously.

"They've taken him down to Casualty."

"A good man, Crosby."

"Er . . . quite," said Sloan, savouring the occasion. Superintendent Leeyes's geese were only swans now and then.

"We'll get whoever did this, Sloan," he said militantly, "if we don't do anything else. And soon."

"Yes, of course," said Sloan calmly. It was a fact of police life that people who killed or tried to kill policemen were usually caught sooner or later. Sooner, more often than not. For some reason too arcane for an ordi-

nary person to explore, those who attacked policemen
in Great Britain ran out of support from friends and
relatives earlier than other wrong-doers did. And more
commonly than with most transgressors someone turned
them in. Perhaps as a penalty for breaking the rules by
which the game of cops and robbers was played? Sloan
didn't know.

"If they so much as touch a hair of his head,"
growled Leeyes, "I'll . . ."

"They've hit it," announced Sloan badly. "Quite
hard. Already." The superintendent's press conference
would come later. He could say whatever he liked at
that. Clichés and all. Now was a time for facts.

"Grievous bodily harm then," responded Leeyes automatically.

"Could be," admitted Sloan. "He hasn't come round
yet. I'm on my way over there now."

"That's right," said Leeyes obscurely. "Close the
ranks."

"We've put out a general alert."

"Good, good. No one else missing, is there?" At times
like this all of the superintendent's flock were dear to
him.

"No," said Sloan, startled. "Crosby and I are the
only two on this job anyway."

"Better write your own report out then before you
leave," said Leeyes lugubriously, "in case anything happens to you too."

"He's only a boy really," said Sloan, heroically sup-
pressing a number of other tempting retorts to this last.
"If in fact it was actually Nicholas Petforth who hit
Crosby."

"Boys," pronounced Leeyes with feeling, "can cause
more trouble then men."

"It may not have been him, of course," said Sloan
fairly. "There's another possibility. All Briony Petforth
will say is that she opened the door of the linen room
and found Crosby there."

"Ah."

"She also insists, sir, that she hasn't seen her brother
since before their aunt died."

"He would always know where to find her though, Sloan."

"I gather," said Sloan drily, "that he is in the habit of coming up on the ward when he wants something."

"Money?"

"Probably. She didn't say."

"I shouldn't be surprised," said the superintendent, who, was, after all, in a better position to judge than most men.

Sloan, momentarily diverted, voiced something that had been puzzling him all along. "I've been thinking, sir, that Beatrice Wansdyke's money must have come from somewhere pretty out of the ordinary."

Superintendent Leeyes snorted gently but did not speak.

"She didn't inherit it," pursued Sloan, "or win it on the pools, nothing's been stolen that we don't know about, the bank isn't unhappy about where it came from . . ."

"If it wasn't for the fact that someone had it in for her over the insulin and the dog," said Leeyes judiciously, "I'd have said the answer was easy."

"Sir?"

"Computer error, Sloan. I had a gas bill once . . ."

"This other possibility on the ward," said Sloan, who had heard about the gas bill before, "is something we've got to think about."

"What's that?"

"I am told that a frequent visitor on the men's surgical ward," said Sloan, "is Inspector Harpe's favourite medical motorist."

"Dr. McCavity?"

"He was a house officer at the hospital before he went into general practise with Dr. Paston," Sloan informed him. "Got quite friendly with Nurse Petforth while he was about it."

"Ah," said Leeyes alertly. The superintendent had never been able to make up his mind if sex was a more powerful ingredient of crime than money. He was, however, willing to consider the proposition at any time.

"But she wasn't having any."

"Like that, was it," grunted Leeyes.

"Turned him down."

"It happens all the time."

"In favour," pressed on Sloan, "of young Dr. Elspin."

"You won't remember this, Sloan."

"Sir?"

"Before your time."

Sloan steeled himself to silence. Every so often some hapless soul at the police station had—metaphorically, at least—to splash his way ashore at Walcheren alongside the superintendent in a wartime landing craft, rifle at the ready.

"There was this radio programme, Sloan, called ITMA."

Sloan breathed again. It wasn't going to be Walcheren.

"They had a character sketch about a young Dr. Hardcastle," said the superintendent reminiscently. "Ivy used to say he was lovely. . . ."

"Being turned down," said Sloan as repressively as he dared, "doesn't seem to have deterred Dr. McCavity."

"He didn't get the message?"

"This last couple of weeks he's been more persistent than usual. Sister Fleming's turned him out of the ward several times even though he's a doctor."

The superintendent stopped thinking about wartime radio comedy programmes. "Are you saying that he might have thought he was onto something?"

"I am merely pointing out," said Sloan astringently, "that his ardour seems to have enjoyed a bit of a comeback recently."

"Love and lolly?" said Leeyes, contemplating this.

"As Dr. Paston's partner he collects a sixteenth of the deceased's estate. . . ."

Leeyes nodded.

"As Briony Petforth's husband . . ."

"A clear way to another eighth," said the superintendent practically. The repeal of the Married Women's Property Act had no more signified with him than with most husbands. "You'd better look into that."

Sloan didn't write his report before he went to the Berebury District General Hospital to see Crosby, but he did telephone his own home.

There was no reply.

* * *

Detective Constable Crosby had come around by the time Sloan reached the Accident and Emergency Department of the Berebury Hospital.

His first words uttered on regaining consciousness had not been notably helpful.

"He just complained about his head," reported Sister Casualty.

Sloan nodded.

"I'm not surprised really," said the sister. "You should see the knock he's had."

Sloan was resigned. "I expect that I'll have to."

"I don't know what he hit me with," complained the patient bitterly. He was lying in an examination cubicle looking surprisingly cherubic in hospital pyjamas. Every now and then he ran an exploratory finger near the back of his head where he had been hit, found afresh that it hurt and took it away again.

"They haven't found a weapon yet," said Sloan.

"Try looking for a sledge hammer," groaned Crosby.

There might well be a Noble Army of Martyrs but quite clearly Detective Constable Crosby of the Berebury Police Force had no intention of being numbered among them.

"He has got quite a contusion there," said the sister fairly. "The doctor's going to look at it in a minute."

Crosby groaned again. "Bury me at Wounded Knee."

"This man who hit you . . ." began Sloan.

"The blighter must have been holed up in that linen room all the time."

"I suppose," said Sloan, "he was waiting for a chance to talk to his sister. If it was Petforth."

"I don't know what he was going to do," Crosby reminded him with a certain savagery, "but what he actually did was to hit me. Hard."

"It's not too serious," said Sister Casualty with professional briskness.

"It's not your head," said Crosby plaintively.

"The man who hit you," repeated Sloan, who had professional obligations too, "did you see him?"

Crosby brought his hand up to the back of his head again. "This is where he hit me. Here." He accidentally touched the spot. "Ouch . . ."

"I've already told you not to . . ." began the sister.

"He got me from behind," insisted Crosby. "That's why I never saw a thing. Except stars," he added mordantly.

"He was waiting in there all right," said Sloan. "He'd been sitting on a pile of blankets."

"Saving his strength," said the victim. "All I can say is that for someone who'd gone native he packed a pretty punch."

"Opted out of society," said Sloan. "That's what he'd done." The real natives of this sceptr'd isle lived in semidetached houses and watched television in the evenings.

"If you ask me," said a disgruntled Crosby, "he'd been practising with a pile driver while he was up on the motorway site. . . ."

Suddenly the curtain of the cubicle in Casualty was twitched back and a very young-looking man in a white coat approached.

Crosby started nervously.

Sloan was near enough to read the taped identification label on his breast pocket. It said "Junior House Surgeon."

"I've just come to put a few stitches in your scalp," he announced cheerfully.

Crosby obviously regarded the cheerfulness as misplaced.

"It *is* Mr. Crosby, isn't it?" enquired the doctor.

All men are equal in hospital.

Or nearly.

"It is," said Crosby in doom-laden tones.

Like steam giving way to sail, Detective Inspector Sloan yielded in the name of the law to the ancient profession of healing.

"I'll be getting along then, Crosby," he said, moving away.

Crosby was still taking in the doctor's appearance. He looked a real infant beside the well-built policeman. He had long wavy hair and sported an amulet with distinctly pagan overtones. He was also trying to grow a beard.

"It won't take a minute," said the young doctor heartily.

Crosby rolled his eyes and muttered something under his breath.

Sister Casualty showed Detective Inspector Sloan out.

"I've noticed the policemen are getting younger too," she said obliquely, walking with him to the door of the department. "And, Inspector . . ."

"Sister?"

"The house surgeon's mother does know he's out."

"Pardon? What was that?"

"Constable Crosby wondered if she knew."

*   *   *

"Of course I don't know what a policeman was doing in the ward linen cupboard," retorted the distraught girl. "And neither does my cousin, George. Do you?"

"No," said Dr. Roger Elspin.

"All I know," said Briony Petforth helplessly, "is that he was there and that I found him and . . ." Her voice trailed away.

"And?" prompted Elspin.

"And that if anything else is going to happen after all this, in spite of what you say, Roger, I don't think that I can . . ."

He interrupted her with, "You've had quite a week, darling, haven't you?"

Her manner changed abruptly. "Oh, Roger . . ."

"What with one thing and another," he said largely. Nearly two years of working in a hospital had taught him the value of unspecific statements that sounded comforting. And of the great importance of always sounding sympathetic. Being bracing made enemies of patients faster than the most painful treatment.

"First poor Aunt Beatrice," she said.

"And now this," he said for her.

"Nothing makes sense any more." She pushed her hair back under her cap. "Why should there be policemen in the hospital at all?"

The obstetrics registrar shook his head. "I don't know."

"And why wasn't Dr. Paston's death certificate for Aunt Beatrice good enough in the first place? Tell me that."

"I don't know." He frowned. "We only had one lecture on jurisprudence when I was a student. It's not enough really."

She shuddered. "Post-mortems are all very well but only when it's someone you don't know."

"That goes for a lot of things," he said soberly.

"I suppose it does." She sighed. "Like illness."

"Like childbirth," said the obstetrics registrar meaningfully.

"Oh, Roger . . ."

"I think we'd better adopt."

"Oh, no, we won't," she said hotly.

"Or do without the patter of tiny feet then and stay childless."

"I don't know about you," she said strenuously, "but I'm proposing to have six babies in quick succession." Her face clouded again. "I don't agree with small families."

"No."

She looked at him. "Roger, you're taking on quite a bit, aren't you?"

"If by that you mean your brother Nick . . ."

"He's a big worry especially if . . ." She fell silent.

"He's old enough to take care of himself, you know," said Roger Elspin.

"I only wish he was," said Nick Petforth's sister practically.

"He's certainly in a spot of trouble if he biffed that young copper."

"I thought he was dead at first," she shuddered. "Now are you sure you want to marry into our family?"

"Quite sure," he said calmly.

"The police wanted to know if Nick had a key to Aunt Beatrice's house."

"Had he?"

"We all had."

"We?"

"Nick, George, and me. Aunt always said we were welcome any time, even if she was out. She was out a lot, you know. She liked to spend her spare time down at the firm's lab working on this theory of hers."

"Turning air into gold."

"It was our home, after all," said Briony, ignoring this, "and anyway she never knew when she might be ill. She was very sensible, you know. Isolde would only attack a stranger so it was all right for us to have keys." She caught her breath. "Roger, I don't understand about Isolde. . . ."

"No. Did the police ask anything else?"

"They wanted to know if Peter McCavity had been up to the ward again. Sister must have told them about that."

"And had he?" asked Elspin quickly.

"Oh, he's always around these days."

"Bothering you?" Elspin's colour deepened.

She shook her head listlessly. "Not bothering exactly. Just around." She looked across at the registrar. "By the way, Roger, someone told me that they'd seen you up on Fleming this afternoon."

He nodded. "I was."

"You were?"

"I came up to snatch a quick kiss between deliveries."

"Oh, I see." She essayed a smile. "It would have had to come out of your ration today."

"I needed a pick-me-up, nurse. It's been a busy day on the maternity unit."

"I didn't see you."

"You had a bit of a flap on," he reminded her.

"That's right." She looked at him, wide-eyed. "Do

you know I'd almost forgotten about that already? And I would never have thought I could so soon. Terrifying, isn't it?"

"That's life."

"He was such a nice man, too, the patient who died."

Dr. Roger Elspin shot a quick glance at his watch. "Talking of patients reminds me that I should have a head coming up to crowning by now."

* * *

"Someone," pronounced Inspector Harpe of Traffic Division, "made darn sure that we linked Dr. Peter McCavity up with that smashed bollard near Ridley Road on Friday afternoon."

"And a man it was to boot," murmured Sloan. "Not a woman." That had been the curious thing. It was the curious things which added up in a case.

"So," said Harpe, "we ran a paint test."

"The good old exchange principle," said the detective inspector.

"We shouldn't get far without it up in this department," said the traffic man.

What Isaac Newton and gravity were to physics so the exchange principle was to police work. Fundamental. Objects could never meet without exchanging something of each other. Never. (Well, hardly ever.) And that usually went for human beings who touched—let alone things that went bump in the night too.

"Paint of car left on bollard?" guessed Sloan. Being a policeman and not a philosopher, he liked to leave the general for the particular as soon as he could.

"Better than that."

"Bit of bollard still attached to car? Oh, well done, Harry!"

Inspector Harpe permitted himself a rare grin of triumph. "Embedded in the headlight."

"McCavity's had another bollard, though, since Friday's, hasn't he?" asked Sloan.

The traffic inspector was unperturbed. Quite clever defence lawyers had been trying to catch him out for years. On oath.

"No, Sloan. The second bollard was yellow. The Friday one was white."

"That helps."

"What I want to know," said Happy Harry, "is whether you want me to run any other sort of test on the man rather than on the vehicle."

Sloan considered this. "He's certainly going to lose his licence one of these days anyway, isn't he?"

"Unless," said Inspector Harpe sourly, "whoever brings him in doesn't play the procedure game properly."

"It's a lot better than it was, Harry," said Sloan, answering the thought rather than the words. Breathalysers had been progress indeed.

"The Leith police dismisseth us," lisped the traffic man mockingly.

"My client," responded Sloan in courtroom tones, "has always had a speech impediment."

"He fell off a chalk line drawn on the floor of the police station."

"My client has a wooden leg. Surely the officer noticed?"

"He couldn't focus."

"An artificial eye."

"Drowsy . . ."

"Tired."

"He attempted to embrace a desk."

"Deeply shocked."

"He was quite unable to complete Rhomberg's test and touch the tip of his nose with his finger while his eyes were shut."

"The officer completely misinterpreted his gesture."

"He was pathologically talkative."

"My client always recites *The Boy Stood on the Burning Deck* when under stress."

"He complained that little green men were running round the charge room."

"Come, come, Officer," declaimed Sloan histrionically, "you must know my client's reputation as a humourist."

Happy Harry grunted and brought the surrealistic word picture to an end. "It's all very well for you to joke, Sloan. Let me tell you that the first man I put the finger on for driving under the influence—he was as drunk as a monkey's uncle—actually fell into the road when I opened the driver's door. . . ."

"And got off?"

"Not a stain on his character. Taught me a lot, did that."

"Has Dr. McCavity any blots on the escutcheon already?"

"Two."

Sloan was not surprised.

"And he's heading for a third," said Inspector Harpe, adding the quaintly old-fashioned phrase, "unless he mends his ways."

Sloan nodded. What the young doctor's resting blood alcohol level was, so to speak, didn't bear thinking about. "Leave it for today, Harry, though," he said, falling back on a police cliché. "There may be graver charges."

Inspector Harpe lifted an eyebrow. "Like that, is it?"

"Too soon to say."

"There have been other medical murderers, of course," mused Harpe.

"You don't need to tell me. The superintendent keeps on about them too."

"Harley Crippen," said Harpe immediately.

"Everyone always says him first."

"Bert Ruxton."

"Nasty piece of work."

"There was a poisoner, too, wasn't there?" said Harpe.

"And how," said Sloan inelegantly. "William Palmer." Madame de Brinvilliers might be *hors concours* as a poisoner but Dr. William Palmer had done his best to keep up. "Palmer the Poisoner, that was."

"That the lot?"

"No, it isn't," said Sloan briskly. "There was Dr. Lamson, who killed his brother-in-law for gain, and Dr. Pritchard, who poisoned his wife."

"Cream," said Harpe suddenly. "Neil Cream. He was a doctor, too, wasn't he?"

"So was Marcel Petiot," said Sloan. "He said he'd killed sixty-three people."

"They've had the training, of course," said Harpe. "By the way, we've had a request for a bobby at Wansdyke and Darnley's for Friday."

"This Friday?"

"They've got some sort of new product shindig on," said the traffic man. "Thought you might be interested. Their works being down near the bridge makes the parking a bit of a problem."

"I wish my problems were only parking ones," said Sloan fervently.

"Good Lord, yes," said Harpe. "I'd forgotten that bit about all your troubles being little ones. How are things?"

Sloan looked at him with dawning horror as he realised that he, too, had momentarily forgotten all about his wife and the unborn baby.

And in favour of murder.

"Fine, fine," he said hastily.

Chapter 14

*For all our cunning, when all's tried and done
That stone won't yield itself to anyone.*

"There is one thing," pronounced Superintendent Leeyes heavily, "that doesn't make sense."

"Sir?" As far as Sloan was concerned there were a lot of things about the death of Beatrice Gwendoline Wansdyke which didn't make sense.

"We still don't know for certain that any of these people really expect anything more than peanuts from Beatrice Wansdyke's estate."

Sloan sighed. There would be no mileage, he knew, in reminding the superintendent that as a motive for murder peanuts were good enough any day of the week. Dotty as it might seem, traditionally the stakes did not have to be as high for murder as they usually were for burglary.

"Not one of them," persisted Leeyes, "has given us the tiniest clue that they know they're in the big-money league."

"Someone hit Crosby."

"People are always hitting policemen," said Leeyes largely. "It's an occupational hazard."

"Someone changed insulin for water."

Leeyes accepted this without contradiction. "Ah, that's different. I grant you that, Sloan."

"It means that the malice was well aforethought," said Sloan. That was something he'd been thinking about quite a lot. The planning. This murder had been well contrived.

"I can see that without the missing insulin there

would be no case to answer," agreed Leeyes, submerging the assault on Constable Crosby's person without a backward thought.

"There isn't exactly a case," Sloan reminded him. "Not yet, anyway. But there will be."

"Up boys and at 'em," murmured Leeyes absently.

"I have been checking on one or two points with the bank, though, sir."

"A clammy lot, bankers."

"There were one or two crumbs they were prepared to let me have."

"Well?"

"They gave me the cut-off dates of their current account statement cycle."

"You could have worked that out for yourself."

"Perhaps," remarked Sloan philosophically, "that's why they disclosed them."

"Big deal."

"And, quite unofficially mind you, we've established the exact date the big money reached Beatrice Wansdyke's account."

"You have, have you?"

"Her bank statements were in the bureau in her sitting room."

"So it wasn't beyond Crosby."

"No." Sloan coughed. "When we tackled the bank again after that they did reveal—saw no harm in letting us know—that the large sum we were—er—interested in was received as one lump payment."

"Some lump."

"Some chicken, some neck," agreed Sloan, adding, "perhaps that's why it attracted attention."

"Nonsense," said Leeyes robustly. "A hundredth part of that sort of lump going into my current account would positively startle the manager."

"Yes, sir." The Sloan family income was modest, too. Police incomes were.

"And when exactly did Miss Wansdyke hit the jackpot?"

"I'll give you one guess," said Sloan.

"Sloan," said Leeyes testily, "are you trying to tell me something?"

"That payment didn't appear on her last bank statement, sir."

"So it's come in since the cut-off date?"

"The day after," said Sloan. "That's when it arrived."

"So it would be how long before she got her next statement?"

"A calendar month."

"Do you mean to say that if for any reason she didn't know about the money it would be the best part of four weeks before she would find out?"

"Unless she went in to the bank to ask what her current account stood at."

Superintendent Leeyes considered this. "Is what you are getting at, Sloan, the idea that she might not have known it was there?"

"All we know is that it wasn't on her last bank statement because we've looked at that. And," Sloan added judiciously, "that she hadn't gone in for being one of the last of the big spenders since it arrived."

"How did you work that out?"

"Crosby again, sir," he said, giving credit where credit was due. "Her cheque book was in the same drawer."

"He might make a detective if he lives long enough."

"Somebody," said Sloan flatly, "tried to see that he didn't."

Leeyes grunted.

"At least," said Sloan, "it explains the Ridley Road life-style. I should say that up until last month she had a Ridley Road income to match."

"The bank," rumbled Leeyes. "Surely they'd have told her that it had arrived."

"They say that they hadn't notified her of its arrival because they had been instructed that no notification was required."

"And they," said Superintendent Leeyes cynically, "always obey the last order too, do they? Who do they think they are? The army?"

"They obey instructions," said Sloan a little wearily. "They don't make decisions." He often wondered if those whose only duty was to carry out instructions ever realised how well off they were.

Leeyes snorted. "In our way of business you have to do both."

"Yes, sir."

"That's what sorts out the men from the boys."

"Yes, sir." There was no absolution to be had from blind obedience to orders in the police line of duty. Sloan knew that well enough. But all the same there was still always hell to pay if you broke the rules and followed your own nose and it didn't work.

And sometimes even if it did.

"If it wasn't for the insulin being tampered with," said Sloan fervently, "I'd have said the money was there by mistake."

"Get anything else out of the bank?" enquired Leeyes.

"Only that the Wansdyke family had banked there for three generations. They didn't seem to mind telling me that."

"That's not information," said Leeyes gratuitously. "That's advertising."

* * *

"No, Inspector," repeated George Wansdyke with some firmness, "I have not seen Nicholas Petforth since my aunt died." He did not sound regretful. "We put an obituary notice in the newspaper and hoped he would see that, though I believe he keeps in touch with his sister, Briony, from time to time."

The businessman was sitting at his desk in his office at the works of Wansdyke and Darnley. At the other side of the same desk, moving restlessly from foot to foot, was Bill Benfleet, the public relations man who had also been there earlier in the day. Wansdyke pushed the piece of paper they had both been studying into Benfleet's hands saying, "Some other time, Bill. . . ."

Benfleet shook his head. "Sorry, Mr. Wansdyke, but no."

"Look, Bill, this really will have to wait for a bit."

"It won't wait," said Benfleet flatly.

"It'll have to," said Wansdyke more than a little briskly. He indicated Sloan. "Can't you see that, man?"

The public relations man stood his ground. "It won't wait any longer. Not if you want it for Friday."

"Of course we want it for Friday," snapped a goaded Wansdyke. "That's the whole point."

"Then"—Bill Benfleet was adamant—"it's got to be done now."

"But . . ."

"I've got my girl staying on to type this tonight," said Benfleet with the air of one unanswerably clinching his argument. "Late."

Detective Inspector Sloan found it in his heart to be sorry for any man caught between the Scylla of his employer and the Charybdis of his secretary.

Wansdyke, too, must have seen the force of what Benfleet was saying. He ran his hand through his hair and capitulated. "You'll just have to do it yourself then, Bill."

"I can't," explained Benfleet patiently. "I've told you before I don't know enough about the product."

Sloan turned his head with Wimbledon-like interest to see how George Wansdyke would take that particular ball.

"Your public relations people don't usually let a little thing like that stand in your way," said Wansdyke with an attempt at lightness.

"I'm an advertising man," Benfleet came back with a straight volley. "Not an industrial chemist."

"Then ask one of them"—irritably.

"Nobody seems to know enough about it to say the right things."

"I'll grant you that," said Wansdyke more gracefully. "It's Mr. Darnley's pigeon really."

"And he's somewhere over the Atlantic," said Benfleet. "I hope."

"So do I. All right, Bill. I'll do it just as soon as the inspector's gone."

Sloan came in as on cue. "We're just checking really, sir."

"Sorry about all that," said Wansdyke as Bill Benfleet withdrew at last. "Friday's the day for a new product launching and we're just tying up one or two loose ends."

"So am I," said Sloan simply.

"What—er—oh, yes, of course, Inspector. What can I do for you now?"

"You can tell me a little more about Petforth."

"Nicholas? There's not a lot to tell you. Typical of his generation, I suppose. Never settled to anything. No money. Not particularly good at school. My aunt always said he had brains and she should know but he never used them that I know of."

Sloan didn't trouble to write down what he was saying. "Did he ever want to come into your firm?"

Wansdyke gave a short laugh. "And do some real work? Never, Inspector. He prefers to live by sponging on his sister and his aunt."

Sloan said nothing. The motorway site hadn't sounded like a cushy job to him.

"Beatrice always had a soft spot for him, whatever he did," said George Wansdyke.

"She's proved that, hasn't she, sir?"

"What? How do you work that out?"

"She left him half her worldly goods, didn't she, sir?"

"Oh, her will. Yes, of course. I was forgetting that."

"Does he know about it?"

"Not from me," said Wansdyke. "I don't know where he is."

"From his sister?"

"Possibly." Wansdyke shrugged his shoulders.

"From his aunt herself, maybe?"

"Perhaps," said Wansdyke. "She might have told him."

"She didn't tell you she had?"

"No," said Wansdyke. "Beatrice only told me that I was her sole executor."

"So Petforth might have known for some time that he was going to inherit?"

"Maybe." Wansdyke pulled his lips down. "Not that half of Beatrice's estate will keep him in comfort for the rest of his days and I suspect that that's the sort of support he's looking for."

Sloan said, "Aren't we all, sir?"

Wansdyke looked up sharply.

"Your new product, sir, that you're launching on Friday."

George Wansdyke smiled thinly. "You win, Inspector. Of course we're hoping that will do the same for us. I must say comfort for the rest of our days would suit us all here at Wansdyke and Darnley very well."

"How near did Miss Wansdyke get to having a press release of her own?"

"I don't really know, Inspector. My partner, Malcolm Darnley, is the technical one—I'm responsible for the business side of things—so I couldn't say for certain how far she'd got. He'd know. They used to chat a lot."

"She spent a lot of time down here?"

"Oh, yes, indeed. It was a fascinating quest for a chemist."

"Something from nothing," said Sloan appositely.

"I think she found it a relaxation after a week's teaching," said the other man.

"She would have made notes."

Wansdyke's face relaxed into a rueful grin. "Inspector, all research chemists make notes. Hundreds and hundreds of them. Filing them, I assure you, is a nightmare."

"Where would they be, sir?"

"Beatrice's notes? At her home, I should think. They're not here."

"Perhaps, sir," he said, "you'd let me know if you come across them." Detective Constable Crosby hadn't found them there but Sloan did not say so. They'd be searching the house in Ridley Road again anyway now that they knew about the insulin not being insulin, so to speak.

"Of course, Inspector." Wansdyke frowned. "Naturally, if you want them."

"Then," said Sloan courteously, "I won't come between you and your press release any more."

* * *

It was the best meal he had eaten for days. Detective Inspector Sloan said as much to his wife as he set his knife and fork down.

She smiled and murmured, "We both had too much."

"Couldn't very well waste anything as good as that, could we?" he said comfortably. "It wouldn't be right."

"It'll be the other sort of waist we'll have to watch soon, won't we?" said Margaret Sloan. "The one that needs a tape measure."

"Fulfilled has two meanings, too," he said, settling into his own fireside chair, "seeing as we're playing with words."

She fetched coffee and poured out two cups.

Presently she asked, "Went the day well?"

Over the years of married congress the two of them had devised an unwritten formula for the policeman's wife's equivalent of the business executive's wife's routine enquiry "Had a good day at the office, dear?" Margaret Sloan never put the question until she had seen to his bodily comfort. She always left out the verbal endearment too. There were other—better—ways of expressing that. . . .

And to her eternal credit she never pursued a negative response.

Today, though, she got a full answer.

"Crosby caught a packet." Her husband told her all about the attack on the young constable's person.

She shuddered. "Poor boy."

"We think it may have been Nick Petforth."

"The nephew?"

"He was around at the time. We do know that." Propinquity came into crime no matter what the moralists said, else why pray to be delivered from temptation?

"Around where?" asked his wife, settling down her coffee cup.

"Fleming Ward."

She frowned in recollection. "That's where the niece works, isn't it? The one I overheard talking to Dr. Elspin."

"It is."

Margaret Sloan stared into the fire and said, "It's

like a horrible mixture of two parlour games. Both jumbled up together . . ."

"Two?" Sloan looked up quizzically. He'd never been much of a man for parlour games. Not of that sort, anyway.

"Murder," she said. "Surely you remember playing that?"

"In the dark," he assured her.

"And . . ." Her voice trailed away.

"And?"

"And"—she didn't even like saying it—"Happy Families."

She got an unexpectedly earnest answer.

"It's in families that there's the greatest danger of murder," he said seriously. Nervous old ladies, afraid to go out in the dark, never believed it, of course. Nobody liked to believe that the greatest danger of murder came from one's nearest and dearest; that home was where the real danger of violence lay. The bedroom for the woman, the kitchen for the man, and the bathroom for the baby—where they were most likely to be strangled, stabbed, and drowned—in that order. The Home Office did their sums and said so.

"Miss Bun, the baker's daughter, and all that," she murmured.

"I thought for a moment," he admitted, "that you were going to say the other game was Consequences."

"I'd forgotten that one."

"It's the one that nobody bent ever plays," he said quickly. "If they did and sat down and worked out all the consequences of what they were doing there wouldn't be any crime and I'd be out of work. . . ." This inability to see the consequences of malefaction was what marked out your criminal.

But not your murderer.

Sloan knew that too.

Your murderer murdered to bring about consequences that were desirable to him.

Which was quite different.

"And Crosby?" asked his wife. "How is he now?"

A slow grin came over Sloan's face. "Better than Humpty Dumpty."

"And all the King's horses . . ." she began.

"And all the King's men—if that's what you call the National Health Service."

"Have put him together again?"

"Well, a young house surgeon was going to have a try. So young that Crosby was affronted."

"Poor boy," said Margaret Sloan again. Ambiguously.

"They're keeping him in hospital, though, tonight, to be on the safe side." His mind still on his own excellent meal, Sloan said, "He won't have eaten as well as this in there."

"No."

Something in the dryness of her tone made him look up, his face crinkling into a smile. "I'll smuggle you something in to the maternity ward, love," he promised, "in a paper bag under Sister Fleming's nose."

"You'll be too busy chasing villains to come to see me," she said mischievously.

"You wait," he said. "I'll be like those natives who camp at the bottom of the bed."

"You haven't seen the ward sister," said Margaret Sloan.

"Not friendly to natives?"

She smiled the rather remote smile of the heavily pregnant. "More coffee?"

"We never found a ransom note for the dog," he said, passing his cup. "I forgot to tell the super that. We did look in the house, just in case."

"You may be sitting in your own home, Detective Inspector Sloan," she observed, "but you haven't really left off working, have you?"

"It's all this nourishment," he said. "My brain is responding to it."

"Coffee coming up." She frowned. "So someone killed the dog for another reason?"

"To stir her up, perhaps. Dr. Dabbe did say a missing dog could upset someone in her state quite a bit, if they were attached to it."

"If Miss Wansdyke wasn't well for any reason," said Margaret Sloan intuitively, "could the dog have given the alarm? It was an Airedale, wasn't it?"

"If it's all the same with you," said her husband, "I'll stick to a St. Bernard when I'm lost in the snow. They've had the practise. You can send one of those with the brandy in that little keg round its neck."

"In the sort of places where you're likely to get lost," she came back smartly, "a working ferret would probably find you quicker."

"That's right—bite the hand that feeds you."

"I like that, Dennis Sloan." She started to struggle out of her chair. "Just you wait until I get my figure back."

"Not in your condition, please," he begged. "Don't do anything rash."

"Rash!"

"The dog," he said, hastily reverting to the late Beatrice Wansdyke, "might have barked if it couldn't get out of the house after she got really ill."

"Except that it was already dead." Margaret Sloan subsided into her chair again. "I wish I didn't feel so much like a stranded whale."

"Or if someone came to the house." He regarded her affectionately across the hearth. "It won't be for long now, love. . . ."

"The Airedale would have barked then," agreed his wife, adding fervently, "The sooner, the better."

"I was thinking," said Sloan, "that it also might have been killed in case if and when anyone called at the house and the dog didn't bark. . . ."

"You've been reading Sherlock Holmes again."

". . . in the night."

"I thought *The Hound of the Baskervilles* was going to come into this," she said, reaching for her knitting.

"Bound to," agreed Sloan gravely.

"I can knit and listen. . . ."

"If the dog didn't bark when someone called . . ."

"Because it wasn't there to bark."

"Whoever called would assume that Beatrice Wansdyke was out."

"And go away again," she said.

"While all the time she was lying there getting more and more ill."

"Poor thing," said Margaret Sloan compassionately.

"You come along to court when the time comes and remind them of that," said her husband. "Usually by the time defence counsel has said his piece on behalf of the murderer everyone's forgotten all about the victim. . . ."

By the time the following dawn had broken Detective Inspector Sloan had forgotten all about the victim too.

For the time being.

Hours later a tiny tug at his shoulder woke him from deep, carefree sleep.

"Have you got indigestion?" enquired a voice in the region of his left ear.

"No," he said sleepily.

"I have."

"Best meal I've had in days," he murmured dreamily.

"I think I ate too much."

"I'm sure I did. And very nice too." He grunted. "What time is it?"

"Two o'clock."

He promptly turned and buried his face in the pillow.

"If it isn't indigestion," said the same voice tightly, "then I think it's the baby starting."

Chapter 15

It's made us squander all we ever had,
Losses enough to drive us mad.

It is a fact universally acknowledged by all experienced policemen that babies, which come in all shapes, sizes, and colours, arrive in only two ways: before reaching the hospital and after reaching the hospital. In the nature of things it is only the first alternative that finds its way into both the occurrence book at the police station and the private nightmares of the officer concerned. It was naturally also the one which weighed on Detective Inspector Sloan's mind as he dressed with speed and backed his car out of the garage with unusual haste (and at considerable danger to the lawn mower).

"If it comes on the way," he joked between lips that had gone unexpectedly dry, "you'll have to christen him after me anyway."

A rather abstracted smile was all he got by way of answer to that.

"It's the done thing," he insisted. Rumour—unconfirmed rumour, it is true—even had it that somewhere down in the town of Berebury was a youth (otherwise to Fame unknown) who as a lusty and precipitate infant had been named after Superintendent Leeyes. Even superintendents, it was conceded down at the station, must have been constables once.

"Have you got my suitcase?" asked his wife more practically.

"In the boot," said Sloan. "Come on. . . ."

"Your supper's in the larder."

"Supper?" he said, momentarily bewildered. "It's the middle of the night. . . ."

"You'll be hungry by suppertime," she forecast. "It's on the middle shelf."

"Do come on."

"Unless you're going to go over to your mother's, of course."

"Margaret Sloan," he said firmly, "are you coming out to the car or aren't you?" This was no time to be talking of mothers-in-law.

"Have you locked the back door?"

"I have."

"Well, what are we waiting for then?" she asked with feminine perversity.

Sloan clamped his lips together.

She was sitting beside him in the car before she said suddenly, "The cat!"

"Out," snapped Sloan.

"I only asked."

"Sorry, love." The cat had had its kittens one night in the spring in the garden shed unbeknown to all until after the happy event. Sloan felt a swift upsurge of admiration of the animal kingdom.

Once put on the main road, he stepped up the speed of the car, sparing an anxious glance to his left from time to time. He started to search around in his mind for something comforting to say . . . the right phrase for the moment. . . .

"I forgot to leave a note for the milkman," she murmured before he could think of the *mot juste*.

"Just asses' milk from tomorrow?" he said, caught off guard.

"You'll only need one pint."

"I propose drinking nothing but pink champagne tomorrow."

"It may be a boy."

"Blue champagne, then."

"Fool," she said affectionately.

"Asses' milk," he said. "I was right the first time."

He negotiated two bends in the road and then drew up as a lonely set of traffic lights showed red. There seemed something faintly idiotic about their stationary

car standing at a halt in solitary splendour in front of a
red light in the middle of the night. He shot a quick
glance at his wife. She seemed all right.

"If the Martians landed now," he said, "they'd have
a job working out human behaviour—us sitting here
like this without anybody about until the yellow light
shows up."

"Until the green light shows up," she said. "I'm not
having Harry Harpe pinning anything on you tonight.
His boys will be about somewhere. They always are."

At right angles to the traffic signals for motorists
were the pedestrian ones, the forbidding red man
dimmed, the permissive green one glowing.

"I wonder what the Martians would make of the little green man over there," he said.

"Jack-in-the-Green," she said absently.

"What?"

"The Green Man. The pagan touch."

"Oh, yes, of course." Their little Red Book of advice
on having babies had been strong on humouring.

"Maypoles, and all that," she said enigmatically.

The red light gave way to amber and then green
while the little green man facing pedestrians was succeeded by the red one. The red man reminded Sloan of
the devil but he didn't say so. It didn't seem to be the
right moment to mention the Prince of Darkness. He
set off down the road again at a more decorous pace
than hitherto. The urgency of his journey had given
way to a thought even more terrifying than that of birth
on the way to the hospital.

False alarm?

Their way led down a hill towards the deserted town
centre. The hospital was the other side of that. The
road went past the police station, its blue light the only
sign of wakefulness in sight.

"I spy blue," said Margaret Sloan. It had been how
she greeted him when they were first engaged.

"I spy black," chanted Sloan.

"I spy a copper with a . . ." She caught her breath
suddenly and broke off in mid-speech, bending for-
wards. He couldn't see her face.

He took his left hand off the steering wheel and put

it over her white knuckles. And he put his right foot on the accelerator.

"Sorry." She took a deep breath and then said, "I'm all right now."

"It won't take long to get there this time of night."

"And at this rate," she said shakily.

He slowed down.

But only for a moment.

* * *

If there is one type of suspect which all the police forces the world over find less difficult in tracking down than any other it is the escapee with nowhere to go. Foxes have holes and birds of the air have nests but with the hearths of home and family well and truly stopped a man on the run is a vulnerable man.

Detective Inspector Sloan found that expectant fathers were similarly without anywhere immediate to go. The journey to the Berebury District General Hospital duly accomplished and the sanctuary of the maternity ward achieved at last, Sloan himself was now at something of a loose end.

At the door of the ward it had been quite kindly suggested to him that he go away and have a cup of tea for half an hour or so. As there had been no information about where he could procure such a commodity in the middle of the night Sloan rightly interpreted this as telling him he wasn't wanted for a little while.

He decided as a first step to park his car.

He steered it around to the visitors' car park, switched off the ignition, and made himself think about that other soul with nowhere to go—Nicholas Petforth. This required quite an effort as his whole inclination was to let his thoughts dwell exclusively on Margaret Sloan. Nicholas Petforth had to all intents and purposes disappeared as surely as if he had been touched by a conjurer's wand. He had not returned to the house of squatters in Luston, he had not been near the motorway site beyond the Calleford Road, he had not been back to Fleming Ward.

Sloan was quite sure of this last.

Detective Constable Crosby had been admitted to the

ward with a bandage on his head and a personal radio in his pyjama pocket. And though the girl herself didn't know it another policeman was keeping a watchful eye on Briony Petforth in the nurses' home. Nick Petforth, though, concluded Sloan, must be somewhere. And as it was by no means a warm night that somewhere was probably under cover. By October even a fugitive from justice needed a roof over his head during the hours of darkness.

Sloan looked at his watch: another twenty-five minutes before he could go back to the ward.

He wound the window of the driver's door down and sniffed the night air. It was distinctly chilly. Not that he was contemplating going for a walk. No policeman who had once done his years on the beat ever voluntarily put one foot in front of the other again except in the line of duty. Sloan had done his share of two and a half miles to the hour, fourteen miles to the day, in his time. More than his share probably, or did everyone always think that?

"And," his old sergeant had said grittily to him on his first day, "if you come back saying you're dead beat I'll run you out of town."

So he hadn't.

He'd finished his first foot patrol and reported instead that as days went it had taken a lot of beating. . . .

A raw constable learned a lot from his first sergeant.

Like the importance of finding out where to get a cup of tea any hour of the night or day.

"Unless you're a good kitchen range-finder, my lad," Sloan could hear him saying even now, his first sergeant, "you'll never make a good copper because you'll always be thirsty. And that's a bad thing."

Sloan wound the window of his car up again and started the engine. He was a pretty poor policeman if he couldn't find a cup of tea somewhere. He turned out of the car park and headed for the town centre again. The blue lamp of the law was still shining above the police station doorway.

The night duty officer greeted him ironically. "We never close."

More importantly neither did the canteen.

A couple of Inspector Harpe's night duty traffic patrol having their rest break nodded to him without curiosity. They knew that the Criminal Investigation Department worked at night too. The phrase "ungodly hours" was no mere slip of the tongue. . . .

Sloan settled himself down in a corner of the canteen with a cup of tea. There was one thing to be said for being here at the police station in the middle of the night as opposed to the middle of the day. Superintendent Leeyes was not usually around in the night on the lookout for fools not to suffer gladly. For some reason the notion of fools set up another train of thought in Sloan's mind. He hoped that they weren't being fools in the case of Beatrice Gwendoline Wansdyke.

The neat elderly spinster and her dog who had inhabited the neat ordinary house in Ridley Road seemed very far removed from exotic sums of money. And yet the neat elderly spinster and her dog were both dead and the neat ordinary house empty. . . .

Sloan set his cup down.

The neat ordinary house was empty.

He pushed his tea cup away and got to his feet. There was just time for him to slip round to Ridley Road before he went back to the hospital and check.

It might not be empty.

* * *

Mrs. Margaret Sloan had her cup of tea brought to her bedside. She was in a nightdress now and lying back in bed.

"More comfortable now are you, dear?" she was asked.

"Yes, thank you." Her face was quite flushed all the same.

"How's the pain?"

"Not too bad." Her concentrated expression belied the words.

The midwife nodded. "We'll give you something for it."

Nonverbal communication ranked high in hospitals. Heightened colour never went unnoticed either.

"Thank you." She caught her breath. "That would help."

"Just relax as much as you can."

Margaret Sloan managed a short derisive laugh.

"I know, dear," said the nurse patiently, "but do try to save your strength all the same. You're going to need it later." She straightened the bedclothes with an automatic twitch in the true Florence Nightingale tradition and went on, "You could probably get a little sleep, too, you know, if you put your mind to it."

"Sleep!" echoed the patient in patent disbelief.

The midwife was too wise to argue. She changed the subject instead. "Your husband'll be back presently."

"I don't know about that," said Mrs. Margaret Sloan. "He's a policeman."

* * *

Detective Inspector Sloan's car was the only one about in Ridley Road, Berebury. He stopped well short of Miss Wansdyke's house and let himself quietly out of his car. He padded noiselessly along the pavement and went straight past the house, noting what he could without turning his head. Save that the window curtains were undrawn, it looked just as did the neighbouring houses. The only immediate difference that sprang to the eye was that there were no empty milk bottles outside the door.

Milk bottles reminded him of home.

And duty.

He took a quick look at his luminous watch. He mustn't be too long about this. He was due back at the hospital pretty promptly. He turned when he got to the end of the road and walked back towards number fifty-nine. The gate did not creak and he was standing outside the front door in a moment.

He still had a key.

So, he reminded himself, did a number of other people.

The lock slid back easily and he was soon inside the

hall. He shone his torch very briefly to get his bearings. He went swiftly through the downstairs rooms first. He wasn't going to have anyone hitting him from behind. That had been a lesson learned a long time ago. He flashed his torch quickly over the kitchen sink and draining board. Traces of human occupation showed up there more often than anywhere else. That had been another lesson learned.

Both sink and draining board here were quite bare. So either there was no one in the house or else they were being very careful indeed. Admittedly the place had the feel of desertion. His torch swept over a dog's food bowl near the stove. Nobody had moved that away yet. Not, he conceded at once, that there had been a lot of time for any tidying up to be done. George Wansdyke, sole executor, had a big business to run, especially with his partner away. An aunt's affairs would have to take their turn.

Sloan moved out of the kitchen and back through the hall. He would take a quick look round upstairs and then get back to the hospital. He put his hand on the newel post and felt with his foot for the first step.

"Don't come any further," said a voice from the top of the stairs.

Chapter 16

Go where they may a man can always tell
Such people by their pungent brimstone smell.

"How is the pain now, dear?" the midwife enquired of Mrs. Margaret Sloan.

There was a significant pause before she could speak. Then she managed to say, "Not too good."

The midwife nodded with the briskness of one not in pain and at once brought into play a piece of equipment which was standing beside the bed. "Take a deep breath of this," she commanded, "when you feel a pain coming on."

Mrs. Sloan reached out hungrily for the proffered mask. Plunging her face deeply into it, she sucked the anaesthetic gas and air mixture with avidity.

"That better?" asked the nurse encouragingly.

She nodded, still clutching the face mask.

When the pain had passed she removed it and asked, "Is my husband back yet?"

"Not yet," said the midwife, adding with uncanny—but quite unwitting—prescience, "I expect he's been held up somewhere."

* * *

Detective Inspector Sloan, father-to-be, swung back to the side of the stairs and out of the direct line of whoever was above. He transferred his torch to his left hand, keeping his right free. The voice had been a youngish one. He decided to provoke it into speech again. He tapped the side of the banister rail with the handle of his torch.

"Don't move," said the voice at once.

Sloan did move. Noisily.

"Don't move, I said," came the voice again. Less assuredly this time.

Sloan stepped around in front of the staircase again. There was a certain amount of thin light coming from an uncurtained window near the landing at the top of the stairs. When he got around far enough to see up in that direction though he was disappointed. All he could make out was a shape standing in a position of vantage at the head of the stairs.

He paused for thought.

There was no chance of rushing someone standing eight feet above ground level. He knew that. Especially with stairs wide enough for only one person at a time. Builders of mediaeval castles had known what they were about when they designed their tiny turret staircases inside their towers. One man with a sword standing at the top of one of these could keep an army at bay. Besides, he, Christopher Dennis Sloan, Detective Inspector, who should know better, had committed the cardinal sin of coming here alone, and without leaving word of what he was about.

So if he failed there would be bureaucratic trouble. Going it alone was countenanced in the police force only when married to success. Hunches could be played by police officers all right—but they had to be winning hunches.

Or else.

Very cautiously he advanced and put his foot on the bottom step of the staircase.

It creaked.

It would.

The figure at the top of the stairs promptly took a step downwards. Sloan could see now that the man's right hand had something in it. It could have been a poker. He decided on a change of tactics.

"Suppose," said Sloan amiably, "you tell me your name."

This arrested the descent.

"Suppose," countered the voice at the top of the stairs, "you tell me yours."

"Police," said Sloan.

A short laugh came from above. "I thought it was either cops or robbers and the silver's not worth stealing."

"Your name," said Sloan again. The superintendent was a great believer in maintaining the initiative and it rubbed off.

"Legion," said the voice promptly.

"I think," said Sloan quietly, "that it's Nicholas Petforth."

"And if it is?" challenged the voice.

"Then we've been looking for you."

"We seek him here," came mockingly out of the darkness, "we seek him there."

"You're wanted for questioning," said Sloan more prosaically.

"I didn't think it was for a dog licence."

"No," said Sloan, "it wasn't." The beginnings of an idea had come to him.

"Coming for me at the squat and then hounding me at work."

"The hospital," Sloan reminded him. In the dim light he was trying to count the number of stairs.

"There, too," said the voice with a distinct note of grievance.

"You led us a real dance halfway round the hospital."

"I've probably caught the dreaded lurgies all because of you."

"That's why you went up to Fleming Ward afterwards to see your sister, isn't it?" He thought there were eleven steps in the staircase.

"She's a nurse," mumbled the voice. "I thought she'd know."

"Got any symptoms yet?" enquired Sloan heartlessly. With sybilline cunning he put his foot on the second stair up from the hall at the same moment as he spoke.

"No."

"Not gone green all over or anything like that, have

you?" The great thing now, decided Sloan, was to maintain the dialogue.

"No," said the figure at the top of the stairs, "and I'm not going to turn into a toad either just for Malcolm Darnley's benefit."

"Come again?" said Sloan. Maintaining a dialogue with the man above wasn't as difficult as it might have been: but it was unexpected.

"Malcolm Darnley," said the voice above richly, "has set up a group to help toads across this new motorway."

"It's in their way, too, is it?" said Sloan unsurprised. He felt for the third step with his foot.

"Cuts right across their patch."

"Pity, that." Sloan was really taking a second look at the landing window. If he attempted to advance in an upright position he would be silhouetted against what little light there was. There would have to be a better way up. He dropped to his knees. The stair he was on creaked as he did so.

"Don't come any further," said the voice hoarsely.

"If," said Sloan with the utmost cordiality, "you're not going to turn into a toad what about being a prince?"

"A prince?" The remark seemed to have caught its hearer off balance.

"Seems as if it's always one or the other," said Sloan, "in all the best fairy stories." He was working his way up the stairs on his knees now. Like the pilgrims did when they climbed the Penitential Steps in the Vatican in Rome.

"Not even to please a fairy princess," replied the voice. Its owner sounded really quite young.

Sloan had to keep silent now. Speech would have betrayed how near to his quarry he was. In fact his only problem was how to keep his breathing under control: it had to be soundless.

"Besides," said the voice, "I think I'd rather be a toad."

As Detective Inspector Sloan tensed himself in preparation for a grab at the ankles of the man standing above he remembered something else about toads: that there was a variety of the species called the midwife toad.

It lent a lot of power to his elbow.

* * *

In a different place and for a different reason some-one else had also been trying hard to control her breath-ing.

Trying harder.

Or perhaps it's just more difficult.

"Don't hold your breath," adjured the midwife.

Mrs. Sloan thought briefly about a suitable retort but didn't make it.

Breath was too precious now to be wasted on words.

Besides, words were magnificently irrelevant.

True she was making a sound of some sort but in a way altogether disassociated from what she was actually thinking. It might have been coming from someone else so little control had she over it.

"And remember to rest in between pains," continued the person in charge in an admonitory manner.

Being in charge, decided Margaret Sloan to herself in a detached fashion, was an illusion. Anyone who thought they were in control of events in a delivery ward was living in cloud cuckoo-land. Events were in control of everyone else. An event, anyway. She took a breath of shuddering proportions, and decided that any-one who wasn't the mother or the baby at a confine-ment was only on the touchline.

Not part of the real action at all.

It was a moment or two before she realised that her immediate world now consisted of more than herself, the midwife, and a gas and air machine. Aware that someone else was standing beside her bed, she turned her head with an effort and consciously tried to focus her gaze on the figure.

Detective Inspector Sloan moistened his lips uneasily. "Sorry I'm a bit late. . . ."

Any husband to any wife.

"Where have you been?" she asked.

Any wife to any husband, as the poet said.

Chapter 17

What about merchants? Lord! They don't maintain
A fixed prosperity, believe you me.

He did set out to tell her where he'd been.

"Nick Petforth's safely in a cell now," he said.

He couldn't tell if she was listening to him or not.

"And a bit worse for wear, I must say."

Or even if she wanted to hear.

"The station sergeant," he plunged on, "didn't like the look of him at all when I took him in."

He had begun by patting her hand, then holding it.

"I told him that he'd fallen down a flight of stairs in the course of arrest, which was true in a manner of speaking."

Margaret Sloan's eyes were closed. He couldn't tell what she was thinking.

"And he said," Sloan told her, "that he'd heard that one before and I could tell it to the marines if I wanted to but that the court wouldn't like it."

Margaret Sloan made no response but she left her hand in his.

Sloan carried gallantly on. "He asked me what I was charging him with. Hitting Crosby, I said. Do you know what he said to that?"

The hand that lay in his tightened but still Margaret Sloan did not speak.

"No?" Sloan grinned. "You won't believe this, Margaret, but he sighed deeply—the station sergeant of all people and you know how strait-laced he is—he sighed and said, 'Inspector Sloan, you don't know how I envy

171

him. Hitting Crosby is something I've wanted to do myself for a long time.' "

Had there been a faint twitch at the edge of Margaret Sloan's lips or had he imagined it?

"Almost worth going on a charge for, he said it would have been."

Margaret Sloan said nothing.

"I know the feeling," said Sloan more to himself than to her.

After that, Sloan, too, fell silent and presently the hand that held his slackened its tension and dropped away.

"She's asleep," pronounced a figure in blue over his shoulder. "We gave her something. You can go away again for a little while. Not too long, mind."

* * *

Sloan looked at his watch. Morning was breaking and the hospital was coming to life again for a new day. He would go to Fleming Ward and visit someone else.

Detective Constable Crosby, tousled hair extruding between layers of bandage, struggled to sit up as Sloan approached his bed. "Morning, sir."

"How went the night?"

"No sign of Nick Petforth," said Crosby, "and his sister went off duty at suppertime."

"He's in a cell," said Sloan.

"Ah." Crosby sank back on his pillows.

"But I don't think he did more than hit you."

"That's enough, isn't it?" demanded the victim, immediately aggrieved. "It hurt."

Sloan looked at the detective constable's bandaged head with a new dispassion. A spell in the delivery room of the maternity ward altered a man's outlook on pain.

"Besides," said the patient, "I didn't get a wink of sleep last night."

"He's admitted hitting you and denied everything else," said Sloan succinctly.

"You can't sleep in a place like this even without a

headache," said Crosby, preoccupied as any other invalid with his own state of health.

Sloan wondered what Superintendent Leeyes would have said to that, and then to his surprise heard himself saying it aloud. He must be getting old. "I don't know what the force is coming to."

"Petforth's got the best motive," said Crosby, reluctantly abandoning the role of valetudinarian.

"The biggest, you mean," said Sloan.

"Half the deceased's estate." Crosby thought for a moment. "And he'd got the means, too, hadn't he, sir?"

"Had he?" asked Sloan.

"If there weren't half a dozen hypodermic syringes sculling around that squat I'll eat my hat."

Sloan nodded. He could believe that half of that lot were on those sorts of drugs.

"And," insisted Crosby, "he'd got the opportunity. Ah, good . . ." His face brightened. "There's the tea trolley. I thought they were never coming with it."

"By opportunity," continued Sloan, smiling winningly at the nurse in charge of the teapot, "I suppose you mean that he had a key to Beatrice Wansdyke's house?"

"I do." Crosby grimaced. "The tea's even worse here than at the station."

"Never."

"Got bicarbonate of soda in it, I expect."

"Whatever for?" said Sloan, startled. He didn't want to be done good to by any hospital so early in the day.

"To make it look darker and go further, of course."

Sloan's mother had never stooped to such tactics. He promptly went off the tea.

Crosby leant back against his pillows with the air of one winding up a case. "There you are, sir. Motive, means, and opportunity—what more do you want?"

"Proof," said Sloan: but it wasn't what he meant.

"Ah." Crosby smoothed down the sheet.

"No," said Sloan, immediately amending what he had said, "that's not true. What I really want to know is exactly where all that money came from and what it was doing sitting in the account of the late Miss B. G.

Wansdyke. . . ." He paused. Somewhere at the back of his mind then something had rung a little bell. He searched his memory but Mnemosyne, daughter of Heaven, mother of the Muses, sat back and answer came there none. "And, Crosby," he added in the absence of elucidation, "I want to know exactly what the hurry was."

"What hurry?" asked Crosby, lending a nice touch of verisimilitude to his remark by lying back negligently in his bed, ostentatiously remote from the pace of life at the police station.

"The hurry about her dying when she did." Sloan regarded the constable straightly: a hospital cut a man off from the world so. "We'll have to get you out of here, Crosby, before the rot sets in."

"I can't see why it was an against-the-clock job, sir."

"I can," said Sloan briskly. "You see, if by any chance it wasn't her money and she didn't know about it either . . ."

"If," said Crosby.

"Then she stood to find out about it pretty soon, didn't she?"

"How?"

"When she got her next bank statement, of course. That hit on your head didn't damage your brain, did it?"

"And," said Crosby with dignity, "the bank statements are due out again at the end of this week."

"Or the beginning of next. You can never be sure with a computer."

"More tea?" enquired a new voice.

"What's that? Oh, no, thank you, nurse. . . . I must be going soon," said Sloan, withdrawing his cup.

"Suppose, though," advanced Crosby cautiously, "she had got her bank statement or happened to enquire about the balance at the bank?"

"Keep supposing," said Sloan. "Suppose for the sake of argument she's an honest woman." Usually, down at the police station their suppositions were based the other way around.

"She sees that there's something wrong," said Crosby,

"when there's that sort
credit."

"And what would sh

"Tell other people
the bank anyway, pr

"Somebody," sai
her to do that. The

"It doesn't ge
Crosby. "Geor
enough when h

"Time," said S
buying time." As a sou
that Crosby lacked some
busy, what with being in sole cha
away and a—what did they call
launching on hand."

"Talking of time," said Crosby helpfully, "i
opening time for Dr. Peter McCavity. And, sir,
don't know how badly Nurse Petforth wants to get married, do we?"

"Or how much any of the others needed their share,"
conceded Sloan, adding, "if the money was really Beatrice Wansdyke's to leave." There was definitely something in the way of thought burgeoning at the back of his mind now. "There's always the possibility that she might have found what she was looking for." Air into money: it was a nice thought.

"If time came into it," said Crosby a little truculently, "it would be because something was going to happen, wouldn't it?" He smoothed the bedclothes in front of him. "Well, nothing's happened so far, sir, has it, and there's nothing due to happen either, is there?"

"Not that we know about," temporised Sloan. He cast his mind over the Wansdyke legatees. Nothing important appeared to be pending. "We don't know everything, of course."

"It's a bit hard," observed the detective constable, following a different tack, "if she's got to die just to stop her beetling round to her bank manager to tell him that somebody's turned over two pages or something. . . ."

...se, does it?" agreed Sloan ab-

...e the quarter of a million pounds did

... "Me, too."

...must use that sort of money," said the
...usiness, I suppose."

...money wasn't lost, stolen, or strayed," as-
...an, "that's pretty well all that's left." The dog
..., too; he mustn't forget that.

... business," said Crosby comfortably. There was
...an five pounds in the locker by his bed.

...etective Inspector Sloan stood up, ready to go back
... the maternity ward. "Business. We'll have to look
...to . . ." His voice faded to a standstill. "Say that
again, Crosby," he commanded, an entirely different
tone in his voice.

"Business," said Crosby. "Big business."

"We were talking about something that might be due
to happen, weren't we?" he said, suppressing a rising
excitement.

"Nothing that we could think of," Crosby reminded
him.

"Oh, yes, Crosby, there is something due to happen."

"Sir?"

"On Friday morning."

"Friday?" Crosby looked up. "Tomorrow?"

"As ever was." Sloan had a memory of not one but
two occasions when a desperate public relations man
had been chasing a managing director about a press release. "Beatrice Wansdyke didn't die because of a clerical error," he breathed with new-found conviction.

"No?" Crosby struggled to sit up in bed.

"No," he said softly. "It was all planned most beauti-
fully, Crosby." Light was dawning fast. Someone had
wanted burial, not cremation. Cremation called for two
medical certificates, not one.

"What was?"

"Oh, yes," continued Sloan to himself, "in due
course George Wansdyke would have indeed discovered
the money and been able to prove that it wasn't Beatrice's. . . ."

"Would he?"

"But by then," said Sloan grimly, "it would have been too late."

"Too late for what?" insisted Crosby, pushing the bedclothes aside.

Sloan wasn't listening.

"Too late for what?" repeated Crosby.

Sloan's mind was racing ahead now with a speed that would have shamed a computer.

"I'm beginning to see it all now."

"I'm not, sir."

"Wansdyke and Darnley couldn't have their new product launching until Friday for a reason."

Crosby merely looked bewildered.

"Because of something that was going to happen to-day, Crosby."

"Nothing was due to happen today," protested the detective constable.

"Oh, yes there was."

"Thursday?"

"Today's Thursday," said Sloan authoritatively, "and something's due to happen. Something we'd forgotten about."

"We knew?"

"Everyone knew," said Sloan. "That was the beauty of it."

"What?"

"Something the murderer was waiting for." He shot a look at his watch and snapped, "Where's the nearest telephone? Quickly."

* * *

Several things happened at once.

Detective Constable Crosby flung back the bed-clothes. Detective Inspector Sloan raced across the ward. A ward maid called Nellie began a stately pro-gression down between the row of beds with a bucket and mop. Sloan side-stepped Nellie but Crosby can-noned into her. Sloan reached Sister Fleming's office and the telephone at much the same time as Sister

Fleming emerged to enquire into the noise and confusion.

Sloan pushed straight past her and grabbed the telephone directory. With savagely controlled speed he started hunting through its flimsy pages, muttering under his breath the while. "Darnley . . . where are the D's. . . . Don't anyone tell me that they're after the C's. . . ."

Nobody tried to do that.

"Mr. Crosby," an outraged sister was saying, "get back to bed at once."

"Darnley," said Sloan again, rapidly running his finger down a column. "Darnley . . . what's his first name? . . . I remember," he said before Crosby had time to speak ". . . it's Malcolm, isn't it? . . . George Wansdyke told us that . . . here we are."

Sister Fleming drew herself up to her full height.

Nobody took any notice.

"Darnley, M.C.P.," shouted Sloan, "Selborne . . . why can't people use street numbers instead of house names? . . . Acacia Avenue, Berebury." He was already dialling as he spoke. "Acacia Avenue isn't as good an address as the one the Wansdykes live at," he remarked as his fingers went round the dialling digits. He heard the bell ring at the other end and answered his own observation with "But then Malcolm Darnley didn't marry a Hartley-Powell."

"Mr. Crosby . . ." thundered Sister Fleming, "what are you doing out of bed?"

The telephone bell rang three times at the house called Selborne in Acacia Avenue before it was answered.

"Mrs. Darnley?" said Sloan with suppressed urgency.

"Speaking." She had a pleasant light voice.

"Do you happen to know which flight your husband is travelling back from the United States on?"

"Who is that?" she asked more sharply. "Do you know what the time is?"

"Police," jerked out Sloan. "Not about an accident or anything." If he believed in crossing fingers he would have crossed them now. "Just a few enquiries."

"At this hour?"

"His flight number," said Sloan martially. "Do you know that?"

"No."

"The time then," said Sloan quickly.

"I do know he's due to land at about seven o'clock this morning."

"Our time?" In his youth Sloan had read *Around the World in Eighty Days*. The last chapter had made a lasting impression on him.

"Our time," said Mrs. Darnley calmly. "Why do you want to know?"

"How is he planning to get home?"

"From the airport, you mean?"

"Yes. Are you meeting him, for instance?"

"Oh, no. He'll have landed by now, won't he?"

Sloan shot a quick look at his watch and groaned inwardly.

"He's coming home by car," she volunteered.

"Whose car?" Sloan fought to keep the rising anxiety out of his voice.

"His own. Ours, that is. I don't drive, you see." She coughed. "Malcolm thinks the fewer people who drive the better, especially wives."

"Where did he leave it?" Sloan heroically refrained from other comment.

"In the airport car park. We don't mind it being out in the open." She laughed. "It's so old that no one would steal it now."

Sloan interrupted her without ceremony. "What's the registration number?"

"Let me see . . . I should know, shouldn't I, after all these years."

Sloan waited. The seconds seemed like minutes.

"But I'm not very good at remembering numbers," she said apologetically. "Is it important?"

"Yes," said Sloan between clenched teeth, adding under his breath, "madam, you don't know how important."

"You'll be able to find it easily enough in a crowd," she said brightly, "if that's what you want."

"How?"

"It'll be the oldest one there."

"Mrs. Darnley . . ."

"Bound to be," she said confidently. "We don't believe in planned obsolescence, you see, so we never
change cars until we have to."

Sloan rigorously suppressed something about not believing in fairies himself and said instead with rigid for-
mality, "Thank you, madam. You've been a great
help."

"Are you sure, Officer, that there's nothing wrong?"
asked Mrs. Darnley.

But by then Sloan had rung off.

* * *

Malcolm Darnley, partner in Messrs. Wansdyke and
Darnley, did not look like an agitator. Therein, as all
experienced bureaucrats and administrators knew, lay
half his strength. His essentially mild manner and con-
ventional dress invariably strengthened his case at public enquiries.

At the moment the archconservationist looked just
what he was—a tired businessman. With jet-lag weari-
ness he walked across the airport car park, humping his
luggage with him. A wasteland, he thought to himself,
as he regarded row upon row of parked cars. Being a
methodical soul, he had made a mental note of exactly
where he'd left his own before leaving on his trip.

Not that he couldn't pick out his own vehicle easily
enough anyway. It was the oldest car in sight. And the
best maintained. He spotted it without delay and
walked towards it with affection. If every owner cherished their mechanical appliances in the way the Darn-
leys did there would be fewer municipal dumps. He
looked at more modern productions of the assembly
line with complacency. They didn't make cars like his
any more.

It was parked some little distance from the entrance
and he picked his way round the rows, wishing his luggage wasn't quite so heavy. He turned his head for a
moment when he heard a distant shout but then carried
on. He had almost reached the row where his own car

was waiting when the shout came again. It was nearer now.

Malcolm Darnley continued walking. After all, no one knew him here. He did just check over his belongings to make sure he hadn't dropped his wallet or anything. All seemed well and he strode onwards.

Next time the shout was clearly audible.

Darnley turned and saw a running policeman. It was, he conceded to himself, an unusual sight. Policemen didn't usually run: something important must be happening. A quick scanning of the horizon did not reveal to Malcolm Darnley what that could be. Shaking his head to himself, he forged on.

The shout came again.

This time there was no doubt as to whom it was addressed.

Himself.

The policeman was running in his direction and shouting at him at the same time.

Darnley had reached his own car now. He dumped his travelling bag down and turned, fumbling in his pocket for his keys. He would just park his luggage in the car. . . .

This time he heard what it was that the policeman was shouting. It was for him to keep still.

Essentially co-operative except in the matter of conservation of the countryside and the preservation of England's architectural heritage, Malcolm Darnley, thorn in much bureaucratic executive flesh, stood still.

As well as the running policeman, other figures were now appearing at the gallop from other corners of the airport car park.

Malcolm Darnley was quite bewildered. He looked around at the car park. It seemed normal enough to him. He cast an eye over his own car. That, too, looked just as he had left it. . . . He stiffened. . . . Well, no, not quite.

He, Malcolm Darnley, had not left a newspaper draped carelessly over the back seat before flying to the United States. Certainly not an Irish newspaper.

The running policeman skidded to a halt beside him

and put out his hand for Darnley's car keys. "If you don't mind, sir . . ."

Darnley surrendered them without demur.

He was no fool. This was no time for protest. Instead he stood back and waited for an explanation. It came from an unexpected quarter. One of the other figures who had converged on his car turned out to be an expert in his own particular rarefied field. Civilised life is under threat in more ways than by the simple despoliation of the countryside. Malcolm Darnley learned that to-day's airport carries its own bomb-disposal expert on the staff.

The specialist's first requirement was that everyone move well back before he commenced operations.

Obediently, Malcolm Darnley—no nonconformist in essentials—joined in the general retreat. They all watched the explosives man working at his lonely job from a safe distance.

It was not long before he reported back.

"If," he said to a bemused Malcolm Darnley, "you had touched your ignition switch you'd have been blown to kingdom come."

"Why?" asked Malcolm Darnley.

Chapter 18

*Sometimes their goods are swallowed by the sea,
And sometimes they come safely back to port.*

Police Superintendent Leeyes was never at his best first thing in the morning. Somewhere about the time when the lark took over from the nightingale his natural acerbity rose. And continued to rise.

This morning ws no exception.

"Will someone kindly tell me," he said with icy impatience, "exactly what has been going on?"

He was sitting squarely behind his desk glaring at Sloan.

Sloan immediately made to speak.

Leeyes forestalled him. "I come in to find a man—Nicholas Petforth no less—in the cells who you"—he flashed an aggressive look at the detective inspector—"keep telling me isn't guilty."

"Isn't guilty of murdering Beatrice Wansdyke," reiterated Sloan: not for the first time.

"And," carried on Leeyes imperviously, "to be given a message over the telephone."

"A message, sir?" Sloan started forward eagerly.

"I pick up that"—here he directed a malevolent stare in the direction of the telephone receiver on his desk which he had just replaced with altogether unnecessary vigor. Telephone cradles did not last long in his office.

"Yes?" Sloan was right on the edge of his chair now.

"To be told, Sloan, something that doesn't make sense."

"What?" asked Sloan urgently. It was all very well

for people to say that a man shouldn't get too involved with his work but . . .

"Why," Leeyes demanded grandly, "should I have a message for you, Sloan, from a bomb-disposal expert?"

Sloan began to speak. "Sir . . ."

"And tell me," carried on the superintendent, "why he should wish you to be told that there was a quantity of explosive packed under the bonnet of a car with the registration number of . . ." He glanced down at the message sheet.

"I know the car," said Sloan weakly.

"And that," said Leeyes, "there was enough of it to be sure of killing the driver."

Sloan relaxed. "We were in time then . . ."

"In time for what?"

"To save a life."

"Ah, yes." Superintendent Leeyes had all the irascible man's maddening imperturbability about the big things of this world. "He said something else too." The superintendent frowned at his own handwriting. "I know what it was."

"Sir?"

"That if the balloon had gone up . . ."

"Yes?"

"They would have been lucky to have found so much as his collar stud."

"Ah . . ." Sloan let out a sigh of pure relief.

"Sloan," he said with mock gentleness: menacingly. "Sir?"

"Whose collar stud?"

"Malcolm Darnley's," said Sloan happily.

"Malcolm Darnley of Wansdyke and Darnley?"

Sloan nodded. "You see, sir, when I came to think of it, it was the only thing that hadn't happened yet."

"What was?"

"His coming home tomorrow . . . today, I mean." That reminded Sloan of something. "Sir, I must be getting back to the hospital as quickly as I can."

"What had his coming home got to do with Beatrice Wansdyke?" insisted Leeyes. You didn't get to be superintendent without being able to override the wishes of other people when it suited you.

"I'm not quite sure . . . yet . . . it was something Crosby said."

"Crosby?" echoed Leeyes in tones of pure disbelief.

"About the source of the money."

"Out of the mouths of babes," conceded Leeyes.

"If it wasn't inheritance or the proceeds of a tidy-sized job . . ." Babes. Sloan kept still with difficulty. He shouldn't be here at all really. Not now.

"We know it wasn't any of them," said Leeyes impatiently. "We checked on all those early on." That "early on" was Tuesday and today was Thursday surprised neither of them. Each criminal investigation had its own timetable: Sloan would not be surprised to know that someone was still looking for Jack the Ripper. There might even be a warrant out for Cain. . . .

"So," went on Sloan, "when Crosby said what about it being big business money . . ."

"I suppose," mused the superintendent, "when you think of some payroll snatches . . ."

"Big business wouldn't think that sort of money so very out of the way," pursued Sloan. "At least, I don't think it would." He had himself been schooled on the principle that murder most foul could be done for a hatpin let alone a hat but it didn't mean that there wasn't an opposite end to the same scale.

"So?" Orders of magnitude didn't interest the superintendent.

"The only business round here that had anything to do with the case is . . ."

"I know," growled Leeyes. "Don't tell me."

"Wansdyke and Darnley."

Leeyes grunted. "That well-known Berebury firm."

"Well known in the plastics field anyway," said Sloan. He'd been doing what research he could in the last half hour.

"I don't see the connection," objected Leeyes.

"Neither do I, sir, yet."

"And I thought"—Leeyes was adept at shifting responsibility whenever he could—"from what you said that George Wansdyke was about the only one who didn't stand to benefit from what his aunt left in her will."

"That was the beauty of the whole thing, sir," breathed Sloan, spoiling the effect by adding in a cautionary way, "I think."

Leeyes started to raise an objection.

"I'm hoping," interposed Sloan swiftly, "that a chat with Malcolm Darnley will put us in the picture."

"And in the meantime?"

Sloan told him exactly what he proposed doing in the meantime.

* * *

Margaret Sloan wasn't asleep any longer.

Far from it.

Sloan had begun to frame uncertain sentences as he hurried along the corridor to the maternity unit. They faded from his lips as he entered the delivery room.

"Margaret . . ."

She put out her hand.

"You got my message," he began as he stepped swiftly to her side.

He had sent Crosby down from Fleming Ward with it, reckoning that, next to a white coat, the wearing of pyjamas, dressing gown, and bandage gave one the easiest entrée to almost everywhere in the hospital. Almost everywhere. Not to this ward, of course. He'd have got as far as the door though. Even Crosby.

His wife looked at him almost without recognition, her mind elsewhere.

"A job," he said uneasily. "I was on a job."

Wordlessly she tightened her grip on his hand.

Someone masked and gowned told him where to stand. He looked up. The voice behind the mask was familiar. He'd heard it before.

"Inspector Sloan, I presume," said the man.

He nodded. It was like studying an Identikit picture without hair, nose, and chin: and as tantalising.

Margaret Sloan was trying to say something.

He immediately turned back to her.

At first no sound came.

He put his head near her lips.

"Never off duty," she whispered, "are you?"

"My dearest love . . ."

He started to perspire.

Those lonely souls who had never travelled far in love missed this road too.

The midwife was saying something behind her mask now.

Sloan moistened his lips. A man tended to forget that the Ship of Felicity once embarked upon berthed here. He wondered if a woman ever did.

"Coming up to crowning, doctor," said the midwife more clearly.

So this was what they meant by that.

Love's majesty wore a crown and this was it.

He found himself taking deep gulps of breath, matching Margaret's. The French had a word for the pain that husbands suffered. . . . Someone had once told him what it was. *Couvade*. It had had no meaning at the time. . . .

There was a moment not long after that when it crossed Sloan's mind that being born from Adam's rib in a deep sleep must be a better way than this.

Once he remembered looking at his watch but it meant nothing now: time didn't enter this world.

It was Thursday, that was all.

Thursday's child has far to go.

A sudden scurrying among the professionals told him this child—Thursday's child—his child—was making a move.

It was just a little later when, though he didn't quite realise it in so many words, Sloan became deeply committed to the Classical Greek School Midwifery. Had anyone asked him then and there he would have opted for his child springing—like Athena—fully armed from the forehead of Zeus.

Presently that feeling, too, passed when they all— man, woman, and child—became submerged in a welter of clinical activity and ordinary human excitement.

Then the man in the mask spoke again. He recognised the voice now. It belonged to Dr. Roger Elspin. He said, "Inspector Sloan, you have a son."

* * *

It didn't seem wholly right that the first person to congratulate him should be a furtive little man lurking outside in the maternity ward corridor.

"What are you doing here, Larky?" asked Sloan from all the eminence of cloud nine.

"Same as you, Inspector. Being a father."

"I'll tell the midwife to keep an eye on her watch."

"Not on my account. I'm going straight these days," insisted Larky Nolson earnestly. "Honest."

"Honest? You wouldn't know the meaning of the word, Larky. . . ." Sloan floated on.

And the second person: a detective constable with a bandage around his head. But fully dressed now. Sloan seized on him.

"Come on, Crosby. We know where to go now."

"Do we, sir? Which way?"

"Wansdyke and Darnley's, of course. Where else did you think?"

* * *

There was a little portable radio on George Wansdyke's desk in his office. It was tuned in to the programme that broadcasts snippets of news as they come in and the latest news every hour on the hour. In between news flashes and weather reports a disc jockey plays pop record after pop record. There was, however, no one in the office listening to it.

"He was here a minute ago," insisted a mystified secretary. "If you'll just wait I'll check to see if he's gone through to the works."

"Thank you," said Sloan, moving over to Wansdyke's desk. There was just one memo on it. It was handwritten and was addressed to Bill Benfleet, Public Relations Manager, and was from George Wansdyke, Joint Managing Director. It was marked URGENT and it read:

Subject: Tomorrow's new product announcement. This is to be cancelled forthwith and all press releases and publicity material recalled at once.

Detective Inspector Sloan motioned Crosby to collect the memo. "We'll need that," he said.

"Exhibit A," commented Crosby. "It's the only one we've got."

"There's an empty insulin bottle," Sloan reminded him, "and some explosive clamped to a car. . . ."

"And a dead dog," added Crosby lugubriously. "I'd forgotten Isolde."

"A funny mixture, I grant you." Sloan frowned. "I reckon this memo was meant to be sent as soon as Wansdyke heard news of the explosion and his partner's death on the radio."

"And it didn't come." Crosby grinned. "Did it?"

"We can't find Mr. Wansdyke," said the secretary, coming back into the room. "I've tried Research and Development—he's often there—and the lab and the moulding shop. . . ."

A telephone rang. She picked it up. "When. . . . when? Oh, I see. Thank you . . . I'll tell him." She put down the receiver. "That was the man on the gate. He says Mr. Wansdyke left just after you arrived, Inspector, by car."

"Which way did he go?" interrupted Crosby.

"He says he took the Kinnisport Road. . . ."

"The hoverport," said Sloan quickly.

"He won't get far."

* * *

The subsequent road chase made traffic history in the county of Calleshire.

"I take it," said Superintendent Leeyes coldly later that morning, "that you are prepared to appease Inspector Harpe. I shall reprimand Constable Crosby myself."

"We got our man," said Sloan simply. It was the police exegesis.

Crosby's turn of speed at the wheel had indicated complete recovery from his head injuries. George Wansdyke's could only point to total guilt. The latter was, however, not saying anything to anyone.

"Which means," declared Leeyes heavily, "that you'll have to do the explaining, Sloan."

"It's easier now that I've had a word with Malcolm Darnley," admitted Sloan. "It was guesswork until then."

Leeyes waited.

"It all happened the way it did," began Sloan slowly, "because Malcolm Darnley had a business trip to the States scheduled."

"Go on."

"That meant that George Wansdyke couldn't kill him when he wanted to."

"Hard luck," said Leeyes vigorously.

"He just wasn't there to be killed," said Sloan. "It all hung on that."

"You couldn't be oversimplifying things, could you?" enquired the superintendent sarcastically. "Why should Darnley come home and be killed?"

"Not long before he went off on this trip," said Sloan, "the firm of Wansdyke and Darnley came up with a discovery. . . ."

"Not Miss Wansdyke's do-it-yourself kit for making money out of air?"

"No. A discovery about plastic—an important one."

"Ah, now we're getting somewhere."

"That's what Malcolm Darnley and George Wansdyke thought—each in his own way." Sloan paused. "The trouble was that their ways were different ones."

"It happens with partners," said Leeyes sagely. "They don't always see eye to eye."

Sloan cleared his throat. "That was a bit of an understatement in this case."

"Especially marriage partners."

"The discovery," said Sloan hastily, "according to Malcolm Darnley was both socially important and highly marketable."

"Bound to be troublesome then," said Leeyes cynically.

"Not so much a discovery," Sloan forged on, "as a new process involving a . . . a"—he shot a quick glance down at his notebook—"a synergist."

Superintendent Leeyes did not speak. He just looked.

"It's like a catalyst but different," faltered Sloan. It was no use. You couldn't bone up someone else's trade over the telephone in a few minutes, especially when that person had just escaped death by a whisker and naturally wanted to know why. "A catalyst," he continued in an unusually hortatory manner, "causes a reaction but remains unchanged by it."

"And a synergist?" enquired Leeyes silkily.

"Causes a reaction but is itself changed in the process. It—er—potentiates things."

"Like murder?"

"This . . . ingredient"—that was an easier word altogether. He would use it from now on. "The ingredient," he continued, "used in this new process they'd stumbled on will make some sorts of plastic eventually decay."

"Is that good or bad?" As far as the superintendent was concerned it was a black and white world.

"Used plastic is a great problem to society," said Sloan, parrotlike. Listening to Malcolm Darnley was infectious. "Your old yoghourt carton stands to last longer than the Sphinx. . . ."

"Well?"

"With this ingredient built in it would gradually become . . . er"—he hesitated before introducing yet another new word—"degradable and so decay."

Leeyes, however, wasn't thinking about words. "This process, Sloan, was worth money?"

"Big money," agreed Sloan tacitly.

"A quarter of a million pounds' worth of money?"

"Precisely, sir." He coughed. "Exactly, you might say."

"What then," asked Leeyes simply, "was the problem?"

Detective Inspector Sloan felt a momentary pang of sympathy for George Wansdyke as he tried to explain. "Malcolm Darnley was a conservation buff, sir. Mad about preserving the countryside."

"We all know that," said Leeyes. "What about it?"

"Malcolm Darnley," said Sloan impressively, "thought that the world should have the process free."

"Pro bono publico," breathed Leeyes, awe-struck, "instead of a quarter of a million pounds?"

"No more plastic cups in the Channel," said Sloan, echoing a fanatic. "No more cows choking to death on plastic bags left in a field. Less detritus for eternity."

The superintendent was considering something quite different—something more in his own line. "There are more ways than one of killing the golden goose," he said. Smaller rubbish dumps didn't excite him. Murder did.

"That's what Wansdyke thought," reported Sloan. The greatest good of the greatest number hadn't suited George Wansdyke at all. "He lost out in the argument with Darnley but he did manage to get him to agree to defer a public announcement until Darnley got back from the States."

"His death warrant."

"Everything was to stay under wraps until then."

Leeyes grunted. "Breathing space."

"He managed that side of things quite well."

"Businesses," said Leeyes largely, "are used to trade secrets."

"Wansdyke apparently made quite a thing of insisting that Malcolm Darnley himself should be the one to do the announcing because of his connections with the conservation lobby."

"Conservation lobby!" Leeyes ground his teeth. "The man won't even let us cut off a branch let alone a tree."

"Wansdyke made out that Darnley would make the better splash in the press and so forth." Sloan was on sure ground here. Twice he'd seen Bill Benfleet, the firm's public relations man, closeted with a strangely reluctant Wansdyke, trying to get him to pass a press release for publication. "No wonder Wansdyke hadn't wanted to say too much."

"Knowing all the time," said the superintendent intelligently, "that there wasn't going to be any disclosing of trade secrets by anybody."

"Not if George Wansdyke could help it," said Sloan, "because he'd gone and sold the process to a big manufacturer while Darnley was away."

Leeyes whistled. "He had, had he?"

"He was in sole charge while Darnley was abroad," said Sloan. "There was no problem."

"Don't tell me," said Leeyes acidly, "that he didn't know what to do with the money."

"In a way," replied Sloan. *Embarras de richesses* was quite often a problem in the criminal world.

"If Darnley was abroad why couldn't Wansdyke have just paid it into the firm's account—he couldn't very well pretend it wasn't the firm's secret, could he?"

"No, it was the firm's secret all right. The people who bought it would have checked on that. Wansdyke couldn't pay it into the firm's account straightaway because Darnley got weekly sales figures while he was abroad and, anyway, anyone in the firm might have mentioned it to him in a letter. . . ." That he also got a cash-flow chart Sloan did not mention. He was a policeman not an accountant.

"What was wrong with using his own account in the meantime then?"

"He shares it with his wife."

Leeyes rolled his eyes at man's monumental folly.

"He could have opened a special account," said Sloan, who had been thinking about this, "but that has the definite look of misappropriation. He needed this transaction to seem quite above board."

"Clean hands."

"Exactly."

"With Darnley dead though," Leeyes reminded him.

"And Beatrice too," said Sloan. "She knew about the discovery, you see. She spent her weekends in the lab by courtesy of Darnley and she knew enough chemistry to understand what he'd discovered. He'd told her about their success."

"So with Darnley and Beatrice both dead . . ."

"And the money back in the firm's account as soon as possible after that," said Sloan.

"Everything neat and tidy for the auditors—that's always important in fraud." The superintendent leant back. "Do you know, Sloan, that you can nearly always put people who commit fraud into open prisons? Funny that they should be that sort of trustworthy, isn't it?"

Sloan kept a grip on his theme. "Wansdyke had already begun to write the firm he'd sold it to enquiring why he hadn't had their cheque."

"Window dressing," said Leeyes succinctly.

"They would say that they'd sent it to the bank as instructed, and the bank would say they'd been given the right name and account number for Miss B. G. Wansdyke."

"And?"

"George Wansdyke would say right name—B. G. Wansdyke—he's Bertram George himself, remember—but wrong account number. The money belongs to Wansdyke and Darnley and he can prove quite easily that it does. It was safe enough, of course, in Beatrice's account while he was sole executor."

"Everyone," said Leeyes drily, "says 'Oops, sorry' and blames the typist. And everything in the garden's lovely again."

"Beatrice had to die too because of what she knew. He was just taking advantage of the fact." Sloan coughed. "We haven't heard George Wansdyke's side of things yet, sir."

"He's not only not speaking to the police"—Leeyes poked at a message sheet on his desk—"he won't see his wife either."

Sloan clapped his hand to his forehead. "Wife! Good Lord, where's the nearest florist?"

"Ah yes," said Superintendent Leeyes pompously, "I hear that Wansdyke and Darnley aren't the only ones with a new product announcement, are they?"

"No, sir."

* * *

Detective Inspector Sloan had someone else to appease besides Inspector Harpe of Traffic Division.

He said it with flowers at the bedside each day.

Margaret Sloan had a lot of visitors. "They're going to get married after Briony's taken her final state," she informed him one day.

"Who is . . . are?"

"Dr. Elspin and Briony Petforth." She smiled dreamily. "He's really very nice."

"For a doctor," Sloan reminded her.

"That will give them a little time to save up." Margaret Sloan paused. "She still gets her aunt's house, doesn't she?"

"Oh, yes," said Sloan drily. "Everything except the quarter of a million pounds goes just where Miss Wansdyke willed it. She only lost out on one thing she wanted."

"What was that?"

"Her wish to be cremated." Sloan shifted uncomfortably. Visitors' chairs in hospitals were not designed for long use. "Cremation means two doctors and a lot more questions all round. Wansdyke didn't want that. He wanted a nice quick death certificate."

"He did it, then? Changed the insulin for water?"

"Oh, yes," said Sloan. "As nice a way to murder as you can find."

"Nice?" She shuddered.

"Nice legally," he said. That means the police didn't like it but the lawyers did. "The superintendent thinks they'll have to go for malice aforethought in a big way."

Margaret Sloan smoothed the edge of the sheet. "And the dog?"

"He killed that, too. He had a key, remember. He didn't want an Airedale barking when Beatrice drifted off into her coma and it couldn't get out. Or if anyone called. Wansdyke had invited Briony to his house on Sunday, by the way."

"To make sure she didn't call on her aunt?"

"That's right. They could have saved her, you know, almost up until the end."

Margaret Sloan shuddered again.

Detective Inspector Sloan recalled himself away from one sort of duty and back to another. "How's my son and heir?"

* * *

On his next visit she asked him about Mrs. Pauline Wansdyke.

"Gone back to mother."

"Poor woman."

"She always thought she'd married beneath her," said Sloan, who had had to endure quite a lot of Mrs. Pauline Wansdyke lately.

"It never does to think that," said Margaret Sloan sagaciously.

"All the other Hartley-Powells said so too."

"That only makes it worse."

"They've traced the explosive that was under the car," he said soberly.

She shivered. "To George Wansdyke?"

"Without a shadow of doubt."

* * *

Another day she had news of Nicholas Petforth for him gleaned from his sister, Briony.

"He's very sorry about it all," Margaret Sloan began.

Sloan grunted. He hadn't a lot of time for young men who hit policemen, and said so now with some vigor. "And without a reason," he added pointedly.

"When he heard the police were asking after him"— Margaret Sloan repeated what an anxious Briony had told her—"he lost his nerve and left the squat and his job."

"Actions speak louder than words," observed Sloan.

"And of course as soon as George Wansdyke knew that somebody was suspicious about something he stirred things up as much as he could in that quarter."

"He certainly got Briony worried," conceded Sloan.

"And Nicholas through her," said his wife. She paused and adjusted a flower in the vase on her locker. "He realises now," said Margaret Sloan, surrogate apologetic from Briony Petforth, "that he was only running away."

"Why?"

She embarked on a delicate secondhand explanation. "There were—er—things going on at the squat that he—er—knew about."

"But didn't want to be asked about."

"They were his friends." She sketched a gesture in the air. "They have their loyalties in those places too."

"Luston Division raided it last night," said Sloan complacently.

"Briony will be pleased," beamed Mrs. Sloan. "That means Nicholas is in the clear, doesn't it? He wasn't really part of . . ." She stopped.

"What was going on?" Sloan finished for her kindly.

"Malcolm Darnley's taking him into the firm."

"There's more than one sort of sentence in this world," he said, amused.

"He says if they send Nicholas to prison he can use his time learning about plastics."

"Condemned to conformity at last." Sloan grinned. "Prison for assaulting a police officer in the execution of his duty would rate more highly at the Luston squat than a job as an executive."

"Malcolm Darnley says," she repeated with a matching twinkle in her eye, "that with so much extra capital in the firm they can afford a few mistakes by a new boy."

"Crosby's head's healing nicely," he said not entirely inconsequentially. "He'll make the christening without a bandage."

* * *

To no one's surprise Inspector Harpe was not as sanguine as everyone else.

"Dr. Peter McCavity's inheritance," he announced in his usual melancholy way, "is going to go the same way as his income."

"Down his throat?" supplied Sloan obligingly. "The way of all flesh was to the kitchen."

"And paying for the damage."

"It will have been George Wansdyke who rang in and reported that McCavity hit that bollard in Ridley Road," said Sloan. Even the outer pieces of the jigsaw puzzle were fitting in now. "On the Friday afternoon."

"Bit of an opportunist your chap, wasn't he?" said Harpe.

"Murderers usually are," said Sloan. "He must have seen McCavity's car around when he was at the house killing the dog."

"There's never any knowing what a drunken doctor will get up to," said Happy Harry censoriously. The traffic man had always been convinced that alcohol was the devil in solution. "If Wansdyke was looking round for someone to take the blame if there was trouble . . ."

"No wonder old Dr. Paston had his worries," mused Sloan. "Got a lot on his mind, I daresay."

"McCavity went the wrong way round the station roundabout last night," said Harpe, who was nothing if not single-minded. "Mark my words, Sloan, that young man's next traffic violation will be his last as a licenced driver."

*   *   *

"Sloan." Superintendent Leeyes pushed the case papers back across the desk.

"Sir."

"I don't like loose ends."

"No, sir."

"Untidy."

"Yes, sir."

"There's something we haven't done."

"Is there, sir?" Sloan allowed himself the luxury of a yawn. He felt as if he hadn't stopped doing things for days and nights. "What's that?"

"Put the coroner right."

Sloan stiffened.

"You might just step round," said Leeyes civilly, "and tell him we were right and he was wrong. With my compliments, of course."

ABOUT THE AUTHOR

CATHERINE AIRD had never tried her hand at writing suspense stories before publishing *The Religious Body*—a novel which immediately established her as one of the genre's most talented writers. *A Late Phoenix, The Stately Home Murder, His Burial Too, Some Die Eloquent, Henrietta Who?* and *A Most Contagious Game* have subsequently enhanced her reputation. Her ancestry is Scottish, but she now lives in a village in East Kent, near Canterbury, where she serves as an aid to her father, a doctor, and takes an interest in local affairs.

CATHERINE AIRD

For 15 years, Catherine Aird's mysteries have won praises for their brilliant plotting and style. Established alongside other successful English mystery ladies, she continues to thrill old and new mystery fans alike.

☐	23668	PARTING BREATH	$2.25
☐	23239	HENRIETTA WHO	$2.50
☐	24083	A MOST CONTAGIOUS GAME	$2.75
☐	24079	PASSING STRANGE	$2.75
☐	24314	A SLIGHT MOURNING	$2.75
☐	23842	HIS BURIAL TOO	$2.50
☐	24316	A LATE PHOENIX	$2.75
☐	23831	THE RELIGIOUS BODY	$2.50
☐	24317	SOME DIE ELOQUENT	$2.75
☐	24078	STATELY HOME MURDER	$2.75

The Caliphate

ANDRÉ
LE GALLO

LEISURE BOOKS   NEW YORK CITY

For Christopher

A LEISURE BOOK®

February 2010

Dorchester Publishing Co., Inc.
200 Madison Avenue
New York, NY 10016

ISBN 10: 0-8439-6305-0
ISBN 13: 978-0-8439-6305-2
E-ISBN: 978-1-4285-0813-2

Visit us online at www.dorchesterpub.com.

ACKNOWLEDGMENTS

All of the events and characters are imaginary—with one exception; Steve is modeled on our son Christopher who died in 2002 and to whom this book is dedicated. The settings and backgrounds are factual. I have personally run clandestine operations in most of the countries where the story takes place. Similarly, although I do not claim to be an Islamic scholar, I studied Islam at Johns Hopkins School of International Studies and lived in Islamic countries for many years. While the Islamic content has been double-checked by others with better academic credentials, I take full responsibility for any error.

I have often been urged to write an autobiography. But there are many biographies available, prompted by a variety of motivations, for those who are curious about the life and career of a CIA operations officer. Although it is natural to be proud of one's life accomplishments, and I am no different, my story would not add much to theirs. A novel allows the author to entertain as well as educate. Fictional characters can say and act out their convictions to reflect their worldviews, which can be centuries apart, as they are in this story. For example, while the structures of our international system are still based on the sovereign state concepts of the 1648 Treaty of Westphalia, bolstered by 19th century nationalism, many Muslims are working toward a borderless world subservient to the laws of Islam—it is not a subject for negotiation. This story is built around this conflict of views. Presenting this issue in a novel was more fun to write and, I hope, will be more fun to read about than eye-glazing dates and treaties.

I wish to thank all those who encouraged me along the way, and for their willingness to spend the time to read part or all of the manuscript, make suggestions, and point out weaknesses: Rita Callahan, Thérèse and Elise, Brittany and Preston, John Panama, Dr. David McCuan, Dr. Barry Goodfield, Denise Constantini, Fred Hill, Philip Giraldi and Philip Gioia. Special thanks to Jeff Cox, successful author in his own right, without whose initial help I probably would not have begun what turned out to be a more challenging project spread over a much longer period than I had anticipated. The book would not have reached publication without the personal interest and generous support of Haggai Carmon, author of the Dan Gordon thriller series. And thanks also to Jordan Rosenfeld who edited the manuscript. Last but not least, thanks to the Dorchester Publishing team, led by Don D'Auria.

I'm very grateful to Porter Goss for his attention-grabbing introduction. Porter, my friend and former CIA colleague, was a member of my Junior Officer Trainee class, a group of dedicated and bright Americans who would have been successful in any career they chose. Our country was lucky that they chose the CIA.

Finally, thanks to my live-in editor, my wife Cathy, who experienced the book's several lives and made many helpful suggestions and corrections, big and small.

INTRODUCTION

André Le Gallo's *The Caliphate* pours out a tale of exciting intrigue too frightening to believe—and too believable to ignore. But you had better believe it because Le Gallo is the real thing. I went to spy school with him years ago. He's a natural, as well as a gifted storyteller. As a long-time, top-ranked CIA operations officer, Le Gallo shares with us both what goes on in the convoluted and treacherous world of foreign intelligence and what might happen if we let our guard down.

Set in the volatile evolving areas of North Africa's Maghreb, a dangerous trail of violence and malevolence takes protagonists Steve and Kella through the sophistication and romance of Paris to the treachery of the Mid-East, areas well known to Le Gallo through his days "in the trade." At every turn the increasingly deranged, fanatic Tariq Al Khalil escalates the stakes to restore the former glory and power of the ancient Islamic Caliphate—no matter what the cost. Le Gallo's portrayal of Al Khalil convincingly reflects the vicious fanaticism of the radical Islamic fundamentalists that we have uncovered since 9/11—and portends eerily those future terrorists who will continue to rally to the bastardization of the Quran by delusional radical leaders with their own agendas.

Le Gallo makes the case why these misguided monsters of inhumanity must be stopped, and gives us professional glimpses of just what it takes in the intelligence world to get the job done. Even though *The Caliphate* is fiction, it captures faithfully many of today's real-world obstacles confronting the protagonists from all quarters. Intelligence officers in our services will relate to wind-shifting bureaucrats and politicians inside the Beltway too timid to reward anything "risky"; hesitant cooperation from supposedly friendly intelligence organizations, which often confounds success; shifting allegiances and devious betrayal by "trustworthy agents"; leaks to the media and sellouts to enemies of important sensitive information by confederates; desperate decision making that must be done on the sketchiest of information; and terrible miscalculations by principal players that can cost innocent lives, if not bring us to the brink of destruction. These are not small matters. Le Gallo does not have to invent these aspects of intelligence work in today's global struggle for a peaceful world future.

He is able, from firsthand experience, to arm his attractive protagonists, Steve and Kella, with natural resource, life experience and acquired skill to meet the unexpected twists and turns in a path that takes them ever deeper into danger. But they are not larger than life. They are credible human beings living out a relationship with each other and struggling against a malevolent force that seeks to destroy them. The excitement is palpable. The outcome is uncertain.

It is a fortunate truth that André Le Gallo's *The Caliphate* is fiction. But the quest for "the new" caliphate by radical fundamentalists is not. Their vision of "restoration" includes full control of much of the geography from the Pacific to the Atlantic, roughly in the Tropic of Cancer—the Philippines and Indonesia through southern Asia, the "-Stans," the Levant (Mid-East), the Horn of Africa, Northern Africa (Maghreb) to sub-Saharan Africa (Sahal). It is a vast area with millions of people, many barely surviving in substandard conditions. While birth rates are generally declining for Western European nations, they are growing in the lands of the envisioned caliphate. Radical Islamic fundamentalists advertise an intolerant, merciless view toward those not totally submitting to their "pure" interpretation of the Quran, the Hadith (the sayings of Muhammad) or all the rules and regulations that have been passed down as "the Law" (Suria) since approximately 650 AD. Even though the radicals are a minority of the world's Muslims, they are a powerful voice and they have found a growing, receptive audience for their corrupted version of Allah's will. There is no room for sanctity of life, equal rights or civil liberty; women are as chattel—or less; Islam is capital *S* Submission, and they decide who must submit to what. A loving, compassionate father god is not included. These people exist. They have struck the innocent countless times already, brutally and with increasingly sophisticated weapons and tactics. And they will strike again! Beware the caliphate!

Porter Goss

Porter Goss lives in southwest Florida, now retired from many years of activity in America's intelligence community. He was the last Director of Central Intelligence (DCI) and the first Director of the Central Intelligence Agency (CIA) under the changes enacted by Congress in intelligence reform legislation after 9/11. Prior to that he served eight terms in the House of Representatives in Washington, including several years as Chairman of the Intelligence Committee. His earlier days as a clandestine services officer in the CIA triggered a keen interest in our national security and an unshakable awareness of how critical good intelligence is for our national well-being.

PART ONE

Allah is our objective, the Quran is our law, the Prophet is our leader, jihad is our way, and dying for the sake of Allah is our highest hope.
—Credo of the Muslim Brotherhood

Fight and slay the unbelievers wherever ye find them.
—Quran, Sura 9:5

CHAPTER ONE

In the darkness of Neuilly-sur-Seine on the outskirts of Paris, Farid stood on the ladder leaning against the wall separating the Saudi ambassador's and the American's back gardens. Wearing designer glasses and dark silk slacks, he looked more like an aging poster boy for the business-casual look than like the typical second-story man. In fact, Farid bin Abdullah was one of the thousands who depend on the patronage of the five thousand royals of Saudi Arabia. A distant cousin had obtained this choice Paris assignment for him. The American's powerful security lights provided an excellent view of his garden and of the double stairway that led from the gravel walk to each side of the patio on the first floor. On the patio, a French window was slightly ajar, as he had been told it was on warm nights. He lifted one leg up and, for a moment, stayed prone on the wall. He was conscious that he was about to leave the diplomatic immunity of the Saudi ambassador's residence to enter the infidel's space. He felt that he was crossing the border between the land of peace, the Dar al Islam, and the land of war, the Dar al Gharb. More accustomed to diplomatic cocktails than to surreptitious entries, he had never been a risk taker. But he was confident in his ability to recognize a low-risk, high-reward mission. Just as he was confident that the warmth of the night was the cause of his perspiration.

Before letting himself down, he pulled the aluminum ladder up. His sweating hands and the unexpected weight caused the ladder to hit the wall. The noise resounded into the quiet night of the residential suburb and was answered by angry yelping several houses away. He froze for a second, looking at the back of both residences, but he noticed no movement. Straining, he brought the ladder down on the American side of the border. He went down the ladder and kept to the narrow grass and dirt strip at the foot of the wall to avoid the noisy gravel as he approached the stairs.

Farid knew that the house was empty. The American's cook, Benjamin, obviously a Jew, had told the Saudi maid that Dr. Coogan was going away for a couple of days and that he, Benjamin, was going to stay with a friend during that time. That was when Farid had decided that this would be the perfect time to carry out Tariq al Khalil's order. He corrected himself; al Khalil, a Salafist, didn't give orders to an officer of the kingdom's Al Mahabharata Al A' amah (General Intelligence Directorate). However, both the international Salafists and the Saudi Wahhabists, who basically agreed on the need for a pure Islam based on the earliest writings, were outraged at Dr. Coogan's public statement that newly surfaced Quranic documents were causing the academic community to question the uniqueness of the Quran, a blasphemous concept. The word of God was unique and unchangeable. There was only one Quran, unlike the Gospels, which allowed the Christians to choose one they liked best. His mission tonight was to find the Quranic forgeries that Coogan certainly kept in his house.

When he reached the French windows, he took off his Gucci belt and folded it into a loop, which he introduced through the slightly open doors and above the handle. He placed the loop around one side of the horizontal handle and pulled up, disengaging the iron rods secured into the bottom and top of the doorframe. He pushed, and both windows opened.

His flashlight scanned the room—a large dining-room table was the centerpiece. Glass-front china and crystal-ware cabinets lined one wall and paintings the other. Documents could be hidden almost anywhere. Luckily, there was no one home and he felt unhurried. He moved to the next room, an office. The walls were nearly covered with photographs of a person he assumed was Coogan with European and Middle Eastern personalities. He first emptied desk drawers filled with business cards, files on investments and newspaper and magazine articles on the Middle East. His heart skipped a beat when he saw one file neatly named *Quran Project*. He opened it, but there was only one letter from the German Order of St. John (Hospitaller), informing Dr. Coogan that documents pertaining to the Quran had been donated to a research institute in Berlin. Nothing new about that. The original information had come from Germany. He guessed that al Khalil had a source in the institute, but that he had been unable to find the documents, the forgeries, in Germany. Farid dropped the file down on the floor.

He was moving toward a file cabinet when he heard a door open downstairs. The click of a light switch followed by the squeaking of the stairs leading up to the office and dining-room level broke the silence. The stairway light intruded onto the file cabinet. His surprise and alarm doubled his pulse. He stepped back into the dining room, away from the stairs. Shocked and angry, Farid's first instinct was revenge and punishment. Bad information was turning an easy mission for which he stood to be rewarded into a possible confrontation for which he had not planned and was not prepared. The stupid maid would suffer consequences. He felt sweat from his armpits and his back start to soak his shirt.

The rustle of soft clothing and of quick breathing forced him back into the moment. He began to move toward the French windows, his escape route. However, this might be his only chance. The forgeries must be found. He cared less about al Khalil than he did of the favors that the Mukhabarat's director was sure to bestow on him if he succeeded. After tonight, Coogan would certainly either hire professional security or bring the documents elsewhere, perhaps to a bank vault. He peered carefully through the doorless entrance of the office, toward the stairs. The light outlined a man in sweats and a T-shirt with long unruly blond hair, probably an American, a domestic whom he could overwhelm easily. It must be Benjamin, the cook, who had lied and was responsible for this crisis. The cook's appearance turned Farid's anxiety into pent-up anger waiting to be released.

The American stepped into the office and put the light on. "Holy shit," he said. He stood in the middle of the room uncertainly, looking at the wreckage on the floor. He looked up, his mouth half-open and his eyes searching into the darkness of the dining room. He took two steps forward and paused. He turned around and stage-whispered to himself, "The police." He moved toward the phone on the desk. Farid knew he had to decide to flee or to attack. He stepped into the office, raised his flashlight and brought it down as hard as he could on the blond head. The plastic lens of the light flew off and the battery compartment broke. Benjamin fell to his knees. Farid looked around for a better weapon, grabbed a desk lamp and again struck. This time his victim fell face forward. Farid leaned down and felt the man's pulse. He was alive but unconscious. A rivulet of blood seeped from his scalp down his face. As it approached his mouth, Farid, captivated, watched the red line go down Benjamin's chin, his throat and onto his T-shirt.

Farid stood with a slight grin, listened carefully and, leaving the lights on, went to the filing cabinet. Drawer by drawer, he quickly examined all the files, dropping them on the floor afterward. He looked at the photos on the wall, took the biggest one and tore the back off. He did the same to several others, with no better results. He went through all the books on the shelves, shaking them with the binding up and dropping them on the floor. He then went up one flight of stairs and found the main bedroom. He ransacked it but found nothing of interest. He moved back to the dining room and examined the backs of the paintings by cutting them out of their frames. Al Khalil's information also had been wrong. In frustration, he tried to topple one of the china cabinets, but it proved too heavy, even in his excited state, to move easily. Before leaving, he took a candlestick from the dining-room table and smashed it into the glass door of the cabinet.

CHAPTER TWO

Steve Church stepped out of the taxi, relieved that the first leg of his trip was finally over. He stretched, feeling all the vertebrae along his six-foot-one spine release, and ran his hand through his short brown hair. He paid the driver and looked at his watch: about ten hours door-to-door from his apartment in Alexandria, Virginia, to his temporary abode in Neuilly. Waist-high crowd-control barriers had prevented the driver from pulling up next to the curb. His temporary address turned out to be between the Saudi Arabian and Moroccan ambassadors' residences. On his left was the Saudi flag, green with an Arabic inscription in white. Steve didn't speak Arabic but knew what it was—the Shahada, the declaration of faith:

La ilaha illa la hu muhammadun rasulu llah. There is no God but Allah, and Muhammad is his messenger.

A horizontal sword underlined the Shahada. To his right was the Moroccan flag, red, symbol of the Prophet's descendants, with a green five-pointed star. Two heavily armed French policemen walked within fifteen feet of the taxi, their eyes cold and their faces like those of poker players trying to decipher their opponents' cards. A van with blackened windows was parked twenty yards away; two helmeted paramilitary policemen were talking to the squad sitting inside.

One of the policemen asked him, "Your identity papers, monsieur." Steve produced his passport and the policeman waved him on. Steve walked up to the door and rang the bell, looking for the key that Dr. Coogan had sent him. No one opened the door and Steve let himself in. He found himself in a small entranceway with stairs in front of him and a door to the right that apparently connected to the garage.

He closed the door, picked up his suitcase and hand carry and started up the stairs, when the front door opened in back of him.

A stocky young man came in. He wore a beret slanted to the right that partially covered a bandage around his head. On the left, his blond hair reached below his ears. They took stock of each other and the newcomer said, "Are you Steve Church? Dr. Coogan told me to expect you. So I came back as soon as I could. From the hospital." He touched the bandage lightly. "You have a key? He didn't tell me."

"Yes, I'm Steve. And you are . . . ?"

"Oh, I'm Benjamin. I'm the cook. I'm actually a student at the Cordon Bleu school. In return for doing the cooking, I get room and board. It's a win-win for everybody, isn't it? Well, it was until last night. Look what they did to me." He took off his beret to reveal a white pad being held in place by the bandage over the shaved right side of his head.

"They? What happened to you? Where's Dr. Coogan?"

Benjamin went up the stairs past Steve, who followed him to an archway that led to the office. "Look." A tornado seemed to have hit. There were papers, books and files all over the floor. "Look at this mess. Somebody came in during the night. I had just come back. My apartment is downstairs next to the garage. I was at my girlfriend's apartment since Dr. Coogan left, but we had an argument." He shrugged, raised his hands palm up and rolled his eyes. "Anyway, I woke up, came upstairs and they knocked me out, but not before I saw this holy mess."

"Are you OK? What did they steal?"

"I bet Achoura let them in. She's the Moroccan maid—comes in at least once a week. We have cops out front 24-7. Only someone with a key could have come in. And she had a key. I called the police, but they haven't shown up. The cops outside said it wasn't their job," he rambled. He blinked rapidly. He licked his lips.

"And where is Dr. Coogan?" Steve tried again.

"Didn't I tell you? He's on a business trip. He left pretty suddenly. Hard to remember now. Two days ago?"

Steve tried to calm Benjamin but decided that only time could help. He wanted to go for a run and take a shower. Benjamin was too agitated to answer questions.

But Benjamin kept talking. "What did they take? I wouldn't know about missing stuff. Achoura is the one who has the run of the house. We won't see her again, I'm sure. Look at this . . ." He led Steve from the office into the dining room. Destroyed paintings and broken glass were on the floor.

"Well, with the police outside, nothing big could have been stolen." Steve grinned. "I just hope the beds are still here. I'll be ready to crash pretty soon. If they didn't steal anything, why did they come? Do you think they could come back?"

"Come back!" Benjamin's eyes had suddenly gotten bigger. "I guess you can take any bedroom on the top floor." He left Steve to fend for himself and went downstairs.

The house had a narrow front on the street and was designed vertically: the garage and servants' quarters at street level; kitchen, living, dining room and a den up one flight;

the master bedroom and a sitting room on the next level; and several bedrooms on the top floor.

As soon as he could, Steve changed and went out for a run, leaving Benjamin to deal with the police, if and when they came. After being strapped in a flying box across the Atlantic, he needed to get out and breathe, to clear his mind. He was mystified by the break-in. If no valuables were stolen, what was the purpose of the intrusion? Had they found whatever they were looking for?

Steve wondered what his absent host was involved in, and where he was. Steve was on a business trip to Morocco. Success in Morocco would give him a step up on the promotion ladder. And hopefully, Morocco would open the door to other projects in the Arab world. He would show his father that there were careers outside of the CIA. He wanted to carve his own path. More practically, he needed to pay off long-standing student and credit-card debts, and he feared that a government salary guaranteed that he would be in debt forever.

But he had gone along with his father's suggestion to stop in Paris and meet his former CIA colleague Ted Coogan, who had left the Agency and, based on his fluent Arabic and PhD in Middle Eastern studies, had gained respectability in European academic circles. He would be an excellent resource on the Arab world, and on Morocco in particular, Marshall had told Steve, who had grudgingly admitted that it couldn't hurt. His father had suggestions for everything.

Coogan and Marshall Church had served together in Morocco under diplomatic cover. Steve wondered if Coogan was still with the CIA.

The Bois de Boulogne was less than fifty yards south of the Coogan house, and Steve's legs were soon propelling him on a path that took him past the Jardin d'Acclimatation and to the allée de Longchamp, where he turned right. A mile and a quarter farther, he made another right to complete a triangle. He looked at his watch—twenty-five minutes, or about three miles, he calculated. It was still fairly early, but not too early for other runners and equestrians. On the way from the airport, Steve's taxi had driven by butchers and fish markets raising their metal shutters. Delivery trucks monopolized the streets. The city was waking up—a great time to run. It made him excited to be in Paris.

Steve stopped in the kitchen on his way upstairs and found a note from Ted Coogan that he hadn't seen before.

> Welcome, Steve. Make yourself at home. Sorry I wasn't able to meet you at the airport. I had to go out of town but will be back before you leave. Feel free to use anything in the house. The cook's name is Benjamin, and the maid is Achoura. Also, I attach an invitation to the American ambassador's residence, if you're interested. Enjoy.

His body was still on East Coast time, where it was the middle of the night. He took a quick shower and lay down for a nap, after which he would be "good to go," an expression he had picked up from his Air Force buddies in Korea, where he had obtained his pilot's license. But before he could go to sleep, he heard the police come in. After a few minutes, Benjamin called him.

"Steve? Steve? Can you come down? The gendarmes want to speak with you."

Benjamin was sitting at the large dining-room table across from a police detective dressed in mufti. The mahogany table was easily large enough for a dinner party of twenty-four. Benjamin said, "Steve, the inspector here wants to talk to you," and then left the room.

The detective extended his hand. "I am Detective Beauvais, monsieur."

Except for his ample girth, testifying that he had not been a street cop for a long time, Beauvais' broomlike mustache and bald head reminded Steve of the Dupond and

Dupont "twins," inspectors from the Tintin cartoons he had loved while living with his family in Francophone countries. After inspecting his passport and flight tickets, the detective asked, "Why are you in Paris, monsieur? Business? Tourism?"

"Vacation. Dr. Coogan is a friend of my father's. He was supposed to pick me up at Charles de Gaulle airport this morning, but he didn't show." Steve remembered his surprise that Coogan might even be late. If he had learned anything from growing up with a CIA father, it was that there was no alternative to operational punctuality; lives depended on it. It was one of Marshall's unbending, and unending, rules.

"And who is your employer?"

At this point, Steve sensed that the detective was well aware of Coogan's prior incarnation. Beauvais might look like a cartoon character, but Steve realized that it would be a mistake to underestimate him. "West Gate Scientific International. We provide consultants, experts, in the area of national defense and crisis management to state and federal agencies in the United States."

"Very interesting. And what is your specialty, Monsieur Church?" Steve guessed from the line of questioning and the conspiratorial smile that the detective thought he had an American intelligence officer on his hands.

"I'm just an analyst. Have you tried to reach Dr. Coogan? He should be informed." Steve surprised himself that he did not tell Beauvais that he was on his way to Morocco on business. There was no secret about it. With annoyance, he recalled another of his father's sayings: don't answer questions that have not been asked, especially when speaking to cops. Another rule, but probably not bad advice.

"Yes. We are trying to reach him. The cook gave me his number."

Two gendarmes appeared on a patio off the dining room

and called the detective, who joined them outside. Steve followed.

Stone stairs led down from the patio to a rectangular gravel garden demarcated by three walls, at the base of which were shrubs and flowers growing in a three-foot-wide ribbon of earth. One of the policemen pointed toward the left. There were footsteps in the dirt around flowers that had not survived a trampling. Steve assumed that the Saudi ambassador had a similar garden on the other side of the wall.

Steve asked the detective, "What happens next? Do you go next door and ask questions?"

"No, monsieur. We don't deal with the diplomatic corps. That's not in our jurisdiction. But, if nothing is missing . . ." His voice trailed off.

Steve guessed that since the evidence involved the Saudis, the investigation was over. He went upstairs. A half hour later, he knocked at Benjamin's door dressed in a dark suit, blue shirt and a tie decorated with a multitude of national flags.

"I'm leaving. I'll be back after dinner."

Not certain that he would get to talk with Ted Coogan, Steve decided to pay a visit to the Institut du Monde Arabe. In the metro, the French president's memorable statement, "We are all Americans!" made immediately following al Qaeda's attack against New York and Washington, came to his mind. How long ago that seemed, he thought. Since then, al Qaeda had inspired and directed attacks in several countries, including Morocco.

The Arab World Institute building seemed to be of recent vintage. His guidebook informed him that the southern facade was a geometric pattern of metallic rectangles, at the center of which was a camera-like aperture that opened and closed according to the available light. He noticed, however, that some were wide-open and others closed. One of the guards explained, "They haven't worked for several years now." The exhibits were disappointingly sterile and bare, as if the funding had run out.

Before leaving, Steve went up to the ninth-floor terrace for a view of Notre Dame across the river, but was turned away. It was closed for a special event. Steve looked past the man at the door, where a group of men dressed in suits were being served drinks and finger food. A cluster of VIPs had their backs to him and seemed to be listening to someone hidden by their bodies. The signs to the cafeteria reminded him that he hadn't had anything to eat since landing.

As he sat, enjoying his tabouli at a plastic-topped table, a light rain drove the VIPs into the cafeteria. The well-dressed group was men only and seemed a bit out of place in the low-ceilinged, self-help cafeteria. Steve noticed that the center of attention was on one man, short but with good shoulders. When he sat down, the group pulled tables and chairs around him. He spoke Arabic, a language everyone seemed to understand. When Steve got up to leave, he saw that the man had a full black beard, an intense gaze and a sharp nose. Steve thought, *This guy is on a mission.* And then he recognized him. Tariq al Khalil had attended the Université Libre de Bruxelles at the time Steve had obtained his master's in international relations there. Steve left without making any sign of recognition. He and his classmates had always thought al Khalil to be from another world. He was obviously more comfortable here than he had been in a strictly European setting.

Steve looked at his watch and decided he could still make the ambassador's reception. The ambassador's residence near place de la Concorde was well guarded, and he had to produce Coogan's invitation to get through the French security gauntlet and then the marines on duty at the door. He knew from the invitation that the reception was in honor of the American deputy chief of mission, Jack Hastings, who was being reassigned to Tel Aviv as the new ambassador.

As he waited his turn to go through the reception line, Steve thought, *Here we go*. He was familiar with the ritual of the diplomatic reception.

He understood that the cocktail reception was the professional vehicle of choice for the members of the diplomatic community. As wandering waiters in their impeccable white jackets circulated with flutes of American sparkling wine they referred to as "champagne" and trays of caviar, the several hundred guests in suits and cocktail dresses were busy playing their roles as diplomats, as spies pretending to be diplomats or as reporters hoping to get a story. In the ecology of these affairs of state, Steve thought, members of the media were as the remora is to the shark. For the French officials, showing up was truly the most important part of their job—they enjoyed being courted. He was sure of one ground truth: the successful players never underestimated the size of the egos in the room.

Out of the corner of his eye, Steve spotted an attractive woman striding across his field of vision, apparently toward a bar set up in one corner of the large reception area. She appeared to be in her late twenties and was wearing a black halter dress that showed off her wide, coppery shoulders. He hesitated a second, his fingers lightly touching through his shirt the wooden beads he wore around his neck, and then directed his steps to intercept her and took inventory of her model's height and poised gait. Unlike many models, however, she was not anorexic; he let his eyes savor the outline of her body. As he got closer he saw that her face was oval, with pronounced cheekbones and full lips, and framed by tumbles of thick, black, wavy hair. Her almond-shaped eyes and tawny skin color suggested Caucasian ancestors wedded to diversity, before diversity became de rigueur.

Still on course, Steve swept two glasses from the tray of a passing waiter and, a second later, handed one to the focus of his attention. "Hi. I'm Steve Church. I'm a guest of the American Embassy, passing through Paris. Which embassy are you with?"

The woman took an instant before replying, looking at him with a frank and bemused smile. "I'm Kella Hastings. Jack Hastings's stepdaughter. I don't remember you coming through the reception line. Don't you know about protocol?"

She smiled encouragingly, Steve thought. He was glad to have passed muster.

"I came late. I did go through the line but I didn't see you either. You must have been on a break. Does protocol allow breaks? Are diplomats unionized? I'm in Paris for a few days, sort of on vacation. I gather that your father is being assigned to Tel Aviv. Are you going with him?" he asked.

"No, no. I'm going to graduate school here in Paris. I'm at the École Nationale d'Administration, better known as ENA. It's like Harvard in reputation." She grinned. "It's also a great way to become prime minister. Over half of France's prime ministers have graduated from ENA. Well, OK, Sarkozy is not an ENA graduate. Paris on vacation? By yourself?"

"I'm actually on my way to Morocco—business trip. Do I detect an accent? What is your first language?"

"I was born in Mali. My birth parents were Tuareg. Have you heard of the Blue People—the Tuaregs?"

"A little. They're desert nomads, right? So this means that your first language was—?" Afraid that he was being too direct, he changed course. "You know, this is turning into more than idle cocktail chatter. What does the future prime minister say to moving the venue of this meeting to a more private location, away from the old folks?" In response to Kella's raised eyebrows, Steve added, "Such as the bar at the Crillon Hotel. If I recall correctly, it's within walking distance, right? OK if I check with you later?"

"Well, maybe. I'm not sure what else is planned tonight," she said, with controlled enthusiasm.

Kella turned back to the reception line. The traffic of arriving guests had stopped and reversed. People with other diplomatic functions to attend were saying their good-byes.

While Kella played her role in the line, smiling and shaking hands, Steve quickly worked the room. He liked the give-and-take and circulated from one group to another. His social skills had caused him to be elected president of his fraternity at Lehigh University.

Eventually, the American ambassador, as host, gave Jack a quick "thanks, good-bye and good luck" speech, and Jack Hastings responded in kind to American, French and other colleagues. The French foreign minister added his own thanks and best wishes to end the official part of the reception.

After the speeches, Steve found Kella in the crowd. "Well, what do you think? There are some important issues to discuss."

"You didn't give up. I'm glad," Kella said with a laugh.

Steve and Kella left together through the security barriers and walked to the Crillon Hotel, nearby on the place de la Concorde.

Kella said, "We'll be lucky to get in. This is a favorite hangout for movie stars, kings, presidents and their coteries, as well as the paparazzi they love to attract."

More parasites, thought Steve.

A waiter stopped them at the entrance to the bar. "Do you have reservations?"

Steve looked over his head and could see that the room was crowded. "Yes, Ambassador Hastings's office called," Steve said. "From the American Embassy," he added. "That must be our table there." He pointed to a small table in the back being cleared by another waiter. The waiter delayed until Steve slipped him a ten euro note, and they sat at a table for two in the wood-paneled bar.

Kella smiled and asked, "Do you always get what you want? What are you going to do in Morocco?"

Steve said, "I had a bright idea—trying to capture part of the Moroccan market. Be careful what you wish for. Now I'm a one-man posse to bring back a contract. But what about you? You have a fascinating background."

"I lived in northern Mali as a little girl, around Timbuktu. Our people rebelled. Tuaregs have never gotten used to the restrictions of borders. Maybe it was like when fences went up in the American West."

"You've come a long way, from Timbuktu to receptions at the ambassador's residence in Paris! How did you do that?"

"During the fighting, the Malian army killed many civilians, including my parents. The Hastingses adopted me from an orphanage run by Catholic nuns in Timbuktu. Jack was posted to Mali during the rebellion."

"I'm sorry about your parents. Are you legally French, American or Malian?"

"My adoptive mother is French. Her maiden name was Joulet. Her father is"—she hesitated—"with the French government. I'm a dual national. Actually I'm probably a triple national." She laughed. "I spent a couple of years in the States. My stepfather insists that I am an American, and that my English should be as good as my French," she said.

After another hour Kella sat back in her chair and said, "You're on vacation, but I have an eight o'clock seminar on the administration of the DOM-TOM. In French that's the Départements d'Outre Mer-Territoires d'Outre Mer. In English, the Overseas Departments and Territories. I think I had better go." She paused and added, "But only if you've finished all your questions."

Steve acted as if he hadn't caught the slight sarcasm in Kella's tone. "Just the name of that seminar is giving me a headache. Wait, I do have one last question. What about the markings on the back of your hand?" Steve gestured to four small black dots arranged in a diamond pattern on the back of Kella's right hand.

"OK, but this is the end of the interrogation. It's the Southern Cross, a small constellation between Centaurus and Musca. In the Southern Hemisphere, it will help you locate the South Pole. I've had this tattoo since I was very young. My mother had the same one. It also has something to do with high authority and status in the tribe and is a symbol of the Tuaregs' mastery of navigation in the desert."

"In my tribe, we have the same thing." Pointing to the watch on his right wrist, he said, "It's called a Suunto X-Lander. I got it at the PX in South Korea."

Kella giggled. "It has so many dials and buttons . . . Can you actually use it to tell time? I don't think I've ever seen one like it."

"It has an altimeter, a thermometer and a compass. Now you could get one with a GPS." He raised his right wrist and glanced at his watch. "Directly north of you there is a tall American named Steve with whom you're going to have lunch tomorrow."

Kella's laugh was brief. "Well, I'm not sure. I have a lot to do tomorrow."

"Oh-oh, a boyfriend on the horizon," he said in mock alarm, surprised at his own words. He hadn't had that concern about anyone for a long time.

"Nothing like that." She smiled at his interest. "I have classes in the morning and I promised to meet a friend in the afternoon. She lives in Saint-Denis. Troubles with her father. I'm not sure that I'm doing the right thing, but I want to try to help her. Her father is superconservative, super-Islamist. He sounds like he wants to go back to another century. Although Faridah lives in the Paris of the twenty-first century, he expects her to behave as if she lived in eighth-century Mecca. In Algeria, where female genital mutilation is not widely practiced, her father had her cut before she was five years old."

Female genital mutilation was the last thing Steve wanted to, or could, talk about. "Saint-Denis, the basilica, where all of the French kings were buried. It's on my list of things to do in Paris. We could meet there after you visit your friend. But first, we'll have lunch. You have to eat lunch somewhere, right?"

"I don't think that's going to work. If you want, we could go to Saint-Denis together. Then, while you go to the basilica, I'll go with Faridah. And we can meet at the basilica later."

Before she got in a cab and disappeared into the swirling night traffic of the place de la Concorde, they agreed to take the metro to Saint-Denis together the next day and see if their schedules meshed on the way.

On her way home, Kella thought about Steve. She was intrigued but wary. She guessed that he was several years older than her twenty-seven years. He had mentioned having lived in Korea, Hawaii, Morocco and West Africa, which appealed to her. He had more than held his own with the diplomats at the reception. At first, she had been a bit put off by his directness. She smiled; he was so American, so different from the French students at ENA, many of whom came from families that would gladly have a monarch rather than a republic. She felt that they had made a connection. He would leave Paris soon. But he was fun and pleasant to be with. She herself felt more confident when she was with him.

Her last thought about Steve that night—and she knew he would have a good laugh if he knew—compared him to a World War II figure whom she had recently studied, General George Patton: forceful, often did the opposite of what was expected, and didn't mind the limelight.

Steve's thoughts about Kella were conflicted. He had almost been engaged a year before, but he hadn't dated since the sudden death of his fiancée. Vera also had been tall and intelligent. He had loved her spontaneity, something he didn't detect much of in Kella. He often wondered whether

Vera might still be alive—he *knew* she would be—if he hadn't been so selfishly focused on high-altitude skiing during their few days in Canada. She had gone off with another group that day, and he had not seen her again. An avalanche had killed them all.

The evening with Kella had started to unshackle his emotions. His hand went up to his neck, and he felt the necklace Vera had found at the hotel gift shop the day before she died. He had worn it ever since.

As he neared the Coogan house, his mind went back to the robbery. Where was Coogan, and what had the thieves been looking for?

Two policemen approached Steve as soon as he got out of the taxi. They recognized him after shining their lights on his face and, politely but firmly, asked him to hold his arms up. They frisked him before they allowed him to go in the house.

The phone rang as he walked upstairs. He took the call in the kitchen. It was Ted Coogan. "Steve, I'm calling from Berlin. I had an accident. Well, not exactly an accident. I'm calling from the Benjamin Franklin Hospital. Someone attacked me with a knife. But he found out that I'm not entirely defenseless." Coogan chuckled. "Anyway, I have to ask you a favor. Take my car—it's in the garage—and pick me up at the airport tomorrow morning. I'll be on Lufthansa 4212, landing at ten A.M."

"Wait a minute. Do you know about the break-in at your house?"

"Yes. I got a call from the French police. Benjamin must have given them my number. But I'm not surprised. It's all related to my trip to Berlin, I'm sure. I'll tell you more tomorrow. Thanks for doing this. I appreciate it. By the way, I'm five eleven, with white hair and glasses. Oh, and I'll be the guy with the cane."

He was barely off the phone when Benjamin came running up the stairs. "I didn't hear you come in. The phone woke me up." He wore sweats and a T-shirt. He frowned, and spoke in a loud voice. "A couple of hours ago a policeman came to the door. He said not to worry. Ha!" He looked up and threw his arms open as if imploring God to be his witness. " *'Ne vous en faites pas monsieur,'* " Benjamin said in a deep voice, mimicking the policeman. " 'We have an unconfirmed report that a terrorist group is planning something soon.' Something soon! Are you kidding? What the hell does that mean? He thought that we should know because of the break-in, he said. As if that explained everything!"

"Well, did you ask him what it meant?"

"Yes, of course. I asked him several times, and he finally said that the terrorists might use a suicide bomber!" His voice had become shrill.

"What else?"

"That it was almost certainly a false report, that it had nothing to do with us and that we should not worry, because there had never been a suicide bomber in Paris. But he was just following orders. In the meantime, they would reinforce the police in the front."

Steve was weary from the long day, but his mind was racing. The knowledge that the break-in and the attack on Coogan in Berlin were related was interesting but did not suggest a line of action. Now a suicide-bomber threat that the police didn't believe in because there "has never been a suicide bomber in Paris"? And then there was Tariq al Khalil's appearance at the museum. He remembered that al Khalil had also gone to school in Cairo and that he came from an Egyptian family, although born in Belgium. So al Khalil's presence at the museum should not have surprised him. He recalled that al Khalil was supposed to be an expert on Islam. Maybe he should talk to him. But he immediately dismissed that thought. Coogan should be able to connect the dots. And then there was Kella. The next day promised to be just as full.

* * *

The next morning, after relishing Benjamin's eggs Benedict, Steve drove to the airport. It took him a few minutes to get comfortable in Coogan's blue Mini Cooper S. The top of his head was only an inch from the small vehicle's roof. He reached Charles de Gaulle, parked and made his way through what had been Europe's most modern airport but now was beginning to show wear. As the crowds walked out toward public transportation, Steve felt he was swimming upstream.

He realized why Coogan had asked to be met at the airport—he walked with a cane to alleviate his limp when he came out of the customs checkpoint. Steve waved and made his way through the crowd. Coogan grinned and said, "Those thugs sent a boy to do a man's job." His grin was replaced by a grimace of pain and a sudden intake of breath as they started to walk toward the covered parking lot. Steve carried Coogan's overnight bag and laptop. "I was leaving my hotel, and he came at me in broad daylight. I was lucky because he showed his knife too early. He gave me a chance to—"

A light flashed on their left. A news photographer said, "Thank you, Dr. Coogan. Mind if I take another?" Without waiting for an answer, he took two more shots. The reporter who was with the photographer stepped forward, put a mike in front of Coogan's face and asked, "How did you feel when you were attacked in Berlin?"

Coogan tried to walk past, but his limp, the gathering crowd and the large reporter planted in front of him made a civilized escape impossible.

Steve wedged himself in front of Coogan. "This is not a good time," he said. "Please excuse us."

The reporter scowled and leaned forward aggressively. "Who are you? Don't interfere with the press."

His face inches from the public's right to know, Steve stepped forcefully on the reporter's foot. "Sorry," he said.

With the reporter now slightly off balance, Steve lowered a shoulder and walked straight through him, with Coogan in his wake. The reporter called out, "*Crétin!* Dr. Coogan, is it true that the attack in Berlin was related to your work on the Quran?"

Coogan kept walking behind Steve and said over his shoulder, "Thank you. Contact Berlin."

Once in the passenger seat of his Mini Cooper, Coogan sighed and rubbed his leg. "Thanks for picking me up. That thug did stick me in the leg." He pointed to his right leg. "No big deal. The hospital bandaged it and let me go. But the painkiller has worn off. Could you reach my bag for me? There's an envelope in the side pocket."

Steve gave him the envelope, and Coogan took two pills, which he immediately swallowed.

Steve drove out of the airport. He asked, "What was that reporter talking about? The Quran project?"

"Right, but first things first. Tell me how I can help you. I understand you're on your way to Morocco. Great country! It was, anyway. Things are changing. What do you hope to do there?"

"My company, West Gate Scientific International, does a lot of consulting for the Pentagon. You know, almost everything is outsourced these days. I've been involved in counterproliferation in Korea and in helping the new North American Command for its first congressional hearings. Now I'll be trying to sell our services to the Moroccan defense establishment."

Coogan shifted in his seat, winced and grabbed his leg as he tried to get in a more comfortable position. "It's OK, I'm fine. The painkiller should kick in soon. Go on. Sounds like your company hired the Renaissance man."

"You sure you don't want to stop? After the 2004 terrorist attack on Madrid that killed one hundred ninety-one people, I learned that the army's European Command was starting to provide counterterrorist training and equipment to

North African countries. Anyway, I put the two together and made a pitch to my boss that this was a business opportunity to win contracts either with EUCOM or with the countries receiving the assistance. Long story short, the idea found traction. Before I knew it, I was packing. Anyway, my father said you were the expert I needed to talk to before I went to Morocco. But this Quran project sounds interesting."

"It's certainly bringing out the nutcases, isn't it? The German order of the Knights Hospitaller recovered very old and very different"—he looked at Steve for emphasis—"versions of the Quran. They might have had them since the Crusades. These predate the official version started under the third caliph, Othman. They were lost during the Second World War, or hidden. The Hospitallers donated the manuscripts to a German research institute. I have been invited to join the research team."

"And why would anyone try to kill you for that? And you said that the break-in was related? How?"

"The Quran is supposed to be the word of God, immutable, eternal, unique—in other words, unchallengeable. A group of infidels claiming that they have different versions of God's word is upsetting to certain Muslim groups, to say the least. And the most extreme, the Salafists, are more than ready to eliminate those other versions as well as anyone who claims they exist. As for the break-in, they must have assumed that I had copies of the manuscripts at home. In fact, I had received one page by e-mail to allow me to decide whether I could handle the skeletal Arabic. But I brought my laptop with me." He pointed in back of him toward his computer.

Steve asked, "Speaking of which, have you ever heard of a Tariq al Khalil? I went to graduate school with him in Brussels. We weren't exactly close friends, but I saw him today, at the Institut Arabe."

Coogan nodded thoughtfully. "Al Khalil lectures and

writes extensively. From a Muslim Brotherhood family, as I recall. His pitch depends on his audience. He tries to be moderate with European audiences, but in front of a Muslim audience, he's a take-no-prisoners kind of guy. Gaining in influence too. I hope my former employers are keeping an eye on him. He has become a leader in Salafist circles."

Coogan smiled, looked at Steve and added, "Your father thought I could give you some useful background before you go to Morocco, so let me fast-forward for you. We are witnessing the renaissance of a religion—no, of an authoritarian ideology. Its proponents—jihadists, Salafists, whatever you choose to call them—honestly believe everyone must fall into line, that it is God's will that we all submit. In the short term they are skillful at perception management, using the Internet, killings, whatever works. In the long term, the only constituency they care about is God, Allah. Those who liked the Taliban will love the new Caliphate, the idea that they're going to re-create the Middle East as a borderless Muslim empire, but only as a first step. My generation struggled against one global ism. Your generation is faced with another. That can be your first lesson on contemporary Islam."

"Are you saying that I'm going to have to deal with these guys in Morocco?"

"Depends. Just keep in mind that the true believers are deadly. They are a small minority of the Muslim world, to be sure. Some say, what, only one to five percent are extremists? That's between fifteen and seventy-five million people. Some of them are in Morocco. That's where the terrorists who bombed the Spanish trains came from."

When they reached Coogan's house, Benjamin met them in the hallway. "Welcome back, boss. What do you think of your Arab neighbors?" Seeing Coogan's expression, he continued, "Oh, you don't know? I thought the police called you. Well, it turns out that the robbers came over the wall in the back, from the Saudi residence. Their footprints are still there. The gang that couldn't shoot straight," he said with more bravado than Steve had seen yet.

Coogan and Benjamin went to go have a look. Steve was anxious to leave to meet Kella. "I'm off to the metro. I promised to meet someone. But could the thief have come from the Saudi residence? What do you think?"

Coogan told him, "We'll talk about the theft later. You look in a hurry. Forget the metro. Take my car if you want. I won't need it for the rest of the day. I'm going to be busy right here." He turned to Benjamin and said, "I'll be here tonight for dinner, but not tomorrow. So just prepare your usual fine cuisine tonight, and Steve can tell you what he would like tomorrow."

"Thanks. The car will be useful, since I'm late."

As Steve turned to go, Benjamin said, "By the way, a reporter called you this morning, Steve. But he didn't leave a message."

"A reporter?" He looked at Coogan. "What did he want?"

"He asked for the person who met Mr. Coogan at the airport. He said that you had given him your name, but that he hadn't had a chance to get the spelling right for the article. So I gave it to him."

Steve and Ted looked at each other.

Steve smiled at the reporter's ingenuity, but Coogan frowned. Steve hurried to the Mini Cooper to go meet Kella, wondering what Coogan looked worried about.

CHAPTER THREE

In Tel Aviv on consultation from his assignment in Brussels at Mossad's European headquarters, David Ben Tov had been summoned by Mossad director Nahum Ben Gal to his top-floor office. Mindful that Mossad's American desk chief often lunched with the CIA chief of station at the Asia House near the Mossad building, David Ben Tov parked two blocks away from the Hadar Dafna Building on King Saul Boulevard. Seemingly a business-office building, the Hadar Dafna was the headquarters of the Ha Mossad, le Modiyn ve le Takfidim Mayuhadim—the Institute for Intelligence and Special Operations—Israel's external Israeli intelligence service.

Ben Tov was in his late forties, with blondish receding hair, light skin, in reasonable shape for his age, and dressed in loafers, cargo pants, a sport jacket and white shirt. He wore no tie, a style established early by the David Ben Gurion tieless generation of pioneers.

The sky was cloudy, threatening rain. Ben Tov quickened his step.

In the elevator on his way to the director's top-floor office, Ben Tov reviewed his operations in Europe to be ready for whatever Ben Gal wanted to take up with him. He ran several agents: a Libyan and an Ethiopian diplomat, a Belgian businessman who did business in Saudi Arabia. The Turkish ambassador was his very good friend, although not yet an agent. He was cultivating the manager of a five-star hotel in Brussels where many Arab plenipotentiaries stayed when visiting Brussels to lobby the European Union. Ben

Tov hoped to be able to plant microphones and cameras in several of the suites. He also had a number of other lesser contacts, including a promising young Palestinian with intriguing family connections. By the time he stepped out of the elevator, he hadn't dredged up any problems that would reach Ben Gal's level.

Ben Gal—tall, still dark-haired although ten years older than David—was dressed in slacks and a shirt with the sleeves rolled up. He walked to greet him from behind his desk and extended his hand. *Good signs,* thought Ben Tov. He had been in Ben Gal's modest office only once before, when Ben Gal's predecessor had told him that Mossad would pay for his last two years of university studies at the University of California, Berkeley, assuming he was accepted. He had met his future wife Rachel there, also a Sabra, and picked up American-accented English and expressions.

Ben Gal moved back to his chair. "I understand that we sent you to Berkeley a few years ago. It's time to amortize our investment, to use your American background for the country. Here is a file I want you to read." He handed him a thick green-colored file. David held it sideways to read the title. *Muslim Brotherhood. Western Europe.*

David, wanting to show he was knowledgeable, said, "I believe that the Ikhwan moved to Europe from Egypt, first to Germany to take advantage of the Muslim émigrés from Russia left over from the war."

"Your target is Salim Salaheldin, the Brotherhood's senior official in Europe. He lives in Brussels. Actually, the real focus of the operation will be Tariq al Khalil. Salaheldin is his uncle and mentor. He has a great deal of influence on al Khalil. And it's al Khalil I'm concerned about. He's young, charismatic, has a following through his academic activities, lecturing and so on, but he's also an activist. Both Salim Salaheldin and al Khalil are related to the Brotherhood's founder. That gives them automatic credentials. The radical Muslims right now are leaderless. Al Khalil badly

wants the job. We're going to help him. I think that we can
control him—well, at least influence him—if we can recruit
Salim. Nature and politics abhor a vacuum. If al Khalil
doesn't take over the movement, someone else will. At least,
if we—that is, if *you*—can recruit Salim, we're in the game.
Al Khalil wants to recreate the old Caliphate. I want you to
keep him as far away from Israel as possible. Have him re-
create his Caliphate in the Sahara. Let him get a tan while
he's doing Allah's work." Ben Gal smiled sardonically.

Recalling Ben Gal's reference to Berkeley, David said,
"Are you saying you want me to put my American hat on to
do this? To pretend I'm CIA?"

Ben Gal smiled. "Exactly. This will be a false-flag recruitment. I will establish a list of the people who will be cleared
for this operation. Until then, you are to discuss it with no
one other than me."

"And do we have reason to believe that Salim can be recruited?"

"It's all in the file." Ben Gal's tone turned abrupt. He looked
out his window at the dark clouds for a second and, in a
more measured tone, continued, "We have reason to believe that Salim's predecessor, also with family connections
to the Brotherhood, met with a CIA officer, Joe DiPietro
from New Jersey."

"What did they have in common, I wonder?"

"Well, it was the Cold War. The CIA wanted access to
the Muslim émigrés from Russia to send them back as
sources. The Brotherhood needed cash and approved the
contact. The Brotherhood also established sympathy in the
CIA by providing occasional snippets of counterterrorist information through their own penetrations of Fatah, Force 17
and other groups."

"Was Salim aware that his predecessor was in touch with
the CIA?"

"That's not clear. You'll have to read the file for yourself."
Ben Gal looked at his watch and Ben Tov took the hint.

"One more thing," Ben Gal said as Ben Tov got up. "Al Khalil has a wife and daughter in Brussels. Find out where and establish their living patterns, school, shopping, friends, you know . . . Could be useful later."

Ben Tov gathered the green file. He glanced out the window before going out the door. The dark clouds were no longer threatening. They had burst, and the wind was whipping the water against Ben Gal's window.

The Boeing 767-300 descended over the Mediterranean as it neared the coast of North Africa toward Algiers. Tariq al Khalil looked out his window and could understand why the French traditionally referred to the city as "Alger *la blanche*." On the northern edge of the green coastal plain, the whitewashed buildings of the Casbah, nestled in an arc overlooking the port and the bay, reflected the morning sun. Several container ships were unloading and two were leaving. Al Khalil noted the absence of cruise ships with satisfaction.

During the flight, al Khalil had been thinking of his last conversation with his wife, Malika. He wanted their daughter Jamila to grow up in a Muslim environment. Malika did not, could not, oppose him. But he still seethed at the deception in her comment, "She will be better off here. She can grow up Muslim, attend the madrassa right here in Brussels." In his absence, she had been invited to a meeting of the International Women's Club by the wife of the Egyptian ambassador, a woman who liked to play bridge with her international friends. Al Khalil suspected that Malika was telling him what he wanted to hear but secretly pined for the life of her Egyptian friend. He decided that he would send them to live in Cairo or Riyadh as soon as he had time to plan the move.

His thoughts wandered when he found a map of North Africa in an Air France brochure in the pocket in front of him. The outlined borders reminded him of the interference of the

Christian powers, and his frustration stayed high. He took a deep breath. In North Africa, it had been France. In other regions of the former Caliphate, it had been Great Britain. The Christians had created the borders to divide the Caliphate into separate countries to divide and conquer. But knowing that he soon would be able to reclaim the populations on the ground below for Islam, he felt empowered. He knew that he could harness the humiliation and the anger of the people to his advantage and fill the current power vacuum in the leadership of the radical Muslim movement. He felt energized.

Al Khalil turned to his Syrian deputy and chief of operations, Hussein al Kaylani. "Petrol and alcohol in those ships. During bad years, the difference between the production and the export of Bordeaux wines from France comes from Algerian wines. Hypocrisy and corruption are the West's capstone principles. A Muslim country in the alcohol business is unacceptable, an insult to Allah, may he favor our actions."

"Yes, that will come. There are more important things . . . I mean, you're right. But don't you think that petrol is where the power is?" Hussein asked.

Al Khalil didn't reply. He thought that Hussein's common sense sometimes made up for his lack of true religious fervor.

They landed at Houari Boumediene Airport. Mediterranean sunlight flowed through large and high windows. Architecturally clean lines offered uncluttered and expansive spaces. Large posters from the Ministry of Tourism greeted tourists in several languages. However, al Khalil immediately felt the embattled atmosphere. The presence of countless military patrols—soldiers walking in pairs with leveled semiautomatic machine guns hanging from their shoulders—sent a clear warning not to abuse the welcome. Al Khalil chuckled. He turned to Hussein and said, "Our Salafist friends obviously have convinced these apostate rulers that their days are limited."

Hussein took his cell phone out of his pocket. "Yes. When the Algerian Salafists became al Qaeda in the Maghreb, they became more aggressive, more deadly. It was a good idea to plan a meeting with them on our way south."

Following a two-hour wait, the Land Rover representative met them on the street side of the airport, explaining the delay as the will of God, *insha'llah.* Hussein took title to the car after another hour of haggling over the final price and a sizeable bribe, or baksheesh.

Al Khalil saw the boxy-looking green car with outsize Michelin desert tires but was only interested in the brand name. As he got in the car, he asked, "Why a British car, Hussein? The British have troops in Iraq; their damn SAS commandos are fighting the Taliban in Afghanistan."

Hussein's shrewd eyes didn't move from his maps as he replied flippantly, "I'm more concerned about being able to traverse the Sahara than who made the car." He looked up at al Khalil. "It's a good car."

Al Khalil gave his deputy a sharp look but said nothing.

They followed signs to avenue Franklin Roosevelt, which became National Road Number 1 and proceeded south. The sign informed them that the distance to Blida was twenty-eight miles. As they neared the entrance to the town, they were stopped at a roadblock. They were let through after a check of their passports. However, off to the side, two soldiers had ordered the driver and passenger of the previous car to get out. There was yelling, and one soldier, holding his weapon parallel to the ground, hit the passenger with the stock of his rifle, stepping forward with one foot for more force. *Just like in training,* al Khalil thought. The passenger fell, his head bleeding.

Hussein, who drove, asked, "How well do you know the AQIM chief, el Maghrebi?"

"Ibrahim el Maghrebi is more of a survivor than a fox. He

was a sergeant in the Algerian army when he tried to enlist fellow officers to his Salafist beliefs. He was jailed, later released in an amnesty and went underground. I agree with him on many things. The execution of uncooperative village officials, as the North Vietnamese practiced, is an effective path to control the population. Since 1991, when they started to fight, they have killed over two hundred thousand. No wonder they convinced al Qaeda Central to incorporate them."

"But will he help us?" Hussein asked. "And does he have the purity of spirit that you seek?" Al Khalil glanced at Hussein; his only response was a thoughtful nod. He knew that Hussein was still trying to convince him of his Muslim motivation.

They found the small grocery store with the safety signal—a Coca-Cola sign in Arabic in its window—which signified to al Khalil and Hussein that the site was secure and that the Algerian police was neither in control of the location nor surveilling it. Immediately inside the door, a bearded guard, holding his AK-47 casually, let them into the smoky and narrow room, where a young boy swept the floor.

After an exchange of greetings, the guard said, "He's up there," and looked toward the ceiling. He shouted, "They're here!" toward stairs in the back of the store. Between coughs, a voice replied, "Bring them up." They walked past shelves lined with bottles of Evian and cans of *petits pois de Clamart* to reach the stairs

Ibrahim el Maghrebi sported an unruly mustache hiding his upper lip but not his tobacco-stained teeth. His dusty brown *jellaba*, the hooded garment that covered the body from the head to the ankles, couldn't completely hide a sturdy physique. Al Khalil could feel el Maghrebi's familiarity with command and easily imagined him in uniform.

"*Salaam alaikum.* We are honored by your visit. Your reputation precedes you. Your family is the royalty of our Muslim Brotherhood. We honor your grandfather, a man with the Quran in one hand and a gun in the other. He promoted the renaissance of a pure brand of Islam to reverse the perversions of Western ideology: Christianity, imperialism and nationalism."

Al Khalil waved a fly away from his face. "You are kind."

El Maghrebi continued, "I'm sorry I have to receive you in this unworthy place. Please understand that we are at war. The next time we meet will be in my palace in Algiers." They both chuckled.

Asked to sit next to his host on a banquette against the wall, al Khalil accepted. A blade of sun cut through half-closed curtains and lit part of the room.

El Maghrebi reached for a pack of cigarettes from a pocket in the folds of his *jellaba* and held it in his hand. He said, "AQIM is on the verge of victory. A few days ago, we attacked a coast-guard installation a hundred kilometers east of Algiers. We killed almost a hundred soldiers. We act in the name of Allah. The time for talk is past. But what can we do for you?" He opened the pack of cigarettes and offered it to al Khalil, who declined, and then to Hussein, who took one. The ashtray next to el Maghrebi was full.

Hussein mentioned the roadblock they had encountered in Boufarik, but el Maghrebi didn't seem worried.

After the required tea and courtesies demanded by Muslim hospitality, al Khalil was soon up and pacing in the small room, his shadow appearing on the far wall when he crossed the narrow beam of sunlight. Al Khalil was not physically imposing, but his coal black beard, aquiline nose and penetrating gray eyes gave him the air of a prophet. Stroking his beard, he said, "We are conscious of your actions. With the help of Allah, the Merciful, the Omnipotent, my Salafist brothers and I will reconquer all the lands of the ancient Caliphate. AQIM will play a key role in North Africa. We will work together. I will bring all of the countries bordering on the Sahara to our cause. You will help us. Acting and preaching must go together."

An hour into the meeting, al Khalil said, "You have been right in not destroying the country's oil industry. We will need it when we take over. But you must do something about the wine—" The phone rang downstairs and the tone of the guard's short questions cut him off.

The guard ran up the stairs. "A mobile patrol is heading this way—one squad with a sergeant. They are now searching the house where Abdullah stayed last month. We must move."

As though having anticipated the warning, el Maghrebi said, "Come, my brothers. Follow us. We will go to another safe house." Out in the street, el Maghrebi, two guards and the boy got into a brown pickup truck. Hussein and al Khalil followed in the Land Rover. A third vehicle followed with four other men. Using back streets, the small convoy circled around the patrol to the northern edge of town and parked on a side street. They walked at a brisk pace for two blocks until they reached a three-story building with a café downstairs, where they went in by a side door and found themselves in an apartment behind the café.

El Maghrebi pulled curtains shut. "I apologize, but this is the life we lead. The military has been searching for us with more vigor since our raid on the coast. Abdullah, the man they are looking for, hasn't been here for a while. They're working from dated intelligence."

El Maghrebi gave his men orders and they started to file out again with purpose, but not before checking the weapons they carried under their *jellabas*. Al Khalil felt el Maghrebi's eyes on him as men pulled the bolts of their AK-47s back and let them slide forward to chamber a round. Al Khalil knew that el Maghrebi respected his intellect and passion and wanted to project his composure under stress.

El Maghrebi said, "We are safe here, but these patrols never come in single squads. We may have to move again. You will be safer if you get on the road. No need to rush, but today is better than tomorrow. I will send another car with you. My men know the desert. And it's always safer to travel with two cars. But first, I have something for you in honor of your visit."

El Maghrebi gave his two guests, who had arrived from Paris wearing rumpled European suits and tieless white shirts, two *jellabas* for desert travel. They both changed immediately.

He then gave al Khalil and al Kaylani each a highly polished teak box. "You did us the honor of asking for our hospitality and help. We are blessed by Allah to join you. Please accept these gifts as symbols of AQIM's unalloyed allegiance. We are as true to Islam as the blades of these two knives."

Al Khalil opened his box and pulled out a Damascus-steel and amourette-wood knife with a contoured gunstock handle. Al Kaylani received a Gerber Trident combat knife with a double-serrated blade. Al Khalil's five-inch blade closed into the handle, but Hussein's gift, with a blade slightly over six inches and a hilt, was clearly a hunting or fighting knife. Each was nestled in a gift box with the same care as an expensive watch.

As they left, al Khalil said, "I'm happy to have had this discussion. We will work well together. Your gifts will be put to the service of the Prophet, the All-powerful, the Compassionate."

El Maghrebi's men led the way out of town and into the desert evening. On the left of the small convoy, the lengthening shadows of the vehicles brushed against the buildings of the town before caressing the sands of the Sahara. Al Khalil soon appreciated that only experienced drivers wary of the perpetual attempts of the sand to cover the road could have driven them safely in the dark. He thought ahead to their next stop on their way to Timbuktu, the oasis town of Ghardaïa, the center of the first fundamentalists, the Kharajites.

CHAPTER FOUR

Kella turned her back on a driver obviously trying to attract her attention. She was at the entrance of the rue du Bac metro station, where she and Steve had agreed to meet. Dressed in loose clothing down to her ankles, she was surprised that she would attract any male attention. Then she heard her name and turned back toward the car parked at the curb to the great annoyance of the cars behind. "Kella, come on before I get run over," Steve shouted. She recognized him and ran toward to the car.

Steve explained the car and, glancing at her clothes, said, "Very chic. Is that the latest Paris fashion?"

"The Saint-Denis suburb is very North African. Faridah told me to dress like this to fit the role of a friend her father would want her to have. The idea is to reassure her father that Faridah hasn't gone to the dark side, that she hasn't rejected her Muslim roots."

Steve nodded and said, "You better give me directions to Saint-Denis."

Kella navigated and continued talking about her friend. She was conscious that she was trying to justify to herself the wisdom of her idea. It had sounded better yesterday, she thought. "Faridah's father is very strict, very fundamental. Now, he suspects that she is not being chaste. She does have a French boyfriend, and her father is assuming the worst. He is talking about moving the family back to Algeria."

"So what do you hope to accomplish? Make a moderate of the father?"

A bit annoyed at Steve's negative tone, she said, "I'm just

trying to help her, show her father that she has decent . . .
well, nonthreatening friends, like me. Faridah said that her
father often beats her mother, on the smallest pretext. He
probably hits Faridah also, although she didn't say so."

"You think that going to their apartment is a good idea? If
I understood you last night, you aren't Muslim . . . well, not
anymore, right?"

Kella took out a scarf from her shoulder bag and refolded
it before putting it back inside. "That's why I told Faridah to
convince her parents to come and have coffee in a public
place."

As planned, Steve and Kella met Faridah at the exit of the
Saint-Denis metro station. Kella made the introductions,
while Faridah appraised Kella's outfit. "Perfect. Except you
do need to cover your head." Kella put on her scarf.

"What if I came with you?" Steve asked. "Are you sure you
know what you're doing?"

As Kella seemed about to agree, Faridah spoke up, turning toward Steve. "Absolutely not. Unless your name is Ahmed
and you're a Muslim. I'm not even sure if bringing Kella is a
good idea. Bringing an American male? That'll burn my father's short fuse in an instant. And by the way, we're going
to my apartment, rather than to a café as you suggested. I
talked to my mother about your idea, and she said that my
father wouldn't do it. So this way is simpler. It's also the only
way."

Kella turned to Steve. "Why don't you go to the basilica
and I'll meet you there in, say, an hour?" Pointing, she said,
"There's a sign for the basilica; it's about five minutes from
here."

Kella and Faridah walked from the metro, past the Hôtel-
de-Ville, toward a row of drab buildings much like those put
up in Eastern Europe's socialist heavens after World War II.
A car full of young men passed. Faridah looked down instinctively, and Kella followed suit. They walked quickly to an intersection and crossed kitty-corner to a faceless apartment

building. Faridah held the front door open. "Le Grand Palais," she said sarcastically. "The security buzzer and combination pad have not worked for as long as I can remember," she added.

Inside, the small lobby's walls and mailboxes were nicked. A graffito in Arabic, ISLAM IS THE ANSWER, was spray-painted on the far wall. "We're on the third floor," Faridah said with a slightly encouraging smile. She and Kella went through the small hallway, which reeked with the odor of urine, and started up the stairs. On the way up, a family passed them on its way down, the mother, dressed in loose clothing that hid her shape, shooing three handsome children ahead of her. The youngsters looked up at Kella with curiosity.

Once they reached the third floor Faridah said, "Wait out here a minute, just in case my mother hasn't mentioned your visit yet." She rolled her eyes and smiled. She walked up to her apartment door, taking keys out of her pocket. The hallway's only light seeped in from a small window at the end of the hall, although Kella noticed a lightbulb hanging from a wire over the stairwell. Faridah turned her key in the first door lock, but before she could find the key for the second lock, the door flew open.

"I was just asking about you!" A dark-skinned, full-bearded, bulky man in his early fifties grabbed Faridah's left wrist and pulled her into the apartment before Faridah had time to say anything. Kella presumed the man to be Hamad, Faridah's father. The door began to shut, but Kella rushed forward and braced her foot at the bottom of the door to keep it from closing completely. At first, she leaned toward the slight opening and listened. She was prepared to walk in, when the angry tone of Hamad's voice stopped her inside the dark hallway.

"You are not the daughter I knew when we lived in Algiers. You have become someone else, someone who shows no respect, a girl who is anxious to show her body. You no longer attend the mosque." Hamad's voice was rising in tone and in volume. Kella felt that he was on the verge of physical violence. She stayed in the hallway, out of sight.

"Stop," Faridah cried. "You're hurting me. Please! Let go!"

Kella could see Hamad standing in front of Faridah in the kitchen. There was a stove on the left, a square table with metal legs and four folding chairs. A woman that Kella assumed was Faridah's mother sat at the table. She wore a loose gray housedress. Along the wall on the right was a narrow but lengthy shelf on top of which she could see dishes and glasses. Under the shelf was a small refrigerator with silverware scattered on it as if Faridah's mother had been interrupted in the act of putting it away. Kella assumed there was a sink next to the refrigerator, but she couldn't see it.

Hamad shouted, "I know that as soon as you got on the metro, you took off your scarf. You went to the Île de la Cité and met your Christian devil. You touched and kissed in public. I know you've done more. And with an infidel! The neighbors know and talk about it. It shames us!"

Kella had originally assumed that Hamad simply wanted to protect a daughter for whom he cared. Instead, Hamad's rantings reflected more concern about what others thought about him. Should she step forward and make her presence known? She was undecided.

In a weak, pleading voice, the woman at the table said, "She is your daughter. For the love of Allah, have pity on your flesh and blood." She sounded upset, but not surprised. Kella wasn't catching every word of the woman's high-pitched and rapid appeal. Kella guessed that much of the woman's speech was in a Berber dialect, from the Kabyle Mountains of Algeria.

Still holding Faridah's wrist, Hamad turned toward his wife, now on her feet and approaching him. Fearfully, she brought her arms up to protect her head. "Fatima, our daughter, may she be forever damned, has soiled our flesh and blood. You know what I must do. It is Allah's will."

"Allah would have pity," Fatima replied in a weak voice.

Kella drew closer. She noticed that Faridah's mother was looking at the top of the refrigerator, and Kella now could see a large knife lying apart from the silverware.

Hamad's voice grew louder. "You whore! You've disgraced us, dishonored me and the whole family!" He pulled Faridah's arm hard toward him, and she lost her balance as Hamad let go of her wrist.

"Filth!" he shouted, as she sprawled on the discolored linoleum floor of the kitchen.

Kella's thoughts raced. What could she do? She looked for something she might use as a weapon, something to hit him with, but she saw nothing. She wished that Steve were here. She didn't move, paralyzed by the fear that she might make things worse for Faridah. She looked at Fatima, trying to judge whether the two of them together could help Faridah. But at that moment, Hamad, his eyes fixed on his wife, turned away from her. He then quickly rotated his muscular shoulders back toward her and, clenching his fist, whipped his right elbow like a piston into her chest. The blow knocked Fatima to the floor.

He returned his focus to Faridah and kicked her in the stomach as she tried to get up. She fell again and brought her legs up and wrapped her arms around her body, trying to make herself as small as possible. Hamad aimed his next kick to her head, which started a slow trickle of blood down her cheek. His strength increased by his wrath, he stood Faridah up and pushed her back until she was wedged against the waist-high refrigerator. She leaned away from him and to the side to avoid the shelf in back of her. For an instant she uncovered her face to look at her mother. Kella felt guilty. Was Faridah looking for her? The blood from her scalp continued to flow down her face, mixing with the tears, and onto her clothes. There was blood on the floor. Faridah shrieked, "You're insane! Stop it!"

"You're going back to Algeria, tomorrow!" Hamad said, his voice viciously calm. "You'll spend the rest of your days atoning."

Thrusting her hands out, Faridah tried to keep Hamad at bay. "Never! I'll never go back there!"

Hamad froze, struck by his daughter's statement. Like a boxer in training, he struck her head and arms with his fists as she tried to protect herself. Faridah let out a piteous wail and, unable to move away in any direction, leaned her upper body back until her head touched the wall behind the refrigerator. Then, pressing her back with his left forearm, Hamad reached behind Faridah for the knife on the refrigerator. Kella saw his rage subside, and another quieter but more menacing emotion took over.

As Hamad raised the knife, Kella sprang forward, no longer able to stand by. She seized his arm from the side with both hands. Surprised, Hamad lifted his foot and tried to kick Kella's knee. But she was too close. With his knife hand still up over Faridah, he swung his left fist into Kella's stomach, hitting the nerve center of the solar plexus. She dropped her hands to her stomach, unable to breathe. Aware that she was now extremely vulnerable, she backed off, still doubled over and breathing in short gasps. She looked up at Hamad, terrified that he would attack her, but he refocused on Faridah. With a violent swing of the knife, he slashed Faridah's shoulder. Her blood sprayed his shirt. He said in a loud voice, "*Allahu Akbar.*" Again, he raised the knife, but Fatima sprang up and hit him with her fists. He shoved her aside. Then Hamad brought the knife slowly and deliberately over his head with both hands, chanting "*Allahu Akbar,*" a sacrifice to his God, and plunged the blade into Faridah's chest again and again, each powerful thrust accompanied by its own "God is greater!"

Kella forced out a scream of horror. To her ears it sounded like a weak squeal. Taking as deep a breath as she could, she managed a louder "Murderer!" Hamad pushed Fatima away and turned toward Kella, the knife still in his hand, blood on his shirt. Their eyes met. She felt the hatred and rage burn into her soul. Acting instinctively, she turned and ran from the kitchen, through the dark hallway and out the door of the apartment.

She pushed past neighbors who had assembled on the landing and took the steps down several at a time, despite her bulky clothing, aware that her life depended upon getting to the street before Hamad caught up with her.

Kella reached the street-level hallway, still breathing with difficulty. She ran toward the entrance but was stopped by four hefty men bringing large boxes into the building. The entrance was blocked from side to side by heavy-looking cardboard containers. One was more than halfway inside and two men were struggling with another. Kella briefly wondered if she could get over the container but was instantly convinced that she could not. She looked around and saw a wood and glass door in the back of the lobby. She ran to it but could not see through the greenish opaque glass. She feared another dead end, but she nevertheless turned the white porcelain handle and found herself in a narrow corridor that led out to a small courtyard. She jogged past garbage cans and entered a corridor similar to the one she had just left and reached the front hallway of the building next door. She kept moving and made it to the sidewalk.

She nearly lost her balance when she saw the movers who had blocked her exit in front of Faridah's building, and barely managed to turn course and run the other way. After a few steps, she realized she had no idea how to get back to the metro. On the way to the apartment, she had been talking and had paid little attention to direction, expecting that Faridah would guide her back. But Faridah was dead. Dead! The thought and the word shocked her. She looked

back for Hamad but did not see him, just a crowded sidewalk
with working people going about their daily routine. Kella's
scarf came undone and she first tried to put it back on, but
decided after a few steps that the effort was slowing her
down, so she crumpled it into her left hand as she ran. The
images she had just witnessed were seared into her mind—
Hamad's face a nightmarish demon's mask, Faridah bleeding and screaming, the knife plunging into Faridah's body.
She was now only fifty yards away from Faridah's building
and already breathing hard.

She ran around a corner, slowed to a walk and put her
scarf back on. No one seemed to be paying any particular
attention to her. She scanned the street for a taxi and tried
to get her bearings. No taxis in sight. She glanced at her
watch, wondering if Steve would still be at the basilica, and
was surprised that less than twenty minutes had elapsed
since she and Steve had separated at the metro station. She
glanced at the Tuareg tattoo on the back of her right hand
wistfully and looked up, hoping to spot the basilica's spires,
but the street was too narrow and its buildings, while not
particularly high, were still too tall to enable her to see anything beyond them.

What she did notice for the first time was the number of
young Arab men on the streets, in small groups. Most had a
cigarette protruding defiantly from the corner of their mouths
as if each were an Ali La Pointe, the small-time thief who had
become the psychopathic hero of the movie *The Battle of
Algiers*, and all with no particular place to go. Every Arab
male on the street seemed like another Hamad, full of anger ready to erupt, if provoked. She saw a sign for the basilica and she hastened her steps in that direction, consciously
avoiding eye contact with any of the loiterers.

She came to an intersection that broadened her line of
sight and saw the market she had passed after leaving the
metro. As she crossed the street she noticed a man walking
quickly, half running, in her direction. He seemed to be

searching over and around the people in front of him. She did not get a close enough look to determine if it was Hamad. Instead she stayed close to the other pedestrians crossing the street, using them as concealment.

At the open-air market, she stopped briefly at a stall and bought a long, dark gray scarf to change her appearance a bit from the beacon of a bright white scarf she had worn earlier. As she completed her purchase, she spotted Hamad. He was scanning the market. Kella moved behind a display of Damascene tablecloths. With the intention of appearing to be just another shopper, she examined the material. She could no longer see Hamad, and she directed her steps toward the metro beyond the Hôtel-de-Ville. As she detached herself from the crowd at the market, Hamad reappeared, now running toward her. Spurred by energy born of desperation, Kella also started running. She looked for a policeman, but the police were wherever the absent cabdrivers had gone. Kella, who had considered going straight for the metro, veered to the right toward the basilica. She realized that she would have no protection from Hamad's violence in the metro unless a gendarme showed up, or unless she could hop on a departing metro with quickly closing doors, both unlikely to happen. The basilica had Steve and Catholic priests, who in her mind stood for safety and sanctuary. Further, there would be tourists, Westerners, visiting the necropolis of the French kings. All in all, the environment would be more protective. She raced to the front doors of the church and went in.

She took a breath and got her bearings. She was in the middle of a thin crowd that was starting to disperse. A Mass must have just ended. Two priests stood in the back of the church, not far from the main entrance, talking with parishioners. Kella looked for Steve but did not see him. The area in which she stood was partially occupied by rows of chairs in the middle, flanked by wide columns rising up about thirty meters toward the vaulted ceilings. Statues and mausoleums took up the far half of the basilica. Not far from her in the public area and on the right was a small souvenir shop. Farther away from her in the center of the mausoleum area, a guide was leading a tour group. Kella started walking toward the tour in the hope that Steve was with the tourists. But a railing about a foot and half high that divided the public area from the tombs stopped her. Kella saw a side door that the tourists must have used to enter and guessed that the ticket booth to pay for the tour was outside that door.

Not seeing any authority who might object, Kella quickly stepped over the railing and headed toward the tour, now behind a large monument with four arches on one side and two on the other. She noticed two effigies inside the monument and with great relief saw Steve listening to the guide and reading an inscription beneath the figures of Anne de Bretagne and her husband Louis XII. Steve saw her, moved closer and, with a false intellectual air, said, "I've always wanted to know more about Anne de Bretagne. Did you know that her marriage made Brittany a part of France?" Kella was not listening. She tried to peer through the openings of the arches but could not see over the effigies inside.

She looked around the monument and was terrified to see Hamad inside the basilica. Kella grabbed Steve's arm and pulled him away from the tour group but still behind the monument. In a low, breathless voice she said, "Steve, something terrible has happened. That's Hamad, Faridah's father. He just killed her. I saw it." A sob escaped, and she put a hand to her mouth.

"Killed her? Is that what you said? No!" He put his arms around her for an instant until she stepped back, having regained control.

Hamad had stopped very close to the spot where Kella had first paused to look at her surroundings. He seemed hesitant to go farther into what to him must have seemed a strange but sacred place.

"I was there. It was awful. I ran. Now he's after me," Kella said.

"That guy over there?" he said looking in Hamad's direction. "Show me."

She pointed from behind the monument. Hamad was moving forward, getting closer to the railing. Kella and Steve stayed with the tourists and their guide as they moved. The tour guide was speaking about Anne de Bretagne's marriage.

Then Hamad, with stains on his clothes, stepped over the railing and came toward them. Steve stepped in front of Kella. A woman who came out of the souvenir shop said in a raspy, vernacular accent that told Kella volumes about the owner's view of Arab immigrants, "*Alors*, look at you! Where are we going—and without a ticket?"

Hamad looked back and spotted the source of the voice, a red-faced female walking toward him, an infidel not fit to clean up behind him. But he felt intimidated.

The woman continued, the superior acoustics of the church lending her words additional authority. "Have you no respect for the house of God?"

Kella watched Hamad's anger turn first to puzzlement, then fear, as he looked to the far end of the church toward the altar and the cross. Then Kella's and Hamad's eyes locked for an instant. She saw him turn away in extreme frustration. With fists tightly clenched and the muscles of his jaw bulging, he strode out of the church.

Steve whispered, "You stay with the tour. I'm going to take a breath of fresh air." Before Kella could reply, he left the group and walked past the woman in the souvenir shop, telling her, "You're right, madame. I'm going to make sure he doesn't hang around the front."

When Steve stepped outside, he saw Hamad standing on the steps that led to the basilica's main entrance, motioning to another man coming in their direction about fifty yards away on the sidewalk. He went up to Hamad, who appeared surprised. Steve said, "I don't ever want to see you again, and neither does the woman you followed here. If either you or your friend"—he pointed toward Hamad's friend, who was now running toward them—"are still here when we come out of the church, your days in sunny France are over, unless you want to spend them in a prison cell."

Hamad reacted instantly with a wild swinging right fist. Expecting it, Steve stepped forward under Hamad's fist and he caught him under the chin with an open palm. The force of the blow was multiplied by Hamad's forward motion. His head jerked back and he fell backward on the stone surface of the parvis. When the other man reached them, Hamad seemed unconscious. Hamad's friend looked down at Hamad, undecided, but reached in his pocket and produced a knife. Steve said, "Don't make it any worse. Take care of your friend. Maybe he'll live." He turned around and went back into the church.

When he rejoined the tour, Steve whispered, "Let's stay with the tour to give Hamad a bit longer." They went downstairs to the crypt. Kella was in a daze. She stayed close to Steve, trying to keep out images of Hamad's knife thrusts into Faridah's body. When the guide explained that Saint Denis had been beheaded in Montmartre in the third century and had carried his head in his hands for several kilometers to this spot, where the church had been built to honor him two centuries later, Kella gasped at the grisly image that reinforced her painful memory.

She asked Steve, "What about her body? What is he going to do with Faridah's body? Steve, I ran away. I ran away." Quiet tears ran down her face. "I want to get out of here."

Steve took her back up to street level and toward the exit. Kella stopped him. "Wait. Before leaving, I want a couple of minutes to myself." She glanced around and walked to a side chapel, knelt and prayed for Faridah. After a few minutes, she stood up. She looked up at a statue of the Virgin Mary in whites and blues with arms out in a welcoming gesture and murmured, "Please care for the soul of my friend, who meant no harm."

Kella met Steve by the front entrance. "You have to tell the police. Let's go to the local police station," he said.

She hesitated a second, wiped her tears, blew her nose and regained her composure. "No. I just want to get away from here. I'll call my father and he'll make arrangements for me to talk to the police later." Seeing the surprise on Steve's face, she added, "As the dependent of an American foreign-service officer with diplomatic status, I'm not supposed to be in touch with the French police without either a consular officer or the regional security officer. My double-nationality status makes things more complicated. It's better if someone from the embassy is with me when I talk to the police."

They went out, looking left and right for any signs that Hamad was near. With Kella clutching Steve's arm tightly, they walked quickly to the parking lot, climbed into the Mini Cooper and left Saint-Denis behind.

CHAPTER FIVE

"Steve, I don't want to go home. Let's go somewhere else. Or let's just drive," Kella said.

It was evening, but the French capital's northern latitude provided natural light late in the day. At first they drove in silence. Then little by little, at times sobbing, at times almost incoherent, Kella relived the horrible memory of her friend's murder. She imitated Hamad's killing motion with her hand, repeating as he had, *"Allahu Akbar."* The retelling was at once traumatic and cathartic for her.

"Steve," she said, "you know that I was initially raised Muslim. But I'm confused. The God to whom Hamad sacrificed Faridah is not the same God I thought I knew."

The intensity of his glance surprised her as he said, "Radical Islamists pray to a different Allah. I should have gone with you . . . I should have gone. Your friend might still be alive."

Kella shook her head. "He stabbed her again and again. There was so much blood. There was a point when Faridah looked for me, I think. She expected me to help her. I tried—" Kella sobbed again.

Stopping at a light, Steve said, "Killing your daughter in the name of Allah! What kind of religion is that?"

"I had heard stories, but I didn't really pay much attention before. I thought these 'honor killings,' as they're called, only took place in the uncontrolled areas, in the mountains of Afghanistan," Kella said, shaking her head.

They had reached the place Charles de Gaulle, and Steve turned onto the avenue des Champs Élysées. Taking his cue from the bright lights and lively rhythm of the wide boulevard, he tried to change the mood. "Listen, you know that I have to leave for Morocco in a couple days," Steve said. "I'm going to drive you home now. But before I get on a plane, I'm going to try to help you forget today's nightmare. I'm going to treat you to the greatest meal you've ever had. Tomorrow night, come to my house in Neuilly and I'll surprise you."

Kella forced a smile.

Steve continued, "It's a difficult time. I'm sorry about your friend. This is the kind of thing one never forgets. But I want to put you on a good path before I leave."

"I know, and I'm grateful. But I don't know if—" She looked over at Steve and put her hand on his. "I want you to hold me," she said.

Steve drove onto a lateral street and stopped. They held each other for a moment. "Thanks. That was good. Until you lose someone, it's impossible to know, to understand, how it feels."

"I know that. I know exactly how you feel. And that's why I'm driving you home right now."

Later, parked in front of her apartment building, Steve said, "A year ago, I took my girlfriend, Vera, skiing in Canada, British Columbia's Purcell Mountains. On the last day, she joined a small skimobiling group so that I could go heli-skiing for the day." He gestured with his right arm, palm out, and looked into the middle distance. " 'Ski on the untouched powder of the backcountry slopes,' the ad said. My plan was to propose that evening. An avalanche . . . I never saw her again. There was an investigation. The guide was inexperienced, according to the report. He should never have taken the group to that area." After a few seconds of silence, he added, "There was someone on the flight the other night who looked like her."

"I'm sorry," said Kella. "What you're saying, I think, is that grief strikes many people. But they go on, like you. And I will too." Neither said anything for a few minutes. "But what can be done about the Hamads of the world? Is your country doing anything? Is France? To stop these barbarian acts?"

"Good question. People like Hamad don't feel controlled by the laws of the state. He gets his justification from Allah. The only interested organizations are the intelligence agencies. But in the U.S., anyway, their main responsibility is to gather information."

Kella got out in front of her apartment building in the sixteenth arrondissement, off the rue de la Tour. Before getting out of the car, she gave Steve a kiss on the cheek. "Thanks. Food is the last thing on my mind, but I'll probably change my mind. See you tomorrow night." She buzzed herself in and disappeared behind a wrought-iron and glass door.

Steve savored driving back to Neuilly. He loved the surprising turbocharged power of the small engine—a kiddy car on steroids. He was glad that Coogan had chosen manual transmission; the six-gear system was smooth, quick and responsive. Although left-handed, he had long ago adjusted to a right-handed world, and the center-console-mounted shifting lever offered no problems for him. Feeling the machine respond to his commands restored a good measure of the control he felt he had lost during the day's events. A good antidote to the high emotions of the previous hours.

In the morning, Steve and his host had breakfast together. French café au lait, croissants, toasted buttered slices of crusty French bread, juice and a jar of peanut butter.

Steve said, "Peanut butter? In France?"

"It's the only thing I miss about American food. It looks like I need to buy another jar. It's only available at Fauchon's, an exclusive shop near the Madeleine. It's right next to the caviar, and almost as expensive," Coogan laughed.

After Steve described Kella's experience, Coogan said, "Honor killings are not all that rare. They just don't get reported. So if there is a hint or a rumor that a female is promiscuous, it becomes the duty, the obligation, of the senior male to either kill her himself or assign one of his sons to do it."

Steve's voice went up a notch. "You don't sound surprised. It's incredible to me that these killings, these *dis*-honor killings, are accepted as part of the landscape. I've even read that in a rape case, the female is usually the one who is punished. I assume, I hope, that the French police will hunt this guy down."

He could see that Coogan was letting him blow off steam. He took a breath, had a sip of the strong French coffee and changed the subject. "What about the break-in? Anything new?"

"The advice from the police and from the U.S. Embassy is to wait for the investigation to take place. As far as I know, the police haven't even contacted the Saudis yet. So I'm going to raise the wall or make it somehow more difficult to get over."

"I don't think you can make that wall high enough."

"You're right. Then I'll just have to mine the flower beds." He chuckled at the idea. "Actually, I'm going to pay a call on my neighbor."

Steve asked, "Why would a Saudi want to break in here?"

Coogan studied his toast before replying. "It's not surprising that the intruder came from the Saudi residence, assuming that the reason for it was to find the Quranic documents. I can't believe that this was an officially sanctioned attempt; it was pretty sloppy. It was probably an overzealous servant. The House of Saud tries to keep everyone happy through handouts. They need the American military but are also dependent on the fundamentalist Wahhabi clerics with whom they have had a Faustian agreement since the 1800s. The Saudis finance the spread of Wahhabism globally, to include madrassas in the United States. But they're also attacked by al Qaeda for being apostates, for being too close to the American 'Jews and Crusaders.'"

Steve reached for the coffeepot and said, "Looks as if, by trying to please everyone, they please no one."

"By the way, you probably haven't seen this yet." Coogan handed him a French newspaper that was folded to a story about the discovery of the documents, complete with pictures of Coogan and Steve at the airport. "They spelled your name right."

"Yes, thanks to Benjamin. With everything that's going on, I don't like having my picture in the paper."

"You're right, and I'm sorry I got you involved."

CHAPTER SIX

That evening, after the police frisked her, Kella rang the bell of the Coogan house under the unwavering gaze of the French policemen. Steve opened the door and, in answer to her curious nod toward the armed security guards, explained, "The Saudi ambassador lives next door. And the Moroccan ambassador is on the other side. I don't know if I should feel safe, or if I'm in the middle of a shooting gallery."

"I can't believe it. They actually searched me."

"Yes. Me too. I'm sorry; I should have warned you."

He led her up the stairs to the den. Coogan had stacked the books and photos in piles since his return. Steve explained, "There was a break-in the other day. Nothing is missing, but they took the place apart."

She sat on one of two leather sofas as Steve opened a bottle of Veuve Clicquot champagne that had been chilling in a silver ice bucket.

Kella said, "A break-in? I saw your picture in the paper this morning. You're famous. Is the break-in connected?"

He handed her a glass of champagne. "That article is trouble. But, there is no fatwa on me yet." He grinned. "But I'm starting to believe that these people are serious. Now they're going to associate me with this Quran research."

"Plus, Hamad, Faridah's father, saw you. I doubt that he reads the French newpapers, but if he does, he now knows who you are. I don't know if he has my name."

They moved to the dining room carrying their champagne glasses. The table was set for two with Baccarat wine glasses, a formal setting of silverware and dishes in a rich gold and red design. She sat down, puzzled by the absence of food smells. Steve went to the kitchen, and soon Kella heard the noise of a dumbwaiter. Steve came in carrying two plates, each with six oysters on the half shell set on shaved ice. He put the plates down and took a paper from his pocket, which he folded in half and placed in front of Kella. It was the menu: belons *mignonettes*, duck à la bigarade with potatoes *parisiennes*, *salade frisée*, *plateau de fromage*, and mousse *au chocolat*. Kella looked at Steve, dumbfounded.

"OK, OK," he said. "I have a confession to make. No, I'm not a world-class chef. A student at the Cordon Bleu school works here in return for a place to stay. I'm doing my best to give him some practice." He smiled at his own humor. He poured Vouvray to accompany the belons, and later there would be a six-year-old Gevrey-Chambertin for the duck course, and a twelve-year-old Château Potensac with the cheese. He knew that he would have to dig deep into his pocket to replace the wines he was borrowing from his host's wine cellar.

Steve had a sip of his wine and said, "You don't have to talk about yesterday if you don't want to, OK? You look worried. We're surrounded by Paris's finest. You met them at the door. Let's just enjoy the dinner. This is the best wine I've ever tasted."

"OK, but I just want to tell you one thing." She got up from the table to get her purse on the sofa and came back, digging around in it. "This afternoon I found my notes from a seminar I attended a couple of months ago on Sharia law in the twenty-first century. I read them over because I want to make sense of Faridah's murder, I guess. I know I'll never really understand or accept it, but maybe I can get some insight into the thinking that provoked it. The speaker was a Salafist born and raised in Belgium."

Steve was surprised. "Belgium? I bet I know him. Tariq al Khalil, right?"

"You're right! Wow, that's an amazing coincidence." She fiddled around in her purse, as though distracted.

"But go ahead. I didn't mean to interrupt. Later, I also have an al Khalil story."

At last she retrieved a notebook. "Let's see—al Khalil, al Azhar University in Cairo and the Université Libre de Bruxelles, where you must have known him. He was, in my memory, supremely self-confident to the point of arrogance—not a hint of uncertainty about him." She looked up. "I remember the way he looked at his audience; it was almost mesmerizing—like a snake hypnotizing its prey."

"Well then, it's definitely the same man I knew!"

"He stressed a couple of key points." She tapped her page where words were dramatically underlined. "First, regardless of time and place, Islam is Islam, given to the Prophet by Allah, and immutable. Any changes are treasonous and constitute apostasy, or *takfir*."

"So, I guess that all interpretations over the last thirteen centuries are out the window. And the last thing they want is a discussion over the reliability of this particular version of the Quran as the word of God," said Steve.

"Exactly. Then, if being a good French citizen leads to being a bad Muslim, being a good French citizen is unacceptable. Here is a quote. 'We are under constant pressure to reform, to modernize, and I can understand this impulse. But the answer is not the modernization of Islam, but rather the Islamization of modern life. Islam is the answer.'"

Steve was actually paying little attention to the duck with orange trimmings that Benjamin had spent hours preparing. "Since Islam can't change, it's up to us to change? So we should all accept Islam, just like that? Not a lot of flexibility. By the way, 'Islam is the answer'—that's a Muslim Brotherhood slogan."

Kella nodded and shifted in her seat. "Someone asked about the oppression of women in Islam. His answer was that Islam has actually been in the vanguard of equality for women, that the Quran has raised them to full status. He quoted from a sura, 33:35. I meant to look it up. Then—and this is why I had to find my notes today—someone else asked, 'If women and men are equal under Islam, would it be all right for women to kill their husbands or fathers if they commit adultery the way that men can commit honor killings upon women suspected of having been unchaste?' "

"That must have hit home."

She had an oyster before continuing. "He almost lost it. He was trying to see who had asked the question. He said, 'You should look at your own society, which debases women by using their bodies to sell cars, to sell anything.' Frankly, he was scary. Finally, he said that what Westerners call democracy is insulting to Allah and to all Muslims. And then he turned and left the room."

"I don't think I understand why. Do you?"

"Well, since our laws are man-made and not straight from God, our laws aren't worth the paper they're written on. Any law other than God's is an insult to God. Right? I'm glad that I don't have to live in his world," Kella said.

Steve took their dinner plates to the kitchen and returned with their desserts. "So, how do you like my going-away dinner so far? How was the duck?" he asked.

"Memorable. I'll tell my grandchildren."

Between bites of mousse *au chocolat*, Kella asked, "OK, your turn. What's your al Khalil story?"

"Somehow, fine food and wine don't go together with al Khalil. I'll make it short." He had another taste of the mousse *au chocolat*. In spite of the topic, the bitterness of the chocolate and the aftertaste of Cointreau liqueur that complemented the duck sauce of the last dish satisfied his taste buds. He put his spoon down and said, "I was a student in Brussels when my father was assigned there at the embassy. He captained the American team in the annual diplomatic tennis tournament and recruited me to be his doubles partner. It turned out that al Khalil was playing for the European team, and I played against him. When a point went against him, he almost brained the referee with his racquet. His partner was barely able to stop him."

Kella said, "Same deal I guess. Western rules, rules that have not come from God, don't have to be honored. In that setting Mr. al Khalil was a misfit."

"You said it. After the match, trophies were awarded and we had dinner. Al Khalil's intense stare caused one of the female guests sitting across from him to move to another table. Al Khalil doesn't know how to behave in the presence of free-range Western women. Oh, by the way, our team won."

Kella took a sip of her Château Potensac. "There's something I've been thinking about all day," she said. Steve gestured with his spoon that she go on. "I want to take a break from school and go to Timbuktu to see my relatives. On the other hand, I can't just pick up and leave ENA. I may have to wait for a vacation or a holiday period when the school is closed. Frankly, I'm having a difficult time making decisions right now."

"A change of scenery might do you good. Why don't you come and visit me in Virginia? I'll be back there in a week or two after my Moroccan trip. I have an apartment, with a guest room."

"Thanks for the offer—it sounds lovely. But I do want to spend some time around Timbuktu where I grew up. My stepparents are off to Tel Aviv and they're busy settling in. They don't need me underfoot. Anyway, we're not going to lose sight of each other, right?"

They got up from the dining-room table and went back to the den, where they sat on the sofa. Steve put his glass down on the coffee table and took Kella's and put it down next to his. Pushing Vera to the back of his mind, he cupped her chin in his left hand and drew closer. They kissed softly. She smiled and said, "I see that free-range Western women don't scare you." Gradually, they slipped lower on the sofa, but shortly, the doorbell rang.

They looked at each other and laughed at the timing of the interruption. Like a software program that is open but not currently in charge of the computer's operations, part of Steve's mind had been thinking of Vera the whole evening. The doorbell was a welcome interruption. Was he betraying her? It had been just over a year. Was he being callous by being attracted to Kella? The bell rang again, and someone pounded on the door with a hard object. He went downstairs and opened the door.

Two policemen held a woman by each arm. She wore a hijab. Steve thought that she looked like many of the women he had seen in Saint-Denis the day before. The older policeman asked Steve, "Do you know this woman? She said she works here."

"You better ask Benjamin. He's the cook. I'll get him. One second."

Steve turned and knocked on Benjamin's door.

"Yes, what is it? How was the dinner?" He smiled proudly.

"Great, but the police want to talk to you."

"Again? Tell them I'm not here."

"No, you better come," said Steve, and he gently pulled him by the arm into the hallway.

Benjamin looked toward the open door and exclaimed, "Achoura! That's her!"

The police asked Benjamin to come outside, and Steve joined them.

Steve noticed there were several police vehicles with their lights on and engines running in the street. He looked to his left toward the Bois and saw that the street was closed off. He assumed that it was closed at the other end as well.

"We arrested this woman before she rang your doorbell. She was acting suspiciously. My men had to restrain her.

Here is what she was wearing under her clothes." He led them to one of the vehicles and pointed to the open cargo space, where one of his men was taking photos of an explosive belt.

Steve went back upstairs and left Benjamin to the tender mercies of the gendarmes. He explained what was going on to Kella. She said, "Like you said, these people are serious. I hope your friend Mr. Coogan is all right. Well, I think better go home. I'll call a taxi." She made the call.

As she gathered her coat and purse, she said, "Ever since my father's reception, ever since I met you, I've been on a roller coaster. Going back to school and normal life in Paris is going to be a relief, and a bore." She smiled. "I don't know if I can return to normal. Faridah's death has changed everything. I'm now anxious to get into the real world. I want to get involved in something more meaningful than studying. I think I'll actually miss you. Who's going to listen to me and get me out of trouble?"

"You're strong. You'll be fine. Think about coming to Virginia. But I admit that I'm not being totally altruistic here." He smiled.

"Thanks. First I'm going to go to Timbuktu as soon as I can. I think that spending some time with my cousin Thiyya, who helped raise me, will be a good thing. I will visit you in the States. I'll work it out, I promise. And I want to take you to the airport tomorrow," she said with a sad smile.

The doorbell rang again. Steve knew that Kella's taxi had somehow made its way through the security gauntlet.

CHAPTER SEVEN

Tariq al Khalil and Hussein al Kaylani followed el Maghrebi's men out of Blida and headed south toward Ghardaïa, where al Khalil hoped to meet with a local leader. They expected to get to Timbuktu in about ten or twelve days, struggling through heat and the occasional sandstorm during the day and stopping in oasis towns at night. So far, the road to Ghardaïa was broad and paved. Both cars were equipped for desert travel, with special sand filters for the air intakes, an extra jerrican of water and another of gasoline in retaining holders on each side, an additional spare tire, and tools that neither al Khalil nor Hussein knew how to use.

Hussein, normally physically unimposing, now was even less so in his oversized *jellaba*. His eyes, slits in his dark face, reflected an alertness and cleverness that some had underappreciated, at their expense. Keeping his eyes on the road and the watery-looking mirages that shimmered in the distance, he asked, "What did you think of el Maghrebi?"

Al Khalil replied, "El Maghrebi said he was a Salafist, committed to pushing the borders of the land of peace back to their former boundaries and to impose Sharia law. I think that he just wants to rearrange Algerian furniture. We will rebuild Allah's house."

Hussein said, "We need activists, doers, more than we need ideologues. Your vision is our guide. I wish we had somebody like el Maghrebi in Morocco."

"You're right. In forging a pure faith, in the heat of fire if need be, to the glory of Allah, the Beneficent, the Merciful, we need no more interpreters of the faith. But we can use all of the el Maghrebis we can find." He paused for a second and then continued, "You're right about Morocco. It's been very quiet. The leader of the cell, Lahlou, is neither a thinker nor an activist. Maybe you should pay them a visit, soon."

The men lapsed into silence. The world was losing its color; everything was becoming a sun-worn brown collage of sand and rock.

Al Khalil dozed off, but Hussein's voice woke him. Hussein gestured at the desert and said, "I hope that you have thought about this strategy very carefully. Is governing this sandbox really the way to recreate the Caliphate that you want?"

Al Khalil looked out the window at the arid, monotonous ground with the occasional group of nomads riding or walking alongside their camels.

He woke from his reverie and looked at Hussein. "The Prophet, may Allah bless him, started from Medina and conquered Arabia. His companions and successors then conquered most of the known world. They started from the desert. We, too, can start from the desert."

The thought provoked a vivid memory of al Khalil's uncle Said and of his protégé Salim Salaheldin, who were the reasons he was now driving through what Hussein called the "sandbox." The decision point for al Khalil had occurred after Said's death. Drinking dark coffee in a Brussels apartment on avenue Albert I, he had listened to Salim, his uncle's protégé and replacement.

Salim was tall and spare. Although dressed in a double-breasted suit, he could have spent the last forty days and nights in the desert. He had a hawkish profile and his hairline had receded to the top of his head. Al Khalil had always thought he dressed like a banker. "What the movement needs you to do in the countries bordering on the Sahara is what your uncle and I did in Europe. Already, we either control or can control entire towns in France, in Holland and Belgium through Sharia law."

Al Khalil knew that immigration combined with a high

birthrate made Islam the fastest growing religion in Europe. He also knew that alienation was driving many immigrants to the mosque. Some immigrants were more Muslim in Europe than they had ever been at home in Algeria or in Pakistan. One only had to look at the growing number of the faithful, especially the young, dressed in Levi's jeans, Harvard sweatshirts and Yankees baseball caps crowding around the mosques of Europe. It was easy to screen and recruit the more zealous.

Tariq hadn't replied right away, thoughtfully taking Salim's cup and his own and refilling them. When he came back with the small, steaming cups with their scent of cardamom, he stood by the window and looked down at the traffic on the broad avenue below. "Isn't putting my efforts in the Sahel a waste of my time when the countries of the Middle East, especially Egypt and Saudi Arabia, are ruled by apostates? Our future, the Caliphate, needs those countries as the pillars of our empire."

Salim had leaned back in his chair. "If you go to Cairo and speak out, you'll be killed just like your grandfather, and what will we have gained except another martyr? Martyrs are plentiful. Besides, playing the Americans' game of democracy is helping us make inroads through elections." Tariq savored the irony of taking over through democracy for the purpose of later imposing the dictatorship of the mosque through Sharia.

Salim had gone on. "Others are focusing on the Far Enemy—the United States and the other Western countries supporting the apostate leaders in the Middle East. If you can bring the populations of North Africa home, the tide will be irreversible. The Near Enemy—the corrupt leaders in Egypt, Syria and other countries—will fall like ripe dates."

He had paused. Tariq felt Salim's eyes fixing on him over his Sèvres porcelain cup. "You will realize our dream of recreating the time of unqualified glory when Islam ruled. Your mission must be to politicize minorities living on the edges of the Sahara. The way to attract them is to provide what they don't have, starting with pharmaceutical goods. Your key to success may start with the lowly aspirin." Salim laughed.

Relenting a bit, Salim had added, "Of course, your work in the Sahel can't take all of your time. It will not help us for you to become forgotten in the sands of the Sahara. You must also continue your speaking and intellectual discourse in Europe. It's what your uncle would have wanted."

Tariq had furrowed his brow as he paced. "Islam is submission. Those who will not become Muslims must still submit— they will acknowledge the dominance, the superiority, of Allah, Lord of the World, the Merciful. Or they will die." Tariq liked Napoleon's characterization of his foreign minister, Talleyrand, as an "iron fist in a velvet glove." Talleyrand had begun his political career in the Church, and al Khalil knew he could also use his religion as the path to power.

Until they neared the *wilaya* of Ghardaïa, the view from the car was made up of rocky, sometimes gravelly ground punctuated by tufts of brownish grass, bizarre black rock formations and leafless shrubs. At the initiative of el Maghrebi's men, they had stopped once, seemingly in the middle of nowhere. However, they had almost immediately been surrounded by a dozen curious nomads. For a few dinars, they had gone about collecting enough twigs for a fire, over which the driver of the lead car had made tea. The nomads had displayed a few items for sale, including "desert roses"— solidified sand shaped in the form of roses by the wind.

The scenery changed as they entered the stony M'Zab Valley, a conglomeration of five walled towns, each built on a hill and dominated by its own minaret. They drove into Ghardaïa, the largest of the five, and followed the lead car driven by el Maghrebi's men. As they passed by the mosque, its height and location symbolic of its importance, it reminded al Khalil of medieval Europe, when the Church dominated society and its cathedrals commanded the skyline.

Later, government buildings had grown higher, and today, all over the world, the highest structures were those of businesses. It was fitting, he thought, that the most horrendous blow against the West in modern times had been the attack on the Twin Towers in New York City.

Tariq noticed the different dress of people in the street. Men wore baggy trousers—beige was a favorite—and flat round hats. There were few women in the street, most totally covered in white cloaks, only one eye visible.

That night, he and Hussein walked back from the house of a religious leader they were hoping would join them, when Tariq said, "I've been thinking about Morocco. What's going on there? I think you made a mistake in appointing this fellow Lahlou to run our operations there."

Before Hussein could reply, they heard singing and shouting. They turned the corner and saw two tipsy Europeans, probably French oil workers from the Total operation in Hassi-Messaoud about two hundred fifty miles to the east. Hassi-Messaoud was Algeria's main petroleum center, operated by French, American and Italian oil companies. These foreign expats did not normally come to Ghardaïa for their R & R. Their companies paid their trips back home for a month before they returned to their oil camps in the middle of the Algerian desert for another month.

In Brussels, when confronted with repulsive behavior, he had not been able to act. Here, he had no doubt as to what he must do.

"Hussein, let's go," Tariq urged. They quickened their step to catch up. It was dusk and very few people were out.

As the Frenchmen became aware of the approaching men, one turned to the other and said, nodding toward Tariq and Hussein, "Look, Arab locals." Addressing them, he said, "We thought your town was deserted. I am so glad to see a human, even an Arab." He winked at his friend. "We came all the way from Hassi. You know Hassi-Messaoud—we're making Algeria rich! What is there to do here?"

To al Khalil, the tone of their voices was insulting. Here were infidel outsiders, exploiters of Arab resources and defilers of Islamic law. Tariq glanced at Hussein. Each understood the other.

In French, Tariq said, "It looks like you're having fun. You deserve it. Hassi must be hard work."

The drunker one said, "Yes." Tariq noticed that the other's eyes were well focused and that he was evaluating the situation.

"You won't find any restaurants open now," Tariq said. "None that serve liquor anyway."

The French spokesman said, "That's right. That's why we're going back to the hotel. My room is the only bar in this damn town. Do you know of any place that's open where we can have some fun? If you know what I mean?"

Al Khalil smiled conspiratorially at the Frenchmen and nodded at Hussein, who couldn't understand French. "We know of a place where you'll have the best time of your lives."

"Well, tell us. I guess you want money," the drunker one grumbled. He reached for his back pocket.

Tariq held up his hand. "Keep your money. We'll take you there because otherwise you won't get in. Besides, that's where we're going."

Once off the main street and into an alley, Hussein and Tariq looked around and seeing no one, on cue, drew the knives Ibrahim el Maghrebi had given them in Blida. Hussein quickly took advantage of the element of surprise. Holding his knife with the point up, he stepped forward and immediately used a killing thrust just below the rib cage and to his right, hoping to drive the knife up under the ribs to the heart. Tariq slashed at his opponent. The two Frenchmen stumbled back, looking for a way to escape. Hussein drew blood but wasn't close enough for the decisive blow. The Frenchmen turned to run, but Tariq and Hussein were quicker and soon had them on the ground. To defend themselves, the Frenchmen turned over to try to grab their attackers' hands or arms or knives.

The Frenchmen were strong and they put up a fight. They yelled for help, but if anyone heard or saw them, they didn't come to their aid. They were, however, at a disadvantage, being drunk and without weapons. Soon enough their loss of blood weakened them. Tariq's fury made him relentless. The drunker Frenchman was on the ground trying to stop Tariq's knife thrusts and was able to get both hands on Tariq's knife hand. With strength born of desperation he began to push the knife away. But suddenly Hussein kneeled over both, and with one swift and muscular motion, he slit the Frenchman's throat. Blood spurted on Tariq's hands and face. They dragged the bodies behind steps that led up to a front door so that the bodies would be hidden at least from one side. Then, quickly, they retreated.

Afterward, Tariq felt immensely satisfied and exhilarated. This was the first time he had felt relieved of the straitjacket he had been forced to wear while living and working in a non-Muslim environment. He was thinking, for the first time, that the advice of his uncle Said was more than just logically sound. He felt purified.

Al Khalil had a mixed reaction to Hussein's performance. He had dispatched his Frenchman in a very workmanlike way. But the lack of emotion puzzled Tariq. The killing of an infidel was one of the greatest acts one could perform in the service of Allah. It had greatly aroused him, while at the same time released the pent-up desire for revenge against the infidels and anger at the European world.

Al Khalil ran his fingers lightly over his cheek and saw blood on his hand. He took a handkerchief and wiped his face and his hands. Their hotel, the Rostemides, although small, was the best hotel in Ghardaïa. Built in the M'Zab style with arches, columns and minarets, it nevertheless had air-conditioning, a pool and a TV.

Back in his room, Tariq put on the TV news while he undressed to wash. Right after the soccer news—Oran 2, Annaba 1—a photo from a French paper appeared as the announcer read, "In Paris, an American working for the CIA died in a hit-and-run accident as he was crossing the street in front of the restaurant that he had just left. This photo of Dr. Coogan and of his assistant, Steve Church, appeared in the French paper *l'Humanité* two days ago when they came back from Germany, where they participated in a slander against the holy Quran. We take you live to our Paris correspondent, Lahcine al Masri."

The image changed to a middle-aged man in front of a restaurant named Chez André. "Dr. Coogan and his dinner companion, Sandrine Légier, had just left the Chez André, a favorite of writers, and were crossing the street right here"—the camera panned to a crosswalk—"when a car came out of nowhere and hit both at considerable speed. The car, described as either a dark blue Renault or a black Peugeot, did not stop. They were both taken to the hospital, but Dr. Coogan died on the way. Wait—" The correspondent pressed his left hand to the earphone from which he was apparently receiving information. "I have just learned that this may not have been an accident. A message from the Global Islamic Front Against Jews and Crusaders now claims responsibility, in revenge for Dr. Coogan's role—" He pressed a finger against the earphone. "Sorry, *alleged* role in the forged CIA documents claiming to be original versions of the Quran. Dr. Coogan's maid was arrested yesterday for attempting to kill him by exploding a bomb tied to her waist. Coogan's assistant, Mr. Church, has apparently fled the country."

Al Khalil watched in rapt attention. He had ordered Coogan's execution. However, he had had to leave before the operation was carried out. He was startled by the second person in the photograph, identified as Steve Church. He had a vague recollection of the American but couldn't place him. He made a mental note that Church had to be found and sent to join Coogan.

Al Khalil wanted to stay another day in Ghardaïa to meet with other potential backers for his vision. However, el Maghrebi's men were on a schedule and explained that they needed to get back to Blida as soon as they got al Khalil to Timbuktu. And with the killing of the Frenchmen, they needed to move on.

The next morning, Tariq, Hussein and the two men on loan from the AQIM had breakfast at the hotel. The dining room was bright with the morning light from large windows facing south. The air-conditoning was on full blast, causing Hussein to sneeze repeatedly. He got up to ask the reception to shut it off and came back to the table. The four men sat at a table on which were dates, oranges, flat bread, jam, a pot of coffee and a can of Nestlé condensed milk with two holes punched in the top.

They were alone in the small dining room until an elderly French couple came in and occupied another table, to Tariq's great annoyance. It seemed to Tariq from the Frenchman's conversation that the man had been a young officer in the French army fighting the Algerian rebels before Algerian independence. In a lowered voice Tariq announced, "I've decided that I have to stop to meet with potential backers in Adrar—"

One of the AQIM men interrupted to say, "That's almost a thousand kilometers south, on the edge of the Erg Chech."

Tariq continued, "In Adrar, I want you, Hussein, to take the Land Rover with one of you"—he pointed at the two AQIM men—"to go on to Timbuktu as fast as you can. You're right, Hussein, nothing is happening in Morocco. Fly there as soon as you can. We need action. I'll continue on with the other car on schedule. I need to gather supporters along the way."

Hussein sneezed. The air-conditioning was still on.

On their way to the cars, Tariq pulled Hussein aside. "Coogan, the American involved in the Quran documents, is dead, *al hamdu Allah*. It was on TV last night. And I recognized the guy working with him from a newspaper photo. I remember him from the university—from Brussels—another American. He was the son of a diplomat. I assume that our friends will have enough initiative to take care of him also."

CHAPTER EIGHT

Steve was in Rabat, Morocco, having lunch at the Marine House, home for the small marine detachment assigned to guard the American Embassy. The U.S. defense attaché had chosen the venue. Air-force colonel Dan Spaceck was in his late forties, tall and tanned, carefully groomed, although without a military haircut, and with remarkably white teeth. His double handshake—left hand on his opponent's right elbow—was firm. Spaceck gave off a cloying scent that Steve guessed must be cologne—it was too late in the day for aftershave. Spaceck's elegant appearance, thought Steve, was in contrast to the rather spartan surroundings. A dour Moroccan cook had prepared and served their hamburgers and French fries from a menu geared to the taste of the young marines who lived there. Steve detected the smell of stale grease when the door to the kitchen opened. He wondered why Spaceck had wanted to meet at the Marine House when there were so many more attractive restaurants in Rabat.

Spaceck took a French fry in his fingers, looked at Steve and asked, "Tell me a little bit about yourself. How did you wind up in Morocco? If you don't mind my saying so, you seem a little young to be talking to the Moroccans about such a major project." Spaceck smiled to show no implied criticism.

Steve hesitated a moment and said, also with a smile, "I guess West Gate thought I was right for the job. And the project is my idea. It seems to me that the Moroccans have a problem here with the radical Muslims. West Gate has considerable experience in counterinsurgency and counter-terrorism. How long have you been in Morocco?"

"Two years. I have another year, probably. I applied to the National War College at Fort McNair in D.C. and I'm waiting for a decision. Where else have you worked for West Gate?" Spaceck asked.

"You'll like the War College. My father did. I worked for West Gate in South Korea, Osan Air Base—"

"Osan! Did you know General Adams? Bruce Adams? He was in my class at the Air Force Academy," said Spaceck, animated.

Steve nodded vigorously. "I worked for him! West Gate ran a major counterproliferation exercise for him. I worked on it for six months just to get it set up and organized, and afterward, another month to analyze outcomes and make recommendations."

Steve didn't mention that what probably had won him the job offer from West Gate was that he had opened a NATO office in Moldova and run it for eighteen months. Nor did he mention the reason for his sudden departure.

Two young Americans walked in. They were in shorts. With their heads shaved on the sides, they could only be off-duty marines. They nodded to Spaceck. "Hi, Colonel. We ran twelve miles this morning, on the road toward Keni-tra. When are you going to join us?" They looked at each other and grinned in a way that told Steve that Spaceck was the last man on earth they expected to take the offer seriously.

Spaceck waved a greeting. "Hi, Mike," without replying to what was obviously a rhetorical question. Turning back to

Steve, he said, "Well, I'm impressed. Adams told me the exercise was a big success. What did you do after Korea?"

"I was assigned to Hickam Air Force Base in Hawaii, working for Pacific Command. And now I'm working out of the Tysons Corner office in Virginia."

Steve guessed from Spaceck's questions that the man wanted to befriend him. Spaceck was of the age and rank when he would naturally be thinking of retirement, and West Gate employed a good number of retired military. Steve wondered if Spaceck was trying to use him as a conduit toward a retirement job, which gave him pause.

He asked, "What can you tell me about the Moroccan brass I'll be meeting?"

"The first thing you need to understand is that, to the extent the Moroccans think about the type of management consultants you're talking about, those guys come from France. Except for the senior staff, the officer corps is now more oriented toward Arab countries. They speak less French and more English. And speaking of the younger officers, some are much more fundamentalist in their religious beliefs than the generals. But don't worry about it. They're more interested in stuffing their pockets than in the five pillars of Islam," Spaceck said with a grin.

Steve wondered at that analysis. He doubted that true Muslim radicals, young or old, could be bought. Besides, bribes were out of the question. Spaceck was becoming less solid by the second.

"Trust me, I know how this place works. Since I know all of these people, I can go to your meetings with you and help you establish that essential personal trust that is so important here. I can open doors for you, and after you leave, I can carry the ball for your company."

Steve didn't want or need the colonel to carry the ball, but he did want to avoid a confrontation. "Thanks. Let me see how the initial meetings go first."

They both finished their coffee, and Spaceck pressed

two of his business cards into Steve's hands. "Call me any-time. And how about giving my card to your boss back in the States? Maybe I'll give your company a call next time I'm in Washington."

They got up to leave, and on their way toward the door, Colonel Spaceck asked, "So your father is in the military? You said he was at the National War College."

"Yes, but he was a civilian. He was with the Agency, the CIA, but he's semiretired and no longer undercover. Rabat was one of his assignments. I was very young. In fact, he's writing about radical Islam and terrorism, and he wants me to scoop up anything I can find in the bookstores on the topic."

"It's still dangerous for people in this country to be writing about the terrorist side of Islam," Spaceck said. "There are Salafists here for sure, but I can't tell you more than that."

Steve said, "Well, thanks for spending the time with me. Appreciated it." Spaceck favored him with another patented handshake, then, as if it were an afterthought, said, "If you hear anything at all about a Tariq al Khalil while you're here, please let me know. He's a Salafist leader with North African aspirations."

"Tariq al Khalil a terrorist?" Steve had no desire to pro-long the conversation any longer, and he restrained himself from sharing what he knew about al Khalil. "Why do you think he's here?"

"I don't know if he is or not. We know that there are Salaf-ists around who look to him for leadership. We just don't know where they're going to strike next."

Steve stepped outside and was half-blinded by the sun's glare. He put on his sunglasses.

As Steve left, he noticed a small pickup truck parked in front of the Marine House next to a brash American car with "arrest me" red metallic paint and a mean-looking grill. Steve guessed that the only person he had seen in the Ma-rine House who could afford the car was Spaceck. He found the choice of car strange for an intelligence collector.

The driver of the truck hoisted a gas cylinder on his shoulder and walked around the side of the building toward the kitchen. The sight reminded Steve that in Morocco, all gas stoves worked off individual butane tanks. For safety reasons, the tanks were normally often outside and grounded to prevent an explosion of the pressurized gas through a build up of electrostatic charges.

Steve walked away feeling that Spaceck didn't fit into a complex North African environment that required cultural awareness and sensitivity. The man was as out of place in Morocco as al Khalil had been in Brussels. His thoughts turned to al Khalil and he wondered how successful the man was at grafting his radical views onto a society with a fairly relaxed view of Islam. And if he was indeed active in the region, what he was doing.

The red car, with Spaceck at the wheel, pulled up as Steve walked back toward his hotel. "Can I drop you somewhere? I should have offered earlier."

"No thanks. It's not far, and I need the walk," Steve answered.

CHAPTER NINE

Following the evening prayers at the Hassan II Mosque in Casablanca, Hussein followed Mohammed Lahlou, the Salafist cell leader, from the blue, white and yellow geometric tile designs of the mosque through an archway that led to several study rooms. Lahlou was a grizzled and sad-looking man who'd spent eighteen years in Moroccan prisons. He looked older than his forty-eight years, the toll of a terrorist life without the inner flame of a fanatic. For both Hussein and Lahlou, their individual trials and lives in the field, in prison or on the run were taking their toll.

Lahlou knew Hussein as a tough fighter, as ruthless in combat as with those in the movement who failed out of personal weakness or insufficient commitment. "Hussein, my brother, your visit honors us. Thanks to Allah for sending you. You are not Moroccan. Do I detect a Syrian accent?"

"Yes. I was born in Aleppo, but my family moved to Hama. My father was with the Brotherhood. Hama was an important political center for the Ikhwan," Hussein said.

"Were you in Hama during the massacre?"

"I was young, but yes, I was there. Those Syrian dogs felt threatened by the Brothers."

"And for cause, as I recall," Lahlou said.

"Old man Assad was so scared for his life that he sent his brother Rifaat to kill us all. First with artillery, then with tanks. After the fighting stopped, they killed all of our fighters and their families hiding in the damaged buildings with cyanide gas. And only then did Rifaat's Mukhabarat butchers arrive to eliminate those who were still alive."

"How many Brothers were lost?"

Hussein felt patronized. But he also never missed an opportunity to contribute to the Assad family dishonor.

"Thirty-eight thousand! May Allah receive them in his house."

"But you survived, *al hamdu Allah.*"

"The soldiers caught me. I was fourteen. They put me to work with other prisoners to clean the streets of rubble and corpses. That's how I found my father's body, may Allah favor him. That's when I made a covenant with Allah to revenge my father's execution."

Lahlou shook his head. "May you achieve your revenge," he said softly.

Hussein stopped walking and held Lahlou by the arm. "Al Khalil is not happy with you. You have put me in a bad situation. I would be sorry to lose you." In giving Lahlou his performance review, Hussein's voice was sad, as if killing Lahlou was an undesirable but unavoidable event. Hussein knew his reputation.

Lahlou said, "Al Khalil doesn't understand what's going on here. The Moroccan police are all over. Security has spies everywhere. But I have not been asleep. I have my own spies, and we are getting ready. You will see."

They resumed walking and entered the back room of the mosque, normally used by preteen students to memorize the Quran. Light green tiles with arabesques covered the lower half of the otherwise white-washed walls. Worn rugs were strewn across the floors. The only furniture was a small desk and chair in one corner. Two men in their twenties sat cross-legged on the rugs, waiting for Lahlou and Hussein. They got up when the two older men came in. They exchanged the traditional greeting, *salaam aleikum*, and bowed slightly, their right hands brushing their foreheads and ending on their hearts. One of the young men wore a faded *jellaba*. He had the typical round Moroccan face and wore tinted glasses that made him look both studious and closed. Hussein thought he looked like an accountant, but Lahlou had told him that he was a law student and an explosives specialist. The other wore stained dark slacks and a gray shirt that once had been white. He seemed to be from southern Morocco, a Berber from the Anti-Atlas Mountains.

"This is Ribb, from the Ministry of Defense—the one I told you about," Lahlou said to Hussein, gesturing toward the man in the stained Western garb. "Ribb sometimes works in the kitchen, often as a messenger, and he unloads trucks. He knows the drivers at the ministry and heard them say they had picked up an American who flew in from Paris, but the American told his driver he had started his trip from Washington," Lahlou said. He seemed pleased and nervous at the same time that he could report on a target of opportunity.

"Repeat what you told me about the American," Lahlou told Ribb.

"I know that one of our drivers picked him up at the airport and took him to the Tour Hassan Hotel in Rabat. The drivers think that he's here to set up a secret project," Ribb said.

"Is he CIA?" asked Hussein.

Ribb smiled. "Of course," he said.

"If he's CIA, why didn't the American Embassy send a car for him?" Hussein demanded.

"The very fact that an embassy car didn't pick him up proves he's CIA," Lahlou said. "He's hiding his American-government connection," Lahlou added, giving Hussein a knowing look to emphasize that he understood CIA methods. Lahlou felt he was playing at the top of his game. He was also nervous because he might be asked to mount an operation against this American. Taking on a dangerous mission had never been Lahlou's strong point.

"Well, I don't know. He could be a nobody. Why focus on him? We would do better to go after the CIA chief in Morocco, or the American ambassador," Hussein said. He suddenly remembered al Khalil's comments about the young American in Paris who was Coogan's helper. He also started putting this information together with a conversation he had had in Paris with a Moroccan diplomat who had met a young American at a cocktail party. The American was on his way to Morocco on business, allegedly. He asked the student with the tinted glasses, "Are you any good with computers, the Internet?"

The law student nodded, and Hussein told him, "A couple of days ago, there was a news report in a Paris newspaper about a Dr. Coogan who was killed by the Ikhwan. The reporter was close; the execution was ordered by al Khalil. Coogan was involved in the forgeries of the Quranic documents. I assume you know about it. There was a photo with the article. I want you to get the photograph through the

Internet. I want to know if Allah is smiling on us and answering our prayer."

The student took his glasses off and wiped one lens with his finger. "I'll make a copy of the photograph."

Ribb, the Berber, said, "I can find out from the drivers when they're supposed to take the American back to the airport."

"I'll get in touch with Tariq and see what he wants to do," said Hussein. "Maybe we can kidnap him and get some of our militants out of jail in an exchange."

"A kidnapping will wake up the whole security establishment against us," Lahlou said. "We would have to take him to Marrakech and have our men hide him. Killing him is simpler and easier. We do it and it's done." Lahlou surprised Hussein by his boldness.

"I didn't ask what would be easier," Hussein said dismissively. "Get more information on him and I'll see what Tariq has to say.

"Take me to my hotel," he instructed Lahlou. On the way, Hussein was surprised at the high number of Europeans, both men and women, in the street shopping or otherwise going about their business. He noticed that most women wore the usual loose *jellabas* down to their ankles, but that many were without veils. Some walked with long strides that revealed their high-heeled shoes. In fact, it seemed to him that they wanted their European fashion to show. He was startled, to say the least, that one woman's high-heeled shoes were bright red. Al Khalil would go ballistic, he thought.

The next morning, Hussein and Lahlou met at the mosque, and Lahlou suggested they go to a café he often frequented. "More comfortable," he said. They walked out of the mosque into the maze of old passageways and narrow streets without sidewalks. Here, Hussein noticed, the occasional European stood out, unlike in the more modern part of the city. On a broader street, they went past a theater playing an

Egyptian movie. The women were all veiled. None dared to wear Western garments, least of all red high heels.

Hussein said, "I sent an e-mail to al Khalil about the American. No answer yet. But I know what he'll say. Do it, with greatest impact. So start planning."

Hussein didn't know Casablanca, but he knew the culture of the Arab world's rabbit warrens, be they called casbahs or medinas. Each political party and labor union had its public fronts and its underground factions. The ruling families, many claiming to be descended from the Prophet, the Arab equivalent of *Mayflower* ancestry, had its alliances based on strategic marriages and grievances going back generations. Each group kept an eye on the others through paid informants, ambitious men aspiring to become members of the organization or family, and others seeking favors. Watching them all was the king's security service. The pecuniary opportunities for clever informants, who frequently were able to sell their information to several paymasters, were abundant. But establishing and violating trusts, the essence of the game, was a high-risk enterprise. Those who did not grasp this ground truth either disappeared or survived as maimed warnings.

Hussein looked about him with the surface interest of a visitor but with the educated eyes of a master of the game. He assumed that their walk was not unobserved. He also assumed that Lahlou had a reason for taking him on this walk through the labyrinths of the old city. Hussein wondered if Lahlou was cleverer than he appeared, if perhaps in this warren he, Hussein, was the rabbit rather than the ferret.

They reached a café, whose owner welcomed Lahlou. Hussein assumed he was part of Lahlou's network. Lahlou led the way inside and they sat at a small table in the back by the wall. The air was heavy with smoke. No women or tourists had ever crossed the threshold. The owner came over immediately with a pot of sweet mint tea and two glasses decorated in imitation gold leaf.

Hussein asked, "What is your source for your information on the American, besides Ribb, I mean?"

Lahlou hesitated a second and replied, "Our informant knows a colonel at the American Embassy. He wants to retire in Morocco after he leaves the air force next year."

"What about the visiting American?"

"Spaceck, that's the colonel, said that the visitor really is a nobody and that he, Spaceck, could get them a better deal on anything they want."

"But is the visitor CIA?" Hussein insisted.

"Oh, here is what my lawyer got from the Internet." He handed the photo and the article about Coogan and Steve to Hussein.

"So, is this the same person?"

"I don't know yet. Ribb will show it to the driver and get back to me."

"Let me know as soon as possible," Hussein said with a slight smile of anticipation.

"All right, I'll call you at the hotel. In any case, Spaceck said that the American's business story doesn't make sense, and that he is too young to have the job he claims to have."

Hussein smiled. This Spaceck character could be useful, he thought. But he also wondered if Spaceck wasn't trying too hard. Perhaps his reasons went beyond money. Maybe Spaceck was the spy. Hussein had survived in an environment rife with duplicity, betrayals and obscure motivations.

That night, Lahlou called Hussein at his four-room hotel in the depths of the medina. "My brother, you were inspired by Allah. You were right."

Hussein answered, "*Al hamdu Allah*. You know what to do."

Before al Khalil answered his first message, Hussein sent

him a second one. "The merchandise is genuine. I will consummate the transaction, which will terminate the Berlin-Paris activity. There is only one God, only one Quran." As an afterthought, he added, "May Allah bless this enterprise."

CHAPTER TEN

In his hotel room at the Tour Hassan, Steve checked his e-mail. He and his father, Marshall, used a still-experimental encryption system developed by the Los Alamos National Laboratory to secure their e-mail communications. Based on his CIA experience, Marshall had said, "Don't write anything that would get sources killed, cause catastrophic consequences or embarrass you or your employer if it appeared in the *New York Times*." Steve had long ago concluded that his father and the CIA had too many rules.

Marshall's last message to Steve said, "Just a reminder to get in touch with my friend Abdelhaq in Morocco. He hasn't seen you since Iran in 1978 or '79. You'll enjoy his hospitality, as well as the best Moroccan meal in the country."

When preparing for his trip from Virginia, Steve had not done enough to set up his schedule in Rabat. But other than the car sent to pick him up at the airport by the Ministry of Defense, the few appointments he had made seemed to have been written in disappearing ink. He spent a day showing up for appointments in Rabat, only to be told by smiling secretaries that either her boss was busy or out of town, or that the very important person for whom she worked would deign to see him very soon, *insha'llah*—if God willed. "Very soon" invariably turned into a wait of hours, and Steve was muttering to himself, "Welcome to the Third World."

He had PowerPoint presentations on the three main topics that he hoped would interest the Moroccans. First, he'd present the accumulated experiences and lessons learned from the U.S. Army special-ops warriors. What they had to say about Iraq and Afghanistan should be of interest to the Forces Armées Royales, the FAR, that was still fighting the Polisario in Mauritania. Second, he would present the use of technology in keeping track of insurgents and terrorists through ground sensors and unmanned air vehicles. And third, Steve had learned that the FAR were planning major relocations of their bases away from the cities to the less developed areas of the country. West Gate had a track record of helping establish new bases in Iraq and of moving old ones in the United States. West Gate could offer people with hands-on experience in all of these areas. Steve was convinced that West Gate could add value to Morocco's military capability and that Morocco's $1.3 billion defense budget could add value to West Gate's bottom line. Steve could already see himself into a new corner office.

Steve went out to see the city before leaving for his first appointment. The taxi took him by his old house, his school, and eventually left him off at the Salé medina. Salé had been a home port to Barbary Coast pirates in the eighteenth century and now offered the best shopping in Rabat. A water seller with bare legs, sandals, a short tunic with red and gold fringes but no sleeves and a large flat hat in several colors from which small bells hung, was trying to attract customers at the entrance to the medina by ringing a bell he held in his hand. Steve went by this Moroccan Harlequin as someone made a purchase. Harlequin unhooked a brass cup from several hanging from a bandolier across his chest and filled it with water from a water skin hanging from one shoulder. Steve entered a narrow alley lined with stalls.

He wandered through the alleyways of the small Salé medina.

He stopped to watch an artisan chiseling intricate

geometric designs on a round brass tray. He could see several finished products hanging in the shop and bought one after a bout of rigorous and expected bargaining. Farther on, he started to bid for a hand-made Rabat rug, blue designs in the center on a field of red, that would have to be shipped. But it was getting late. He suspended the negotiations and went back to his hotel.

Once in his room, he wanted to check his PowerPoint presentation one more time and went to his laptop. It had been turned off for the last two hours but was surprisingly warm to the touch. Concerned, he quickly went through the password and thumb-print identification procedure and satisfied himself that his presentations were still there. It seemed unlikely that the hotel maid had been surfing the Internet or that she could even get through his biometric security software. He returned to his dresser and wished that he had paid more attention when taking fresh clothes from the drawers. He couldn't be sure, but on closer inspection, he thought that his clothes were not as he had arranged them when taking them out of the suitcase. He had brought brochures to leave behind after his meetings and, on checking them, was sure that someone had been through them; they were definitely out of order. He found no other suspicious indications but wondered whether he should have "trapped" drawers and doors as he had seen in the movies. Nothing had been stolen, as far as he could tell. He was annoyed that one of his father's stories forced itself on him. From his service in Romania, he had concluded that if a surreptitious visitor has taken nothing, it is most likely that he has left something behind. Steve started looking for microphones halfheartedly and self-consciously, a bit embarrassed. Wasn't this just another of his father's rules? Still, he felt uneasy.

The next day, Steve walked out of his hotel toward the center of town and went into a shop. Several singletons came in after he did—two men and a woman. None paid attention to him. He went out, walked two blocks to another shop and again observed people who came in shortly after he did, ostensibly looking at the merchandise. None was a repeat. He figured that the people he was looking for were probably young men, which allowed him to eliminate 75 percent of his possible surveillants thus far. He went to one more shop and he had a repeat, a young Moroccan in sunglasses, a New York Yankees T-shirt and Nikes, easy to remember. He then took a cab to the Mausoleum of Mohammed V, the monarch in power when Morocco became independent in 1956. There he told the driver to wait, and went up the marble steps of the white crenellated mausoleum past a guard in red, with a white cape, black boots and a green fez. The guard's rifle looked very much like an M1, the U.S. Army's primary infantry weapon in World War II and Korea. As a member of Lehigh's rifle team, he had seen but never fired the weapon. He wondered if that was the vintage of the average FAR weaponry.

At the top of the steps, he looked back at the surrounding ruins of the old mosque on which the mausoleum was built and noticed New York getting out of a cab in back of the one Steve was still using. New York had a friend, same age, about twenty-five, also slight of build but at least five ten. Steve concluded that the unwanted attention was not a mugging in the making. They didn't seem threatening; they apparently just wanted to keep him in sight. He cut short his surveillance detection, went back to the hotel to pick up his briefing materials and headed for the ministry, positioning himself in the backseat so as to keep his eyes on the cab's rear- and side-view mirrors. A white Fiat shepherded him from the hotel to the ministry.

He arrived early for his meetings and drank more sweet tea than he really wanted while he waited. He sensed a changing attitude for the better from the outer offices. The Moroccan officers liked that he had been in Morocco as a young boy and that he was familiar with their country. His presentations were also creating interest.

The colonel with whom he had met walked him out of his office and gave him a promising handshake as he left, further bolstering Steve's confidence. His next appointment was at a training camp—not far from Rabat, he had been told—whose commandant was interested in West Gate's interactive software, Urban Warfare Tactics for Small Unit Leaders 2.0, not at the top of Steve's priority list. Nevertheless, it was a useful entrée to the training side of the FAR.

The ministry car assigned to him was waiting. They left at ten twenty-five. As they headed out of town, Steve heard something loose in the trunk clanging against one side and then the other on the turns and over bumps, as if the spare tire was not well secured. They were not quite beyond Rabat's city limits when the driver received a call.

"Mr. Church, General Labibi has asked me to bring you back to the ministry," the driver said. It was ten thirty-eight.

General Labibi was one of the heretofore-unavailable principals. Steve hoped that Labibi's sudden interest meant that his project was picking up traction with Labibi's superiors. Steve decided to go back. He told the driver, who parked in the street outside the ministry entrance, "I'll be right back. Keep that air conditioner on. I think something's banging around in the trunk—can you hear it? Is it the spare?"

The driver merely shrugged.

Steve was inside General Labibi's outer office for no more than five minutes when he, and most likely everyone else in Rabat, heard a thunderous explosion.

Shards of glass from the window flew across the room like arrows seeking their targets. A uniformed officer fell to the ground with a glass shard in his neck. The building rocked. Inside the offices of the ministry, the blast was followed by several seconds of total silence. Steve, the secretary to whom he was speaking and the dozen officers and secretaries either sitting or walking through the office froze as if the projector depicting their lives had stopped. They looked at each other questioningly for another second. Then the choreography broke down. The slow learners rushed to the windows, others attacked the telephones and a few ran out. Steve heard a secretary stage-whisper, "It's a coup!" The room reeked of fear born of confusion and uncertainty.

Since everyone was ignoring him, Steve extracted the glass from the fallen officer's neck, grabbed a Moroccan flag from the wall and gave it to him to stop the bleeding, and walked out, anticipating the damage, but uncertain just how bad it would be.

In spite of his expectation, the sight of the wreckage stopped him in his tracks. A half dozen people had reached the site of the explosion. Some had started to help the wounded. He walked the spot where his car had been, through still-falling small debris and dirt. He put his handkerchief to his nose. It was abnormally quiet, as if the noise from the blast had stopped everything and everyone in the city. The only sound came from the several people on the sidewalk; the injured were moaning. He could see a deep hole in the street where the car had been parked. The twisted metal remains of the car were scattered over the street and the sidewalk as far as he could see. The chassis, on its side about twenty feet from the hole, burned fiercely at the base of a tall plume of black smoke.

He turned away from the heat of the burning fuel. His eyes scanned the bodies of the victims to try to find the driver. Drawn by dark trousers at the bottom of a garden wall adjacent to the ministry building, he walked around the bodies of the victims. He reached the dark trousers. The lower half of his driver's body was at his feet. A white hip bone contrasted with the intestines partially spilled on the ground in a widening pool of blood. The blast had pulverized the driver's head and upper body. One shoe was missing. Steve's insides tightened. He doubled over and vomited violently.

The constriction of his abdomen closed his eyes, but he still saw the legs with the missing shoe. Suddenly it overlaid with a memory from Moldova several years before. He was looking at the body of his friend and Russian translator Misha, his head oozing blood from two small holes, his legs outstretched, one shoe missing.

Assigned by NATO to open an office in Chisinau, capital of Moldova, he had been driving with Misha to go meet with leaders of the breakaway Transnistria Republic on the eastern side of the Dniester River. At Misha's initiative after driving for two hours, they had stopped at a village for coffee.

A waiter came to take their order. Misha said, "You need to taste mamaliga. *It's a local dish. I ordered it for you."*

After the waiter left, Misha picked up the menu and laughed. Reading from the back of the menu, he said, "Romanians have odd proverbs. Listen to this one: Muncat bine, baut bine, dimineatsa sculat mort. *It means, he ate well, he drank well, in the morning he was found dead." He laughed and shrugged his shoulders.*

The waiter brought their coffee and their orders. Steve tasted his mamaliga *and said, "This tastes no better than it looks. It's cornmeal mush, right?"*

Misha finished his coffee first and said, "I'll meet you by the car. Take your time. Have the last gogosh." *He got up and headed for the men's room, and Steve reached for the donut that Misha had put on his plate.*

The waiter was not in sight, and Steve waited for the bill. Eventually, he went to a heavyset and heavily made-up woman sitting behind a small counter near the door and paid. As he turned toward the door, he heard two popping noises, followed by the sound of a car accelerating out of the dirt and gravel parking lot. When Steve reached his car, Misha was dead.

The next few hours had been a blur. The police had questioned him extensively about Misha, his background, his friends. Steve knew that Misha had been in Afghanistan serving with a unit of the Soviet Spetsnaz, the Soviet Special Forces. Misha had talked about it openly. He had even given Steve his former uniform, at the time a souvenir of the Cold War.

A police inspector had said, "Your translator was a KGB officer. How could you not know that?" Another had said, "This Misha was just another Russian trying to get rich by running guns to the secessionists."

His NATO boss had brought him back to Brussels twenty-four hours after the killing. Steve had forever been sorry that he had not stayed and seen the investigation through. He felt strongly that Misha would not have betrayed him. But Steve would not have been surprised if Misha had been involved in the arms trade.

Steve came to believe that the Moldovan government had killed Misha and had orchestrated the subsequent character-assassination campaign. Steve was convinced he could have done something for his friend had he stayed.

He shook off the memory and stood up. People continued to spill out of the ministry. Sirens wailed in the distance. With all the resolve in his body, he pledged to avenge this mindless act of terror. At the same time, he looked around with new apprehension. Who were these people? Why was he of such interest? He busied himself trying to help the wounded until ambulances arrived.

Hussein had driven from Casablanca to Rabat in record time and was soon in Lahlou's apartment in Rabat's New Medina. He was halfway up the stairs when the scratchy recorded voice of the muezzin called the faithful to prayer from overstressed loudspeakers at the top of the nearby mosque. He joined Lahlou in prayer as soon as he entered the one-room apartment.

Hussein held his anger in check until the end of prayers. "You are an incompetent idiot! You told me you had it planned to the minute. Now, not only is this American still alive, you've made us look like fools."

Lahlou, shoulders sagging, said, "It was fate. The American returned to Rabat. He got out of the car."

"All you did was kill a Moroccan government employee, wound a few others and demolish one of the king's cars. May Allah have mercy on you!" Hussein said, unable to keep his voice and anger down.

"We used a timed charge. It was set with a ten-hour delay at one o'clock this morning. Ribb knew that the American had an appointment and would be in the car for about forty-five minutes on the way to the military camp where he had an appointment at eleven fifteen. Very precise timing. Not my fault. It was Allah's will," Lahlou said. He was sweating.

"A timed charge? Are you crazy? A timed charge robs you of control over the time of the explosion. Why didn't you set off the explosion remotely? Further, why did you involve the ministry? You could have killed the American in his room, on the street, anywhere. Why in a government car? Now military security is going to take this as an attack on them and put all of our people under great pressure!" Hussein thundered.

Lahlou shook his head. "Security doesn't know anything about the identity of our militants. We're underground." He wiped his face with a handkerchief. The pitch of Lahlou's voice went up as he continued his bluster. "They'll huff and puff for a couple of weeks, and then everything will be back to normal. Besides, we have our own informants in military security."

"I want you, Ribb and your so-called explosives expert, and anyone else who knows about me, to get out of town and go into hiding. I'm leaving the country first thing tomorrow, while I still can," Hussein said.

CHAPTER ELEVEN

In Marin County, California, Steve's father, Marshall Church, just back from the gym, prepared for a TV interview. He looked at his red-walled office and didn't even try to organize the papers and books on and around his desk. What might appear as confusion to an outsider made perfect sense to him.

Since the CIA had approved Marshall's request to drop his cover, the San Francisco media had discovered him and regularly contacted him anytime there was terrorist-related news. Marshall initially found the sudden attention gratifying. But he became less available when he saw how the media cherry-picked sound bites to fit the anchor's agenda.

The phone rang. "Marshall, how are you?" It was Abdelhaq al Fassi. Marshall had recruited Abdelhaq for the CIA during the 1978–79 Islamic revolution that overthrew the Shah when both Marshall and Abdelhaq, a Moroccan intelligence officer, were posted to Tehran. They had contacted each other following their respective retirements, and their friendship had grown, transcending the typical case officer–agent relationship. "Abdelhaq, we're all fine. In fact, my son Steve is in Morocco on business. I was going to call you myself to tell you," Marshall said.

"Well, it's Steve I'm calling about. I haven't spoken to him yet. But something has happened. Military security is talking to him, and that's why he hasn't had a chance to call you himself."

"What in the world does security want with Steve?" Marshall asked.

"An IED blew up a Ministry of Defense car he was using. Steve wasn't in it at the time. He's OK. We think it was a Salafist operation. It just happened, so we don't know much more than what I've just told you," Abdelhaq said.

Marshall's grip tightened around the phone. "Don't keep anything from me."

"Well, I've been away and just came back to town. But security heard from one source that there was Islamist interest in an American who was supposed to be a recent arrival and a CIA officer. I'm not connecting this with Steve right now, but who knows?"

"I assume you'll see him soon?"

"Consider it done. His company must think well of him to send him on such an important business mission by himself."

"To tell you the truth, Abdelhaq, I sometimes don't recognize him. He always tested and interviewed very well, but school bored him. Too many rules, he said. He was stronger on the people side."

A few minutes later, the doorbell rang. Through the window Marshall saw the TV crew. He first straightened a small frame. It read, "WE FACE A HOSTILE IDEOLOGY, GLOBAL IN SCOPE . . . RUTHLESS IN PURPOSE AND INSIDIOUS IN METHOD. UNHAPPILY THE DANGER IT POSES PROMISES TO BE OF INDEFINITE DURATION. Farewell radio and television address to the American people by President Dwight D. Eisenhower, January 17, 1961."

He put on his blazer before realizing it was the one with the Knights of Malta crest on the pocket. He quickly changed his jacket and then put his tennis racquet in a closet out of sight next to a German Heckler & Koch G3 rifle that had hung in his office until recently. His wife had finally convinced him that it made their home look too martial. He opened the door.

Bruce, the Channel 32 producer, and his cameraman came in. Their white van with the dish antennae was parked in his driveway. Marshall brought them upstairs to his office. He knew they preferred his office for these interviews because of the large framed 1676 map of the world decorated with likenesses of the rulers of the time, and a large globe on a wooden stand.

"Thanks for letting us come out," Bruce said. He was in his early forties, with short dark hair, just under six feet and fairly trim. With the long sleeves of his checkered blue and white shirt rolled up, Bruce was all business, but in a smooth, nonconfrontational style. "We'd like to talk to you today about the latest terrorist video that al Jazeera aired last night."

The cameraman set up his equipment and aimed his lens on the globe, with a close-up of the Middle East. Marshall sat with his back to his desk and to the map. Bruce asked, "Last night, Zawahiri again mentioned their goal to recapture Andalusia. That's been a theme in al Qaeda's public statements over the years and one that we have not explored. What is that all about?"

Looking into the camera, Marshall said, "Until a Frankish army stopped it in the eighth century, Islam expanded by force of arms into the vacuum left by the virtual disappearance of the Roman Empire. For several hundred years afterward it continued to rule over Spain, which they called Andalusia. The Islamists now claim all of the countries in their former Caliphate, from Spain to Bukhara, Tashkent, the Philippines and Burma."

Bruce said, "Of course, they can't be serious. The world has changed."

Marshall replied, "In his last statement, the Prophet Muhammad declared that Allah had ordered him to spread the faith to all corners of the earth, to bring Islam to all unbelievers. This is taken literally by the radical Muslims."

Marshall pointed to the portraits on the map. "This fellow on horseback, Muhammad IV, between Louis XIV of France and Pope Innocent XI here at the top, was the Ottoman caliph. After conquering Baghdad in the thirteenth century, the Turks established the Muslim capital in Istanbul, and until Attaturk shut down the concept of the Caliphate in 1924, the Arab lands were basically Turkish provinces. Then, in World War I, the Turks were on the wrong side, after which the British carved up the Ottoman Empire into new countries. The fundamentalists have never accepted the partitions. But that's a topic for another time."

After the interview, Marshall called Steve, who picked up on the second ring. "Steve, what's going on?"

"Hi, Dad. Moroccan security wanted to know anything I could tell them about the explosion, which was nothing. I did tell them that I thought I might have been followed." Steve recounted details of the men who'd followed him.

"Keep in mind that there are a lot of criminals out there looking for rich Americans," Marshall said. "They're usually focused on tourist sites. But if they meet the time and distance test—if you see the same people in separate locations over time—then they're probably professionals and have interests other than just stealing your wallet."

"One of the security guys debriefing me, Driss Benjelloun, looked uncomfortable. He squirmed when I told them about the surveillance. I got the feeling that he knew more than he was letting on. Security offered to give me a bodyguard if I wanted one. I said no. But I have the feeling that they'll keep an eye on me anyway."

"You should just get the hell out of Morocco," Marshall told him. "In the meantime, get in touch with Abdelhaq right away. I just spoke with him by telephone. With his background and his contacts, he should be able to help you out and find out what's really going on."

"What should I do if I'm under surveillance again? Tell me how to lose them," Steve said.

"In your case, go to the nearest authority—the police or the embassy. Usually, if the surveillance is official, it's best to ignore them and lull them to sleep. Convince them you're not a threat. If the surveillance is official, you really can't escape them except for brief periods. They'll simply bring more resources to bear. But these guys tried to kill you, Steve. This is serious. I want you to get on an early plane."

Steve said he would think about it.

After hanging up, Marshall reflected on what he knew from both Abdelhaq and from Steve. Should he go to Morocco? Was Steve safe by himself? There was no hard indication that the attack was against Steve. The car could have been a target of opportunity based on the hope it would kill an important general. If the Salafists were targeting Steve, what was the reason? It didn't make sense that it was just because he was an American. There were plenty of Americans in Morocco. Maybe they thought he was selling weapons.

Could Steve, untrained in basic intelligence tradecraft, handle this situation? He knew that Steve was not averse to physical risk. But this was clearly different. Marshall recalled that Steve's Myers-Briggs test results had painted him as extroverted, sensing, thinking, perceiving and the "ultimate realist." Objective, analytic, yet spontaneous and action-oriented. A good formula for assessing the danger and acting accordingly. Marshall understood the frailty of psychological assessments, but in this case, he felt confident that Steve would make the right decisions.

Morocco was Abdelhaq's turf. He and Abdelhaq had faced danger together, and he knew the man to be cool and decisive when necessary. Marshall figured he would probably get an ulcer worrying, but he decided to stay put.

CHAPTER TWELVE

When Steve opened his hotel door, he was face-to-face with a smiling man about his own height. A ring of gray-white hair circled the bald top of the man's head. He had a bushy gray mustache and wore tan slacks, a lightweight dark blue jacket and a loose checkered tie that exposed the open top button of his dark blue shirt.

Steve took some clothes from the easy chair and motioned for Abdelhaq to sit down, while he sat on the bed.

Abdelhaq glanced around the room and his eyes came to rest on Steve. "It's a pleasure to meet you as a young man. I first met you about thirty years ago in Tehran. I spoke to your father yesterday."

"My father told me to be sure and get in touch with you while I'm here. Although he wants me to leave on the next plane." Steve smiled. "He spoke highly of you. You know about the explosion?"

"That's why I'm here. I'm in charge of the investigation. I need your help. Please tell me everything you told security. This is looking more and more like the work of the Salafists."

Steve gave him every detail he could remember, and then said, "Salafists, Salafists! That's become a mantra. A couple of weeks ago, I had barely heard the term."

"Do you know about this article? Do you know that Dr. Coogan is dead?" Abdelhaq asked as he handed Steve a copy of the article naming him Dr. Coogan's assistant.

"Dead?" Steve exclaimed. "What happened? He was slightly wounded by some nut who attacked him with a knife in Berlin, but I didn't think it was serious."

"This was a hit-and-run later claimed as an execution by a Salafist cell. Since you're identified as Coogan's assistant, you were probably the target yesterday. What's your role in this Quranic-document affair?"

Steve recounted what Coogan had told him and added, "But I was never his assistant. I was just visiting him for a couple of days." Steve took a deep breath and stood up. He went to the window and looked outside with a slight frown. He turned around and said, "I want to help catch whoever did this. The IED killed people, innocent people, just people walking by. These were senseless murders. I want to help send those guys away for a long time." Steve looked Abdelhaq in the eyes to make certain he understood his commitment.

"What you can do is to stay here and finish your business. Right now you're our only connection to those who blew up the car—until the interrogations that are going on now shed some light on all this."

Steve mulled that over for a moment. "Like a tethered goat to attract the lion. Can you protect me?"

"I'll have you covered. The minute you leave the hotel, I'll have discreet protection on you."

"Isn't this ironic? I came to sell expertise on counterterrorism, and now I'm in the middle of a counterterrorist operation."

"Don't worry, we have our own counterterrorist experts."

"Are your Salafists homegrown?"

"In a way, you can compare them to the old Communist parties. Like them, they have local activists, and they have a unifying ideology that comes from outside. This time, instead of Marxism and Leninism, the dogma is subverted from the Quran, written for seventh-century Bedouins. The radicals claim that it has all the rules that humankind needs. In American terms, it's the Constitution, the Bible, the Bill of Rights and the rules of the Securities and Exchange Commission all rolled into one. But they regard man-made laws to be sacrilegious, to be an affront to Allah."

Steve nodded. "A constituency of one, Allah. Well, I assume that you have a plan, other than dangling me out there to draw their fire, right?"

Abdelhaq smiled. "You remind me of your father. He's more concerned with the practical than with the philosophical. As a matter of fact I do have a plan, and it should allow you to leave when your business is concluded, whether we have arrested the terrorists or not. You stay in Morocco for a while, go about your business normally. Your continued presence should bring the bad guys out. You'll be protected, don't worry."

"My father trusts you, so I do as well. Plus, I still have work to do with the Ministry of Defense."

"There is a Moroccan proverb that tells us, 'If you know his father, you may trust his son.' I know you will do the right thing in a crisis. The minister knows about the threats against you. Go to your meetings. You'll be protected. And don't worry—you won't lose your contract."

"And . . . ?" Steve said. Despite Abedlhaq's reassurances, he felt unsure.

"First thing in the morning, I want you to go see a friend of mine, a photographer, in Fez. He'll fit you with a disguise and an alias, including a passport that will allow you to leave the country 'black'—that is, in a way that will hide the fact that you've left. We don't want to drag this out too long. Marshall would not allow it." He smiled. "If we don't catch them soon, you can still leave the country in a few days. I assume the Salafists have their sources and will know as soon as you go through airport controls if you go under your true name. Their searching will make them more visible to me."

Steve was off to Fez in a rental car the next morning. He frequently glanced into the rearview mirror but could see no car behind him. On one hand, if there was a friendly tail on him, he was happy that they were so invisible, so professional. But was there really a friendly team keeping an eye on him?

Once in Fez, he parked near the Palais Jamai and headed for the photographer's shop. He was thirty seconds away from the car when he abruptly turned around—he had forgotten to lock the car. When he reached it, a man in his midtwenties wearing a black long-sleeve Nike sport shirt and sunglasses, and with long curly black hair, was peering into his car. He turned away as soon as Steve came into view. Steve watched him get into the back of a black BMW. Steve concluded the car must have just reached the large parking lot, as its engine was running and he could see two people in the front. Steve almost gave a friendly wave to the occupants of the car but restrained himself—it might not be professional to wave to your guardian angels.

He directed his steps toward Fez's medina in search of Daud, Abdelhaq's friend, and his shop. The air was heavy with the scent of jasmine. Cascading bougainvilleas lit up the whitewashed walls with brilliant shades of crimson, orange, yellow and purple.

The alleys of the medina were crowded with merchants and tourists. Young children wove in and out on their way to the bakeries, balancing wooden boards on which rested round loaves of unbaked bread. A donkey carrying cases of Coca-Cola in wicker baskets strapped to his sides rocked and rolled down the alley, forcing Steve to step into a shop that sold brass and copper trays. Since the donkey effectively blocked traffic, Steve had time to look at an artisan etching geometric designs on a tray with a hammer and a center punch. He resumed his walk, steering clear of the leather tanning area because of its smell of urine and noxious chemicals. But he did like the smell of finished leather in an alley specializing in belts, saddles and *babouche* slippers.

He walked into the photographer's shop, where a young man in Western slacks and long-sleeve shirt approached him. Steve asked for Daud, the owner. With a knowing smile, the salesman went to the back of the store and disappeared behind a dark curtain. Daud came out quickly. His gray hair and gold-rimmed glasses gave him the air of a professor.

In a low, conspiratorial voice that made Steve feel more nervous than secure, he said, "We cannot meet here. Maybe someone has followed you." Looking toward the front of the shop carefully, Daud guided Steve beyond the curtain with great respect. Steve followed him into a long and narrow room, past boxes and files that overflowed the narrow shelves. Daud managed to squeeze in between the wall and a large wooden desk. He sat behind it and invited Steve to take a plastic chair in front. Steve noticed *HMS Invincible* inscribed on the front of the desk.

Peering from behind a twenty-four-inch cutting-edge flat-screen iMac computer, Daud spoke in French. "Yes, the desk comes from a sunken British ship. My father, may Allah keep him, bought it in Tangier many years ago. His Excellency, Mr. al Fassi, has of course told me you would come. We need to go to my house, where I will outfit you with all you need. To avoid bringing troublemakers with you, you will follow my directions exactly. There is one long street with nothing but brass plates, lamps and decorations of all kinds. Do you know where it is?"

"Yes, I was just there," said Steve, remembering the Coca-Cola donkey.

At that moment, the young man from the front of the shop joined them and stood by the curtain, keeping an eye on the shop.

"Start from the east and walk west. My son Youssef"—he pointed to him—"will be at the far end of that alley. If Youssef detects no surveillance behind you, he will run his hand through his hair. That means you're OK, no one is behind you, and he will lead you to my house."

Youssef stepped closer to Steve and said, in good American-accented English, "If I do not signal, that means you are being followed. You should then enter the last brass shop on the left side of the alley and quickly walk to a door in the back before any surveillants draw abreast of the shop. The door will lock when you close it behind you. A guide will be there to take you to my father's house."

Daud gave Steve precise instructions on how to get to the alley. He said it would take him about twenty minutes.

Youssef added, "Don't deviate from that route. There will be friendly eyes on you at key locations until the final checkpoint, when you will see me."

Steve had not gone farther than the first hunded yards of his choreographed walk when he sensed rather than felt something in back of him. He instinctively put his hand on his wallet and closed his fingers around a small wrist. He turned to find a young boy at the other end of the wrist. The boy began yelling in Arabic, "American, American, money for my mother, in *hôpital*!" Steve retrieved his wallet and was about to focus on the little Moroccan thief, but his attention was diverted by a millisecond sighting of Curly, whom he had seen hovering around his car. Steve thought he had seen him behind a group of Japanese tourists—not a wise concealment choice for a full-size Moroccan. But he had disappeared. Likewise, the boy had taken advantage of Steve's distraction to make his getaway. Remembering Abdelhaq's assurances, he was tempted to believe that Curly's presence was a positive sign. However, he was getting confused.

When Steve arrived at the end of the surveillance-detection route, he was relieved to see Youssef run his fingers through his hair. Youssef walked Steve quickly into the heart of the old quarter. As they went by the old, and historical, Karaouine Mosque, Steve wondered if this was the smartest route. If Salafists or their sympathizers were around, they'd most likely use the mosque as their Fez head-quarters. He put his head down and kept walking; it was too late to change routes, and he had no choice but to trust Youssef.

They walked down an alley flanked by windowless walls about three stories high and came to a nail-studded wooden door with a large iron lock and handle. The door opened instantly when Youssef tapped the palm of his hand against its surface. They stepped into a world out of *The Thousand and One Nights*: a lush garden, a riot of greens and yellows and pinks, surrounding a bubbling fountain. Several dark-skinned servants hurried about. Daud welcomed him and ushered him inside a room bordering on the garden.

Daud was the perfect traditional Moroccan host. He placed loose tea, lumps of sugar, and sprigs of mint in a sil-ver teapot. At his signal, a servant brought boiling water, which Daud poured in the pot. After pleasant conversation concerning the history of Fez, Daud took the teapot and poured first with the spout close to the glass, and gradually extended his arm to produce a long stream of steaming tea between pot and glass, never spilling a drop. They each drank the traditional three cups.

Then Daud introduced Steve to what he called his atelier, his workshop—an office-sized room with dozens of wall-mounted wooden drawers and cabinets, a square work ta-ble on one side, running water and a waist-level counter on the other. Out of one cabinet, inside of which were smaller pull-out drawers, he selected pairs of glasses. He tried sev-eral on Steve and finally selected a highly noticeable black-rimmed pair. He then looked at Steve's hair and opened another cabinet, inside of which were rows of wigs on wire wig stands.

He explained to Steve, "The idea is to make you look older and give the observer something to fix his attention on away from your basic unchangeable *physionomie*—your height and bone structure, for example. We could change those also but not in a couple of hours, as Mr. al Fassi wants, and not on such short notice."

He outfitted Steve with salt-and-pepper hair and a severely receding hairline. Steve looked in the mirror and saw himself aged fifteen to twenty years—an expert job, he thought. Daud took his picture with the disguise on for Steve's new Canadian passport, then removed the disguise, explained to Steve how to put it on and slipped it into a small cloth bag. He went into an adjoining room for a half hour and came back with the passport.

He told Steve, "You are a Canadian tourist, Ian Ross. You came from Paris five days ago. You're on your way to Dakar, Senegal. The passport has the French, Moroccan and Senegalese stamps and visas that you need. You were born in Toronto. That will explain your accent when you speak French. I cannot help you with your Canadian past. You will have to create that yourself, based on what you can convincingly talk about. You must memorize all this information. It has to come out instantaneously if needed."

Steve said, "Abdelhaq is lucky to have you as his friend. How can I thank you?"

Daud held up his left hand, palm toward Steve, and said, "Not your worry."

Steve thanked him again and shook his hand, and Youssef walked with him back to his car. Steve was now extremely aware of his physical environment, but he didn't spot Curly.

On his way back to Rabat, Steve noticed a black BMW 740 that stayed doggedly behind him. Whether he sped up or slowed down, the car stayed within sight. Since this tail didn't seem to be hiding, Steve assumed it was the friendly, protective team sent by Abdelhaq, probably the same BMW he had seen in the parking lot when he had arrived in Fez.

On a straight stretch of road, the BMW sped up and was quickly behind him. There were no other cars on the road. The black car swerved to the left to pass. In his driver-side mirror, Steve noticed that the black car's windows on the right, on his side, were open—the hair of the man in the back was blowing around. His mind quickly processed the information and concluded that the face and hair belonged to Curly. He checked his mirror again and saw movement. A hand appeared from the front passenger-side window, but it was not waving in friendly gesture. Steve caught sight of the barrel of a gun. Instinct powered by fear made him slam on the breaks. The BMW shot past him. He heard the popping of the shots. Most of the bullets flew over his car, except for one that scored a long gash across the hood. As the shots punched past him, Steve pulled the hand brake and whipped the steering wheel to the left, triggering his car to skid into a 180-degree turn even as it continued down the road. Steve had his hand on the brake, ready to release it, when the car went off the road onto the dirt and grass strip punctuated by poplars every fifty yards. Steve regained control, released the hand brake, drove the car back on the asphalt and accelerated toward Fez at full throttle.

Steve knew that heading in the opposite direction was the only way to put more space between him and the BMW. Without a weapon, surprise had given him perhaps a minute advantage. He was around the first turn and the black car had disappeared from sight. He had a good head start.

He saw a sign: KHEMISSET—3 KILOMÈTRES. To reach Khemisset before the BMW became the most important goal in his life. He urged more speed from his car. There was no one else on the road except for the occasional *jellaba*-clad peasant walking alongside the road with his donkey, carrying farm produce. Steve stayed in the middle of the narrow road and took the turns as fast as he could. The BMW had more horsepower and soon appeared in his mirror. But he reached Khemisset with about a quarter mile lead. He hit the brakes and turned onto a side street, passed a restaurant-hotel sign and furiously jammed the car into the parking lot in back. He grabbed the keys and the bag with his disguise and went into the building through the back door. He entered the kitchen, where he saw only one person, the cook. Steve put his hand on his heart, smiled at the cook, said, *"Labess-alik,"* a Moroccan greeting he had picked up, and kept moving. The cook barely paid attention to him. Steve went through the only other door and saw the letters *WC* on a green door on the left.

He hadn't anticipated that he'd ever have to use his disguise, but now he was glad to have it. In a few minutes, a middle-aged man with a receding hairline came out of the bathroom and walked through the dining room and out the front door. Steve reasoned that with his car in the back, this restaurant would soon be the object of a search. With his eyes out for his pursuers, he walked down the street and soon found a taxi with the driver asleep in the front seat. The driver demanded an absurd sum to drive him to Rabat. Steve, not in the mood to bargain, got in the backseat of the yellow Simca and cut the sum in half. Steve told the driver, "I'll give you the entire amount if you can break the world's speed record on the way to the Tour Hassan Hotel in Rabat."

Only a few minutes later, Steve knew he had made a mistake. The driver had already used two of their lives passing trucks around blind curves.

But the Simca was no match for the BMW. Fifteen minutes later, the black car appeared. The hit team drew abreast of the Simca, and two faces peered out of the open windows, hands held out of sight. Steve knew what they would see: a sleeping passenger in black-rimmed glasses, the back of whose graying head was leaning against the far window. The BMW dropped back. Steve glanced at the side-view mirror and saw the BMW pull off the road, turn around and head back toward Khemisset to conduct a more thorough search. He breathed a sigh of relief, though his body was still wired with adrenaline.

As Steve neared the Tour Hassan he wondered about the wisdom of returning to his hotel. Had the guys in the black BMW called ahead? Would he have a bad surprise waiting in his room? What did he have there that he couldn't live without? He had left most of his cash and American passport in an envelope in the hotel safe, for one thing. But he had his credit card and alias passport with him. He decided to go in, retrieve his stuff and check out that evening. He didn't think this group was seeking martyrdom. If and when they tried again, there would be an escape route in their plan, which probably meant no attack in a public place.

In order to gain entrance to the hotel without being challenged at reception, he had put Daud's disguise back in its cloth bag and out of sight by the time he walked through the lobby. He tried to record everything he could see without obviously moving his head. A thousand thoughts and possibilities were going through his mind. Everything and everyone was suspicious. What about the guy in the white *jellaba* just sitting in the lobby, not even pretending to read a newspaper as they did in the movies? On an impulse, he went to the reception desk and told the clerk that he would like to stay a week beyond his original reservation. Steve thought that would allow his adversaries to think they had plenty of time to plan their operation. He didn't want them to do anything hasty. With an officious smile, the clerk said that would be no problem, and he made a notation.

Steve went up to his room, gathered some essentials in a small bag and left his suitcases, most of his clothes and his toilet articles. He would go to another hotel—that should buy him more time. He knew there was a Rabat Hilton. There would undoubtedly be shops there where he could get what he needed.

He called Abdelhaq. A woman answered in Moroccan

Arabic, then in French. Abdelhaq was not home, and Steve left a message: "Steve will be at the Hilton." He hung up and cursed himself. Someone might have been listening. He wondered about the hotel receptionist. Steve took a deep breath. *Think clearly,* he told himself. *You cannot afford even one mistake.*

He went back downstairs and asked for access to the safe, explaining apologetically that he wanted to place other personal documents in the care of the hotel. In the privacy of the small closetlike room provided for this purpose, he extracted all of his cash and passport from the manila envelope, replaced it with hotel stationery and a thick leaflet from the Moroccan Office of Tourism to give the envelope some weight, sealed it and gave it back to the clerk.

Steve went out through the ornate lobby. He looked across the street before making a right turn up the slight incline of the rue Chellah and noticed another BMW with three men inside. This car was dark blue. The one in the back was hard to see. They seemed to be looking at him. He made his way around the corner to find a taxi before the blue car made its way around the block. He tried to remember what his father had said about surveillance. Where was Abdelhaq? Whatever happened to his vaunted protective team?

He went into a bookstore to plan his next move, where he picked up a guidebook. He should not have left the hotel without a firm plan as to how to get to the Hilton. He was deep in thought when someone whispered his name, making him jump. It was a smiling Abdelhaq, who wordlessly guided him to the blue BMW waiting outside.

They drove past the palace, and past the Zawa Theater. Abdelhaq pointed out the small airport behind the Rabat Hilton where King Hassan II had always kept a plane and crew for a fast getaway in case of a coup. Abdelhaq's house was in the Pinede section of Souissi, named for its ever-greens.

Abdelhaq pointed to an inscription by the front gate: VILLA LEILA. "That's my wife's name." He smiled. "We bought the house just before I was assigned to Tehran." They walked through a spacious marbled entrance, and Abdelhaq led Steve to a wood-paneled living room that looked out on a rock garden. They sat on banquettes against the wall.

Steve brought him up to date about the events on the road back to Rabat and asked, "What happened to the protection you promised?"

"It's been a full day for me too, Steve. We interrogated all the drivers and mechanics that had access to the ministry cars. All but one, that is. And we pretty much concluded that he was the one who placed the bomb in the car. Anyway, we're looking for him. He'll lead us to the rest of his group. The bottom line, as you Americans like to say, is that the protective team assigned to you was led by Benjelloun, the Salafist penetration of our service," Abdelhaq said.

Abdelhaq stood up. "How about some dinner?" He opened the sliding glass doors to the dining room, and a maid, head covered and with fading hennaed designs on her hands and feet, soon came in with a tagine. The couscous was already on the table. The maid removed the onion-domed top of the earthenware dish to reveal steaming chunks of lamb mixed with prunes, sprinkled with sesame seeds and almonds. Abdelhaq poured from a bottle of Gris de Boula-ouane, a Moroccan rosé with an alcoholic content that matched the strong tastes of the dish. The aromas of saffron and cinnamon caused Steve's stomach to signal that it had been a long, eventful day with little food. They both helped themselves directly with their fingers. Abdelhaq took the couscous with his fingers, rolling it into a ball, a feat that Steve didn't even attempt.

Steve said, "Tell me about Benjelloun and his gang. Is he now under arrest?"

"We're still looking for them. I suggest that you stay here tonight. Now that we know who to look for, you should leave Morocco. Since you told us he was in Khemisset a couple of hours ago, my people are looking for him right now. It shouldn't take long. We'll get you on a plane out tomorrow. But it would help my investigation if the Salafists think you're still here. Some might do something else to reveal themselves. You can leave as a Canadian tourist in your disguise and with a Canadian passport."

"That guy Benjelloun was part of the security team that I met with. He seemed very uncomfortable when I told them I knew I was under surveillance," Steve said.

"Your antennae are obviously better than Benjelloun's boss's in security. He should have pegged Benjelloun as a problem. That cretin comes from a politically connected family, so he may have gotten into security through the back door. He's a problem we will deal with," Abdelhaq said, with a scowl.

After the meal, Steve and Abdelhaq returned to the banquettes, low to the floor and with an abundance of backrest pillows. Steve was beginning to feel safe and relaxed for the first time all day. "I know you and my father met in Iran, but I was too young to know you then. How did you meet? What were you two doing?"

"If your father hasn't told you himself, it's probably not my role to talk about it. I only will tell you that I probably owe him my life. At a roadblock, he wrested a rifle—I remember it was a German Heckler & Koch G3 rifle, standard issue for the Iranian army at the time—from the hands of the leader of the thugs who wanted to take us prisoners. You can ask him for the details."

"Well, I can tell you also that my father has the greatest respect for you," Steve said.

The next day Abdelhaq took Steve to the airport at five A.M. for his Air France flight to Paris. Abdelhaq's people, in plainclothes, were on both the public and the passengers-only sides of the passport check-in booth and security-control area. Steve was wearing his disguise. Steve went through police and customs control with his fake passport with no problems.

Abdelhaq took Steve to the VIP lounge and took his Canadian passport. "It will be easier for you now to travel under your true name. Ian Ross is registered on our airport records as having left Morocco today. That fills our need. If anyone is looking, you are still here. By the way, did I tell you that we arrested Benjelloun and his crew, the team that tried to shoot you? After we knew from you that they had been in Khemisett, it was easy to find them."

"Was that the whole cell? Is everyone under lock and key?" Steve asked.

"Unfortunately, the leaders, one named Hussein, a Syrian, and Lahlou, a Moroccan, were able to leave the country. We're dealing with the most dangerous and the most ambitious Salafist group. Their leader is Tariq al Khalil. He sometimes masquerades as a moderate intellectual, as you know."

"Al Khalil again!" Steve cried out. He told Abdelhaq how al Khalil's name had come up during his lunch with Colonel Spaceck.

"Today, we asked your embassy to send their defense attaché home. That was your friend Spaceck. He was part of the problem. It seems that he fingered you to Benjelloun as a CIA officer."

Steve, eyebrows raised in surprise, said, "Why the hell would he say that? I never had a good feeling about that guy. He seemed out for the main chance. I wouldn't be surprised if this was just the tip of the iceberg."

Steve's flight number was called out over the loudspeaker as boarding. Abdelhaq briefly gripped his upper arm and said, "I want to thank you for the part you played in getting rid of this Salafist cell. It's not over, but we've got a line on the others. We've gotten you a seat in first class, by the way."

He gave him a fatherly hug and told him to give his greetings to Marshall.

Steve sat back in the Airbus that would take him to Paris on the first leg of his trip back to the United States. As the two Pratt & Whitney 6122 engines lifted the aircraft up to its cruising altitude of thirty thousand feet, Steve became aware of his heartbeat—it was normal for the first time in several days. He felt good that he had been able to draw the Salafists out of their holes, even if it was by playing the role of the tethered goat that Abdelhaq had chosen for him. He had taken a measured risk, which he now realized had been based on the false information that Abdelhaq's men would protect him. But he had made his own luck.

Later, on his connecting flight to Washington Dulles International Airport from Charles de Gaulle, he realized that he had learned something else about himself. Being a successful businessman would never be enough. He needed to be a part of something bigger.

CHAPTER THIRTEEN

Al Khalil entered the impoverished town of mud and sand that was Timbuktu and likened its decay to the decay of Islam. He knew that twenty-first-century Timbuktu was a far cry from its days as a center of trade and scholarship. A visitor needed to bring the history of Timbuktu with him or be disappointed. The Malian Office of Tourism claimed that the oldest Islamic law library in the world was in Timbuktu. Although the United Nations and private foundations were providing resources to keep this institution from disappearing completely, it was only a dusty shadow of its former self.

Al Khalil found it hard to imagine that the town had once been fabulously wealthy and that pirogues loaded with gold from the Malinke Empire of Sundiata Keita had once come up the Niger River to meet the caravans from Libya and Egypt carrying spices and other goods.

His cover, his front organization, was the International Muslim Relief Agency. His office occupied a mud-walled building distinguished from similar buildings only by a green banner with the initials IMRA. Warm breezes pulled on the banner's loose ties.

The day after al Khalil's return to Timbuktu, Amadou Sangaré, al Khalil's moneyman in Mali, came to report. The year before, Sangaré had brought the director of the Morila gold mine on board. The mine had had an output of eight hundred million dollars that year, and Sangaré made sure that a 10 percent tithe was embezzled and placed in Tariq's Swiss bank account. There were gold mines on the other side of the Guinean border to the south and west of Timbuktu as well, and Sangaré hoped to be able to work similar arrangements there.

He stepped around people waiting outside in the shade of the building and went into the IMRA offices past a guard sitting in the open doorway. The IMRA offices were surprisingly well furnished, a step up from the bare Malian government offices. Several Afghan rugs were on the floor, Arabic posters of Cairo's Al Azhar Mosque and Jerusalem's Dome of the Rock hung on the walls, and instead of the usual photograph of the current Malian president on the highest place on the wall, green Islamic calligraphy spelled out the word *Allah*.

Sangaré walked by the case handlers talking to their applicants and knocked on the door to an internal office. He wiped the sweat from his face on the sleeve of his boubou before walking in. He exchanged greetings with al Khalil and went to an open case of water bottles in the corner of the room, grabbed one and took several swallows. Al Khalil sat behind a table rather than at an office desk. In the corner was a locked metal cabinet. Because graven images were too close to Jahiliya image worship, his secret was locked in the file cabinet. It held two prints: an inexpensive engraving of Sheikh Abdelkader al Khalil, who had fought and died at the Battle of Tours in 732 AD, when the Muslim armies had been beaten back by a man who would become Charlemagne's grandfather, and another of Sheikh Tariq ibn Ziad, the Berber warrior who had led the Arab armies across the Strait of Gibraltar into Europe in 711. Both were in the style of Jacques-Louis David's painting of Napoleon crossing the Alps, a victorious warrior on a white horse. The hill, or *jebel*, overlooking the straits crossed by Tariq ibn Ziad and his men had been named Jebel Tariq, later corrupted to Gibraltar. Out in plain sight on Tariq's desk was a sign in Arabic quoting his grandfather, the founder of the Muslim Brotherhood.

It is in the nature of Islam to dominate, not to be dominated, to impose its laws on all nations and to extend its power to the entire planet.

Al Khalil looked up and said, "Amadou, what's going on at the mines? The gold you're getting for us is helpful. But you know that's not why we're here. The gold is only a means to an end." Tariq looked down at papers in front of him, but before Sangaré could say anything, he stood up with his hands on the table. "We need more recruits among the miners—not only in the gold mines but the salt mines in Taoudenni. We need to organize special indoctrination for the more susceptible and transform them into dedicated warriors. We need to identify individuals from these groups for special training. They're perfect recruits for our army. We must go faster." His tone was commanding.

"I know that, and I'm working on it," Sangaré said defensively. "But these people are not like us. They're Sufis. They even drink beer. They would rather play soccer than go to the mosque."

"At this rate, it's going to take a hundred years. I'm taking the recruitment function away from you and giving it to Mohammed Lahlou. Maybe Moroccans are better at talking than at operations. You keep your focus on the money."

Four days later, Lahlou walked into the IMRA building and went directly into Tariq's office. Tariq closed the top drawer of his metal file cabinet and turned around to witness an agitated and sweating Lahlou.

"I spent the last couple of days at Taoudenni, like you told me. I think we're wasting our time there. The workers are the scum, the rejects, of every other possible employment possibility. Taoudenni used to be for political prisoners working off their sentences. I'm sure some stayed, if they didn't die first, because that's the only thing they could do."

"All right. Let's forget about Taoudenni. But I wouldn't bring up Morocco if I were you."

"Going after that American so quickly, with no information and no planning, was not my idea. I could have done it very well by myself, and our best penetration of security, Benjelloun, would still be alive today and working for us," Lahlou said.

"If you're such a smart operator, how is it that you spent eighteen years in prison?"

At that point Hussein came in and sat down. Tariq could see that Hussein had better news than Lahlou, whom he waved out of his office.

"I'm making arrangements for the Gao meeting next month," Hussein said.

Tariq tapped a finger on his desk. "I was just going to ask you about that. It's going to be the first meeting of all of my key Salafist leaders from the Atlantic to the Indian Ocean. I want to give them my orders for the next twelve months. Is everything ready?"

"Remember the Tuareg rebellion a few years ago?" Hussein asked. "One of the concessions given to the Tuaregs was that the Malian army would decrease its presence in the northern region of the country. One of the forts they closed down was the one in Gao. That's where we'll meet. It used to be a French Foreign Legion fort. I told the Malian colonel in charge of the Gao military district that IMRA needed it for its annual Saharan Conference. He'll take five thousand to make it happen and clean the place up for us, but you know he's going to pocket most of it."

Hussein went to get himself a bottle of water.

"Good, Hussein. I want you and Lahlou to make all the arrangements."

Tariq paused and looked down toward his desk, on which several papers were lying. Frowning thoughtfully, he said, "Now, I keep hearing about the Crusaders—the Western missionaries, and what they call NGOs. How many are there in this area? What organizations do they belong to? Are they having any success turning our people away from Islam? Getting the Western influence out of our lands is our first priority. We need to eliminate these proselytizers. These infidel missionaries think that their blessings increase with their difficulties? I want to heap such blessings on them that they go straight to their heavens!"

Tariq got up from his desk and walked toward the door. Hussein followed as Tariq said, "Hussein, work on it. Give me a plan. It shouldn't be that hard. How many of these foreign preachers could there be? They need to be encouraged to go home."

Tariq opened the door and Hussein left the office, saying, "You're right. Eliminating the competition—priests and other do-gooders—should not be a difficult challenge."

Using more force than necessary, Tariq closed the door hard behind him.

* * *

Later that day, Tariq took a plane to Paris via Bamako for a speaking engagement. Hussein knew that he also would stop in Brussels to see his wife Malika and daughter Jamila. Tariq had confided that he would probably send them to live in Cairo. In his absence, Hussein had time to reflect on his role in Tariq's grand design. His objective had never been religious. He wanted to take revenge on the Syrian Baathist leadership. He would have been perfectly happy and fulfilled to shoot the entire Assad family, starting with Rifaat Assad, who had led the attack that killed his father, and now Bashir, the former president's son, who had taken over the country on old man Hafez Assad's death. Creating a new Caliphate was much bigger, too grand an idea to hope for and probably too vast to even begin to contemplate.

When recruited by Tariq, Hussein's mind had focused on only one thing: Tariq's promise to overthrow the Syrian regime and install a leader who would be loyal to the new caliph. But the Assads still ruled Syria. No country had yet been folded into Tariq's grand scheme, although potent groups within each of the Sahel countries professed an allegiance to the Salafist banner. The meeting in Gao would be critical for the continued success of Tariq's movement. He decided he would stay with Tariq. His was the only game in town, for now.

CHAPTER FOURTEEN

Steve and Marshall were on the CIA campus in Langley, Virginia, about to enter the Old Headquarters Building. Marshall had mentioned Steve's brushes with radical Islamists in Morocco to his colleagues at the CIA who wanted to hear about it firsthand. They passed a statue of Nathan Hale. "Why Nathan Hale?" Steve asked. "Wasn't he captured and hanged by the British? There must have been more successful American spies."

"Yes, of course. But as the first spy to be executed for the United States, he stands for the patriotism and bravery of clandestine operators over the years."

In Steve's absence, to-dos from other projects had accumulated in his Tysons Corner office. The catch-up work weighed like a millstone. Steve already suffered from the boredom of too many hours spent writing overdue periodic progress reports and attending staff meetings; the routine was almost numbing. He was also frustrated over the lack of news concerning Coogan's death. The good news was that to everyone's surprise, the Moroccan Ministry of Defense had already asked that West Gate send a team to Rabat to begin the next phase of the negotiations. But Steve's job as the initial developer of the project was over for the moment.

As they walked over the CIA seal in the marble lobby, Steve saw on his left the bronze statue of Major General William Donovan, an Irish Catholic from Boston who had become the most decorated soldier of World War I and then founded the OSS, predecessor to the CIA. To his right was the Memorial Wall, with eighty-eight stars symbolizing the CIA officers who had died in the line of duty and whose names could not be revealed.

"I have friends among those stars," Marshall said. "I've been lucky." He paused and added, "And so have you."

They went up several steps and turned into a small room, where a guard was waiting for them. He checked Marshall's badge, gave an "escort required" badge to Steve and led them to an open elevator being held for them. They exited on the fifth floor directly into a conference room, thus avoiding the need to share corridors with undercover intelligence officers of the National Clandestine Service who might be leaving on secret missions the next day.

"Hello, everyone. I'm Isabel," said a black-haired woman with lively dark eyes and a broad smile, seated at the large conference table. "I'd like you to sign several forms, Mr. Church," she said, pointing to Steve.

Marshall interceded. "If that's a secrecy agreement, Steve is here not to acquire information but to share it."

"He still has to sign them." She pushed them forward, and hesitating just a second, Steve signed them. Rules and regulations—he shook his head slightly.

Isabel then led them to a windowless conference room where four people waited for them. On one wall was a row of portraits that reminded Steve of the photos of Bogart and Bacall in movie-theater lobbies. Certainly less glamorous, but he assumed these people were stars in the world of clandestine operations.

As they sat around the table, one of their hosts, a woman who seemed a bit younger than Steve, greeted them. "Hi. My name is Nicole. I'm with the Maghreb section of the Directorate of Intelligence." She looked to her right. "And this is Jason. He's with the National Center for Counterterrorism. He focuses on radical Muslim terrorism. I don't know if you realize it, but you're one of the few survivors of a Salafist attack. In fact, you're the only one I know of who lived through two attempts—two in less than a week, a record. We're interested in anything you can share with us. For example, in hindsight, were there any indications of surveillance or any other interest in you beforehand?"

After recounting his story, Steve said, "So in a nutshell, yes, there were signs. Somebody went through my stuff in the hotel, I had company for sure when I went to the mausoleum, but I thought that Curly and his friends in Fez were on my side. The Moroccan police must have all those guys in jail by now."

Jason, his dark hair lightly spiked, said, "This definitely sounds like Tariq al Khalil's style. We knew they had a cell in Morocco, but it hasn't been very active."

At that point a slim woman in her late thirties came into the room. Marshall said, "Steve, this is Therese LaFont, the chief of the Africa Division of the National Clandestine Service." Steve recognized her from the last photograph on the wall. She had short blonde hair and was elegantly dressed in dark tailored slacks and jacket, with a white silk blouse. She gave Steve a firm handshake, saying, "I only heard part of your story, but that was some driving. The only thing that's going to keep your father from going to jail for sharing our methods with an unauthorized and uncleared individual is for you to come to work for us." She laughed.

Steve managed a laugh too. "My father showed me how to do that maneuver on a vacant lot in an old Ford. It stuck with me, luckily."

They spent the next few minutes focusing on the respective roles of Benjelloun as the Salafist penetration of the Moroccan security service, Spaceck's over-the-top zeal in trying to gain favor with the Moroccans to build himself a retirement sinecure, and Abdelhaq al Fassi's continuing value to the king.

"I understand, Steve, that you know Tariq al Khalil?" said LaFont abruptly.

"I met him a couple of times when I was in school in Brussels," Steve replied. He noticed that the meeting was moving beyond his Moroccan experience.

Nicole and Jason left the room, and the two officers who had been sitting against the wall moved to the table. LaFont introduced them. "This is Philip, branch chief for the Maghreb, and Mel, West African–branch chief." Philip, average height, average weight, dark hair with specks of gray, could have been any age, thought Steve. He was the original gray man who would be undistinguishable in a crowd. Mel was a heavyset woman in her fifties with white hair. She was draped in an abundance of striped fabric.

Philip said, "According to our information, al Khalil has a

front in Timbuktu called the International Muslim Relief Agency. From there he is trying to establish a base for radical Islam in the entire Sahel, across North Africa, especially in countries with weak governance. His tools are his academic reputation, his Muslim Brotherhood ties, plenty of money and the willingness to use physical violence. He is starting to make an impact. His goal is to establish a new Caliphate in the Sahel and grow it to include all of the Middle East."

Philip turned to Mel, who asked, "Steve, at West Gate International, do you need medical clearances before you travel?"

Steve, puzzled by the non sequitur, nodded. "Why do you ask?"

Philip shot a frown in Mel's direction and took the conversational lead back. "Al Khalil recently traveled through Algeria with his operations chief. While he was in Ghardaïa, a major town in the northern Sahara, two French oil workers were killed for no known reason. We suspect that his presence in the area was not a coincidence."

LaFont leaned forward. "We have no one who can give us an eyes-on-target view of his setup in Timbuktu. Islam, radical or not, is not a topic the Malian government wants to talk about with us. You know, I assume, that Mali is a Muslim country. I'll be up front with you, since you're family." She glanced and smiled at Marshall. "Our eventual goal, of course, is to have a source in al Khalil's office, in his group. So what we need to get started is a general overview—who these people are and what they do. Of course, names, identifying data and assessments would be great."

Steve glanced at his father, leaned back and said, "I definitely want to help. What I've seen and learned in the last month has convinced me that the Salafists are a threat." He hesitated and added, "But if you're thinking I can get this information for you, you've got the wrong guy. I have no idea how I would go about it."

"Well, you could do more than you think just by visiting him in Timbuktu. It's just to give us context. The biggest thing we'd like you to do, that we would appreciate your doing, is to meet with al Khalil once or twice under some pretext. Hopefully you could go to his IMRA office and take a look around. We'll take it from there."

"What do I tell my boss at West Gate? I do have a day job."

Marshall, who had let the conversation take its course, now jumped in. "Your people just told us that the cell that attacked Steve in Morocco came under al Khalil. Now you want him to walk into al Khalil's office? Why does that make sense to you?" he asked, looking at LaFont and the two other CIA officers.

Philip answered. "Yes, we talked about that and we reviewed the communications between al Khalil and the Moroccan cell. They never mentioned Steve's name per se. The cell leader in Casablanca and al Khalil's operations chief, who was in Morocco at the time, only mention a young American who worked for Ted Coogan."

Marshall looked a bit surprised. "That's new. When did you have those messages? Why weren't they available while Steve was in Morocco? If you knew that he was in danger, why didn't you take action to warn him and get him out?" Marshall slapped his hand on the conference table with restrained anger.

"We didn't have those messages until after the fact, unfortunately. Sorting and translating and then figuring out where the information should be sent took the National Security Agency a bit too long to make it actionable. Further, we didn't know who the messages were about, either, until you told us what was going on, Marshall," LaFont said, shaking her head.

"When will the NSA understand that its information is not just for the historical record?" Marshall asked.

LaFont nodded in sympathy and turned to Steve. "I hope you don't mind . . . We've already talked to your boss at

West Gate. He said that he would reluctantly lend you to us, but he wants you back. Sounds like he's got you on the fast track."

Mel, who had been silenced earlier, came back to the charge. "Before we let you go overseas on our behalf, you need to be medically cleared. We'll sign you up for a full physical next week. Secondly, I don't know what it's like in the private sector, Steve, but here you'll have to keep a tight record of all the expenses you expect to get reimbursed. And we'll need receipts. We'll buy your flight tickets, of course. We'll get cheaper government fares."

Steve thought he was in the presence of a frustrated accountant. "Mel . . . It is Mel, isn't it? I admit that I'm new at this, but right now I think it's more important that I—that we—focus on the actual mission."

Marshall looked at LaFont, then at Steve, and said, "Welcome to the government, Steve. For the privilege of taking risks on behalf of your country, you get to spend more time filling in forms than you do on actual operations." Turning back to LaFont, Marshall continued, "But since Mel brings up the issue of money, keep in mind that Steve, if he agrees to do this, will still be paid by West Gate, since you've already made the arrangement. He won't be paid by the Agency. In other words, you're getting a freebie, so—"

LaFont frowned at Mel. "Of course, and we appreciate it. I agree. We'll minimize the paperwork."

Mel frowned and said, "I only thought that since Steve's new to the government, he should know the rules."

LaFont looked at her watch and got up to leave. "Steve, thank you for your willingness to help us. I suggest that the next step is to train you on basic tradecraft, especially agent assessment, reporting, and show you what we've got on your new best friend, al Khalil."

She left the room and they laid out a training program for Steve.

As they were leaving the CIA's Langley campus, Steve

asked his father, "What's with this Mel? I've met a lot of your CIA friends. She's not like them."

"No, she's not," Marshall commented. "The Agency is so thin that it's taking people like her with no overseas experience in order to staff the desks. I heard she comes from HR and spent some time with the Recruitment Center. She's obviously big on process."

Steve laughed. "If people like Mel are the face of the CIA for new applicants, the Agency has more problems than I thought." Left unsaid were internal warning signals that he was entering a situation with more rules and oversight than he wanted.

Chapter Fifteen

That evening, Marshall drove Steve to a CIA safe house in the Virginia countryside where he would live during his brief training period. They soon got off the highway and drove across familiar rolling hills. Although it was dusk, Steve could make out the large estates and forested properties. The training safe house turned out to be a comfortable six-bedroom house on twenty wooded acres. An unobtrusive fence surrounded the property. In the front, the white crossbuck fence was the same type used by the horse farms in the area. The front gate was a simple white wooden pole with a counterweight dropped across the entrance road to bar vehicular access. It was controlled remotely by the authorized visitor or by security from inside the grounds.

Marshall said, "The periphery of the property is guarded by concealed sensors and cameras monitored from a separate building recessed just inside the tree line. The office of security normally keeps a unit of guard dogs on the grounds. I want to remind you of a couple of things that you already know, which may come up early in the training. First, remember that the CIA is not part of law enforcement. It doesn't have the power to arrest and doesn't fall under the Department of Justice. Also, an agent, in CIA parlance, is a foreign national recruited to steal secrets for an intelligence officer. The media still uses the FBI meaning of the word, which describes the FBI staff officer who investigates and makes the arrests."

They turned into the driveway as Steve said, "Don't worry, Dad, I won't embarrass you." Inside, Steve resented his father's assumption that this talk was necessary.

After a week during which Steve had been introduced to basic tradecraft topics, such as the spotting, assessing and developing of potential agents, Marshall came by after Steve had had dinner and was going through French language cards—French on one side, English on the other. "Sorry to interrupt you. I thought I'd come over and see how you're doing and whether you need anything, since you're not allowed to leave."

"I guess these French irregular verbs will just have to wait," Steve said, and put his cards aside.

Marshall moved some books off a chair and sat down. "I have something to ask you. You know that two years ago I was initiated into the Knights of Malta, an organization created in Jerusalem in 1099. I think you would make a great addition to the Order, and I would be proud to sponsor you. The investiture is scheduled to take place at the Church of the Holy Sepulcher in Jerusalem. The ceremony itself dates back centuries—a lot of tradition there."

Steve had avoided following in his father's wake. But he was intrigued by the offer. "What is the purpose of the Order, exactly? What do you do?"

"Exactly?" Marshall grinned. "We raise money for wounded veterans from Afghanistan and Iraq. That's what my chapter does anyway. Each chapter has its favorite cause."

"Sounds like a good cause. Let me think about it. You think I qualify to be a member?"

"Well, there's no test, if that's what you mean. It is a Christian organization—it started in the Holy Land during the Crusades. We look for professional people who have attained a high level of accomplishment in their field. And the usual qualities . . . you know, trustworthiness, integrity, the usual personal values."

Steve looked serious. "I'm just getting started. I don't have accomplishments."

"You're wrong about that. But it's also for people who we think have all of the personal attributes and who we judge will become successful. And that's you. Am I wrong?" He grinned again.

Steve didn't want a confrontation with Marshall at this point. In fact, the offer actually sounded interesting. It sounded even better when Marshall added, "While we're in Israel we can visit some of the Crusader castles—all part of the Order's history."

The next day, Steve met his new instructor, Juan, dressed in boots and cammies. Juan had black hair and a squat build. Steve learned over the next forty-eight hours that Juan was a former Special Forces master sergeant who had trained counternarcotics forces in Colombia and Mexico. Juan told him, "I'm going to introduce you to weapons and explosives. We don't expect you to use them, but you need some knowledge for defensive reasons."

That day, Steve fired the Glock and other personal weapons. He was shown the various improvised explosive devices used by international terrorists and how these groups built and used car bombs, a weapon of choice in the Middle East.

On the way back from the range in the old Ford Fairlane assigned for his training by the base's administration, Steve asked, "What about butane bombs?"

"Yes, I heard about your experience in Morocco. Using the pressure inside the butane cylinder multiplies the force of the blast severalfold—more bang for the buck. I understand they used Semtex to set it off. I'm not surprised. Remember Václav Havel, who became president of Czechoslovakia? He said that during the Cold War, his country had sold or given enough Semtex for the world's terrorists to have an ample supply for the next hundred and fifty years."

The next day, when Juan picked up Steve, he told him over coffee at a table in the kitchen, "Today, you make an IED and set it off. Like yesterday, the purpose is defensive. The rule of the range is that the student picks up his own duds. That means that if your device doesn't explode, it's your job to go pick it up. Nothing new about that—sort of like packing your own parachute."

They drove out to the range, and following Juan's directions, Steve timed a six-inch piece of fuse, which then allowed him to cut a length that would burn for forty-five seconds. Steve held the cap up to his eyes and crimped the metal around the fuse.

He pushed the cap into the C-4 and walked it out about fifty feet. Then he lit the fuse, turned around and walked back with a determined but unhurried step. Juan had taught him that when dealing with explosives, one needed to be calm and measured.

They both got into the bunker and watched through a quartz bomb-blast window and waited for the blast. Juan looked at his watch and said, "It's been two minutes. Wait another minute and then go get it." Juan watched Steve closely, Steve assumed, for any signs of fear or nervousness, but he was determined to show none.

A long minute went by. They were waiting and watching through the window. Juan looked at his watch and said, "Time." Steve started out of the bunker.

Juan said, "Don't worry. We've only lost a few students. Besides, it would look bad on my record. Seriously, I'll go with you, Steve."

"No. I don't need any special favors. If the SOP is for me to get it, I'll get it," Steve said. As he walked out of the bunker, the instructor followed and quickly caught up with him. Having Juan beside him made Steve feel that the danger was acceptable: here was someone whose expertise was explosives; he wouldn't be there if he thought the risk were high.

They walked toward the IED, both watching closely for telltale smoke. Steve and Juan stood for another second by the IED before the instructor picked it up and pulled the fuse out of the detonating cap. He gave the whole package to Steve and told him, "The problem was that you didn't push the fuse into the cap firmly enough. Also, we normally use two fuses and two caps for insurance, but I didn't tell you to do that this time. The problem was in part mine. That's why I came with you." He had Steve do it again with two detonator caps, and this time the device exploded, sending a cloud of dirt and rocks up into the sky.

As they left the range, Juan said, "Now that I gave you instructions on what headquarters thought you should know, tomorrow morning I'll show you what headquarters should have told me to show you. Ever hear of nonlethal weapons? Sounds like an oxymoron, but the military has been doing a lot of work in this area, and so have we. We've adapted the technology that the military needs to stop a crowd at a distance without shooting and reduced it to something you can carry in your pocket, with a range of thirty feet. It's called a pulsed-energy projectile, or PEP. I'll show you after breakfast tomorrow."

Steve left the next day at ten o'clock after two hours of instruction on the new personal weapon.

Chapter Sixteen

Kella ran down the stairs as fast as she could. The fear of Hamad behind her coursed through her veins. To get away from him, she thought of jumping down from landing to landing. Was it possible? She jumped and came down lightly. But Hamad jumped after her. He reached for her. She felt the touch of steel on her back. Was the knife in her back? Somehow she knew that her blouse had been cut open. She kept running down the stairs. For her life. How many flights of stairs so far? How long would it take to reach the street? She lifted up her robe with one hand to go faster. Hamad yelled, "Whore! Whore!" She tripped and Hamad suddenly was on top of her; he straddled her. She was terrified. Was he going to rape her? She couldn't move her arms or legs. He raised the knife and shouted, "Allahu Akbar." His face was a demon's mask. The knife came down slowly but inexorably toward her heart. His face was closer, grimacing with anger with the effort. Was she dead now? Bells were ringing. She must be in the basilica of Saint-Denis.

The ringing woke her up. She was in a sweat, her head turning from one side to the other. Her heart pounding, pounding, told her that she was alive. Her phone was ringing. She put her light on. It was six thirty in the morning.

It was Steve. "Hey—I was hoping to catch you at home

before you left for the day, so I stayed up late. I'm in Virginia, at home. I've been thinking about you. How are you?"

"I'm OK. Wait a minute, I'll be right back." She went to the bathroom and washed her face.

Returning, she put the phone back to her ear. "It's early here, you know. But I'm glad you called. I'm OK, but to tell you the truth, I have problems concentrating . . . In my studies, I mean."

"I have the remedy. A trip. I've just accepted a temporary freelance assignment as a photojournalist. I'm going to do the definitive piece on the Tuaregs. Come with me."

"What? The Tuaregs? It's been done already," she told him, laughing.

"Maybe, but not like I'm going to do it, because you're going to be my secret weapon. How about going with me? What better guide could I have? You even speak Tuareg, don't you? Have you already taken your trip to Timbuktu? I hope not."

"It's Tamasheq—the language, I mean," she replied. She was glad to be distracted from her nightmare of Hamad, but Steve's call was doubly welcome. She was attracted to the prospects of traveling with Steve in her native land. Yet she felt she had to put up a little resistance. "Steve, it's a wonderful offer, but I can't just pick up and leave my studies at a moment's notice. I was planning a visit to my relatives in Timbuktu, but not this afternoon. Are you going through an early midlife crisis? I thought you liked your job."

"Trust me, Kella. I know this is sudden and you've got a ton of questions. I'll answer them all when I see you in Timbuktu. Think of it as fate. Think Lady Luck and the spirit of adventure. Think Baraka."

Without too much effort, Steve convinced Kella to join him, and they agreed to make their own separate ways to Timbuktu and meet there a week later.

In coordination with the central cover staff, Marshall, Philip and Mel had settled on Steve's cover. Sitting in the cover staff's conference room, Yukio, the cover officer, said, "Your photojournalism cover will give you a reason to be in Mali and to make contacts with just about anyone in the Timbuktu area. And it will provide a pretext to contact al Khalil and IMRA, which presumably provides assistance to Tuaregs."

"What about sending Steve into the lion's den under his true name? The Salafists targeted him in Morocco. They know his name. Everybody has his name. It was in the newspaper," Marshall said.

Mel interjected, "I'll get the forms from State for Steve to fill out."

Steve spoke up. "I can't very well contact al Khalil using an alias, since we've already met."

Yukio said, "An alias passport at this late date is out of the question anyway. Passports are controlled by the State Department with an iron grip. You wouldn't believe the red tape."

"Listen, since I have to travel in true name, and since I have to meet al Khalil in true name, I'll use my middle name, Christopher, when making contacts in Mali, just to keep a lower profile," Steve said decisively. "I have a hard time believing that al Khalil has anyone actively screening the names of everyone arriving and leaving Mali; the risk must be minuscule. As far as Tariq himself, I'm sure I can convince him that I have no involvement with the Quran documents." *If I can actually reach him,* he thought.

When the meeting was over, Marshall pulled Steve aside out in the hallway. His father's face was drawn and serious. "As usual, the real cover will not be what the CIA provides, but what you can do with it and how you conduct yourself," Marshall said.

With Marshall's interference, Mel was forced to let Steve plan and buy his own flight tickets. Mel was only looking at the cost to the government, but Marshall had pointed out, "All tickets bought at government fares are so labeled and will give Steve away."

Steve flew out of Dulles on a five-and-a-half-hour night flight to Paris, had breakfast at Charles De Gaulle airport during the four-hour layover and read and dozed during the eight-and-a-half-hour flight to Bamako. As they flew over the hundred-mile-long ergs and then the massive dark and rocky plateaus of the Anti-Atlas, Steve was struck by the vast desolate space and wondered how anyone could survive down there.

The moment Steve stepped out of the plane at Bamako Airport, the acrid smell of smoke filled his nostrils. He had expected the heat and the poverty. He knew that with few paved roads, it would be dusty. But he knew that he would always associate the burning smell with Bamako.

Upon arrival at the Hotel de l'Amitiée he made arrangements to rent a Toyota Land Cruiser for pickup in Timbuktu. In answer to Steve's question, the desk clerk told him, "The smell, monsieur? Ah, you mean you smell smoke? That's from the fields, monsieur. They burn the old crop." He looked at Steve as a kind teacher would at a student with limited intellectual ability.

As prearranged, Steve met the CIA's local chief of station, Rod Descouteaux, at his home on the banks of the Niger the evening he arrived. The purpose of the meeting was simply to give Steve a local contact in case of problems. Rod was in his thirties, tall and thin, with sandy hair combed straight back. They sat outside on a patio lit by the dining-room lights. Outlined against the moonlit sky were hundreds of fruit bats flying over the river.

Sipping a dirty martini, Rod said, "I appreciate your help. IMRA is an information target, but I have had problems just getting access, let alone recruiting anyone in al Khalil's group. Since you already know al Khalil, it should be simple. You meet him once or twice, take his temperature, take a look at his operation and you're done."

"I don't guarantee anything, but I'll do my best," Steve said.

Before Steve took his leave, Rod told him, "You should call on the cultural attaché at the embassy tomorrow. It will reinforce your cover. He's in charge of contacts with the media for the embassy and might know some people who could open doors for you in Timbuktu for your photo shoots."

Before getting on an Air Mali flight to Timbuktu the next day, Steve stopped by the American Embassy, a white-washed building that had once been a bank. He told the cultural attaché, a bearded, rather short and rotund African American, about his photographic assignment. In return, he received the names of a couple of Malian officials in Timbuktu who might be helpful. The attaché, a friendly and outgoing bon vivant, walked him out to the street, and laughing, he said, "Thank God that my great-grandfather was a slow runner."

"What do you mean?"

"Nothing really." Seeing Steve's puzzled face, he added, "Only that I'm here today as an American diplomat rather than in the ranks of the local unemployed, getting picked up by government trucks for unpaid labor only because one of my ancestors got caught and was sold to the slave traders on the coast."

As his Antonov An-24 landed in Timbuktu, Steve noticed the rusted wreck of his plane's twin that had been pushed to the side of the runway. After checking in at the Bouctou Hotel, he followed Rod's advice and hired a local driver. By any measure, anyone born and raised in Mali was not half as expert behind the wheel as the average Westerner. He hired a Tuareg named Atrar, who had driven a truck in Marseilles for five years and spoke decent French. He soon realized that along with Atrar, he inherited the driver's wife, young son and brother.

When Atrar showed up to take Steve to a Tuareg camp

outside of Timbuktu, he came with his brother, Izem. On the way out, Atrar proudly told Izem, who sat in the front passenger seat like a security guard, "Tell Monsieur Christophe, go on."

Izem appeared initially reluctant but said, "I am a soldier. Ever since I was a young boy. When we fought the Malian army, maybe fifteen years ago, I rode with my brothers. It is our history, to fight. At the beginning we won. We knew the desert. But too many Malians—they took over the wells."

Steve asked, "And what did you do after the fighting? Were you a prisoner?"

"No, never. Many of us made our way to the military camps on the other side of the Libyan border. At first, the Libyans didn't know what to do with us. But they saw that we were good soldiers. They trained us, gave us guns, and we became part of the Libyan army. We patrolled the Libyan desert and then we fought in Chad."

Again prompted by Atrar, Izem said, "My name means lion in Tamasheq."

Steve realized that Izem could be useful to him, although he didn't yet know how.

Later that day, Steve began to establish his cover credentials as a photojournalist.

Back in his room, Steve sent his first message to CIA headquarters in Langley. Using steganography, Steve was able to hide his message in the photographs that he took that day. His e-mail, which he sent to an ostensibly commercial e-mail address, summarized his visit to the Tuareg camp, and the attached photographs hid his real message. Steganography was the modern version of microdots. Steve had the option of hiding his messages in graphic images, websites, or recorded music. In view of the questionable reliability of the Malian telephone system, Steve was communicating to the outside world through his handheld Iridium 9505A satellite phone.

He first called Kella from his hotel-room phone. The phone made clicking noises for so long that Steve assumed that the call was being relayed through Paris. Eventually, after finding stairs that led to the flat roof of the small hotel, he called her using his satellite phone, which could not be used inside. He reached her quickly and they made plans for dinner that night at the Poulet d'Or, not far from the Petit Marché, an open market.

When he found the restaurant and sat at a table for two, Steve learned that the Poulet d'Or, or Golden Chicken, took its name seriously. Fried and boiled chicken dishes accompanied by couscous monopolized the menu. He was ordering Gazelle beer from Senegal when Kella came in. He took in her harmonious curves as she approached. She was conservatively dressed in jeans, sandals and a military-style long-sleeve shirt with epaulets. He had looked forward to this moment, and he was not disappointed. He hoped that he read the same conclusion in Kella's smile when she seated herself at the table.

Suspecting that Steve's apparent change in career was a result of the events in Morocco, she asked, "Did you leave West Gate?"

Steve replied, "No, I'm just taking unpaid leave. The Moroccan project is moving along nicely. My part is done. I ran into a magazine publisher and we just clicked. He said he was looking for a freelance photographer who could write and had overseas experience for a project that would last a month or so. When he said the focus of the article was going to be the Tuaregs, I told him that he had found his man."

"You're full of surprises. I can't stay here a month, though. I've got ten days."

"Well, let's make the most of them. By the way, the name I'm using here whenever I don't need documentation is Christopher—my middle name."

Reacting to Kella's questioning glance, he added, "Well, OK, I'm a little nervous that the same guys who tried to get me in Morocco might somehow learn I'm now here. If you don't mind, I'd like you to call me Christopher in public—in fact, all the time here."

"Sounds mysterious. I never thought of it before, but are there Salafists here too?" She glanced around the restaurant.

"Are you ready for this? I learned that Tariq al Khalil is here running a social-welfare group."

"You're kidding. What happens if he learns you're here? What about the publicity surrounding you and the Quran documents?"

"For now, I'm just going to get material for the magazine. It may turn out that going to see him with my cameras may be the best defense. What about the relatives you want to find?"

Kella looked at him with one eyebrow raised like a question mark. Steve didn't respond and she said, "Thiyya is my birth mother's cousin. Her husband is Azrur. Other Tuaregs will know them. It's a small tribal community. I've been thinking about spending time here with them ever since that day when Faridah died. They're my closest birth relatives. Besides, I'm sure that they'll be able to help with your article, and I hope to write a paper for school out of this time in Timbuktu."

"OK, I'm good to go. How do we start looking for them? There's a lot of desert out there. Your Imazighen relatives could be anywhere."

"I'm impressed. You've been doing some reading. Did you also know that *Imazighen* means free and noble people? You must have read some of Timbuktu's history. Do you know about Mansa Musa? He was a fourteenth-century Malian emperor who made a pilgrimage to Mecca with sixty thousand men and twelve thousand slave girls. His baggage train included eighty camels, each carrying three hundred pounds of gold. He spread so much gold in Egypt that the price fell and didn't recover for years."

"Sounds like something out of a movie," Steve said.

Steve drove her back to her hotel, the Hendrina Khan. On

the way, Kella said, "Here is a bit of trivia for you. Remember A. Q. Khan, the father of the 'Islamic Bomb'? This is his hotel. He named it after his Dutch wife."

Steve stopped in front of the hotel. "Fascinating." Under the gaze of the hotel guard and doorman, Steve kissed her good night. As he drove away, it occurred to him that he was now thinking of Vera *after* rather than before the kiss.

The next day, Kella went to the Catholic orphanage from which the Hastingses had adopted her. The building was fairly large, including a dormitory for fifty children, two classrooms and an office. A sandy courtyard surrounded by a seven-foot wall was full of running and laughing children. Next to the courtyard was a church. Mother Superior Catherine was still there, surprised and pleased to see her.

"Oh, my dear!" she exclaimed. "I still remember how the Hastingses fell in love with you the moment they saw you, especially Madame Alexandra. Your stepfather held a very important position at the American Embassy in Bamako, you know. He came to Timbuktu to take care of any American citizens affected by the Tuareg rebellion. And when Madame came with him, I made sure that she saw you. Somehow I just knew that she would want to adopt you."

"My stepmother said that you had warned her that Tuaregs are very independent people," recalled Kella.

Mother Catherine laughed and said, "That is true. I didn't want her to be surprised. I also told her that your DNA was quite a mixture of European, Berber, Arab and Negro, and she said that explained why you were such a beautiful child. She promised to bring you up in the Church," said Mother Catherine. "Has she?"

"Yes, Mother Catherine," Kella replied just as seriously. "I would like to get in touch with my birth relatives while I'm here. How do you think I can find them? I suppose they're still nomads and moving around quite a bit."

"Start with the marabout, a Muslim holy man very close

to the Tuaregs. He knows everything." The mother superior told Kella how to find him.

Steve made calls to the Office of Tourism in order to establish his official presence in Timbuktu and try to avoid the high degree of red tape he had been warned about by the cultural attaché. Then, wanting to begin both his cover and his CIA assignments, as well as try to get a fix on Kella's relatives, he went to the airport to rent a plane.

The airport was deserted, other than a few Malians who seemed to call it home. He headed for the control tower. It was an incongruously elegant piece of architecture consisting of a long neck rising out of an administrative building at a sixty-degree angle to support the control room forward of the tower. *Overdone,* thought Steve. *Like having an army to protect a bank with no funds.*

He reached the control room but found himself alone. He eventually went back to his car. Just as Atrar was putting the car in gear, a pickup truck pulled up. Steve told Atrar to wait. He got out and went up to the other car as the driver stepped out. He was in his late twenties and sported a stubble of beard. Steve determined immediately from his speech that he was Australian.

"No, mate, there are no Hertz Rent-a-plane outfits here," he told Steve. "The only private aircraft at the airport is shared by several NGOs. That's nongovernmental organizations to you, mate, if you're new. It's a Cherokee Six, a Piper. You're talking to the owner and pilot. I'm Campbell," he said. "What is it exactly you want, Yank?"

Steve explained his photojournalist status and said he wanted to use the aircraft for half a day or so for a reconnaissance of the area around Timbuktu, looking especially for Tuareg camps he could visit by car later.

"I've got a pilot's license and could fly your plane, but for the first time, I could use a pilot who knows the neighborhood."

"You've got a deal, mate. How about tomorrow morning?" Campbell asked after they settled on the price.

"Great. There'll be one other passenger."

Campbell walked toward the field while Steve told Atrar to drive back to town.

CHAPTER SEVENTEEN

Steve and Kella waited at the airport for Campbell. When he showed up, forty-five minutes late, Steve thought he smelled the sweet odor of marijuana from Campbell's clothes. He leaned in for a closer look. His eyes were indeed a bit bloodshot. "Have a late night last night?" Steve asked, wondering if the Aussie was 100 percent together.

Steve saw Kella's concerned look and squeezed her arm in reassurance.

Campbell laughed, "The biggest secret about Timbuktu is the party scene. I'm not staying here for the money."

They got settled in the Piper Cherokee, a six seater, with Kella sitting behind the pilot. She said, "We're looking for a place just north of Lake Faguibine. Do you know where that is?"

"Yes, it's west of here about a hundred miles."

"Then I'd like to fly over any Tuareg camps within, say, a hundred-mile radius of Timbuktu," Steve said.

"You got it." Campbell pushed on the throttle.

The plane picked up speed down the runway, and Steve quickly sensed that something was missing—he hadn't seen Campbell go through the takeoff checklist. With the plane still on the ground but gaining speed, the engine sputtered for a couple of seconds, but resumed its normal operation. Steve, on the pilot's right, looked at Campbell and said, "What's that?"

Campbell didn't answer. He pulled back on the control and lifted the plane off the ground. At three hundred fifty feet in altitude, the engine coughed again, alternating between no power and normal function for several seconds and then stopping completely.

Kella leaned forward. "I don't like this. Christopher?"

At almost the same time, Steve said sharply, "We'd better land." He expected Campbell to keep going straight and land on the hard desert floor in front of the runway. Instead Campbell initiated a sharp turn to the right.

"No, we're not high enough!" Steve yelled, and wrestled the yoke from Campbell's control to get out of the turn before the plane stalled.

"Oh, my God. What's going on?" Kella shouted from the back as she looked at the ground rushing toward her.

The plane swiftly lost lift and altitude as the wings became almost perpendicular to the ground. Kella yelled, "No!"

Campbell, fighting back Steve's pull on the yoke, shouted, "Drongo Yankee," but Steve was too strong and Campbell relinquished his hold. The plane was only thirty feet from the ground before Steve managed to return the wings to a horizontal position. Their sharp descent became a glide toward the sand.

Steve glanced down at the fuel-selector controls and noticed the setting was all the way to the left, on the off position. With his left hand, he quickly moved the setting to number-three position, the left main tank, going right past the number-two setting for the left wing-tip tank. Barely ten feet off the ground, the engine came back to life. Steve moved the throttle forward, at first gently, but when the wheels touched the ground, he forcefully pushed on the throttle and the Piper jumped up, the engine no longer coughing. At a thousand feet, Steve turned the plane around and circled the airport but kept climbing. He reached two thousand feet and the engine seemed to be functioning normally.

"What do you say? The engine sounds OK. I vote for going on. The sand looks pretty hard. If we have to, we could glide down. Your radio works, right?" Steve said.

Campbell nodded but without enthusiasm, and Steve added, "I'll do the piloting and you be the navigator."

"Look, Yank, I'm still the captain," Campbell protested, his face white and sweaty.

"I know that, and you are in charge. But you have to agree that you're not at your best this morning. Right? That must have been a hell of a party last night. You don't put a plane in a tight turn like that at less than at least seven or eight hundred feet, and we were barely off the ground, with no power! You could have killed us. You're still under the effect of whatever you smoked." Steve smiled at the Australian to keep the situation as calm as possible. "Let's watch that fuel-selector switch. Did you gas up this morning? Are the tanks full?" Steve asked.

"The tanks are not full, but we've got at least two hours of gas. OK, OK, head directly west at two hundred seventy-five degrees," Campbell replied. Steve was sure he didn't want to lose the fee.

"How did the fuel selector get to the off position?" Steve asked.

"You must have hit it with your knee."

"I don't think so," Steve said firmly, looking at Campbell, convinced now that Campbell hadn't gone through his checklist.

Steve looked back at Kella and gave her a reassuring smile. "You OK back there? Having fun yet?"

She did not smile. "This is not a joke. We almost crashed. I think we should go back and forget about this."

"We can do that," Steve said. "But I think we fixed the problem. The fuel selector was set on an empty tank. We're

OK now. Right, Campbell?" Campbell said nothing, sulking. Steve again looked at Kella. "I'm for going ahead. We're OK, really. I've got things under control."

"I hope one of you knows what he's doing," said Kella.

Timbuktu was still visible to the north as they flew over a track that headed first to the west and then to the southwest, paralleling the Niger River. As far as the eye could see, the only traffic consisted of one truck heading west. However, there were scattered small groups, some with a camel or a donkey or two. Soon Lake Faguibine was visible in the distance. Indeed, on the northern side was an outcropping of rocks rising a couple hundred feet above the desert. Between the northwest side of the lake and the rocks were palm trees and bushes. Steve lowered his altitude and could see several camps among the trees. The black tents, the whites and blues of the men's clothing and the blacks of the women's, together with the green of the vegetation were in stark contrast to the otherwise-monotonous color of the sand.

"They're Tuaregs," Kella said. "That's where the marabout told me I would find Azrur and Thiyya."

Steve came down to a hundred feet above the camp and waggled the plane's wings in a friendly gesture. "Here, put an *X* on the map so we can find them again," he said. He then pointed the plane on an azimuth of forty-five degrees, heading toward the oasis of Dayet en Naharat, to start a wide northern arc around Timbuktu. They soon reached the track that led to the oasis and followed it north until they overflew it. They then headed directly east and soon reached the oasis of I-n-Alei.

Off to the east about four miles, sand and dust swirled into the sky. Curious, Steve headed for it, skirting the cloud on its southern side. A convoy of trucks and jeeps apparently coming from I-n-Alei was at the source of the disturbance. The trucks were loaded with barrels and with goats and cases of vegetables.

"Where do you think they're going?" Steve asked Campbell, who shrugged.

"I'm not sure I want to know. They look military—probably the Malian army resupplying its desert troops somewhere," he said.

"Well, let's see," Steve said as he directed the plane to follow the desert track being used by the convoy. Thirty miles farther, flying at a thousand feet, they could see the outlines of a camp. There were vehicles, several large tents and a group of men in single line getting food and water—a chow line. It was lunchtime. There was another group doing push-ups and calisthenics. Steve could also see an obstacle course and a rifle range. The men in line had weapons, and a few pointed them toward the plane. Others waved their arms for the intruder to leave their space, and still others appeared to be shouting. A black flag flew at the top of a pole in the middle of the camp.

"What's that?" asked Kella from the back of the aircraft. She leaned forward and pointed to the far end of the camp, where they could see an airstrip about a thousand feet long. As Steve looked toward where she pointed, a small plane about half the size of theirs was taking flight from the airstrip. Steve banked the plane to circle the camp and headed higher.

"Looks like a UAV, an unmanned air vehicle. It's too small for a pilot. But big enough to carry other stuff, like cameras, machine guns, even missiles," Campbell said. "I'll take over here. I feel fine," he added with a new air of authority, and Steve reluctantly relinquished control of the plane to the Australian.

The UAV was also gaining height, and it soon was only about a half mile away but clearly heading toward the Piper at an altitude of thirteen hundred feet, only two hundred feet below them. As it got closer, they noticed it had no identifying number, only a black rectangle on its tail.

Campbell climbed to keep some distance from the UAV

until the ground controller made his intentions known, which he did quickly. Heading toward them at a right angle, the UAV shot a hail of bullets their way. Steve was able to see that the bullets were high, because some of them were tracers, bullets modified with a pyrotechnic charge that burn brightly, making the path of the bullet visible to the naked eye and giving the shooter a way to correct his aim.

Campbell headed higher while Steve got out his camera and shot photographs of the camp and of the UAV that continued to follow them, firing an occasional burst.

"Let's get out of here!" cried Kella. This was advice Campbell took gladly, and he pointed the aircraft south, gaining speed. After ten minutes, the UAV turned back.

"What the hell was that all about? I never saw that camp before," Campbell said. "What kind of flag was that?" he asked.

"It only needs a skull and crossbones," said Steve, suspecting that they had just flown over a Salafist installation, an open secret the Malian government was choosing to ignore.

On their way back to the airport, they flew over Timbuktu. It was clearer from the air that the city of legends was struggling to survive. The sands of the Sahara, with the patience of centuries and the power of the wind, were trying to smother the city. Houses on the outskirts of town acted as a barrier to the slow but irresistible juggernaut of rock ground by the elements into tons of minute granules and moved at the command of the wind. Heading north was a caravan of at least fifty camels, with two Tuaregs walking in front and a few others near the middle and the rear of the caravan. Steve wondered if they were going to Morocco.

After a surprisingly smooth landing, Campbell said, "I went through a difficult patch back there, but hey, thanks, mate, I don't know what happened. I couldn't think straight. I shouldn't charge you anything for this flight, but you have to understand, my bank account is a little low right now."

Kella got out of the plane as quickly as she could and, without another word, headed toward their car.

"Well, it was a memorable flight. I don't like getting shot at," Steve answered. Boy, had his life changed. His CIA briefings had obviously been incomplete. He wondered what other surprises were out there.

CHAPTER EIGHTEEN

The next day, Steve and Kella had breakfast together at her hotel, the Hendrina Khan. They were planning on an early start, and the dining room was otherwise empty. They sat at a table against the wall. Kella's black hair was pulled back. Steve noticed that her only makeup was a light trace of lipstick as protection against the sun. She looked rested and fresh faced. She wore khakis, and a white T-shirt over which she had an open light blue shirt with long sleeves. She rolled them up above the elbow, where she buttoned them down.

She put her tan bush hat on one of the other chairs at their table and took a sip of her orange juice. "I'm really excited about seeing my cousins again. This is going to be a good day. Do you think we'll get there today? I don't know about you, but I don't ever want to fly with that Aussie again. Yesterday was a miserable day. I thought we were going to die before we even left the airport."

"I'm sorry. But we did find the Tuareg camp. Your marabout knew what he was talking about. We should get to your relatives early tomorrow."

Atrar loaded their backpacks, two large plastic containers of water and a cooler that Kella had found in the Timbuktu market, in which she stocked flat bread, fruits and a chicken she had convinced the hotel to cook for them. At the time, Steve had said, "That cooler looks ideal for the beer," but he lost the argument and sent Atrar to find another cooler. So they left with his-and-hers coolers.

The camp was about one hundred miles due west as the crow flies. However, by land, it was more like a hundred and fifty miles, since Atrar wanted to use tracks as long as he could before heading out across the desert. On the way, Kella talked about her early childhood as a nomad, tending the goats, pounding millet into meal, seeing the world from the top of a camel when the clan changed grazing areas and desert wells and, when possible, attending school. "As a kid, I did a lot of walking when we changed grazing areas. Now I'd rather ride, thank you very much. Although I do jog for exercise, I really hate it—so boring."

Steve asked, "What about women's role in the tribe? You hinted at it in Paris. It sounded very different from the Muslim tradition."

"You're right. In the Tuareg tradition, ancestry flows through the female line. My mother and her mother always had positions of leadership. That didn't mean necessarily that I would also have been a tribal leader. But in a way, it was mine to lose."

They spent the night in Goundam, a town surrounded by several lakes created by the Niger's annual floods.

Before they left the next morning, they had coffee at their hotel on a deck overlooking a tributary flowing into the Niger where a family of hippopotami was bathing. A young American couple joined Steve and Kella. The man wore a white shirt with a pouch slung across his chest bandolier-style. The woman wore khakis and a long-sleeve shirt, also white. It seemed big for her, as if it belonged to her companion. The newcomers introduced themselves as John and Elise West, a brother-and-sister team of the Church of Jesus Christ of Latter-day Saints—Mormons—in the last few days of their two-year proselytizing mission.

Steve asked the waiter to set the table for two more people.

John said, "All Mormons go on a twenty-four-month mission normally right after high school. We took French at Highland High School in Salt Lake City. Then, before we left Utah, we picked up some Bambara, the dialect of the dominant Malian tribe, at the LDS language center. Elise has a knack for languages and she learned Tamasheq after we got here."

Kella and Elise exchanged a few words in Tamasheq, each surprised and delighted that the other spoke the language.

"We could have been sent to Poughkeepsie or to Vladivostok . . . just about anywhere," said John.

The waiter poured coffee for the four of them.

John continued, "But we were sent to Mali, and here we are, on the edge of the Sahara. We normally work out of Beautiful Downtown Timbuktu-on-the-Niger."

Elise said, "I've dreamed about a mission like this since I was fifteen. It's important for all of us to spread Jesus's word."

Kella had been listening closely, leaning back in her chair. She took a sip of her orange juice and asked, "This is so interesting. Are there other Western organizations around Timbuktu?"

Elise answered, "There are at least a dozen NGOs in Mali with different goals: humanitarian, medical, religious and sometimes political. The United Nations has its groups. The United States has the Peace Corps. Médecins Sans Frontières is here. Cuba has medical technicians, and the International Red Cross also."

Steve looked at his watch and asked, "How about Muslims? Have you met anyone from IMRA?"

The Wests glanced at each other, and John said, "Yes, Sunnis. They don't mix with the rest of us. Although their boss, Tariq al Khalil, claims Belgian nationality, I've heard that he has little use for Europeans. We've never met those people."

"But what do they do here?" Steve persisted.

Elise said, "They're supposed to be helping the people in the region with health and social services, and they use that as a springboard to urge their audiences toward a pure brand of Islam. Rumors are rampant that they have a dark side, that the Malian authorities don't dare interfere in their activities and that they're forming a secret army."

"Are they successful?" Steve asked, looking at John.

"I'm not sure. The brand of Islam around here is more basically Sufi than strict Wahhabist, so there is natural resistance. The strict Muslims don't even believe that the local Muslims are Muslim at all because their religion has marabouts, saints and they worship images. Some of the rumors about IMRA claim that they are responsible for the deaths of several of these holy men who were not interested in the IMRA version of Islam."

The Wests offered to introduce Steve and Kella to their world by inviting them to their going-away party the following week in Timbuktu. Many NGO workers would be there, as well as Malian employees and friends. Kella and Steve accepted the offer.

From Goundam, Atrar left the track and headed straight west in the desert and then found a path on the western side of Lake Kamango that took them north toward Lake Faguibine.

In midafternoon Atrar stopped the car and pointed toward the horizon. Steve took out binoculars and said, "It sure looks like the camp we saw from the air."

Kella asked, "Can I have the binoculars?" In the far distance she saw dark rock outcroppings above the desert floor. After a few kilometers of rough, off-road driving, she saw a track heading up a long, sloping incline, and at the top, between the two lakes, a number of horizontal slashes in the landscape as the land rose again.

The Tuareg camp was at the bottom of the outcroppings. Atrar stopped the car beside a steep rock wall. A hundred and fifty feet away a dozen camels looked down at a herd of cattle drinking in clusters from metal drums almost completely buried in the ground. A barefoot boy in a loose white garment that covered him to his elbows and knees used a stick with his left hand on a short-horned bull that, with the exception of his black nose, blended with the hard-packed brown sand. In his right hand, the boy held one end of a rope that curled almost down to the ground to a tight noose around the animal's horns. The bull's long, muscular neck held his head low, but his eyes looked up to his left, and his horns were at an angle that pointed the left horn directly at the boy's waist. Another rope tied to his horns trailed on the ground behind him toward several branches planted in the ground like tent poles the height of a man. A pulley hung under the apex of the branches over a well. Kella realized that it was the boy's job to draw water from the well.

The animal suddenly swung his horns toward the boy, who nimbly jumped out of the way. A blue-clad adult shouted at the boy, who stepped behind the bull and hit him several times with his stick. The bull's defiance flagged. He pulled, and the rope tightened behind him.

Kella and Steve followed a path around the rock wall. A young boy about seven or eight ran up to them and said, "Welcome," in Tamasheq. Kella replied with the normal courtesies of the desert and asked him about Azrur and Thiyya. "This way," he shouted as his bare feet took him running and bouncing like an eland up the path.

"Oh, it is so familiar," said Kella as they followed the boy. "I can't help but remember my own childhood."

The boy had run ahead to the campground, a wide plateau with perhaps fifty tents made of black animal skins with open sides. As Steve and Kella entered the camp, a couple emerged from their tent. The man was tall and wore a beige robe. His head, nose, mouth and neck were covered by a long indigo cloth. His eyes inspected them quickly, but he did not put down the thin lance, one end of which he rested on the ground. The woman wore a black turban and a loose sleeveless indigo overgarment with large openings for the arms. Kella yelled, "Thiyya!" and ran toward her. They hugged closely, speaking in rapid and joyous exclamations. Azrur was more reserved, but his words welcomed Kella. Both were in their early fifties.

Thiyya had an air of supreme self-confidence without the sharp edges of the dictator. In another age, thought Kella, she could have been an ambassador or led a salon in late-seventeenth-century France—a Tuareg Germaine de Staël. Kella smiled, her eyes moist. Thiyya's eyes were like dark brushstrokes. When not speaking, her lips were were pressed softly together. Her skin was the color of cinnamon batter. Kella wondered at the absence of wrinkles. Kella remembered Steve and introduced him as a group gathered around.

Thiyya announced to all, "Kella is my cousin's daughter. Her parents were killed by the army during the troubles. She is my blood." Then, she took Kella's right hand and raised it for everyone to see the four black dots arranged in a diamond on the back of her hand. The effect was to have the women call out happily to Kella, while the men crowded closer to have a better look at Kella's hand and throw looks of suspicion in Steve's direction.

Thiyya made tea and served biscuits with goat cheese. Later, Azrur took Steve and Kella to the well at the edge of camp.

Kella said, "Azrur's great-great-grandfather, by the way, led a Tuareg army that fought the French army at the Battle of Goundam in the 1890s. I should have told you when we were there." Knowing Kella was saying something about him, Azrur looked in their direction, and his eyes were made narrower by what Kella knew to be a smile.

Steve said, "Tell him it's an honor to be his guest. What about your name, and Thiyya's? Do they mean something in Tamasheq?"

"*Thiyya* means beauty, and Kella was the daughter of Tin Hinnan, a Tuareg queen."

"I'm impressed. Both of you were well named."

Later that night, after small talk, Kella and her cousin drew aside, while Azrur and Steve stayed by the fire.

Kella told her about the horrific scene she'd witnessed in Paris. Thiyya hung her head while the story unfolded. As Kella finished recounting the story and the reason she came to her cousin for comfort, Thiyya opened her arms and held them out to her. The young woman slid over to her and rested against her bosom as Thiyya's arms folded around her and rocked her gently. Kella cried softly.

Thiyya said, "We Tuareg women have never let ourselves be dominated by the men. When the Arabs came and imposed their religion, the Tuareg tribes fought them, but there were too many. But we hang on to our culture. We Tuareg women are the equals of men; in some ways our situation is even better. We can decide whom to marry, and we can manage our own wealth. Our marriages are monogamous, unlike Muslim practice." She guided Kella to a corner of the tent where some blankets were laid out.

On the evening of the next day, Kella's cousins organized a tribal feast in Kella's honor. Goat and camel steaks cooked on a wood and dried-dung fire to eat, and for drink, they offered goat and camel milk. Steve had Atrar bring Gazelle beer from the cooler he had left in the Land Cruiser.

However, the main event was the camel races. Steve seemed amused when Kella translated the good-natured ribbing from her cousins.

"They recall that I grew up riding camels and have insisted I participate," she told him with an expression caught between amusement and dread.

"Well, I'll be cheering you on!" Steve said.

"I'll wave to you so you can recognize me in my blue robe."

Steve pointed to his cameras. "You'll be the star of my article."

Kella watched Steve and Atrar drive their car close to the starting line. Steve opened the sunroof and readied his cameras. There were fifteen contestants. Most riders, men and women alike, had sticks for riding crops, but only the men were veiled. Kella's mount was easily the largest animal on the starting line. She assumed that her cousins were being the perfect hosts, or perhaps Kella's noble lineage gave her certain rights.

Men, women and children had lined up on the side of the ad hoc racecourse. Kella guessed there must be at least a hundred people waiting, talking, with occasional ululations of jubilance from the women. Both the men and women were in colorful billowing robes.

Suddenly, the mounts were off. Both riders and watchers were in the moment. The excitement was palpable. Just about everyone was yelling, and the riders encouraged their mounts by slapping their sticks against their sides.

Kella did not have a good start, and she was in the middle of the pack for the first fifty yards. But the long white legs of her camel gobbled up the ground and gained yard after yard on the leaders. Finally, the race was between Kella and another woman on a sandy-brown camel, who used her stick with vigor. In a nose-to-nose finish, it seemed to Kella that she finished a close second.

As the camel folded its ungainly legs and Kella dismounted, Steve hurried over to her. "Wow, that was close. This is serious competition. You looked a mile high up there on that beast. The way it was rocking and rolling, I don't know how you stayed on," he said.

"This is not as easy as I remembered. Another fifty yards, though, and I would have won. Don't you think?"

Steve laughed and said, "I'm certain of it."

Before they left the next morning, Thiyya took Kella to her tent, opened a wooden box and took a bracelet out. Thiyya's face, always reflecting control over herself and her immediate environment, looked solemn. The unusually stern set of her eyes and mouth presaged something important. Kella wondered how she did that without gaining a wrinkle.

"This bracelet belonged to your mother. It has been passed on from generation to generation since before any of us were born. According to the legend, retold by our tribe's storytellers over the years, it belonged to an ancient Tuareg queen. Now the bracelet belongs to you."

Kella remembered that her mother used to wear a gold bracelet during important occasions, but she never knew the story behind it. "Thank you, cousin. What else can you tell me?" she asked.

"There is another story that an American ship captain who was shipwrecked off the coast long ago and sold inland into slavery was also one of your ancestors. He was the first outsider to reach Timbuktu and leave alive. He was ransomed by a British official in Morocco and returned to the United States. And when the French soldiers were here a long time ago, one of them stayed and married into the family. You are Tuareg royalty, with an American and a Frenchman, maybe more, in your family tree," Thiyya told her.

"Not too different from my current life. I have a French mother, an American father. Except, you're all the royalty I need," she said, and hugged Thiyya.

CHAPTER NINETEEN

A knock on al Khalil's door interrupted his thoughts. He had been analyzing IMRA finances and found them coming up short. Hussein walked in and al Khalil closed the computer. Before Hussein could speak, al Khalil said, "We have to find ways to raise more funds. Our donors are going to sleep because they think we're going to sleep. I have to pay new recruits—fighters, martyrs, politicians, imams. Incoming funds are not sufficient. We have another year at the most."

Hussein tried to interrupt. "I understand—"

Al Khalil put his hand up. "All of our income from private and public sources, from secret sources and so on, is not enough on which to build the renaissance of Islam." His eyes transferred to Hussein the burden of action.

Hussein said, "I do have good news. One of my sources, a Malian who works for a Canadian NGO, told me that the missionaries are having a big party tomorrow. A lot of Western infidels are also going to be there. Is this the opportunity you've been looking for? It would be easier to hit them all at once than to kill them one by one. What do you think?"

"Yes, I've been urging you to do just that for some time. We need a highly visible operation, and a *successful* one, to attract funds. Attacking a few missionaries is thinking small. We need a bigger, much bigger operation to regain our funding." Hussein and all his other assistants were small people with small ideas. Al Khalil resigned himself to this incremental action for now. He willed himself to be more positive. Perhaps Allah was smiling. "What do you want to do? A bomb in the middle of the party? Who do you plan to use?"

"A bomb means finding someone with natural access to the location, or a martyr. We don't have time for a bomb operation. And I have better uses for my fighters than blowing them up. This is a soft target, the softest. I say keep it simple. Two men with AK-47s can walk in and mow them down. Direct and short, with immediate results."

Tariq smiled at the picture Hussein was painting. He said, "Dahmane is well experienced in this type of work. I trust Dahmane. Although he's Malian, he's a Fulani. He claims ancestry from the Quraysh, the Prophet's tribe. He shares my vision. After this, we'll give him more responsibility. And give him another fighter."

"Yes, I want to give him Karim, the Algerian. It's time he got more directly involved, and I think he's ready. He's still young but he has had combat experience in Algeria."

Tariq drew himself up and declared, "This will send a message to the infidels that they are not wanted here. They need to go home. They have to get out of Muslim lands. Make sure the operation is clean. We want no repercussions, although our friends in the police won't investigate very hard. It should be like target practice. AK-47s against unarmed missionaries at a party." He chuckled, and Hussein joined in.

Hussein left and al Khalil went back to his Excel spreadsheet.

The world had to pay attention, or he would never replicate the work of the Prophet. People were apathetic, too inured by selfishness and the media's constant focus on irrelevant problems. Only a major action on the order of Hiroshima would wake them up.

He had had several false starts in his efforts to acquire nuclear materials. He had lines out in several directions to obtain the means to make the nuclear splash that would bring the apostate rulers to his door. He thought of the underground storage at the training camp. He still didn't have the right people to help him use the large amount of yellowcake he had hidden. He couldn't do it all. His focus was in establishing a base in the Sahel states of Africa. Influencing the local authorities through bribes or coercion was working, but too slowly. He leaned back in his chair and looked at the posters of Jerusalem and Cairo on his wall.

When Steve and Kella arrived at the NGO warehouse where the going-away party was planned, tables and chairs had been rearranged. The cases of bottled water, blankets, medicine and tents had been restacked in the back. Each group had brought food and drink.

John and Elise were already there, as was Campbell. An old Charles Aznavour song was playing in the background. Tables along one wall were for the *mechoui*—lamb slow-cooked over a wood fire—and grilled capitaine, the huge freshwater fish from the Niger River. Along another wall was a table laden with fruit, chicken, dates, teas and soft drinks. Soon the room was full of laughter from several dozen people who were celebrating a job well done and wishing bon voyage to good friends. Each new arrival brought more food and drink. Steve heard at least a dozen languages being spoken, with English dominating. "Quite the international group," he said to Kella.

Frank Sinatra replaced Aznavour until a live Tuareg musical group, called Tivaren, began to play and sing. Steve told Kella, "My driver's brother Izem met the members of this band when he was in the Libyan army. Many of the Tuareg rebels went to Libya after the rebellion. As a favor to him, they came to help the international workers celebrate."

Kella replied, "I like their music. It's called *ishoumar*, a mixture of traditional Tuareg music, John Lee Hooker and reggae."

Steve and Kella soon served themselves and went to find

seats. But almost as soon as they sat down, Kella said, "Oh, I'm going to go say hello to Elise. I'll be back."

Steve tasted the *mechoui* and looked around for something to drink. He saw a large white plastic cooler underneath a food table near the front wall and got up, hoping that he would find a beer. The space was alive with music and conversation. He looked back to spot Kella as he walked toward the cooler. She was half-kneeling by the Wests, who sat at a center table in the back. He bent down to open the cooler and was reaching for a beer when the staccato sound of gunfire suddenly dominated the room. He dove to the floor and shouted, "Get down. Get down." Steve could see that many had not immediately recognized the sound of gunfire. They seemed almost paralyzed. He looked up to see the legs of two men walking down the center of the warehouse. Looking up a bit more, he saw them firing AK-47s, one firing from the center to the right and the other to the left. The gunfire had plunged the party into total chaos. Most people were now on the floor. Steve could see that a few in the center had been hit by the steel-jacketed bullets. A Malian waiter and a Canadian with Médecins Sans Frontières were down and not moving. Few in the middle of the room were not wounded. He couldn't see Kella.

The sound of the guns punctuated the screams of pain and terror. Tables, chairs and other furniture were knocked over. Dishes, glasses and bottles exploded and crashed to the floor, spraying their contents and shards of glass around the room.

He crawled closer to the entrance and noticed that he still had his bottle of beer in his hand. The gunmen were past him but still firing mostly to their front and side. He was in back of them and to their right. He again looked for Kella near John and Elise with mounting anxiety. He could easily have run out the front door and tried to get help. The gunfire continued in shorter bursts, and he saw one assailant drop an empty magazine clip and reload. Unconsciously, Steve knew the gunman had sixty more shots, and there was no time to look for help.

From the first bursts of AK-47 fire, even as he plunged to the floor, Steve remembered that his explosives and weapons instructor had given him a concealed self-defense weapon on the last night of training. He turned to one side on the floor in order to get his hand in the pocket where he had placed the device when getting dressed for the party. He took out what appeared to be a Montblanc pen but was a still-experimental pulsed-energy-projectile gun. He turned the top quickly to the left, felt it click, pointed the top of the pen toward the closest assailant but stopped when he realized his hand was shaking. He quickly got to his knees, steadied his left hand on the back of a chair and pushed the clasp firmly inward. The pulsed energy immediately superheated the air and moisture around the target with a flash of light and a loud bang. The effect was not exactly what Steve had expected. In training, both light and sound had been twice as great. Nevertheless, the whole room instantly froze in time, its population temporarily deafened and paralyzed. The gunman that Steve had fired at appeared unsteady on his feet. He looked as if he was about to drop his weapon—he was holding it limply. For an instant, the only sound was from the Beatles, singing "Help."

Steve recovered first. With adrenaline pumping, he sprang to his feet and rushed toward the second gunman, who was starting to drop to one knee, his hands going up to his ears as if to protect them from another explosion. He still held his weapon. Steve's tackle took the gunman down.

Simultaneously, a shot rang out and the attacker immobilized by Steve's weapon fell over backward. As the man fell, his carotid artery, pierced by the bullet, began to pump blood from his body in cadenced spurts. Steve quickly got his adversary facedown and seized his weapon. He looked up and saw Izem about to fire a second shot. But his target was down. "Tie them up!" Steve yelled to Izem, and directed one of the waiters to help him.

Steve then went to look for Kella at the Wests' table. He first saw Elise bending over her brother John. She looked at Steve and said in shock, "He's dead. John is dead."

Steve bent down and felt for a pulse. However, he could only hear and feel his own heart. He moved his hand from John's throat to his chest but felt nothing. He asked Elise, "How about you? Are you hit?"

"My brother is dead," she said in a low monotone, eyes unfocused. "We were going home tomorrow."

Steve saw Kella under the table. Blood colored the loose white shirt she wore over her halter top. "Don't move," he said. "How are you?"

"I don't know yet," she said. "I can't move my arm." Steve helped her up to one of the chairs. She was holding her left arm. Blood seeped onto her slacks. Steve took off his belt and used it as a tourniquet around her upper arm.

Izem had tied the surviving terrorist's hands behind him and was now tying him to a chair. The wounded moaned; a woman shrieked in shock, and her friend joined her in sympathy; some cried over their dead friends; some were in a helpless daze. Steve saw that two men, whom he knew to be part of the Médecins Sans Frontières group, were trying to help the wounded. The floor was covered with broken glass, food, dishes and silverware, forming islands in the middle of a crimson-tinted mixture of blood and Orangina soda.

"Take this guy to my room and keep him there until I get there," Steve told Izem. "See what information you can get out of him in the meantime. Do not turn him over to the police. I'm going to take Kella to the hospital." Steve found Atrar, assembled Kella and two others who had been wounded, and hurried to the hospital. There were as yet no police sirens to be heard.

CHAPTER TWENTY

Kella, with a crewman in a flight suit on one side and the French Embassy nurse on the other, walked under the tail and up the loading ramp of the French air-force cargo plane—a C-160 Transall, according to the crewman who had met her and Steve inside the terminal. It was dark, but she could see the outline of the high-winged aircraft outlined by red lights on its wings and tail, a tail that seemed to be two or three stories high. The pilot had not shut down the two engines, and Kella tried to protect her face from the sand blowing toward her with her right hand. Her left arm was in a cast. The hard soles of the crewman's shoes against the metal of the ramp punctuated the noise of the engines. Steve followed Kella, carrying her suitcase, which she had, with considerable misgivings, asked Steve to pack for her while she was at the hospital.

Before being hustled out of the plane, Steve, almost shouting to be heard over the noise of the engines, said, "This is the best thing for you. We're lucky this plane could pick you up. You need to get to a real hospital. Your grandfather the general will take care of you. Call me when you land."

Kella was in pain. She winced as she tried to fit into the uncomfortable seat. "Take care. You should really leave too. Don't interview al Khalil. Stay away from him. They're killers."

Steve gave her a quick kiss on the lips and went back out the loading ramp, which closed quickly behind him.

Once the plane reached cruising altitude, the nurse took

a look at Kella's temporary cast. She said, "My name is Viviane. We're the only passengers. I'm here just to take care of you until we get to Paris. I think that your cast is OK until then. If you're in pain, I can give you a painkiller if you want. It will put you to sleep. This flight doesn't have a movie, so you won't miss much."

Kella swallowed the pills that Viviane gave her and slept until they landed at Vélizy-Villacoublay Airport outside of Paris, where an ambulance was waiting for her. She was taken to Val-de-Grâce Hospital, usually reserved for the military. Kella was accorded the luxury of a private room.

One evening a week later, during dinner at her grandfather's comfortable apartment on rue de Longchamp in the upper-scale sixteenth arrondissement, Kella's grandfather, General Joulet, asked for a full account of what had happened to her in Timbuktu.

Kella poured coffee for the two of them and recounted her trip and the events that led to the NGO party and the terrorist attack. "My friend Steve then took me to the Timbuktu Hospital. The doctor was Cuban, but he spoke English with a New York accent."

The general said, "Yes, Cuba has sent doctors and medical technicians all over the developing world. During the Cold War, that niche belonged to the Bulgarians."

"But the X-ray machine didn't work. So he thought I should go to Dakar or Abidjan, because the bullet fractured the bone. It wasn't a clean break. Dr. Delforge said that I was lucky that the bullet missed the brachial artery. My arm is now held together by a plate and screws. My luck was that you were able to get me on that cargo plane. I am very grateful to you, Grand-père."

Pointing to the sitting room, Joulet said, "Let's go sit over there, Kella. Take one of those pillows"—he pointed to a sofa—"to put under your arm."

After Kella got herself situated in an easy chair, Joulet

brought her a cup of coffee and put it on a small table to her right.

"Will you be able to return to your studies soon?"

"I've been thinking about that. Forced bed rest does that. I don't know what's happening, but in the last few months I've seen my best friend murdered by her father, and I've been shot at and had my arm broken."

"You've been in more danger in the last few weeks than most people in their entire lives. You can stay away from these dangerous people and get back to your main task, which is to graduate from the ENA," her grandfather replied. "I've been in touch with the president, a friend from my riding club. He agreed to give you extra time to finish your year's assignments. As soon as you're well, you can go back to school and the slate will be wiped clean. You'll be on the same schedule to graduate as the rest of your classmates, at least those that have made the grade."

"Thanks very much, Grand-père, but I don't think that's what I want to do anymore. I've thought a lot about this. What is the connecting thread between these events that have turned my life upside down? Both were connected with the *intégristes*, the jihadists. They are struggling and fighting amongst each other and now we, the West, the Christian world, have become targets."

The general smiled at her and said, "Now you're beginning to sound like my analysts. Except that you're more direct. The only way they know how to write is to start with 'On the one hand' and then qualify their conclusions with 'But on the other,' so they're never wrong. An American president, Truman I think, said, 'Give me one-armed economists.' Anytime you want to leave school, I have a job for you as a counterterrorism analyst."

Kella laughed at the idea. "I appreciate the offer, but I don't want to sit in a cubicle at a computer all day long. Rather than analyze, I'd rather get the information that someone else can analyze. If your analysts get the wrong information, the end product is not going to be useful, right? But frankly speaking, I'm not sure I'm that kind of person—a collector I mean, who can convince others to steal secrets for me."

"Well, if you prefer, after you graduate you can join the diplomatic service and play an important role in this issue, which is the central global issue of your generation—how the radical Muslims are going to fit into the current century, or how they're going to force the rest of us to live in their century. And their clock is no later than the thirteenth century, at most."

"Grand-père, I don't think the diplomats have done much. They all gather at the UN, sign meaningless resolutions, and then they go to their next cocktail parties in their chauffeur-driven cars. No, I think intelligence is the place to be in this fight. It's more significant, has more impact. So, can you help me?" Kella asked.

General Joulet spent the rest of the evening trying to dissuade Kella. In the end, she said, "I'll be thirty years old soon. I've seen my friend killed and been attacked by the same ideology. I'm not going to sit back and pretend none of this happened and is not happening to others every day. You said yourself that it's the most important issue that my generation will have to deal with. I want to make a difference, and this is where I want to do it."

CHAPTER TWENTY-ONE

A day after the Salafist attack on the foreign-aid personnel, Hussein brought Karim to al Khalil's office, and in answer to questions, Karim recounted the operation. Al Khalil sat behind his desk and Hussein sat in front of it. Karim stood in front of both. He played the role that Steve, whom he knew as Christopher, had outlined for him, although he believed that the advice was obvious.

Waving his arms as he talked, Karim nearly shouted, "Dahmane told me this would be easy—convincing foreign Crusaders to go home. If you had planned this operation well, you would have known that the party was going to be guarded. Everybody was shooting at us. Dahmane shouldn't have died. I was almost killed. You should have told us that there would be guards. Everybody was shooting. They even had hand grenades," he said.

"It was Allah's will," Hussein replied. "Dahmane died a *shahid*'s death. May we all be as fortunate." Karim uttered, "*Allahu Akbar*," in automatic response.

Karim exaggerated his account according to Steve's instructions. Also, he wanted to underline that his survival was due to his own skills and that the operation was not the walk in the park that everyone had expected.

Al Khalil picked up a copy of *L'Essor.* "This morning's paper reports that in Canada, France, Switzerland, the United States and other countries where the NGO's central offices are located, the media has the foreign ministries under siege. I think NGOs will be more careful to keep their people out of our lands in the future."

Hussein drank from a plastic water bottle. "Timbuktu is now full of diplomats and newspaper people. The hotels are full."

Al Khalil leaned back in his chair. "Yes, I know. I already received phone calls and gave a couple of interviews. I'm putting our IMRA work up front, but I'm also explaining how unnatural it is to have missionaries among our believers. We can take care of our own."

Karim walked to the wall on his right, picked up the only other chair in the room, brought it near Hussein and sat. "What about the police. What do they know?"

Hussein said, "Don't worry. They have no leads. The eyewitnesses were too shocked and busy trying to survive to be able to give the police any useful information or accurate descriptions. Dahmane carried no personal documentation and has not been identified. There will be an investigation to satisfy the foreigners, but all will go back to normal soon."

"The objective was to chase the missionaries out," said al Khalil. This was a sign, Karim thought, that al Khalil was closing the books on the attack. "Some are dead and the rest are leaving. Even some of the NGO people are packing, *al hamdu Allah*. The results are even better than we planned. Next time, Hussein, get more firepower on the target, just to make sure."

CHAPTER TWENTY-TWO

Steve hurried to his hotel room after getting Kella onto the French military plane, an hour and a half after the terrorist attack. Izem was threatening to burn off the soles of Karim's feet, using the finest interrogation methods he had learned in the Libyan army. So far, Karim, tied to the only chair in the room, had admitted little other than that he was Algerian. Steve told Izem to go outside and wait.

Steve said in French, "Well, I guess the next step is to call the police. How do you think you'll like the salt mines in Taoudenni?"

Karim looked frightened. "It wasn't my fault. I was forced to do it," he said.

"Forced to kill innocent people? Who forced you?" Steve asked.

"They are not innocent. They are forcing good Muslims away from Allah. They are saying lies about the Prophet."

"Really? Did you hear anyone at that party say anything at all about the Prophet?" Steve asked.

"They are bad people. They should not be here. They have to leave. This is not their country."

Steve repeated his question. "Who sent you? Who do you work for?"

Karim considered his answer. "I'm thirsty. I need water." He glanced toward the bathroom.

Steve leaned down from his chair, pulled out a soda from the small room refrigerator and handed it to Karim. "There's an opener on the side of the fridge," he said, pointing.

Karim, still tied to the chair, shrugged. "I can't."

Steve grinned and said, "Oh, I forgot. Well, for the time being, you'll have to stay thirsty. Who sent you? It's me or the Malian salt mines."

"I work for IMRA. Either I do what they say or they kill me, so I do it."

"IMRA? The IMRA that does social work among Muslims? Tell me who heads IMRA. Why the killings?"

"I told you, to make the missionaries and the other foreigners leave. We got our orders by Hussein."

"And he is . . . ?"

Karim shifted his weight a bit on the chair. "He's Tariq al Khalil's deputy."

"So, the missionaries and the others were shot because they are foreigners. What about the Malians you killed? And what about you—is this your country? I thought you told my friend that you came from Algeria, right? Why are you here?"

Little by little, Steve pulled Karim's story out. Karim had been a young student in a village outside Oran when the Salafist Group for Preaching and Combat, which later became AQIM, raided it. Karim's teachers, French and Algerians who were deemed too Westernized by the Salafists, were among the over two hundred thousand people killed over a period of several years.

Karim said, "One day they came when we were in class. They killed all the teachers. They took nine of us with them. They put us in dirty chicken coops for two days without food or water before taking us out one at a time. We all agreed to become their soldiers. Before we knew it, we were ambushing Algerian patrols.

"I was arrested once and spent six months in jail at Sidi Bel Abbès. It was difficult; two of my friends died there. But they let me go after a year. Later, I went to the Sudan and I met Lahlou—he's a Moroccan at IMRA—at a training camp. He recruited me for IMRA."

Steve stood up. "I find your story interesting, but I don't see why I shouldn't just turn you over to the Malian police. You killed some people today, including Malian Muslims. I don't know how your religion works, but I don't think that killing other Muslims is the way to heaven. Nor is killing Malian citizens the way to live a happy life in Mali."

"I don't want to go to jail. Please, I beg you. Let me go. What do you want?"

"Well, there's nothing you have that I want. You think you can help me? How?"

"I will tell you about IMRA. What do you want to know about IMRA?"

"I'm just a photographer. What makes you think that IMRA is of any interest to me?" Steve moved to the window and looked out.

"You're an American. I know that al Khalil hates Americans. You are a Crusader; otherwise you wouldn't be here, in a Muslim land. I will tell you what al Khalil is doing and planning," Karim said in a rush.

Steve, still standing, pointed to Karim. "You're a murderer. I should just turn you over. I don't know. I don't care about your information. But maybe I know someone who does. Maybe I can put you guys together. In the meantime you can talk to me. Let's try it. If your information proves to be good, and you don't lie, then we have a deal. If you're speaking the truth, then I'll say nothing to the police. But in case anything happens to me, I'm giving everything I know about you to a friend in the American Embassy in Bamako. And if something happens to me, the police of the world will be after you. But my friends will get to you first. I guarantee it."

"May Allah, the Merciful, the Beneficent, favor you," he said in Arabic. Reverting back to French, he said, "If Hussein or al Khalil find out, they will kill me on the spot. This is very dangerous. But I will do it."

"I want to see you right here in a week." Steve looked at his watch. "I want to see you next Thursday at six fifteen."

Steve handed Karim the soda on his way out. Before he let Karim take the soda, he had him repeat the time of their next meeting.

Karim showed up. He had thought about it all week and had concluded he had little to lose. He was confident that he could meet Steve and have no one the wiser. Rotting in Taoudenni was not an attractive alternative. And if it didn't work out in his favor, Karim thought that he could kill the American. He would thus get rid of one person who could identify him, and also get credit with al Khalil for eliminating a Crusader who was also a spy, like all Americans in Muslim lands.

In spite of his outward self-confidence, Karim was nervous when he reached the hotel. He rehearsed the story that Steve had given him. *If you're stopped downstairs, say that you're a guide and that I want to hire you, and don't give your real name.* But there was no one at the desk. He went straight to Steve's room. Before he knocked, Karim wondered whether the Tuareg who had first brought him to the hotel the week before would be there.

Steve let him in and they first talked about Karim's

debriefing following the attack on the missionaries. Karim said, "All is good. Al Khalil and Hussein are happy with me."

Steve asked, "Well, what do you think you know that would be of interest to me?" as Karim knew he would.

"I know many things that are of great value. Very important things. IMRA is strong because al Khalil knows Islam, and Islam, through the Quran, is the word of Allah as told to the Prophet." Karim wanted to make a strong impression on the American. He had no clear plan but felt that this could be the opportunity of a lifetime. In weighing the risk of meeting with Steve again, Karim had concluded that he would not be in this situation if Allah had not first willed it.

Steve asked, "So, what is special about IMRA?"

"Al Khalil talks a lot about Hamas in Gaza and about Hezbollah in Lebanon. We are just like them. You know, one side helps the poor and the other gives them guns to fight and die for Islam. Like me. One day I will die for Islam and go to paradise." He smiled in that knowledge.

Steve's expression was puzzled. "Where do IMRA funds come from?"

"I don't know. Only al Khalil knows. And maybe Hussein. I cannot help you. I'm sorry. Wait, maybe I could steal some documents from al Khalil's office."

"No, don't do that. Don't take any papers and don't ask questions that you would not normally ask, for now."

After an hour and a half, Karim had given Steve the names of all of the people he knew in IMRA, the names of IMRA supporters and sympathizers in Timbuktu, and that al Khalil was planning a big meeting in Gao. He said, "It is time that I go back. Or maybe someone will ask where I am."

"You're right. Next time, in a week, let's talk about the camp up north."

Karim left without acknowledging that he knew what Steve was talking about.

On his way back, Karim thought about Steve not knowing

if he was a savior to be embraced or a danger to be eliminated.

Steve moved their next meeting to an abandoned Tuareg camp two miles outside of Timbuktu. He told Karim, "This is for your protection." Karim preferred the abandoned camp to the hotel. He was confident but also knew that he would be summarily executed personally by either al Khalil or Hussein if they learned he was meeting with this American. No cover or pretext would be good enough.

Karim was fifteen minutes late. To explain his lateness, he told Steve, "You said to come after dark," a directive that Karim had thought to be gratuitous at the time.

"It's important to do things exactly as I tell you. For your safety. It's been dark for an hour. How did you get here and what is your cover for being away from IMRA?"

"I walked. It's not far. Sometimes, I go see a girl I know." He smiled at Steve, who chuckled back.

They were sitting on the sandy ground of a three-sided corrugated tin shelter. They heard voices, and Karim stood up to look toward the source of the sounds. He saw a small fire about thirty yards away. The camp was apparently not totally abandoned. Steve stood up and motioned to Karim. "We're moving. Come on."

They walked quietly to Steve's car, keeping the shack between themselves and the campfire. In the car Karim said, "So maybe this was not the safest place?" Steve did not respond.

They spent the next forty minutes talking in the car while making their way slowly back toward the town. The night sky was bright, and Steve, with directions from Karim, could drive without lights. Though they saw no other vehicles, there were a few people walking toward Timbuktu. Karim understood that Steve didn't want to give them opportunity to read his license plate.

Steve said, "Tell me about the camp in the north."

"Oh, yes. I go there sometimes. It is for training. We bring new fighters there."

"Are there any secret storage sheds or underground warehouses?"

Karim said, "There is an underground room. It's locked. No one except al Khalil and Hussein are allowed there. I think that's where they keep the gold. You know, from the mines?"

"And where do the weapons come from?"

"From many places. Like deserters. A long time ago, several trucks delivered weapons and ammunition from Libya. But not for a long time. We have many weapons, but we always need more ammunition. Al Khalil has contacts. Some Malian officers sell us ammunition from their warehouses. I know that al Khalil's go-between with them is a man who owns a hotel, the Khan Hotel, I think."

Steve made sure there was no one on the street and he let Karim out of the car.

Two weeks later, again meeting in the car at night, Karim handed Steve a typewritten document. "I was in al Khalil's office this afternoon and he went to the bathroom. I saw a file on his desk and this was in it, the list of all the imams in the region who are paying *zakat*, a tithe, to IMRA."

"This is useful, Karim. But I told you not to take that kind of risk. What if al Khalil notices and decides you were the only one who could have taken it?"

"Don't worry. He won't notice."

"I worry about you, Karim. By the way, I want to pass on thanks to you personally from John Littlecorn, the head of American intelligence. Some of your information has reached him and he wants you to know that he is appreciative. He wants to know what he can do for you."

Karim didn't read newspapers and did not follow international politics. However, the name John Littlecorn was well-known throughout the Middle East. He often accompanied the American president on his trips and had once successfully mediated a dangerous hostage situation— dangerous for the hostages and for the terrorists.

Karim was enormously pleased. Little by little, he had learned first to trust and then to like Steve. That Littlecorn knew of him and was extending compliments and thanks was because of Steve.

"I am honored that he even knows I exist."

Steve said, "It is important for my country to understand the Muslim world. Otherwise, it will make mistakes. You are now someone who can help us reach that understanding."

Karim listened. He understood that the United States had awesome power, that what the United States did could affect the lives of people all over the world. "I want to help make things better. I don't ask Mr. Littlecorn for anything."

Steve said, "Remember when you told me about your family in Oran? What is your little brother's name? Hassan? What do you hope for him, Karim?"

Karim's eyes watered at his brother's name. Hassan would not live this life. He would obtain a proper education. He would become a pharmacist. He remembered that was Hassan's dream, a dream they both knew at the time was just fun to talk about but not any more realizable than, for example, living in their own house.

"Yes, Hassan. I haven't seen him in a long time. He is smart. I want him to go to school, maybe a school in France."

Steve turned left to avoid the more populated part of town. "Listen to this and tell me if you agree. I want to open a bank account for Hassan. Every month that we work together, I will put money in the account. You can have it whenever you want. By the time Hassan can go to France, you'll have some money to give him, or to your mother, if Hassan doesn't want to become a pharmacist anymore."

When he left Steve that night, Karim hoped to be able to

work for him for a long time. He was motivated to do whatever Steve asked. At the end of the day, Hassan and his mother would have a better life. He would make it happen. He looked upon Steve as his mentor, as his big brother.

CHAPTER TWENTY-THREE

Once Langley was satisfied that Karim was a viable, responsive agent, Steve received instructions that read as follows:

1. WE WISH TO REPLACE SBCALIPH/1'S [the cryptonym, or code name, assigned to al Khalil by the CIA] CURRENT SATELLITE PHONE WITH ONE WE WILL PROVIDE. HE IS USING A CIPHER THAT IS TAKING TOO LONG TO BREAK IN A TIMELY MANNER. THE REPLACEMENT TROJAN HORSE WILL SEPARATE AND TRANSMIT HIS OUTGOING AND INCOMING MESSAGES TO US USING AN ENCRYPTION SYSTEM WE PREFER.

2. TO THAT END, HAVE SBCALIPH/4 [the cryptonym for Karim] COLLECT THE FOLLOWING INFORMATION REGARDING SBCALIPH/1'S SATELLITE PHONE:
   A. MAKE AND SERIAL NUMBER.
   B. TELEPHONE NUMBER.
   C. COLOR AND ANY MARKINGS THAT SBCALIPH/1 MIGHT HAVE ADDED, SUCH AS HIS NAME OR THE TELEPHONE NUMBER OR ANY OTHER IDENTIFYING MARKINGS ON THE INSTRUMENT.
   D. SIMILARLY, HAVE HIM IDENTIFY ANY ACCESSORIES THAT SBCALIPH/1 USES WITH THE PHONE, SUCH AS BATTERY CHARGER, EARPHONES, ETC.

3. FURTHER, DETERMINE WHERE SBCALIPH/1 KEEPS HIS PHONE IN THE OFFICE, HOW HE CARRIES IT WHEN HE TRAVELS,

WHETHER HE EVER LEAVES IT AND WHERE WHEN AWAY FROM
HIS APARTMENT AND OFFICE.

4. BASED ON THE ABOVE INFORMATION, PLS SUBMIT OPERA-
TIONAL PLAN TO REPLACE THE PHONE AND ADVISE SOONEST.

5. REGRET THAT COS BAMAKO IS UNAVAILABLE TO ASSIST IN THIS
OPERATION.

6. FILE: SBCALIPH.

Steve had been able to obtain the requested information.
Al Khalil's satellite phone was a Globalstar, but there had
been too little time left before the Gao conference to replace al Khalil's phone with a CIA "Trojan horse." Steve liked
the idea. He had heard during his short training that the CIA
elves were adept and creative technicians. There should be
little left to know about IMRA and al Khalil's plans and activities after combining Karim's inside information with in-
tercepts of his satellite phone.

Steve decided he had to go to Gao to try to effect the exchange away from Tariq's home field. He read the last sentence of the message to mean that given his inexperience,
the plan had been for Rod to come and run the switch operation. Steve felt good that CIA headquarters had enough
confidence in him to go ahead without Rod's assistance.

CHAPTER TWENTY-FOUR

On Monday, Steve arrived at the Hotel Atlantide in Gao, a
major desert town farther down the Niger and to the east of
Timbuktu. Izem met him at the airport.

As they walked outside to catch a taxi, Izem said, "The
hotel was named after a story of our people. Do you know

Atlantis? It was a big city on an island a thousand years ago. Then the desert came, the water went away. The island is now the Ahaggar Mountains, over there." He pointed to the northeast. "In the Sahara."

They got into a taxi and Steve said, "You mean in Algeria? So you could be from the old civilization of Atlantis?"

Izem smiled with pride. "We are an ancient people."

They stopped in front of the hotel, a one-story building behind a low decorative barrier on which sat several young Malians. The roof was surrounded by a white balustrade. They walked past the young men, who stopped talking and looked at Steve with what he thought were barely repressed urges to assault him with once-in-a-lifetime proposals. He guessed that Izem's presence was keeping them from trying their luck. In the lobby the overhead fans turned noisily but too slowly to interfere with the squadrons of flies patrolling the superheated air of their domain.

"How about waiting for me here while I go check out the room?" Steve asked Izem. "Then I'll see about renting a car, and you can show me around."

By the time Steve got the car it was midafternoon. Nevertheless, they had time to go see Gao's main and only tourist attraction, the Tomb of Askia, an imposing seventeen-meter high pyramidal structure dating from the fifteenth century, identified for preservation by the UNESCO World Heritage organization. It was the last resting place of Askia Muhammad, a Songhai emperor who had made Islam the official religion of his empire. Steve also couldn't resist taking photographs of a mosque whose only claim to fame that his photos could document was a minaret with the unmistakable profile of an aroused penis.

Izem snickered when Steve took photos of the unmistakable phallic symbol. "Are they like that in America?"

"They're much bigger, especially in Texas." Steve motioned how big with his arms, causing Izem to do a 360 on one foot and laugh while touching his crotch.

Through his camera's lens, Steve noticed that the shadows were lengthening, and he became concerned about the light. "Izem, did you talk to your friends? Can I go visit with them, and take pictures?

"Yes, we can go now if you want."

The Tuareg camp resembled the one near Lake Faguibine: tents of black leather, tops and sides on sticks and branches planted in the ground, goats and camels off to one side. The young children ran and played games among the tents, and the women and the older children gathered firewood, carried water from the well or cooked dinner over an open fire.

The chief, the *amenokal*, welcomed Steve. Izem pointed to Steve and said, "He is my *patron*, my boss, Monsieur Christophe." The *amenokal* was a couple of inches taller than Steve. His robe hinted at a rather bony body. What Steve could see of his face when he loosened the *tagoulmoust* to eat or drink was all angles and planes.

With Izem as translator, Steve said to the chief, "Those are very stylish sunglasses." The *amenokal* took them off and proudly said, "Yes, Italian." Steve could only guess as to their provenance, but they undoubtedly added to the *amenokal's* aura of leadership.

Steve spent the rest of the day with Izem's friends, taking pictures and eating the evening meal with them. He was impressed by the Tuaregs' appearance. Their comportment conveyed pride. Since they stayed veiled most of the time, Steve found it difficult to read their expressions. Their eyes were cautious. He found them less forbidding when they lowered the blue cloth that hid the lower part of their face to eat and drink. Their unusual height was accentuated by their *tagoulmousts*, or blue veils and turbans that enveloped their heads and necks. The seven-foot lances and the rest of their medieval weapons, swords, knives, that they still occasionally carried as they did this day—probably at Izem's request, Steve thought—magnified their physical presence.

To show off his knowledge, Izem said, "Christophe, show them the pictures on your computer." To the delight of his audience, Steve then put on a slide show for the *amenokal* and his men from the shots he had taken that afternoon.

Before Steve left their encampment, he gave the *amenokal* a bag and said, "Here are some things that I thought would be useful to you: tubes of antibiotic ointment to treat basic cuts and wounds from infection, and special eye ointment." Steve had learned that many of the Tuaregs, especially the children, suffered from conjunctivitis and other eye ailments.

He handed the chief a box and said, "You might also find these walkie-talkie radios useful for communication in the desert."

As the chief opened the gifts, he handed them out. Their examination was a communal experience. Steve asked, "Izem, what are they saying?"

Izem replied, "They say that America should invade Mali," and they laughed.

Steve had another bag for the kids—hard candy and a few inexpensive compasses. On their way to the camp, Izem had told Steve, "Give the compasses to the kids, not to the chief. He might get offended. He doesn't think he needs a compass, I'm sure of that. But, somehow, the compasses will in the end belong to the adults."

Before Steve left, the *amenokal* asked him to wait, and in a few minutes someone came to hand him a package wrapped with string.

The chief said, "You have won many friends today. Izem was kind to bring you. Think of us as your family in the Sahel."

Steve left in the dark as the Tuareg men stood in front of their tents and campfires. He felt deep sympathy for them. The Tuaregs had been important actors of the region's history, but they had been bypassed and had become victims.

Steve thought that instead of giving candies to the kids, he should have given them books.

The following day, one day before Tariq and Hussein were to arrive, the advance team of Lahlou, Karim and several additional men who would act as gofers and security guards arrived in Gao.

Steve's first priority was the satellite phone. He only had a few days to come up with a plan and to execute it. While Steve avoided rigid structures and planning, looming dead-lines energized him. He already had three-dimensional plans of the fort from CIA headquarters. He still needed al Khalil's schedule and information on the whereabouts of his satellite phone at any given time.

Steve was in his room when he heard an urgently furtive knock on the door. He let Karim in and they shook hands. "I'm picking up mineral water from the hotel, so I have very little time," Karim said.

"OK. Any word from your mother and from Hassan? Is the family all right?"

Karim smiled. "I don't hear from them often, but I was able to arrange a phone call with Hassan from the Oran Telegraph and Telephone office. He sounded good."

"I'm glad." Turning to business, Steve said, "Do you have a list of the attendees to the conference?"

"Not a list, but I know the names."

Steve wrote them down as Karim recited them.

"Is everyone still scheduled to arrive tomorrow?" When Karim nodded, Steve produced two oversized tacks and said, "These are miniature microphones. What I want you to do is to stick one in al Khalil's room and the other in Salim's room. Out of sight, of course. Behind or under a piece of fur-niture, for example. You explained to me before that Salim is important, maybe the elder statesman of the group, right?"

Karim, gratified that Steve took his information and per-sonal comments seriously, smiled his assent.

Steve didn't explain that each "tack" contained not only a mike but also a transmitter and a five-hundred-hour battery.

Before Karim left, Steve said, "Come back when you can. Until you have some sort of schedule, I'll stay pretty close to the hotel. I need to know where everyone will sleep and the schedule for the whole conference. This is going to be the most important thing you have done so far. But also the riskiest, so don't take stupid chances."

Steve had urged caution before but was always concerned that Karim's self-confidence and zeal would make him step over the line and make a fatal mistake. Steve knew enough by now to realize that in this business, there were no second chances.

Within two hours, Steve had a brief background on all of the expected Salafist chiefs, all on the CIA list of active radical Muslim terrorists.

Karim was able to come late that evening. He told Steve, "The guards wanted me to get them beer."

"What will al Khalil think about alcohol at the fort?"

"It will be gone by the time he lands." Karim laughed.

With the plan of the fort in his mind, Steve debriefed Karim and quickly determined the use of most of the rooms. Al Khalil had a two-room ground-floor apartment in the central tower, originally used by the fort commander. The only other room in the tower on the ground level was larger than the apartment and had been used as an armory in the past. Now it was used for storage and contained odd pieces of furniture, much of it broken. The rest of the tower was taken up by a stairway to the top, punctuated on several landings by narrow openings in the outside wall designed to be used by armed defenders. Steve had noted that there was a small room on the second landing, but its use then and now was difficult to discern.

* * *

Steve met Hank, a CIA technician carrying the replacement satellite phone, at the airport on Wednesday. As they got in Steve's car, Hank, in his forties with a light, Irish complexion, didn't beat around the bush. "I have never run an operation headed up by other than a seasoned case officer. But I'm told you're good, so I trust we can work together."

"I'm glad you're here. I gave the quick-plant mikes to Caliphate/4 yesterday. He should have placed them by now."

Hank nodded. "I'll set up the listening post in my room. From there, the conversations will be transmitted automatically by satellite to CIA headquarters, translated and sent back to me via Inmarsat. I'll test the system today. I gather that we don't have much time. Which is fine with me. I've been in some godforsaken places but"—he looked out the window at the arid scenery—"this has to be the worst."

Steve asked, "Hank, how long will you need, once we get Caliphate/1's phone?"

"Count on one hour. Could be less, could be more—depends. I also want a chance to call headquarters if any special problem comes up."

Hank received the first transcript shortly after he set up his equipment. Since Tariq and Hussein were scheduled to arrive by road later the same day and Salim was not due until the next day, the main purpose of sending a transcript back at all was simply to test the system. While the little audio pickup was clear enough, the transcript showed that Murphy's law applied universally. A desk that had been in Salim's room had been moved. Unfortunately, Karim had planted the tack microphone underneath that desk. It sounded as if it was now located in the room where the Salafist leaders would eat their meals. Rather than have Karim take the risk of moving the tack microphone, Steve looked on the bright side: the new location might provide interesting conversations among the Salafist guests. He therefore decided to leave well enough alone, and Hank agreed.

During their Wednesday meeting, Karim told Steve, "Tariq and Hussein are here. Tariq used his satellite phone almost right away to call Salim. He doesn't get here until tomorrow. The only time when Tariq doesn't carry the phone with him is during prayers. He leaves it in his room, I think."

With a hand-drawn sketch in front of them, Steve said to Karim, "OK, show me the room assignments."

Acting like a zealous pupil, Karim asked, "Do you need to know about locks? There are no locks." His face brightened as if he were personally responsible for this fact. "Most rooms have no windows, except high up, like in the room where I sleep with three others." After trying to understand the sketch for what seemed to Steve like an unusual length of time, Karim pointed to his room triumphantly. "Is this the tower? Yes, you go in over here"—he pointed—"and al Khalil sleeps here. He has a window. It opens on this side. It's a real window."

Steve asked, "Does his window open? Or is it one of the high ones you can't reach?"

"He has a desk in front of the window and he can see the courtyard from his desk." He smiled and looked very pleased with himself.

Steve smiled in return and gave him a pat on the back. "That's good, Karim."

Together they decided that the best time to effect the transfer would be during the Friday prayer. Al Khalil, they hoped, would leave the phone in his room, or he would give it to Karim when Karim served as his bodyguard, as he sometimes did during that midday period. Karim would take the phone to Steve when everyone else was in the mosque, a room in the fort that al Khalil had so designated. Hank would then make the transfer, and Karim would take the gift from the CIA elves back to the fort.

CHAPTER TWENTY-FIVE

On Thursday, Hussein went to the airport with Karim, the driver, to welcome the Salafist leaders. Hussein saw a tired, rumpled and short-tempered group. One of the new arrivals looked in the van and, looking toward Hussein and Karim, said with an Egyptian accent, "There was no water on the plane and now you have no water for us. Can things get worse?" Neither Hussein nor Karim replied.

The promising outline of the Hotel Atlantide prompted the Egyptian to say, "At last, a place to stretch out and have something to drink." But Karim continued past the hotel and about a mile out of town to a high-walled structure.

Hussein, who sat on Karim's right up front, turned to the men in back of him and said, "That's where we're staying. Not far from town and very secure. We have it to ourselves."

"I'm sure we do," said Talal Kawar, who had identified himself to Hussein as the Jordanian Ikhwan chief. He wore black pants, a blazer and an ascot. His shiny black hair was combed straight back. The scent of his cologne wafted throughout the vehicle.

Hussein said, "It was built and used by the French Foreign Legion. It was ceded to the Malian army after independence."

The fort was the same color as the sand that surrounded it. On one side grew several tall palm trees, creating shade for a small group of blue-clad Tuaregs sitting on the ground while their camels looked haughtily down at the world. A solid black flag with no design was waving in the intermittent breeze from the top of a crenellated tower rising from an inside courtyard. The tower and its flag dominated the external walls in the style of medieval castles. A massive front gate and a row of vertical slits about halfway up were the only openings in the fifty-foot-high wall.

Karim took the new arrivals to their rooms. These had uniformly high ceilings, with one small barred window about fifteen feet above the floor. The furniture consisted of a cot with a burlap-covered straw mattress, a chair and a small desk, on top of which was a carafe of water and a plastic glass. Down the narrow corridor were a common toilet and a separate washroom with several large jars of water.

Tariq greeted each of the delegates as they came into the former military fort and, during the rest of the afternoon, visited with them individually. Everyone took note that al Khalil took a brief walk in the courtyard with Ibrahim el Maghrebi, the Algerian AQIM leader, before taking him to his room. He said to Hussein, "Have somebody bring us some tea. I want to share some of our financial realities with my brother Ibrahim."

At sunset, they all came together for prayers, after which they broke up into informal groups until dinnertime. They prayed again at nightfall. Everyone was awaiting the next day, Friday, when Tariq would give the *khutbah*, or sermon.

Steve and Hank also waited for the *khutbah* that would give Karim his chance to steal the phone. Late in the day, they received a partial transcript from Langley of the take from the tack mike in the canteen. They were in Hank's room. He sat in the easy chair and Steve sat on the bed. Altough Hank had a portable printer, Steve read the transcript on Hank's computer.

VOICE NUMBER ONE: I don't understand why we can't meet in Paris or in Geneva. Next thing we know we'll be whipping ourselves bloody like Shiites.

VOICE NUMBER TWO [identified as AQIM chief Ibrahim el Maghrebi]: Stop whining. In Algeria we're fighting with bullets not with cocktail shakers.

VOICE NUMBER THREE: As long as we settle on positive action, I don't care.

VOICE NUMBER ONE: We all know the problem we have to solve. Not enough funding and not enough progress to show—one leads to the other.

Steve said, "My guess is that al Khalil was not there."

Hank commented, "Is al Khalil the main actor in this play? I'm surprised we received this transcript so fast. Once the National Security Agency in Fort Meade receives the signal, it has to find it among millions of messages, process it and get it to the CIA building. In this case, because we're trying to do this as close to real time as possible, we have a translator working on the Arabic text at CIA. Then it goes to Africa Division, where someone has to read it and decide who needs to see it. You should feel lucky. Your operation is getting priority attention."

On Friday, Tariq made his awaited sermon in the mosque room. "Glory to God most high, full of grace and mercy," he began. He then preached on the remembrance of Allah before launching into the substance of his message. "You have seen our banner, our black flag flying from the tower. Some of you know that it is a replica of the Prophet's battle flag, may Allah sustain him. It was the Quraysh tribal banner, the flag the Prophet flew during his military conquests. We will use it to come from the desert as he did and vanquish the apostates, the false leaders of the lands that used to be in the fold of the Caliphate. The lands now outside Islam revere ways that are depraved, trivial and wanton. Their people revere the false gods of materialism and technology. They spend more time taking care of their lawns than they do trying to please Allah, the Most Blessed, the

Merciful. Satan is their only God, temptation their opiate. Jews are in the positions of power. Their very existence is an insult to Allah, may he favor our ways to please him.

"We are Allah's soldiers, his disciples on earth. Islam will rule all of mankind. Only through jihad can we bring about the rule of Islam on earth. Jihad is not only the sword; it is also the war to bring about mental and intellectual devotion, most importantly subservience, to Allah.

"Islam is the complete answer. It will bring all people from the darkness and into the light."

The rest of al Khalil's speech was borrowed from the Ikhwan's master plan, couched in dialectical rhetoric reminiscent of the *Communist Manifesto*. With the final goal of establishing an Islamic state, Tariq struck his familiar themes of temporary cooperation with nationalist groups, the avoidance of unwinnable confrontations and the support for jihad across the Muslim world. He also encouraged the use of the Palestinian cause, the use of social, health and educational institutions to create local Islamic centers of power, and the use of self-criticism and constant scientific evaluation. He reminded the congregation that he would be talking with each and looked forward to their specific recommendations for implementing his plan.

But he reminded everyone that that the immediate need was for more funds.

At the Hotel Atlantide, Steve and Hank waited for Karim to show up.

Hank said, "Where is your boy? He should have been here an hour ago. Either he got caught or he got cold feet. It's going to be no good if I have too little time. I told you an hour."

Steve caught the implication that Hank had lost his trust in him, that he was not a "real" case officer, not one of the elite operations officers from the Directorate of Operations, the CIA's small but defining segment—what his father, Marshall, always referred to as "the tip of the spear." What was he doing in Gao anyway? Maybe he was in way over his head, as Hank seemed to believe.

He left the room and bought cigarettes at reception. From a nonsmoking family, he had smoked somewhat in college, all part of becoming independent, and had smoked in Moldova, but not since then. He walked outside, vaguely conscious of the harsh taste of the dark tobacco in his unfiltered Gitane Brune, only thinking of where Karim might be. *I told you a thousand times to be careful, Karim,* he thought. *You're too macho, trying to prove something. It's not worth it if you get caught.* The air had cooled with the sunset, but he was still sweating, and not entirely from the temperature. He wondered if he, too, was trying to prove too much.

Steve went back inside. He found Hank checking the Trojan-horse phone. One half of the plastic outer shell was facedown on the small table, and Hank was examining the electronics laid bare.

Steve looked over Hank's shoulder. "Maybe Tariq's speech was declared a command performance that everyone had to attend."

Hank didn't look up. "Did you give him a cover, something he could say in case he got caught with the phone? Did you give him a logical reason? How was he supposed to explain it?"

Steve said, "There's nothing he could say." He felt guilty that he had not discussed possible worst-case scenarios with Karim. But there was so little time. Had Karim been caught? Was he, Steve, responsible? Was Karim even alive?

They took turns staying in Steve's room, going to dinner separately. Around ten thirty, they gave up.

After his Friday sermon, al Khalil met with all of his leaders in the canteen. An unusual discussion took place, reflecting discord in the ranks, bordering on a minor rebellion on the part of Talal Kawar, the Jordanian, and Walid Fahmy, the Egyptian. Since each enjoyed close ties to the Muslim Brotherhood, Tariq listened. Karim and several other guards and helpers sat on a blanket in a far corner of the sparsely furnished room. Al Khalil and his lieutenants sat at a long wooden table cluttered with cups, plastic bottles of water, tea, coffee and two platters of finger food—dates, peanuts, mango slices and sugar biscuits on one and slices of dried fish on the other. The one ashtray was overworked for the task at hand, since they all smoked, el Maghrebi incessantly. Cigarette butts surrounded the table.

Fahmy was a beefy individual dressed in suit pants and a short-sleeved Hilton Pyramids Golf Resort polo shirt. He said, "As you have explained to us in the past, Sheikh al Khalil, the subversion of the Sahelian countries is a worthy objective. And it will happen. But to go forward, we need funds, and in spite of our efforts and of blessings from Allah, progress is slow. Our financiers expect results in their lifetime. We need a splashy event that the world will notice. If it happens in Egypt, the population will respond. Egypt must be the core, the focus of our action. It is the rock on which we can lever the entire Middle East."

Kawar, the Jordanian, had taken his ascot off and was fanning himself with a magazine. "Jordan is one of the few remaining kingdoms left in the world. It is ruled by an illegitimate dynasty installed by the British. Over half of the population in Jordan is Palestinian. We'll have a groundswell of support if we strike in Amman."

Hussein, who usually said little in these strategy sessions, saw an opening to achieve his life goal. "The Assad family has killed many thousands of our Muslim brothers in Syria, my father among them. What could be more right, more pleasing to Allah, than to strike the Assads?"

El Maghrebi, who had been quiet, pinched his cigarette from his lips. "You all need to do more than talk. I only hear planning for possible future actions coming from most of you." He took a long drag on his cigarette. "You need to start somewere. Nothing will take place unless you take military action. There is no better time to start than right away. We in AQIM are the only real revolutionaries. You can come to Algeria and I'll show you. But leave your fancy clothes home."

Fahmy and Kawar answered in loud voices, speaking at the same time. Kawar said, "You are so successful that you have to live in the desert and move your camp every day." Fahmy said, "In my country, open warfare is not the answer."

Al Khalil stood up so quickly that his hand brushed his cup from the table. It broke as it crashed against the hard floor. "I have listened to all of you. We will have a strategy before we leave. The Sahelian initiative must go on. But I agree that it is a long-term program that is too subtle for our donors, who suffer from strategic myopia."

Salim was at one of the tables but had said nothing. He got up to leave with al Khalil.

Karim knocked on Steve's door at eleven thirty P.M. "Here it is," he said with a nervous smile. "I couldn't get my hands on the phone until after al Khalil went to bed. He always opens his window at night and he keeps it on his desk right under the window. I have to get back right away before anyone notices. I'm the night guard tonight. I'll come back for the phone in a couple of hours, whenever I can. The phone needs to be back in his room before he gets up for morning prayers." And he was gone. Steve's questions remained unasked and unanswered.

Hank first looked at all the external aspects of the device to see what he had to do to make the CIA gift identical. He noticed a slight nick on the side of the gray Globalstar 1700 and carefully nicked the new one identically. He plugged al Khalil's satellite phone in his computer and, using CIA-developed software, quickly found al Khalil's password, *1141346*. Hank then transferred all the settings in Tariq's phone to his computer and from his computer to the new phone. He placed the old battery in the new phone as well. He needed no advice from CIA headquarters, but called his support team in Langley to inform them that he had finished his task. After a few questions to double-check his work, his CIA team signed off. And the waiting resumed.

About an hour and a half before sunrise, Steve was forced to conclude that Karim had run into an obstacle and wasn't coming back to pick up the phone and return it in a way that al Khalil would never know that it had left the fort. If al Khalil noticed that his phone was missing, Karim would immediately be under suspicion. Steve left the hotel with a bundle under his arm. Before getting in his car, he looked to make sure no one saw him and dressed in the Tuareg robes and sandals that he had found in the package given to him by the Tuareg *amenokal* earlier that week. He made sure that his *tagoulmoust*, his headdress, hid as much of his face as possible. He then headed out for the fort with the CIA phone.

There were no streetlights, but his headlights and a star-bright night sky provided good visibility. Once out of town, he turned off his lights. Campfires dotting the night landscape helped to keep him on the sandy track, and the luminous screen of his GPS kept him on direction. He left his car about one hundred and fifty yards from the fort under an ancient and gnarled baobab tree, a remnant of the time when the Sahara was green. Several goats were also under the tree and moved to make room for Steve's car with the utmost reluctance and bleats of complaint.

The front gate of the fort was open. He took a wide turn to his right in order to approach it from the side, where there were no entrances. There were three or four camels near the corner of the side and front walls. Camels were valued property, and their owner, probably close by, would not take kindly to having his means of transportation, his source of milk and his investment threatened or even disturbed. Further, he had learned that camels were as ornery as they were aloof and might complain loudly if they thought he was invading their territory.

He walked toward the front gate, staying close to the wall. Voices came from inside the gates as he approached. He moved forward slowly and silently, extremely conscious of the sound his sandals made in the sand. The voices became louder. Two men stepped out of the fort through the front gate and continued talking. Steve was close enough to recognize Karim. Steve waited until Karim was looking in his direction to loosen his blue *tagoulmoust*. Hoping for recognition, he then pointed to his right. Karim apparently understood; he and the other guard started walking slowly along the wall, away from Steve.

Steve had had no particular plan when he headed to the fort, except to find Karim somehow and hand him the satellite phone. He now understood that Karim could not leave the other guard without a very good reason, and that he would have to return the phone himself. Steve looked inside the gate to see if anyone else was in the courtyard and walked in with an air of bravado that he did not actually feel. From Karim's information, he remembered that al Khalil normally kept the phone on a desk inside his room at night. With the layout of the fort in his mind, he headed toward the tower in the middle of the courtyard. It was still dark. There was no movement in the courtyard. When he made his way into the corridor leading to al Khalil's room, he saw the door was closed. He placed his hand on the door handle but hesitated and instead went back outside and looked for the window he hoped would be open, substituting for air-conditioning. The window was where he thought it should be, and while the bars were close enough together to keep a body from entering, they were wide enough for the phone and his arm. When he got close enough, he used a pencil flashlight to look inside. The bed was near the wall to the right of the window. In the bed, he could see a body turned toward the wall—he assumed al Khalil. Under the window was the desk. He reached inside and put the phone carefully on the desk.

As he withdrew his hand, he heard shoes crunching in the sand from the direction of the front gate. He quickly walked around the tower and went into the corridor in order to stay out of sight of anyone in the front part of the courtyard. With pounding heart, he stayed there for about a minute, noting that the sky was getting lighter. It couldn't be long before the morning prayers began, when these corridors would fill with bodies and he would be seen. The sound of voices growing louder told him people were approaching his location, and he felt trapped, but he retreated farther inside. He guessed that someone was supposed to wake up al Khalil. He went up the stairs to stay out of sight as a man in a *jellaba* came into the corridor. Instead of stopping at al Khalil's door as Steve expected, the footsteps began climbing the stairs, pushing Steve farther up and giving him the feeling that he was losing his avenue of escape. At a steady pace, sweating with anxiety, he ascended the stairs until he saw the door to the room that he had earlier noticed on the plans. With his small flashlight he scanned the room for a hiding place, seeing only empty ammunition boxes, coils of rope in one corner and a large piece of black cloth on a table crowded with old candles and booklets yellowed with age. The black cloth, he realized, was a flag. It occurred to Steve that perhaps that flag was raised every morning. He grabbed a coil of rope and kept going up the stairs and hoped to find a place to hide at the top.

The platform at the top was larger than it looked from outside and could accommodate fifty men firing on attackers below. But it was wide-open. It was still too dark to see the ground. He looped and tied one end of the rope through an iron ring just below the top of the five-foot-high wall around the platform and then threw the rest of the rope over the wall, but he couldn't see if it reached the ground. Steve briefly considered waiting in ambush for the guy coming up to put his flag up; surprise would be on his side, and he was confident that he could overcome the flagman. But would he have to kill him to keep him quiet? He went over the side and held himself steady about ten feet down by wrapping his legs around the rope. After the flag was up, Steve thought he might be able to come back up and escape down the stairs. However, he might run into someone else in the tower, maybe al Khalil. He started going down and soon he could see the ground. His rope was about twenty feet short of the sandy courtyard. Without any other options, he continued to go down hand over hand. With just two feet of rope left, he noticed a shooting window below him. He was able to wedge first one leg, then the other into the opening of the window. He let the rope go and was able to grip a ledge immediately above the window. Then he lowered his grip to the window, got his legs out and lowered his grip to the bottom of the window. From there he swung himself away from the building and dropped.

The noise attracted attention from a man coming into the courtyard. Since Steve was dressed as a Tuareg, the man shouted and rushed toward him threateningly. Until that moment, although his heart had been beating at twice its normal rhythm, Steve had felt in control, unseen, invisible and almost invulnerable. Now that he was under scrutiny, he went into fight-or-flight mode. With a head feint to the right, Steve ran to the left, heading for the open gate. Not used to running in sandals, he almost fell but regained his balance, and holding the hem of his ankle-length Tuareg robe in one hand, he headed for his car as fast as he could, knowing this could be a life-or-death sprint.

By the time he reached the car, there was more than one voice yelling behind him, but he didn't look back. His car was now surrounded by several nomads who, with their goats, were examining the car. One was conducting his inspection from inside. Steve had left the car unlocked with the thought that he might need to leave quickly and now wondered if it had been a huge mistake. As they saw this mad Tuareg moving toward them at flank speed, however, the goatherds stepped back. Steve threw himself into the car and started it as quickly as he could get the keys in the ignition. His backseat inspector jumped out when the car started moving, falling on a bleating goat that had been busy nibbling at the tires.

As the car started to move, an SUV came tearing out of the fort and picked up the two men running after Steve. He took off with the SUV in full pursuit. He first headed back toward town, but going to his hotel would simply delay the inevitable confrontation. He glanced down at his watch compass. As he drove, he thought that his Tuareg costume would minimize the seriousness of the incident in the minds of the Salafists only if his American status was not revealed.

He turned off on a track heading north toward the Tuareg camp he and Izem had visited on Monday. The sun was coming up over the curve of the horizon when he reached the encampment. He sounded his horn as he drove the last fifty yards, stopped the car and ran toward the tent of the *amenokal*. The chief analyzed the situation in a moment with uncanny precision and called out his warriors, many of whom were already up around their campfires. Several of his men answered his summons armed not with their medieval swords and lances, but with guns of various vintages. The armed Tuaregs surrounded the SUV. Loud words were exchanged. The SUV turned around and headed back to the fort. In that place and at that moment, the Tuaregs ruled.

CHAPTER TWENTY-SIX

The conversation following al Khalil's Friday sermon in Gao had been spirited, and sometimes acrimonious. Salim had listened, but without hearing the details of the conversation. He had heard all this before.

The arguments triggered the memory of similar conversations years ago when he was Said's right-hand man, later his deputy, and eventually his replacement. Then, the mission was to spread the Muslim Brotherhood's organization and concepts throughout Europe. The movement had profited from an unlikely base—Muslim soldiers from the Soviet Red Army, captured by the invading Nazi blitzkrieg in 1941. Mostly from Central Asia, up to a million soldiers agreed to fight for Hitler. At the end of the war, many had been transferred to the Western Front and were captured by the British and American armies, thus saving them from immediate execution by the Soviets. Said, the Brotherhood chief for Europe, accompanied by a young Salim, showed up in a Cadillac and donated a thousand marks when a former SS imam announced at a public event that he planned to build a mosque in Munich. The enemy of my enemy is my friend; the Muslim Brotherhood was as strongly anti-Communist as Communism was atheistic.

Following the inpromptu meeting in the canteen, Salim and Tariq walked outside in the inner courtyard. The sun had set, but it wasn't entirely dark. Tariq said, "You understand that we need to establish a strong base. A strong Sunni base. The Shiites are growing in influence. Our Sunni faith is losing its traditional dominance. If democratization catches on, then keep in mind that including Iran, a Shiite country, there are about a billion and a half Shiites in the world. Make no mistake, they're waking up. Sometimes I think that we should first take care of the Shiite apostates even before we focus on the Egyptians, Syrians and others who call themselves secular. Besides, the Syrians who are run by the Alawite clan are also Shiites. The only alternative operation I would consider would be a major strike against the Zionist entity. That would create great popular support and a way to obtain a nuclear weapon, which would get us the respect we want."

Salim replied, "You have given me much to think about. Let us talk again in the morning."

During the night, Salim called David from his room. The next morning, Salim took Tariq for a walk in the courtyard. Salim wanted to continue the trend of thought that Tariq had initiated the night before, which David had found fascinating.

They walked in the courtyard until the midmorning prayers.

When Steve received the transcript from the miniature mike in Salim's room, he was at first puzzled. Salim, whom he knew to be the European Ikhwan chief and al Khalil's advisor, had called a man named David and given him a summary of the day's discussions at the fort. Significantly, Salim had said, "Tariq is thinking of redirecting his focus toward Iran. What do you think?"

David had encouraged that line of thought. At the end of the conversation, Salim said, "I understand. The kind of attack you suggest will please everyone and will do Tariq a lot of good as well." All Salim had to do now was to convince al Khalil.

CHAPTER TWENTY-SEVEN

Following his return to Timbuktu from Gao, Steve felt he had more than accomplished his mission. Back in his hotel room at the Bouctou, he used his steganography system to hide his message in his scenic photographs of the Tuaregs.

> STRONGLY RECOMMEND THAT I TURN OVER SBCALIPH/4 TO BA-MAKO CHIEF OF STATION, RETURN TO THE U.S. AND TERMINATE MY PARTICIPATION IN THIS OPERATION. BELIEVE THAT PURPOSE OF MY MISSION HAS BEEN ACCOMPLISHED.

Steve could read Mel's negativism in the reply:

> BAMAKO COS IS TO DEPART SHORTLY AND WE HAVE DECIDED TO PUT SBCALIPH/4 ON ICE. PLS SET UP APPROPRIATE RECONTACT ARRANGEMENTS IN CASE SB/4 IS NEEDED AT SOME POINT IN THE FUTURE.

He was soon at CIA headquarters, being debriefed again. Steve and his nemesis Mel, the West Africa branch chief and the Queen of Anal, as he thought of her, Philip, the Maghreb branch chief, and Marshall were in the same windowless conference room as before.

Mel, true to her nature, said, "I don't understand why you recruited CALIPH/4 without express authorization from headquarters, from me. Associating with terrorists is not right. You saw him kill people. And that report about the hidden gold . . ." She gave Steve a condescending smile. "We call that RUMINT, intelligence from rumors." She wore the same dress with broad stripes as before, hardly flattering to her ample figure.

Before Steve could reply, a sudden cannon-shot sound came from an eighteen-inch square door in the wall that Steve hadn't seen before. He almost dove to the floor, thinking it was gunfire.

Marshall said, "That thing was built around 1961 when the building was constructed. I don't know why it's still in use. But it does keep most people from dozing during staff meetings."

Just then Therese LaFont came into the conference room, followed by a bevy of people. She moved to the center of the room and said, "Congratulations, Steve. CALIPH/4 was one of the best recruitments I've seen in my career. You saw an opportunity, you kept your cool, literally under fire, and you made quick, good decisions. We're all proud of what you did. You might think about a career as a full-time intelligence officer with this agency. As a result, you not only gave us a view of the target, as we asked, you went above and beyond and actually recruited the source we needed. For that, we're awarding you the Intelligence Commendation Medal." It was about five inches in diameter and bronze colored. The center design was a four-pointed star.

LaFont read the certificate that accompanied the medal. "For performance of especially commendable service for an act or achievement significantly above normal duties, which results in an important contribution to the mission of the Agency."

Everyone present, including a tight-lipped Mel, came around to shake Steve's hand.

Following the ceremony, Steve and Hank were joined by Philip, whom Steve had typecast as the little gray man the first time they met. Steve asked him, "I understand from Hank that al Khalil's satellite phone password was a seven-digit number. Did it mean anything?"

"Like his social-security number you mean? The number

was 1141346. Most likely, those are two dates using the Muslim calendar. The first one, 14 Anno Hegirae, or 732 AD, is when the Muslim armies were defeated at Tours in France. The second number, 1346 AH, or 1928 AD, is when al Khalil's granduncle founded the Muslim Brotherhood."

Philip nodded and smiled. "Excuse me," he said, and moved away.

Marshall asked, "Are you ready to leave? Maybe we shouldn't have come together—you could have stayed longer. But I'm in no hurry. This is your party."

Steve glanced around the room and took in the animated conversations. How many knew the Salafists firsthand and how many thought of them as an intellectual challenge to slice and dice in think pieces that were steps up the promotion ladder? He thought of Hamad's barely contained rage in the basilica. He thought of the sounds of the AK-47s and of the bullets hitting the bodies of his friends in the Timbuktu warehouse. He could see the muzzle of the gun barely sticking out the window of the BMW in Morocco. The catalyst who formed and harnessed the ideology behind these actions was Tariq al Khalil, the guy who had almost brained the judge at the tennis tournament.

Steve said little until he was in the car with Marshall, driving off the CIA campus. "You know, I don't think that the CIA is fighting the same battle as al Khalil."

CHAPTER TWENTY-EIGHT

Captain Lucien Roger was in his DGSE office when his outside line rang. He turned to pick it up, letting his eyes stop for an instant on a large photograph taken when he was still competing after graduating from France's elite equestrian academy at Saumur in the Loire Valley. The horse's head and front legs were already over the obstacle, and he, in the uniform of a cavalry lieutenant, was looking straight ahead, holding the reins and a riding crop.

He put the phone to his left ear. The agent on whom the captain was building his career, Tariq al Khalil, said, "We're staying at the fort just outside Gao."

"Isn't it an old Foreign Legion fort?"

"I suppose. It is not as comfortable as a hotel, but at least we have total security. Except from thieves—but even hotels are not safe from thieves. There were differences of opinion from my Egyptian and Jordanian chiefs. As usual, they want action closer to home. They are like children. They don't understand."

"By the way, how's your friend Salim? Was he at the conference?"

"Yes. He mostly listened." Al Khalil was still mulling over what he wanted to reveal to Roger.

After he hung up, Roger glanced at the photograph again. He brought his hand up to the right side of his face and felt the frozen muscles under the skin. His fingers felt the rictus-like smile forever painted on the right side of his mouth. The photograph had captured his last triumphant moment. Visitors often commented on it in admiration. What no one knew was that the fall that had caused the right side of his face to become paralyzed had occurred a second after the photo had been taken. His future fame and glory, so certain in that photo, had been destroyed in the next heartbeat. He knew that he was ordained to win the next Olympic jumping competition. But life had played a dirty trick on him. He was hell-bent to substitute the life that had been taken from him unfairly with success in other ways. He felt confident that he was owed big-time and that he need not play by the same rules. He knew that he was different, that he was gifted and that laws and regulations were for others.

The army had sent him to study Islam and Arabic, first at the Institut National des Langues et Civilisations Orientales, called by its students Langues O', and then to Tunis, where the DGSE had an Arabic-language school. From the school, he had been recruited by the DGSE, Service Action, the DGSE's special operations branch backed up by the Eleventh Parachute Regiment of the French Foreign Legion.

As a student of Islam, Roger had managed to meet al Khalil and eventually convinced him to provide information on radical Muslim movements. In time, al Khalil had grown in stature, and he was offered participation in alluring financial propositions. Roger often profited personally from these opportunities. Al Khalil had become more than just an agent in Captain Roger's life. In a way, the money he made from these deals made up in small part for the life that had been taken from him.

PART TWO

*It is in the nature of Islam to dominate, not to be
dominated, to impose its laws on all nations
and to extend its power to the entire planet.*
—Hassan al Banna, Founder of the Muslim Brotherhood

*Those who know nothing of Islam pretend that
Islam counsels against war. They are witless.
Islam says, "Kill the infidels."*
—Ayatollah Khomeini, Qom, 1986

CHAPTER TWENTY-NINE

The morning after his telephone call with David, Salim took Tariq for a walk in the courtyard. Salim said, "The insights you shared with me last night are worthy of a great leader. You are right that the Shiites are gaining in political significance, thanks in part to the Americans and their 'one man, one vote' concept. Taking care of the Shiite problem is major. However, it will follow as night follows day once we take care of the Jew problem. In the meantime, instead of striking against Iran, perhaps we can use its international capabilities to our advantage. Our funders and backers will be happier if we score directly against the Zionist entity. Or against its American parent."

Those had not been David's instructions. On the contrary, David had told Salim to support a strike against Iran. But Salim had turned David's words over in his mind for most of the night. It was one thing to give the Americans information on the state of progress of the Sahelian enterprise. It was something else to do their bidding against another Islamic state, even if it was Shiite. The advice he was giving Tariq was his own, not David's.

"What are you suggesting, Salim?"

"That we give Islam a victory against Israel in its own land. Hijacking an El Al plane or attacking an Israeli Embassy has become routine, unexciting. A strike in what they call their homeland will renew your mandate as head of Islam's hopes. And I'm not talking about blowing up a pizza parlor."

"Salim, you are inspiring me. But how can we be

successful, where the Palestinians have failed? Or even against the United States, now that their guard is up?"

"Nothing is impossible, Tariq, if Allah is with us, and he is. Now is the time to activate one of the support cells in America. In fact, we could have a two-track strategy. Prepare for both an operation in America and another in Israel. At the right time, we will choose one or the other."

Al Khalil said nothing for several minutes, picking up sand and letting it run through his fingers. Finally he looked at Salim. "No. We can not dissipate our resources. We must exert all of our forces on one target, and that target has to be the Zionist presence on our land. Hamas will help us. We have many Ikhwan brothers in Hamas."

It was time for midmorning prayers. They stood up and went to the mosque room.

CHAPTER THIRTY

Justin, a member of the Paris CIA station, rushed to reach the Grand Hotel on rue Scribe near the Opéra in Paris. He crossed rue Auber and was soon in front of the baroque facade of the Grand Hotel. Before he walked in, he rechecked the picture in his pocket to imprint the target's features firmly in his mind. He spoke into what appeared to be a cell-phone headset but was an encrypted surveillance-communications device. "This is Blue Hunter. I'm in place. I'm about to go inside. Anything new on target location? Over."

Joyce, in the Paris Station's communications vault, answered, "This is Hunter Control. He has not moved. Over." She was sitting in a room crowded with stacks of communications gear operated by two men busy with their duties.

"I have not heard from Red Hunter or Green Hunter. Are they in place? Over."

"They are on their way. They should check in with you in the next five minutes. Out."

Joyce called Justin to join her in the Paris CIA station's communications vault. She said, "Typical headquarters bugfuck. They knew this guy was going to have an ops meeting in Paris because they've been monitoring his phone conversations. They also knew from the GPS device in his phone that he was here. There was no need to wait until now to tell us. Now it's a fucking emergency." She was reading a computer screen. "Wait a sec. Here, copy down these coordinates: 48.52345N–2.2250E. And find out where that is."

Justin took the numbers, opened the heavy steel door and felt the air inside decompress. He went to a wall map of Paris hung in his cubicle that was marked with small colored flags showing safe houses, hot spots where there were more likely than not to have concentrations of police such as banks, embassies and official buildings, and the areas where CIA officers were conducting operations during the week.

He went back inside the vault and told Joyce, "It could be the Opéra or the Grand Hotel on rue Scribe."

"Well, the signal has been transmitting from that spot since last night, so we'll assume that he spent the night at the hotel and not at the Opéra. Headquarters switched the signal to transmit once every thirty seconds instead of once a day, when he was in Africa. He, by the way, is CALIPH/1. I'll give you his photo, true name and basic bio in a minute."

"I'll get ready and we can move out as soon as Larry and Doreen get here. Where the hell are they anyway?" Justin asked. He looked at his watch. It was eight thirty A.M.

Joyce said, "They were up half the night keeping tabs on FARC visitors from Colombia. It looks like the French government is negotiating with the FARC over hostages.

CALIPH/1 could start moving any minute, unless he likes to sleep late. I'll tell Larry and Doreen to go directly to place de l'Opéra. You can connect with them after they get there. You're Blue Hunter. Larry will be Green and Doreen will be Red. Go."

Justin walked into the hotel and made a quick recon. When he was with the marines in Iraq, *recon* meant skulking in the streets of Fallujah fully armed and anticipating hostile fire at any second. This was much better, without giving up the feeling of contributing to something greater. His earphone suddenly came to life. He took a quick scan of his immediate surroundings and was satisfied that no one could overhear his conversation.

"This is Green Hunter. We are approaching place de l'Opéra heading east on boulevard des Capucines. Over."

"This is Blue Hunter. No sight of him yet. But be aware that the hotel has exits on rue Scribe, at the corners of Scribe and Capucines, and of Capucines and Auber. There may be another one on the northern side, but I haven't had time to check it out. If he takes a taxi, they're on rue Scribe by the main entrance. Over."

Justin walked through the central part of the ground floor, a vast sitting area lit by an equally large skylight. One dining room was round, with balcony-type French windows thirty feet up. Another dining room was flanked by tall cream-colored Greek columns going up toward a Sistine Chapel–like ceiling. Justin was searching for an informal breakfast restaurant where he thought his man might be having coffee, when he spotted him.

He again looked around before he said, "This is Blue. He is walking toward the Scribe side, probably for a taxi. Pick me up at the corner of Scribe and Capucines. Over."

"Roger, out."

With Larry driving the ten-year-old white Renault Clio hatchback with custom BMW 3 engine installed by CIA technicians to give the little car a dependable source of power, they followed al Khalil's cab down rue Royale through place de la Concorde and west along the Seine River until they reached Passy.

"Hunter Control, this is Blue Hunter. Target took a cab to the sixteenth arrondissement and went into a building on rue Chernoviz next to a grammar school. Red is on the street and we are around the corner on rue Raynouard. Over."

Joyce said, "This is Hunter Control. Determine identity of target's contact. Out."

An hour later, Justin reported back to Joyce. "Hunter control, this is Blue. Target just exited the building with another male in his late thirties to midforties. Right side of his face . . . I can't describe it exactly, but it's unusual. The right of his mouth is up like he's smiling, but he's not. Looks like he could star in a horror movie. We'll try to take photos."

Using the cameras in the side-view mirrors, Doreen and Justin were able to take the photos they needed as the two men walked to a neighborhood restaurant. The unknown male eventually broke off from al Khalil, and the team followed him to his car and continued to tail him.

As they drove by the porte de Bagnolet metro station, Larry said smiling, "I think I know where our friend is going." When their quarry turned left on boulevard Mortier, Larry added, "I knew it. This guy is DGSE. I can't believe it. CALIPH/1, a terrorist by any measure, is an agent of French intelligence."

During their meeting in the safe apartment on rue Chernoviz, al Khalil had not revealed his major change in direction. Instead, he solicited funds. Captain Roger's reply was, "We already give you more money than I can account for to my supervisor. Why do you need more money?"

"We are really making progress. You know that unless I gather the extremist imams under my tent, someone else will. And French interests will not be safe."

"What about that American professor killed in Paris? We know that was you. You're not living up to your side of the bargain."

"We all know that he was a CIA spy operating in France, so I did you a favor as well. Besides, we never agreed that Americans in France were included under 'French interests.' I'm keeping my jihadists under control. Unless I can pay them and show that we're active, they're going to go elsewhere or go out on their own, and your churches and malls and official buildings and metros will be see one firebomb after another. Who do you think has kept suicide bombers away from France?"

Al Khalil knew Roger well enough to understand that he wanted to continue the relationship. Roger's financial and career advantages were at stake.

Commandant Leroux had to do what he most disliked about his job as head of the DGSE's Technical Directorate—ask for assistance from the DGSE's sister service, the DST—the Direction de la Surveillance du Territoire, France's internal-security organization. He made the call to Lacoste from his boulevard Mortier office. "We have intercepted a new signal that will be of interest to you. We have been tracking it for several weeks through our intercept site in the Kourou Space Center in French Guiana. It was an encrypted microsecond burst. Unfortunately, there were much higher priorities for the use of our Cray computer here. However, yesterday—no, two nights ago—our center on the Oregeval Plateau at Alluets-le-Roi picked up the signal, but now it's more frequent. Instead of once a day, the signal is transmitted once every thirty seconds."

Lacoste interrupted. "Probably a simple locator transmission. If we can't break the encryption, we should be able to find out where it's coming from."

"You may be right. In any case, the source seems to be within our borders, and that's why I'm calling."

"Just send me everything you have. It would have been better if we could have had it earlier. It may be too late to make any arrests now. We'll see."

Leroux hung up. He wasn't interested particularly in an arrest. The DST, as part of the Ministry of the Interior, were just cops, he thought. Promotions were based on collars. He shook his head. The better way was to let the agent run, and discover his entire network.

CHAPTER THIRTY-ONE

Kella was in her cubicle at her new job in the DGSE building, which so far was bare of any personal items, such as family photos or favorite decorations. Most of her new colleagues were men, about half of whom were in uniform. The atmosphere and the corridor decor were also strongly military. Her feelings about that were fairly agnostic. Her parents had been killed by soldiers, but her grandfather was a general. She was the object of considerable curiosity. After all, the boss was her *grand-père*, she was a woman and she was an ENA graduate.

She had been looking forward to this moment since she learned that her request to be assigned to the Maghreb, or North African, section had been successful. The "Cimeterre" file was on her desk. She opened the red cover of the Tariq al Khalil operation and, excited, began to read. She noted the romantic inference of the name, meaning scimitar, and its invocation of the Muslim conquests that had made this Arab battle sword notorious.

After her DGSE junior-officer training, she had gone through a series of interims in each of the five directorates:

Strategic, in touch with the users of the information to determine its adequacy, relevance and timeliness; Intelligence, the HUMINT collectors; Technical, the intercept operators, France's equivalent to the American National Security Agency; and Operations, or "Action," the special military groups organized into maritime, air and ground divisions.

The file was organized chronologically, with the most recent reports on top. She flipped to the back and read Captain Roger's version of the recruitment. It read well. Roger had been adept at meeting and developing al Khalil. In time, al Khalil had shared information about the leading personalities of terrorist groups in Indonesia, the Jamaat al Islamiyya, whom he had met in the Afghan training camps. After the Bali bombings, Roger had claimed credit for al Khalil's information that led to the eventual arrest of Abu Bakar Bashir, the Jamaat leader. She was shocked to learn that the DGSE funded al Khalil to the tune of twelve thousand dollars a month. Several assassinations in northern Mali and in other countries of the Sahel were attributed to al Khalil's group by other sources. However, there was no reporting on those assassinations from Roger. Roger's reporting on the IMRA activities in the Sahel focused on social services and health care. It seemed that al Khalil was also obtaining funds from the gold and uranium mines of West and Saharan Africa. Some of his military training camps were identified, including the one she and Steve had overflown. She found no mention of his use of unmanned air vehicles.

She went back over the assassinations reported on by other sources and noted that it included Tuaregs. She looked at the bracelet given to her by Thiyya and had mixed feelings. Was she on the wrong side?

"How are you doing, Kella?" A tallish man in uniform stepped into her small space. He wore jump wings and several decorations. She had met him fleetingly during her first day on the job. It was Commandant Jocelin, the Maghreb section chief. She wasn't sure whether to get up, but he sat down in a chair beside her desk. His long legs took up the rest of her space.

"Just fine, sir. I'm starting to review the Cimeterre file. Very interesting."

"Yes. You have to meet Captain Roger. He's the case officer. What do you think of the case so far? Cimeterre is very knowledgeable and has saved French lives. He's given us information that has helped us prevent several attacks against French targets."

"I'm reading it chronologically and I haven't gotten very far yet. Isn't al Khalil a member of the Muslim Brotherhood, and hasn't it been behind several terrorist events?" she asked.

"That depends what you mean by *terrorism*. Besides, al Khalil has agreed not to operate in France," he said. She was not happy with that answer. It was too reminiscent of paying tribute to the Barbary Coast pirates several hundred years before. Or of paying off a gang so it wouldn't rob your store. Concerned that she might have to reveal what she knew about al Khalil's activities, she decided not to pursue the topic. She knew that perhaps she shouldn't hold back, that after all, she was part of the DGSE. And then again, the DGSE was presumably better informed than she was, and too many comments from her might suggest that she was not a team player, or that she was not sufficiently sophisticated to understand that al Khalil had his uses.

Jocelin got up. "Well, keep reading. I'm glad you're with us and I look forward to a major contribution from you. I look forward to your ideas."

After his departure, she noticed that the file contained information from other intelligence services, including Israeli and Egyptian intelligence. Typically, those reports showed al Khalil unequivocally as a terrorist. However, the word *self-serving* was liberally sprinkled in the margins of these reports by Captain Roger and reflected the view in the DGSE that both the Israelis and the Egyptians had their own reasons to cast aspersions on al Khalil.

The most recent reporting on al Khalil was from his case officer, Captain Lucien Roger, who had met him in a Paris safe house located on the rue Chernoviz a few weeks before. Al Khalil's Paris visit had involved both the Technical Directorate and the internal French security service, the DST, the Direction de la Surveillance du Territoire. She read about the signal that was eventually traced to Tariq's satellite telephone. According to the report, Roger was extremely skeptical that the signal, if there was one, was originating from anything his agent was carrying or wearing, which, if he was correct, would imply that something had gone wrong with his case. His only suggestion was to continue to monitor the signal to determine without doubt where it came from and, if indeed it was related to al Khalil, to try to piggyback on the signal as a check on the location of their agent. However, the counterintelligence staff had the power to override him and did; if there was some sort of beacon in the phone, it indicated that another intelligence organization had gained access to the phone and might have done more than just plant a location device in it. It was decided to steal the instrument and force al Khalil to buy another one. "Stuff" happened in urban areas, and Paris was no exception. Al Khalil would not question such an incident.

A few days later, Commandant Jocelin called to ask Kella to come to his office, one floor up. The secretary nodded that she could go in. Jocelin sat behind his desk to the right of the door. On the wall behind Jocelin was a map of North Africa and a military-unit insignia. The man sitting in front of Jocelin's desk got up as Jocelin said, "Kella I want you to meet Captain Lucien Roger. I'm sure you saw his reports in the Cimeterre file."

Kella glanced at the captain and her gaze became embarrassingly fixed on the right side of his face, frozen in a permanent grimace. However, considering the way the captain had looked her up and down—the "elevator look," she thought—the grin appeared to her more like a leer. He said, "Allow me to express my deep pleasure at having you on board. I heard you graduated from the ENA, whose graduates don't normally end up with us. It is truly an honor. I have to assume that you're being groomed to be our boss in very short order." The sarcasm was not lost on Kella, who was aware that Roger had noticed her staring at his face.

Jocelin's voice allowed her to wrest her eyes from Roger's face. "I saw you looking at this when you came in," he said, and pointed to the insignia on the wall, a blue triangle with the point down, in the center of which was a flame in the middle of a green and red rectangle. On the left was the number two and on the right was the suggestion of a deployed bird wing. "It's from my old unit, in Corsica, the Second Airborne Regiment of the Foreign Legion—great outfit."

"I assume that jumping out of perfectly good airplanes is not a requirement for me," she said with a grin.

Captain Roger, who was dressed in civilian clothes, said, "It depends on the mission, mademoiselle."

Jocelin shooed them out of his office. "I have another meeting. But you'll be working together, and I assume that Captain Roger has a lot he wants to share with you, Kella."

They moved to Roger's office, on her floor. Sitting across from Roger, Kella said, "That's a wonderful picture. Is that you? Growing up in Mali, I don't think I ever rode a horse. A camel, yes. A horse, no." Roger turned away from the photograph without answering, and Kella felt uneasy. She went in another direction. "I was reading the Cimeterre case since I'll be doing the operational support work. Al Khalil looks like an interesting person. Do you think he's truly under our control? Also, I was wondering about that signal. What do you think that's all about?"

Roger appeared startled. "What? You've been on the desk two minutes and you're already questioning me? I recruited him, and he's one of the best sources we have."

In the face of his defensive attitude, she clearly had to be more sensitive and diplomatic.

Before she could try her new tack, Roger continued in a calmer tone, "I'm not convinced that the signal is coming from his phone. Those techies have it all wrong. I'm opposed to mounting an operation to steal it; it's a waste of manpower. I could just ask him for it. But the DST boys have their best team on Tariq. They're going to borrow that satellite phone and examine it. It's probably going to create a diplomatic incident." He shook his head and rolled his eyes.

Roger questioned her about her African background, her studies and her parents. In a few minutes, Kella felt that she had been wrung dry by an expert. Finally, he said, "We need to continue this conversation later in a more relaxed atmosphere," which she took to mean that she was dismissed and that he meant to go further than just leer at her.

As she walked out, she noticed another photo on the wall. Roger in a black and gold uniform, spurs and a cocked hat, holding a horse by its reins. Unlike Jocelin, proud of his former unit and what it stood for, Roger was very much about himself. And from the way he had reacted, she concluded that he was not comfortable in his skin.

Maurice, the burly DST team leader, waved to Paul, farther down the rue de Courcelles. They were on al Khalil. Their assigned objective was to separate him from his briefcase, where, they knew from the DGSE, he carried his satellite phone. Al Khalil had come out of the Saudi Arabian Embassy on avenue Hoche and was proceeding north on rue de Courcelles. Although Roger had briefed the team that al Khalil usually took taxis in Paris, he seemed headed toward the Courcelles metro entrance, and Maurice sent two of his men ahead into the metro station. The team also knew from tapping his hotel phone that al Khalil was scheduled to make a presentation at the Salle Pleyel that afternoon. The two surveillants preceded al Khalil to the platform that would put him on the metro heading west toward Charles de Gaulle-Étoile. By the time the subway pulled in to the Courcelles station, Maurice had maneuvered three men in front of Tariq. He and Paul were immediately in back of him. As Tariq stepped onto the metro, he was prevented from moving forward by the three men in front of him who, their backs to him, barely gave him room to step on board. The wagon was fairly crowded, and as the team had hoped, he didn't push forward. Just before the doors to the metro started closing, the two who stayed on the platform acted in unison.

A few minutes before, Maurice had summarized the choreography for his team. "The first action is to keep him very close to the door. The second action has three movements. That will be you, Paul, and me. We don't get on the metro, but we'll be immediately behind him as he gets on. You'll be on the left. Movement one, stick him on the left side with this pin to get his attention away from the briefcase; second movement, I tear the briefcase from his hand; third movement, the doors close and the metro takes him away from us and his briefcase. It's over and we have his phone."

As planned, Paul stuck a needle in al Khalil's left buttock. Al Khalil yelped in pain, turned to his left and looked behind him. As his shoulders started their rotation, Maurice, on Paul's right, seized al Khalil's briefcase with both hands and wrenched it away. The doors of the metro closed within a fraction of a second and the metro pulled away.

Al Khalil shouted, "They took my briefcase. Stop the train, stop the train!" People looked at him strangely. The three men in front of him moved away in different directions as if to avoid getting involved with this helpless and indignant foreigner, probably an Arab. "Serves him right," one muttered to no one in particular.

Chapter Thirty-two

Hussein saw Karim outside the IMRA building sitting on the sand in the shade of the building, his legs crossed in front of him, with a small group of IMRA militants.

"What are you doing?" Hussein asked.

"I'm waiting for the boss. He wants me to drive him to the northern camp."

"Come inside."

Karim got up and followed him past several desks busy with welfare recipients into a far corner, where there were two empty chairs away from everyone. Hussein said, "We don't have enough people at the camp. You have enough experience now to help out with the training. Also, talk to Rashid up there. He'll tell you where you're needed most. When you go up there with Tariq, take another driver to bring Tariq back."

Karim was pleased with the increased trust being placed on his shoulders since the attack on the missionaries and the NGO workers. He gave some of the credit for the new mindset to Steve. He had taught Karim to be less passive, to recognize when he had choices and what they were. Being at the camp meant more responsibility, perhaps more independence and probably more choices. He came to believe that his meeting with Steve had been meant to take place; Allah had clearly willed it. Such a life-changing event didn't just happen. It had to be part of a greater design.

At the desert camp, Karim immediately became aware of the almost uninterrupted whining sound of small engines being operated at high speeds. He went toward the noise and found the airstrip. He counted five small planes that were flown remotely. Karim was fascinated by them and began to spend as much time as he could around the camouflage netting under which the unmanned air vehicles, the UAVs, were hangared.

Karim knew that Rashid was in charge of the camp, which also included the obstacle course, the runs in the desert and the other physical training, as well as the weapons familiarization and their firing. Rashid's priority was clearly the UAVs. He left the other activities to others.

One day, after Karim came back from a run with the trainees, Rashid, a Moroccan Berber in his forties with a dark complexion and a high forehead, called out to him. "Karim, I want you to clean the engine of this drone. I'll show you how, and then you can finish it. These things weren't made for a desert environment. Unless we can keep the sand out, it's going to destroy the engines." Rashid spent two hours with him answering Karim's questions on the workings of an internal-combustion engine.

A couple of days later, Karim made a point of sitting with Rashid at dinner. He asked, "Where did you learn about UAVs?"

"Actually, I'm self-taught on the UAVs. But I attended a technical school near Casablanca, and one day I was given the chance to take an exam for one place at a French aeronautical school near Toulouse. The test was given in Algeria and Tunisia as well as Morocco. The school offered one slot to each country. Well, I went and studied in France for two years."

"Why didn't you stay? I would have stayed." Karim spit the pit of a date out of his mouth.

"After the formal training, all of the French students were offered jobs in the French aircraft industry around Toulouse. The three of us kept getting turned down because we were Arabs."

"The French are pigs," Karim said. "So, what did you do? Go back to Morocco?"

Rashid laughed. "Well, I felt isolated. The French students didn't let us, the three Arabs, hang with them. One day, for something to do instead, we went to the mosque. And we went back the following week." He reached for a piece of chicken in the plate of couscous. "I don't know what happened to the Tunisian and to the Algerian, but I found that the Salafists liked me. Eventually, I was introduced to Hussein when he was traveling through France, and he brought me to IMRA."

Karim became Rashid's best student, and at Rashid's request, Hussein told Karim to stay at the camp as an assistant. Karim felt that he was heading upwards. He asked Rashid for manuals, which he pored over, asking a thousand questions about the UAVs. When Rashid taught him to pilot the little planes by remote control, Karim was as happy as he had ever been. Under Rashid's tutelage, Karim became an accomplished UAV pilot.

One day, under the camouflage netting, Rashid told Karim, "Our UAVs are not the most recent technology, but we don't need the latest technology. Our planes have the capability to carry out multiple functions, including real-time or photo surveillance. Next week, I want you to help me experiment with different payloads."

"OK. What kind of payloads?"

"I'm going to adapt them to carry a number of different things, since I don't know what the mission is going to be yet. I want to know where to place the camera, sensors or weapons. Right now, we don't need the specific payload, just their weight and size." Rashid stood by one of his UAVs. He leaned down and touched its wing.

"Are they going to be flying bombs? Like the Americans' smart bombs?" Karim asked.

"Don't know yet."

Karim came to the conclusion that Steve would want to

know about these little planes and he started to mentally inventory them. Rashid had obtained the first UAV, the Mirsad-1, from the Lebanese Hezbollah. Rashid told him, "This one became famous when the Hezbollah used it against Israel during the 2006 war."

Rashid had four other UAVs, all obtained, Karim learned, through a retired American officer now in the arms business. Three, an IAI Harpy, an RQ-2, and an RUAG Ranger, had originally been developed in Israel. The Falcon was Jordanian, a joint venture between the King Abdullah II Design and Development Bureau and Jordan Aerospace Industries, according to Rashid. The Ranger was the closest to looking like and being a real airplane. Karim's favorite was the RQ-2, bought and used by the U.S. Navy, which would retrieve it on board with the use of a net. With a wingspan of almost seventeen feet, it was no toy. But Karim found it easy to maneuver, and he loved to fly it around the skies of the Sahara, spotting caravans either in the distance or directly under the craft through its live TV system. With the ability to fly up to fifteen thousand feet, it was unseen and unheard by people on the ground.

Karim made no notes, remembering that Steve told him it was too dangerous, but since he worked with the planes on a daily basis, he found it easy to remember every detail. One day, Allah would put him back in touch with Steve. In the meantime, he continued to practice his remote flying skills over the Sahara.

CHAPTER THIRTY-THREE

Steve went back to his West Gate job following his return to the United States and the award ceremony at CIA headquarters. His division chief, Charlie Van Diemen, a retired airforce colonel, walked into Steve's windowless office. "You did it, Steve. We just received the first payment from the Moroccans for a two-year program to renovate Ben Guerir Air Base for fighter aircraft of the Moroccan air force."

"That's great. I discussed that project with the Moroccans, but I never had the chance to go down there. Ben Guerir was used to support the Space Shuttle program for a possible abort landing. I suppose we have other options these days."

Van Diemen pointed to a plaque on the wall of Steve's office addressed to *Boy Genius*. He said, "They were right." The plaque was from the Fifty-first Fighter Wing at Osan Air Force Base in South Korea, where Steve had worked on counterproliferation for two years. "I really didn't think you could do it. Breaking into a new market already dominated by French companies seemed like a long shot. But you certainly did it. If you can do it there, maybe you can do it in other countries as well. Don't unpack."

Steve knew that he was highly thought of by his company. However, now that he was back at work, he was away from the action. He had mulled his options over several times. Joining the CIA full-time was one. However, he was extremely reluctant to have to depend on people like Mel. And there were too many rules. Maybe a large organization had to dumb down its regulations to protect itself from the lowest common denominator. He hadn't yet decided how to keep to his goal to resist the Salafists, al Khalil especially. But he had not dismissed it.

Later, Steve's West Gate office phone rang. It was "Mel from the office," as she identified herself. That Mel, who didn't think that he was a "real" case officer, should call meant that there was a serious problem. "We were wondering if you could come today. This afternoon would be all right." Steve looked at his watch. It was already early afternoon and he had a load of things to do.

"I could come in the morning." Not wanting to go through the hassle of the security checks and badging, he asked, "How about if you came out to Salona Village? We could have coffee."

They met at the Seven Seas Restaurant, owned by a retired CIA officer and a favorite of CIA employees, since it was only five minutes away off Dolley Madison Boulevard. When his father was in northern Virginia on consultation, the restaurant was a favorite venue for his ROMEOs— retired old men eating out.

When Steve went in, he immediately spotted Mel, this time in a different tent dress but, as usual, one of many colors. *Great disguise for a spy,* Steve thought. Sitting with her was a young man in a dark suit—Josh, a trainee. Mel had told Steve on the phone that he would be with her. Steve slid onto the red-leatherette-covered bench of the booth across from Mel and Josh under a large poster of Pete Sampras. After the introductions, Mel said, "Therese LaFont asked me to talk to you about taking a trip back to Mali. To see CALIPH/4."

Both Mel and Josh already had a cup of coffee and a menu. A waitress poured Steve a cup as soon as he sat down. "I don't need the menu, thanks," he said. "Go ahead and order if you want. Coffee is all I'll have." He looked at his watch.

It had been three months since Steve had last seen Karim. "How is he?" he asked.

"We had a turnover in Bamako. Rod was reassigned. The new chief of station contacted CALIPH/4 and ran him for two months. First, our new chief of station said that he really had not been properly recruited, that he was not a fully responsive agent when he first met him." Mel's look challenged Steve to rebut her statement. Josh stirred his coffee.

"Not responsive? He stole al Khalil's phone for us! How responsive can he be?" Steve's voice was a bit louder than necessary. He looked around, but no one seemed to have noticed.

"Well, Therese thinks you should go over there and try to revive the operation."

Steve asked, "How is the satellite phone I gave to al Khalil working out? I hope you're getting some good info."

Mel said, "I can't talk about that."

"Why not?"

"Well, you're not cleared, not anymore."

Steve was getting irritated at Mel's narrow view of life and her mindless rigidity. He saw no sense in prolonging the discussion and he said, "I'll have to talk to my boss. I'll let you know. I have to go back to my office."

They walked out together, Steve giving Mel a wide berth. Mel said, "I'll see you back at the office, Josh. I have to run an errand." She was parked on the left. Steve and Josh walked to the right toward their cars.

Steve said, "How long have you been with the Agency?"

"Three months, sir. I was in classes until last week. This is my first interim assignment. Then I'll have three more months of classes and another interim with another directorate. Then more training."

"How do you like it so far?" Steve felt sorry that Josh's first job was under the worst manager in the Agency.

Josh smiled. "Not exactly what I expected. But I read the SBCALIPHATE file. That's how I thought it would be. What you did in Gao was amazing, just like a movie."

"What's your take on CALIPH/4 and this new case officer, then?"

They were standing by Josh's car, an Audi convertible. Josh took his jacket off and swung it over his shoulder. "I haven't met the new Bamako chief—his name is Gregory— but I heard about him. A short man with a tall ego and ambition to match, I gather. He and CALIPH/4 didn't get along. I shouldn't be judging, but it seemed to me that he laid some over-the-top requirements on CALIPH/4. When CALIPH/4 couldn't produce, Gregory terminated him."

"What about the money we owed him? We were putting his money aside each month."

"I don't know about that."

"Good luck to you," Steve said abruptly. "Don't let Mel get you down."

"Thanks, sir. I'll be on this end answering your mail if you go back out. You can count on me, sir."

Josh opened the door to his car, and Steve walked away toward his.

Steve went to Van Diemen's office as soon as he returned to the West Gate tower. He said, "I just had coffee with the Agency's West African–branch chief. They want me to go back to Mali."

Van Diemen frowned. "For how long?"

"I don't know. I'm guessing a week or two."

"The last time, the request for your services came to me from the West Gate CEO. It can't be that important this time. We're going to ignore the request unless the CEO calls. I don't mind helping out, but we need you here. Well, actually not here, exactly. Sit down."

Steve sat on a sofa and Van Diemen came from behind his desk to sit on an armchair at a right angle to the sofa. Like many of the offices at West Gate, Van Diemen's office was decorated by plaques and insignias of air-force units that more or less outlined the office dweller's career.

"You did well on that Moroccan deal. You'll get a considerable bonus. People like you. You establish trusting relationships easily. That's a definite strength. I'd like you to try some of your magic farther east. We've got a lot of contracts in the Middle East with our own Department of Defense, but so far only with the American military. Well, with the Moroccan exception, thanks to you. I'd like you to focus on the mother lode, on Egypt and Israel. U.S. taxpayers are sending more than two billion dollars to Egypt each year in economic and military aid. And a bit more to Israel. Do you think you could go over there and help them figure out how to spend it? I can set up some meetings at the Pentagon for you to get you started. As you can guess, DOD has been working with the Israeli Defense Forces forever and with the Egyptians since the 1979 Camp David Accords, when our government really opened up the purse strings—the reward for making peace with Israel. Anyway, some of my contacts over there can give you the lay of the land, and hopefully some names in Tel Aviv and Cairo. I would start with the Egyptians."

Steve listened to Van Diemen's suggestions, all the while thinking about what he had just learned. Not only was Mel incapacitated by a by-the-numbers way of thinking in a profession where wide mental horizons were absolutely necessary, but her field counterpart Gregory seemed blinded by ego and ambition. Steve was arriving at the point where he still wanted to stop al Khalil but didn't think that he could do it through the CIA, and was angry that the commitments made to Karim apparently were not being carried out. He wondered if somehow he could help Karim and also do something to slow al Khalil if he traveled. He couldn't do anything from his West Gate office.

"You know me. Anything to get out of the office."

Later, he also wondered if he could manipulate this trip into a visit with Kella.

CHAPTER THIRTY-FOUR

Kella now had dinner at least once a week at the Joulets on rue de Longchamp. The general's wife had excused herself, knowing that Kella and her husband were about to talk shop. General Joulet had Courvoisier in a large brandy glass.

Kella said, "I've been through the training. Now I'm on the Maghreb desk, except that we pretty much also run the Cimeterre case, even though it's in Mali—it's so close to the AQIM group, el Maghrebi and his thugs. I've gone on an orientation trip to Algiers. I'm providing operational support to DGSE officers in the field. Yet I don't feel that I'm accomplishing much." She took her earings off and held them in one hand. "To be frank, I'm somewhat disappointed in the people I work with. Most of them are military, and they can't wait to get back with the troops. They're not happy in an office environment, that's obvious." Noticing her grandfather's frown, she added, "Commandant Jocelin is different. He's OK."

She chose not to reveal the growing tension between her and Captain Roger. In spite of their age difference, the captain was showing a strong personal interest in Kella.

"Keep in mind that you're a junior officer fresh out of training," the general said. *As well as a woman and a civilian in a military culture,* she thought.

Kella asked, "When I was in Timbuktu, I learned that al Khalil has UAVs. In fact, I must have told you, one of them shot at our plane. I haven't seen anything like that in our files. I wonder why." The general blinked in surprise, but she didn't know quite how to interpret his reaction.

Joulet swirled the brandy around in his glass and took a sip of his Courvoisier. "There have been rumors of UAVs in North Africa, but as far as I know, no hard information. Did you raise this with your supervisor?"

"I did, but he didn't seem surprised." She didn't want to speak out of school about Captain Roger. However, she didn't feel that her question had been welcomed. On the contrary, Roger had acted defensively, as if threatened.

When she drove home that evening, she still was unsatisfied that the DGSE was the warhorse she needed in the fight against the Salafists. She wanted to speak to Steve.

Chapter Thirty-five

Najib Salah fell into step with his brother Mahmoud as they walked toward Gaza City's Oriental market. They had run into each other leaving one of the Hamas government buildings and were making their way to Najib's apartment on the other side of the market. They were both in their late forties, although Mahmoud was a year older. His black hair was graying on the sides and he was stockier than Najib. While Najib, a former teacher, looked every inch the intellectual, Mahmoud had always been more physical. They were both senior members of Hamas. The Muslim Brotherhood's military wing had operated in Gaza since the late sixties, and had become Hamas in 1987. Since then, it had grown into a hydra with political, social and military heads. Najib was with Hamas's social services. Mahmoud was with the military wing, the Izz al Din al Qassam, and a member of the al Qassam council, as well as a respected operational chief. Like many of his colleagues, he had spent time in an Israeli prison. He was picked up after having planned an operation that had killed five Israelis and seven Arabs on a Tel Aviv bus by using a suicide bomber. Hamas had determined that Shin Beth, the Israeli internal-security service, had learned of Mahmoud's role through a low-level Hamas militant, who was quickly executed by Mahmoud's men. He had been freed in an Israeli-Palestinian exchange of prisoners. Mahmoud often joked that his suicide martyrs were smarter bombs than the high-tech so-called smart bombs of the Jews. Mahmoud, Najib and the two guards all wore wraparound sunglasses.

Since the withdrawal of Israeli troops from Gaza and the January 2005 elections giving the prime minister's post to Hamas, political disagreement between the religious Hamas and the secular Fatah forces had grown into a civil war that had become an all-out war in which Hamas overwhelmed Fatah forces and took over Gaza. Mahmoud had been one of the three military leaders, each one in charge of the fight for each of the three Fatah security compounds.

The street was flanked on each side by six-story whitewashed apartment buildings. Colors were provided by the tenants' drying laundry hanging from windows. A multitude of wires and cables, many jury-rigged by utility customers who preferred not to pay for telephone and electricity, seemed to tether the buildings together. As they walked down the street, Mahmoud's bodyguard stayed within five yards of the brothers, and Najib's bodyguard either followed or led in a looser formation, but never farther than twenty yards away. Both had their semiautomatic rifles at the ready, not an unusual sight for a population in constant conflict with Israel and with each other.

Mahmoud's eyes constantly shifted, alert to possible threats. From scanning apartment windows, his eyes went skyward, looking for an Israeli UAV he knew had to be above them, monitoring Gaza City.

Najib said, "I am telling you that it's not a desert-agriculture experimental station. If it is, it's also a cover for something else.

"I've driven by that installation for the last two years many times on my way to Ashdod, and I've seen vehicles and people coming in and out. Those people don't look like farmers to me. They could be professors. Some look military. I saw men dressed in civilian clothes, but I could also see they were wearing military boots."

"Any guards? Any uniformed military?" asked Mahmoud.

"No," answered Najib. "But remember the hitchhiker from Nablus I told you about? He had worked as a laborer in this installation. He was telling me about the size of the watermelons. He thought that the place was a front for some sort of Rafael project."

"Rafael? You mean Rafael Armament Development Authority? You didn't tell me that before. Rafael does all of the Jews' secret weapons work. It could be important after all," Mahmoud said. "We definitely would have the world's attention if we destroyed a Rafael site. They built the Jews' nuclear bomb. We could easily get funding for an attack against the Jews' nuclear programs. In fact, against any research site. What led him to think this place is connected to Rafael?"

Najib took off his sunglasses and wiped his face with a handkerchief. "Well, he's not one hundred percent certain. He is sure that it's more than an agricultural station. For example, he's been in some of the buildings and he was surprised how few people were there, compared to the cars parked outside. He saw a lot of people go in, but he saw very few people inside. One more thing. It's very close to the Palmachim Air Base, in Yavne, where the Jews have their rockets, and Nahal Soreq, the nuclear center. So it's logical for them to have this secret base close to these other secret projects," said Najib.

"The Jews often build their secret laboratories, their essential military offices, underground. That would explain where they all went. We do the same thing; if it wasn't for our tunnels, we couldn't smuggle weapons or people to or from Egypt," Mahmoud said with a chuckle.

"When the Jews started their nuclear center at Dimona, their cover was that it was an observatory, because of the dome shape of the first building. They also floated the story that the other buildings were part of a textile center. So this so-called agricultural station could very well be something else. If we can collect more information, I'll propose a specific operation to our leadership. This could be big. I wouldn't be surprised if the decision is made at Hamas headquarters in Damascus. The Syrians or the Iranians would help. But I'd rather work with our Ikhwan brothers in Cairo—I'm thinking specifically of Walid Fahmy. He's a doer. He's aggressive and he's in touch with Tariq al Khalil. He won't hesitate to help us. The Brotherhood was there at our creation; it will want to take part in what will be a major blow against the Zionists."

Mahmoud dropped his Camel cigarette butt and lit a fresh one. "Isn't the irony delicious? The Jews helped the creation of Hamas, or facilitated our initial existence in Gaza, in the belief that Hamas would weaken the PLO. Now we have actual control of the movement, and the PLO is nothing. We own Gaza; we will own the occupied territories of the West Bank. The Jews have outwitted themselves."

Several boys were playing soccer in the street. By accident, the ball was hit toward the Salah brothers and one boy came running after it. Mahmoud's bodyguard quickly blocked the ball and kicked it back, shouting, "Stupid boy. My trigger finger is very nervous. Don't ever kick a ball toward someone with a gun."

They reached the market and turned in between stalls loaded on one side with dates in wooden boxes and on the other with raisins in flat cardboard containers. They crossed the market and continued their conversation amid the smells and sights of the temporary stalls. The strong and earthy smell of cumin competed with the lighter but equally fragrant sage and the smoky aroma of paprika. Rusty saffron sat next to vats of green and black olives.

Both Najib and Mahmoud believed that in their own way, they were working so that the people behind these smells and colors could one day have the opportunity to support their families in dignity and under the laws of Islam. To reach that objective, the nonbelievers in and out of Gaza would have to submit and, with Allah's help, would submit.

They were still a block away from Najib's apartment building when they emerged from the market, one bodyguard now twenty feet ahead and the other in back but much closer. There was only light traffic as they started to cross the street. Suddenly a burst of gunfire erupted and the front bodyguard went down. Another burst quickly followed as both Najib and Mahmoud dove to the ground. People on the near side of the market were all on the ground. Guns appeared in multiple hands. Several single rounds were fired, coming from the market. The Gaza population had much experience with random acts of violence, and weapons were plentiful. The attempted hit soon led to indiscriminate firing.

The assassin had mistimed his hit. If he had waited for the Salah brothers to reach the middle of the street, they would have had no cover. Instead, they had only just emerged from the market and started crawling quickly back toward the stalls. Najib was bloodied but moving. The rear bodyguard had come from behind and was down on one knee, looking for his target. He spotted the gunman lining up his own weapon to fire again, steadying his aim and using a metal light pole for cover. Both fired at almost the same time. The hit man fired at the retreating brothers in a scattered spray that belied his professional preparation. A shot hit the would-be assassin in the shoulder, causing him to spin and lose even the slim protection of the pole. The bodyguard then fired again at the now-easy target and cut him down.

Mahmoud leaned down to look at Najib's wound and muttered, "The al Aqsa Brigade. I thought we had killed all those Fatah dogs."

The next day, Mahmoud went to visit Najib at the Shifa Hospital. From outside, he could see that most of the windows were shattered. Inside, the walls were dirty, and too many people waited for medical care by doctors who were often forced to first take care of those most likely to live. But Najib's and Mahmoud's status as senior Hamas officials guaranteed priority attention.

Najib was sitting in a green plastic chair in a room with ten beds, all of them occupied by patients with more serious problems. His upper body was encased in a cast to keep his shoulder and arm immobile. Mahmoud said, "*Al hamdu Allah*, you're looking fine, brother. If the doctors are done, you're better off coming home. I'll ask for some painkillers and we can go."

He disappeared and came back ten minutes later. "The doctor said that the hospital is virtually out of supplies. He had four of these pills. He said that each should last about two hours, but to make them last as long as possible. He has no more."

As they walked out, Mahmoud said, "Are you OK? Listen to me. This cowardly al Aqsa attack has convinced me to act against that Rafael installation near Ashqelon. By winning the elections, we used the democratic weapon. We won international credibility. But we're not going to get the Jews out through elections. The armed struggle continues to be the key. Look at the increased status of Hezbollah after their month-long fighting with the Zionist army in Lebanon. We can complete our capture of the Palestinian heart and mind with a major victory over the Jews. Your discovery of a Rafael installation is the ticket. I need first to get the political support, and then I'll collect the operational information for a plan. I'll get Walid Fahmy or Talal Kawar, or both, the Ikhwan chiefs in Egypt and Jordan, to put me in touch with their boss, Tariq al Khalil. My guess is that he wouldn't mind making headlines about now."

Najib walked firmly with Mahmoud out of the front door of the hospital but winced in pain as someone in a great hurry came in and pushed past him. Mahmoud put his hand on his holstered gun, but Najib restrained him with a stern look and a firm "No."

After they were down the steps and on the street, Najib said, "Military operations are your responsibility, not mine. But my sense is that Hamas is going to let al Khalil fund this operation, so you would be wise to get in touch with him soon."

Mahmoud had called a meeting of the Izz al Din al Qassam Council. They were on the second floor of an apartment building in Gaza City in a one-bedroom apartment that belonged to one of the council members. They were all sitting at a wooden table, each with either water or tea. As usual, the smoke was thick.

Mahmoud had already given its five members the background of the operation. "With the help of our brother Arabs who work in Israeli vehicle-registration offices, and using surveillance as well as the Internet, we have been able to connect vehicles that entered the agricultural compound with personal addresses. From there, using the utmost discretion, we were able to determine that the drivers of these vehicles habitually went from their homes to the Dimona Nuclear Center, to Israeli Defense Forces headquarters in Tel Aviv and to major defense-related companies, including Aeronautics Defense Systems Ltd in Yavne, Elbit Systems in Haifa, and Tadiran Communications in Petah Tiqwa. All of these companies produced high-tech items for the IDF, Israeli Defence Forces. None had any connection to agriculture." He stopped to take a puff of his cigarette and gather his thoughts.

"We have concluded therefore that we were right, that the agricultural center is a front for a secret defense installation operated by the Rafael Armament Development Authority. I request the authority of the council to contact Tariq al Khalil through our Muslim Brotherhood friends to propose he funds and provides the men and materiel for an operation against the secret installation in Ashqelon."

He stopped and had another puff, waiting for the council's reaction. Since Mahmoud had already briefed and obtained the support of each individual member of the council, he expected approval, and he was not disappointed.

On his way home, Mahmoud planned how he would exit Gaza without alerting Israeli authorities. He would go out through one of the tunnels under the Egyptian border, he thought. The sea was too well patrolled by Israeli gunboats. He would lay out the information first to Walid Fahmy, the Ikhwan chief in Cairo.

Chapter Thirty-six

Steve mulled over his options as he drove to his apartment. As usual, the GW Parkway was crowded with commuters. Van Diemen wanted him to prepare for another trip, to Tel Aviv and to Cairo. Should he try to fix the operation in Timbuktu? The car on his right, a silver SUV, pulled even with him, although he could have kept moving ahead another twenty feet in the daily driving competition over inches. This unusually laid-back behavior interrupted Steve's thoughts and he looked at the driver, a dark-skinned man with jet-black hair, who had been looking at Steve but turned his head back to the front. He was alone. Steve took note of the car and dropped back to see its license plate. *Probably nothing*, he thought, but he maintained a closer eye on his environment as he drove home. The silver SUV pulled ahead of him and took the Roosevelt Bridge exit while he stayed on the parkway toward Alexandria.

He parked near his apartment thirty minutes later and wrote down the plate number. He wasn't sure whether to follow up on the SUV. However, his recent experiences in Paris and Morocco didn't allow him to dismiss it. He would keep the number until he decided what to do.

He changed into running shorts and went out, again considering his situation. He was doing well at West Gate. He probably would be offered a higher position and a better salary in the near future. Should he fit a trip to Timbuktu to see Karim on his way to or back from the Middle East? How did West Gate fit into his determination to do something concrete, something that would blunt the ambitious plans of the Salafists and their killing spree? He no longer wanted to put his life in the hands of people like Mel—and now, this Gregory. This meant that his work for the CIA was over. But how could he possibly fight the Salafists single-handedly?

As he closed in on his apartment after a seven-mile run, he saw the silver SUV turn into his street half a block away. He ran past his street and made two rights, which brought him to the head of his street, where he stopped. The silver car was nowhere in sight. He nevertheless ran past his street again and came at his apartment from the back by cutting through a neighbor's backyard. He wondered if the Salafists, armed with his name and picture from the Paris newspaper, had tracked him down. It would have been easy to do. All they needed was a phone book.

Once upstairs, he called Gordon, an FBI agent he had met at the gym, and left him a message.

He took a quick shower, put on old jeans and grilled a steak, taking care to season it liberally with plenty of garlic, and then prepared a salad. He opened a beer. The scent of the garlic quickly took over the kitchen, and Steve felt that his problems were no longer insurmountable.

Beer in hand, he went to the living room, sat at his computer and sent Kella an e-mail:

Hi, I'm making plans for a Middle East trip. Any chance we could meet? Paris is not on my itinerary for obvious reasons. If it doesn't threaten to discombobulate your life, how about meeting me in Geneva? We could have some fun and I have an idea that needs the intellect of an ENA graduate. All this on the assumption that you're not yet president.

Gordon called back. He was home. "Hey Steve, what's going on?"

"Just one second." Steve took his steak off the grill and came back to the phone. "I have a favor to ask. Did I tell you that I was actually famous? That I appeared in the international press?"

"You mean the Quran project? You didn't say a word about it to me. I know about it anyway. The FBI knows all, sees all."

Steve then related his suspicions about the silver SUV and asked him to trace the plate.

"I can do that. You think they're that organized that they would follow you to the ends of the earth to get you? Probably not. But I'll do it. In the morning."

Steve went to bed feeling calm.

Gordon called the next day. "The SUV was a rental. However, I found out that the guy who rented it is on the terrorist watch list: Rafiq Jallad, AKA Jabril al Jihad. He's been here two years, from Tunis. Unemployed. Lives in Herndon and frequents a mosque in Herndon that is a center of Muslim activists. He has a bank account and he gets money from a bank in Qatar."

Steve said, "Activist! I love your official euphemisms. Is that a politically correct term to stay under the ACLU's radar?"

"You're welcome. This guy is probably part of a support mechanism responsible for surveillance, renting safe apartments and cars, etc. The hit team arrives after all the groundwork is done."

"So, what are you saying? Don't worry because the hit team is not here yet? Are you going to arrest him?"

"He didn't do anything illegal. I'll pay him a friendly visit, which should calm him down. In the meantime, maybe you could live somewhere else for while."

Steve felt hunted. These guys didn't give up. It only reinforced his determination to take the initiative. The next day, he moved into his father's town house and decided to move up his trip to the Middle East and Geneva.

Two weeks later Steve was in Cairo with two days of meetings left on his schedule to try to move the Egyptian military toward West Gate's services. At Van Diemen's recommendation, Steve stayed at the Talisman Hotel de Charme on Talaat Harb Street. It called itself a boutique hotel, and Steve assumed that Van Diemen had chosen it because it was cheaper than the grandiose Hilton and Marriott, where most American businessmen stayed. His main point of contact was an Egyptian armor colonel with a Sandhurst pedigree. Steve concluded that as a "Yank," he had the wrong accent to be taken seriously by this Anglophile colonel. He would find someone from the West Gate staff with a British background.

Checking his e-mail after he returned to his room, he found that he had a message from Kella that said in part,

How about meeting in Geneva next week? I can get away from Thursday through Sunday. I have to be back at work Monday. I have another message for you.

Last time I was in T, I met with Mother Catherine. She
had a message for you from someone named Karim,
who needs to hear from you urgently. Who is Karim
and why don't I know him?

Steve was nonplussed by mentions of Mother Catherine
and Karim and himself all in the same sentence. Perhaps
he hadn't been as clandestine as he'd thought after all
while he was running Karim. He replied,

You caught me in Cairo, where professionally speaking, my progress is underwhelming. But at least no
one is trying to kill me. Your message raises a thousand questions on how people in your message are
connected.
    Later.
    P.S. It's OK to pass my cell number to Karim. Maybe
I could stop in Bamako on the way back home, but I'd
rather not.

Steve got Karim's call the next day. "Monsieur Christophe. I am so happy we are talking, *grand merci à Dieux*,"
he began.

Steve picked up on the French equivalent of *al hamdu
Allah*, also "thanks be to God." He wondered why Karim
wasn't using the Arabic version, as he had so many times
before.

"And I am happy we're talking also. It has been a long
time. How is your brother?" Steve replied, mindful that even
in urgent situations, family was always the conversational
priority.

"Oh, my brother, he is dead. He was killed in a firefight
between Algerian soldiers and the Salafist rebels, the AQIM.
I don't know what happened. He was supposed to travel to
France the next day. I wanted him in France working while
I earned enough money to send him to America. But Monsieur

Gregoire, he is not a good man. But that is not why I need to talk with you. I think that something important is going to happen. I remember that you said to never talk about these things on the telephone, so I don't want to. But how else can I tell you? I am flying *avions sans pilotes*, and they will be part of the plan, I think."

Steve was thinking fast, balancing the need to finish his business in Cairo and his plans to go to Tel Aviv next against what he was learning from Karim. "If you have any excuse to go to Europe, I could see you there next week," Steve offered hopefully.

"How did you know? I am traveling to Geneva with Hussein next week. He is taking me with him because I know about these planes without pilots, and Rashid is traveling. He wants to buy some more."

He told Karim, "Since you're probably going to be busy during the day, would it be better to meet at night, do you think?" He waited for Karim to answer, but Karim hesitated.

Steve continued, "Take this down. I'll be in the bistro section of Le Chat Noir, rue Vautier, in the Carouge section, at eleven in the evening on Tuesday. It's a jazz cabaret. Look it up in the tourist information they will have at your hotel. If one of us can't go, then I'll be at the place du Marché, also in Carouge, not far from Le Chat Noir, the next day at ten in the morning and the day after that. Do you know were you'll be staying?"

"No, Monsieur Christophe."

"It's important for you to come to Le Chat Noir—the first meeting. There is a bistro and a nightclub. I'll be in the bistro. At eleven. Do you understand?"

"Yes, of course."

"OK, I'll see you on Tuesday night."

Steve arrived in Geneva on Monday morning. In the afternoon he took a cab to the Carouge section and had the cab drop him off at the place du Marché, about three miles south of the southern tip of the lake. He walked the three blocks to Le Chat Noir and ordered an Orval beer in the bistro section. He followed a sign down a circular stairway for a visit to the men's room to case the nightclub on the same level.

His waiter seemed in his early twenties, with dark hair that was a bit too long to be neat, and intelligent eyes. Steve said, "Not too crowded tonight."

"Tomorrow night is when it's going to be crowded. The club usually serves up alternative music. But tomorrow is for local rock/pop groups. Who knows, maybe someone will be discovered." Although Steve had spoken in French, the waiter replied in English.

"Are you a student?"

"Yes. Tell me if you need anything. My name is Luke." And he left to attend to other customers.

Before leaving, Steve paid with his credit card.

The following night, Steve returned to Le Chat Noir and sat at the same table. But the atmosphere, dominated by the loud rhythms and sounds of people talking and laughing downstairs, was radically different.

At eleven thirty, on the off chance that Karim had somehow walked past him, or rather improbably arrived early and was in the nightclub area, he went downstairs. The decibel level increased geometrically with each step. It reminded Steve of the increasing water pressure on a diver going deeper. The loud funky music came from a trio on a stage lit by a square framework of overhead lights. The rhythmic dissonance of the band moved the profiled bodies on a small dance floor. But only the band was visible. The rest of the room was dark. As he headed back toward the bathrooms, a man with a black muscle shirt with twin lightning bolts, leather wrist bands and a belt made of three-inch-diameter iron links came downstairs and went by him toward the pulsing pandemonium of the club. Steve went back upstairs.

A few minutes later, the band stopped playing and Steve went back downstairs. The lights were on. He could now see that a car, highlighted by colored spotlights, hung from the ceiling. Underneath the car was Karim, near the dance floor, sitting with an older man, wiry with hard features, who Steve assumed was Hussein. There were no unoccupied tables near Karim. Steve assumed that Hussein must have seen his picture, and he knew that he was taking a chance that Hussein would recognize him. There were about a dozen people standing, perhaps waiting for a table to clear, and he went to stand near them. He would wait for an opportunity when Karim was alone.

Steve saw that Luke was on duty, and he intercepted him as he went by. "Do you think a table might clear soon?" he asked. Steve quickly considered and dismissed the thought of sending Karim a message through Luke—too many things could go wrong.

Luke recognized him, smiled and gave him a victory signal. A few minutes later, Karim summoned Luke to his table and whispered something in his ear while pointing at Hussein. The three of them smiled conspiratorially. Five minutes later, Luke brought their drinks. Hussein tasted his and grinned at the waiter in thanks. Steve was guessing that there was more than Coke in that glass. Maybe it was a *Mazout*, he thought, Coke with a shot of scotch, a drink popular in Morocco.

Steve decided to make his move before the lights went out again. He walked near Karim's table but kept in back of Hussein. Karim glanced up and Steve headed toward the bathroom, hoping that Karim would follow for a quick meeting, during which they could decide whether and where they could safely meet before Karim left Geneva.

In the bathroom, he got busy washing his hands after confirming that he was alone. A mop was leaning in a far corner. A few seconds later, the door opened and Steve looked in the mirror in front of him expecting to see Karim.

Instead, a determined-looking Hussein came in. He began washing his hands next to Steve and said in French, "Haven't I seen you before? You're a famous person. Am I right?"

Steve assumed that Hussein was trying to confirm his identity before killing him. "No, I'm not famous."

Hussein, between Steve and the door, continued, "Don't be modest. Yes, I know who you are now. You were in a French newspaper, yes?"

Steve stepped back from the sink and turned to the left to get around Hussein and leave. But a hunting knife appeared in Hussein's right hand. Hussein blocked his exit.

"You're making a mistake. I'm not the person you think I am." Steve tried to keep his eyes on the knife and still look around for a weapon. The utility closet was behind Hussein. However, he remembered the mop leaning against the wall beyond the stalls. He started backing up. Hussein was in a crouch now with his knife held low, his thumb up and his left arm extended toward Steve.

Hussein said, "You will no longer insult Islam by claiming that the Quran is a fake." He lunged forward, sending the knife on an upward arc meant to penetrate under Steve's rib cage.

Steve jumped back and caught Hussein's wrist in the V of his two open hands, with a thumb on each side. He gripped the wrist tightly and kicked Hussein in the crotch, then swung Hussein's arm over his head in a 360-degree turn. In one motion Steve forced the arm up behind Hussein's back with all of his strength. They both heard a crack and Hussein grunted. The knife fell. Steve picked it up and let Hussein go. Hussein was still on his feet and he turned to face Steve, holding his right arm with his left hand, his face a grimace of pain. But he made no sound.

At that moment, the man with the twin-lightning-bolts muscle shirt walked in and stopped at the sight of Hussein and Steve facing each other, the air virtually crackling with tension. In French he said, "Dirty Arab. These Arabs don't belong here, eh? Let me help." He started taking the chain from around his waist with relish.

Steve said, "Thanks. But I think that's enough. He learned his lesson." Steve took his opportunity and left. Those two deserved each other, he thought. He saw Luke in the hallway and stopped him. Now that the fight was over, Steve found himself breathing in quick shallow breaths. "Call the police. There's a fight in the bathroom." He stopped a second to take a breath. "Here, that's for my bill." He handed him fifty Swiss francs.

The band was playing again and he couldn't see Karim, but he headed toward his table. Karim wasn't there. He went back toward the hallway leading to the bathroom and saw him going toward the men's room. Steve stopped him and brought him to the protection of the dark.

"Your boss tried to kill me. Where were you? The police are coming, so you want to get out of here. Listen," Steve said quickly, recalling the message that he had planned to give him. "I'll be in the lobby of the Hotel Beau Rivage, quai du Mont-Blanc, tomorrow between eleven and eleven thirty. When I see you, I'll get up, and you follow me at a distance. Don't talk to me. If you can't come then, I'll wait for you in the lobby of the Palace Hilton between five and five thirty, also tomorrow. They're major hotels. You'll find them. OK? Where are you staying?"

Karim nodded, and gave him the name of a small hotel near the Cornavin railroad station. They had been together for less than a minute. Steve left by the back door that opened on the parking lot after repeating his instructions.

He waved a taxi to the Montbrillant Hotel. He walked to the Cornavin railroad station and took a taxi to his hotel, the Ramada Encore, back in the Carouge district. If the police were looking for him, they would undoubtedly find him, but not right away. He would have time to meet with Karim and, with any luck, then meet Kella. His hand traced the edge of Hussein's knife under his shirt with both satisfaction and apprehension.

The next day, as agreed, Steve waited in the atrium of the Hotel Beau Rivage. Behind his *Journal de Genève*, he was inspecting the rose-marble columns and the tapestried walls when he saw Karim walk in. Steve folded his newspaper after he was sure that Karim spotted him, and walked out toward the river shuttle service in the back. The boats, called *mouettes*, or seagulls, provided convenient transportation across the lake and were part of the city's public-transport system.

As instructed, Karim followed him from a distance, giving Steve a chance to take a position on the boat from which he could observe the back of the hotel, as well as the people boarding the boat. Steve was looking for anyone paying undue attention to Karim, an obviously young Arab. As he waited for Karim, Steve wondered if he had made a mistake directing Karim into an environment where a young Arab man might stand out, especially to the hotel security staff. Steve hoped that Karim would be invisible among the 40 percent–foreign resident population in Switzerland. Swiss hotel security staffs profiled their foreign clientele out of necessity. Steve had noticed several Arab men in the atrium wearing the ankle-length galabia and the kaffiyeh head covering. The hotel clearly did not discriminate among its wealthy clients, no matter where they came from. But Karim would not fool anyone into believing that he was a rich Arab sheikh in Geneva on business.

Karim boarded the boat, and Steve noticed a well-dressed man who seemed to have his eyes glued to Karim's back. He stayed on the dock until the small boat pulled away and began to cross the river. Apparently satisfied that Karim was no longer his problem, the man turned away and headed toward the hotel. His obvious interest in Karim marked him as a man comfortable and secure in his operational environment, not a foreign-intelligence officer or agent. Steve pegged him for a retired cop now working for hotel security.

Steve and Karim were leaning over the side of the boat as they talked. "How much time do you have? What happened last night?" asked Steve.

"Hussein saw you and recognized you. I told him to let me go and kill you. He liked that but he said, 'No, I'm going to do it this time, to make sure.' There was nothing I could do. He told me not to move. When I went to get him, somebody was hitting him with a chain. I stopped him. The police did come, but about twenty minutes later. They arrested the guy with the chain who was beating up Hussein. Hussein is still in the hospital, broken arm." Karim smiled at Steve. "The Swiss guy said he hadn't done it, that someone else had been fighting Hussein before he went into the bathroom. I heard him give the police a good description of you, even that you were an American. Did *you* break his arm, Monsieur Christophe?"

"I didn't have a choice. What's your schedule?" Steve could see from Karim's expression that he had gained status in his eyes by surviving Hussein's assault.

Karim looked questioningly at Steve. "You could have killed him. That's what he told me."

Steve glanced at the other passengers on the boat to confirm that no one was paying attention to them, and took Hussein's knife from his jacket's inside pocket.

Karim exclaimed, "That's Hussein's favorite thing, his knife."

Steve held the knife for a few seconds before throwing it into the lake. Karim gasped involuntarily.

Steve asked, "What about your schedule?"

"We're leaving tomorrow, I think. I will go get him at the hospital this afternoon." Karim grinned. "The only thing Hussein asked me to do was to buy him Swiss chocolates."

"How about your brother? I'm so sorry. Tell me what happened."

"I don't have the details. There was a firefight. He was in the wrong place. He never hurt anyone. He was a good person."

Steve knew how much Karim's brother meant to him. He touched his shoulder. "I'm so sorry." Seeing that Karim was not going to say anything further about his brother, he asked, "What happened after I left Mali?"

"Your friend Monsieur Gregoire didn't like me. He asked me to tell Tariq that an American from the embassy wanted to talk to him and to bring Tariq to a meeting with him, with Monsieur Gregoire. That was like asking for my own execution. He didn't want to talk about how I was supposed to do that and still stay alive. He said I was not worth the money and that you had been too generous. So that money you said was being set aside, is it gone? Did Monsieur Gregoire keep it for himself?"

The boat was nearing the fountain, and tourists came to their side of the boat to see it up close. Steve overheard someone say the jet of water was over four hundred feet high. Steve could see that Karim was enthralled, and he let him take in the sight.

"No, I don't think he stole it. Don't worry, I'll get that money reinstated. And start thinking of yourself. That money wasn't just for your brother. It was for anything you wanted to use it for—your mother, maybe yourself?"

And then he turned to business. "So, tell me about your planes." He let Karim talk, asking infrequent but targeted questions to keep him on track. But a major piece of the puzzle was missing. Hussein had not divulged what they were getting ready for.

They arrived to the other side of the lake and walked up the quai Gustav-Ador to a park on the right where they sat. Small children and their nannies seemed to be in the majority. After five minutes, Steve got up, concerned about sticking out. They resumed their walk.

"Hussein has stopped talking about operations in Niger

or Mauritania or those places. He and al Khalil have another objective in mind ever since Gao. But I don't know what it is. Hussein talks to me. He trusts me. But he's not talking about the final objective. No one knows anything. Only al Khalil and Hussein, and they're not telling the rest of us. Oh, and he has a new recruit, Habib, a Tunisian who studied in America. He's a scientist. Anyway, Tariq and he have long conversations. I don't know about what," Karim said.

"Since we've been here in Geneva, Hussein slipped once and told me that I would be taking my UAVs off a beach, close to water. At first I thought the plan was to use the UAVs like smart bombs. But now I don't think so. Rashid, the UAV *patron*, he said the targets would be about twenty-five to thirty-five kilometers away," Karim added. "We're buying more UAVs here in Geneva. The sales agent is an American. I met him with Hussein yesterday. His name is Spaceck. Hussein calls him Colonel, which pleases the American, I can tell. The new UAVs are being shipped to Cyprus, and from there . . . I was able to learn that they will be shipped on a second leg, to Alexandria, Egypt, but I don't think that's the final destination."

"Could the target be in Egypt? Where do you think they'll go from there?" Steve asked. Karim shrugged.

Before they ended their meeting, Karim had promised to find a way to send an e-mail to Steve with additional information as soon as he found it.

Kella arrived the next day, Thursday. Before going to meet her at the airport, Steve checked out of the hotel. During the night, he realized that he had made a mistake by paying for his first visit at the Le Chat Noir with his credit card, which Luke could easily find if the police asked for it.

He watched her stride toward him. Without wearing heels, she still could see over most of the other passengers coming out toward the luggage area and the exits—beauty in the middle of an otherwise unremarkable gaggle of humanity. "You don't know how good it is to see you."

She responded with a radiant smile and a kiss. He said, "There's been a little change in plans. We're going to a village at the base of the Alps, on the other side of the border in France. Do you have any luggage?" He led her toward the central part of the airport.

"Of course I have luggage. I thought we were staying in Geneva, in the Carouge district. I was looking forward to it. It's supposed to be old and eclectic and fun. In other words, it's not totally Calvinist."

"That's why I wanted to talk to you."

She said, "You mean to discuss Calvinism? I thought this was going to be a romantic weekend."

"Well, that's certainly not excluded. Sit here a second," he said as they reached a restaurant with tables adjacent to the passengers' main route to and from their gates. "Here's what we're going to do. Take a cab to the main bus station and take a bus to a village in France. Something has happened. The police are looking for me, and I'm not interested in trying to convince the Swiss authorities of my innocence."

"What did you do? Double-park?"

"This is serious. Another Salafist came at me with a knife. It's a long story. I'll tell you everything when we're alone."

"No! Are you all right? Why are you running, if someone attacked you?" She looked at him a second as if wondering whether to speak her mind. She said, "If I didn't know you better, I'd say you were living an exciting fantasy life. Tell me, are you still a photojournalist? Or are you into some other 'temporary' profession? Is this some CIA mission?"

"No. But that's sort of what I want to talk to you about . . . but later. Let's get out of here. Too many cops in airports."

They followed the crowd, retrieved Kella's luggage and

took a cab to the Gare Routière. "I checked my suitcase in here before going to the airport. While I get it, how about finding out about buses to Saint-Genis-Pouilly in France?" Steve asked. "It's probably about fifteen or twenty miles. If I rent a car, the police would find me in a second. From everything I've heard, the Swiss police are a very thorough lot. And the incident was important enough for a paragraph in the *Tribune de Genève*."

Kella said, "I could rent a car in my name."

"Let's keep it simple. For now, we'll use public transportation. Maybe you can rent a car in France."

The bus crossed the border without stopping, and in forty-five minutes, Steve and Kella were in a larger town than Steve had anticipated from his quick Internet search. They quickly settled on the Kyriad Genève Hotel. Steve commented, "This could be a Holiday Inn."

When they checked in, the lady at the counter asked, "Are you with the CERN? Do you have your discount card?"

Kella replied, "No, madame, we're tourists."

On the way to their room, Steve asked, "CERN? What is it?"

"It's the European Organization for Nuclear Research. A CERN representative spoke to us when I was still at the ENA. This is their headquarters. If you thought there were too many cops at the airport, wait till you see this place. I imagine it's crawling with security."

They had not been able to talk on the bus, and after freshening up, Kella said, "Should we go for a walk? This may be like a Holiday Inn, but the mountains are pretty."

Once outside, Steve asked, "I don't think you ever told me what your job was. Didn't you say a long time ago that it was time for true confessions? Except it wasn't. I think that now, it is. Do you work for your grandfather the general? It's an important question."

They turned up route de la Faucille, walking slowly. She held his hand.

"I'm the one who should be asking questions, don't you think? What was the photojournalist story you told all of us in Mali? Weren't you then working for the CIA?"

It was now late afternoon. A gray cloud cover had turned black. The breeze from the southwest had picked up. Almost imperceptibly, they picked up their pace. A light cream-colored sweater was draped on Kella's shoulders, with the sleeves tied loosely around her neck. She stopped to put it on.

As she put her arms through the sleeves of her sweater, Steve said, "Because of my father's connection, the CIA asked me to try to get some basic information on IMRA and al Khalil—because I had met al Khalil before in school. But as things worked out, I didn't have to meet him. Probably a good thing, since the Salafists all think I'm the devil. Then I went back to work for West Gate. And that's what I have been doing. So, your turn. Who pays your salary?"

"I did join the DGSE after graduating. But I would be fired if they knew that I was sharing this information with anyone, especially a foreigner."

The admission opened a floodgate, and Kella told Steve about the Cimeterre file and Captain Roger, al Khalil's DGSE contact.

"The DGSE is paying al Khalil? He's a killer!"

Kella nodded and said, "But not on French soil. That's the deal."

"Bullshit. They killed Ted Coogan in the middle of Paris."

"But he was an American." Steve was about to explode again when she added, "I'm giving you the DGSE rationale."

Steve had noticed two police cars go by in their half-hour walk. He became self-conscious and they turned off on a street with less traffic.

"I want to stop, or slow down, the Salafists. But I can't function under the myopic rules of the CIA bureaucracy.

I gather that you feel the same way about the DGSE. Am I right?"

"Well, I don't feel that I'm contributing much right now. That's for sure. And the DGSE is not going to do anything against the Salafists. At least not until they attack French interests directly. What's your idea?"

Steve said, "That we work outside of government rules and constraints. Watching the Salafists is not enough. They killed your friend Faridah in Paris and my friend Ted Coogan. They tried to kill me . . . let me count . . . three times. And you told me that there had been more murders. Al Khalil has a free pass. And that really pisses me off. It's not right."

"How can we possibly stop them? By ourselves? We don't have the resources. What do you want to do exactly?"

Steve stopped and took her arm. "At least slow them down. To make this workable, we can take small bites. For example, just publicizing al Khalil's activities in Mali would be a start."

"You mean bring public attention to the camp and hope that governments and organizations then take action, having been shamed into it?"

"Right. That would be a start. Let the media do its job, inform the public." He looked up at the sky. "Let's turn around. It looks like those clouds are about to burst open." He steered her toward the hotel at a brisk pace.

It started raining. In a few minutes, it would pour. They were now close to the hotel and they ran at an easy pace that Steve thought Kella, who had told him that she hated to jog, could sustain.

The almost continuous rain and thunder of the night made Kella snuggle closer to Steve under the covers. The weather didn't improve the following day. They stayed close to the hotel and discovered to their dismay that it offered no Internet access. After breakfast in the hotel restaurant, they each brought a cup of coffee to their room.

Kella said, "You told me about Karim and the satellite phone last night. What about Izem?"

"Yes, I think Izem is ready to help. We could use him inside al Kahlil's group. Since Karim seems to be specializing on those UAVs, having Izem help us from the inside of the fighters' group would be good. Do you think you can pull rank as a Tuareg queen the next time you go to Timbuktu?"

"What do we want him to do?"

"He already has military experience, and Hussein would love to pick him up, I'm sure. He would get paid whatever al Khalil pays, plus later, I think I could talk somebody in the CIA into rewarding him. Communications will be a problem. Neither of us lives in Mali. And I doubt that Izem knows about computers. That's something you would have to explore with him. What do you think? Of course, this would be outside of the DGSE as much as it's outside of the CIA. Your Captain Roger can't be witting."

"With Izem inside the fighters' group, we should be able to prevent some of al Khalil's murders. I'll talk to Izem on my next trip."

Steve finished his coffee. "For the first time, I'm beginning to feel that I'm getting some control over events. Until now, we've been like corks on the waves."

"Do you feel like you're creating a new intelligence agency?"

He moved toward the bed. "I'm not that ambitious. But we can't just sit on our hands and watch the CIA and the DGSE simply monitor this movement that is trying to change the world as we know it, thinking it's getting direct orders from God."

She moved toward the bed from the other side. "Do we know what we're doing?"

Steve reached for her from across the bed. "The biggest

mistake intelligence agencies usually make is to not coordinate, to build Chinese walls between each other. Let's work on that."

Lightning lit up the sky. A second later, thunder shook the windows of their room.

CHAPTER THIRTY-SEVEN

Tariq walked into Salim's stylish avenue Louise apartment in Brussels, an environment more suited to his tastes than the camps in the African Sahel. He noticed a framed painting on the floor leaning against the wall and picked it up—a crowd of villagers around a horseman in the center and huts on the sides. "New?" he asked. Salim took it from him and said, "Brueghel the Elder." He disappeared for a moment in a side bedroom and came back empty-handed.

Salim motioned for Tariq to sit. "We haven't seen each other for far too long, my son, since Gao. I hope you are well and that Allah is watching over you," he said.

"He is indeed, my father, he is indeed, *al hamdu Allah*. I have been traveling more often—Cairo and Amman to examine operational possibilities there more closely with our Ikhwan Brothers, and to the kingdom."

Salim smiled. "Ah yes, Wahhabist Central. Did they agree to augment our funding?"

"Not enough. But they will after we show that we are the principal players."

"What about Israel? Are you in touch with Hamas? In Gaza?"

"I have sent them a message. We must succeed there. With Allah's help, I will create a firestorm, a final Armageddon, for the Jews."

CHAPTER THIRTY-EIGHT

In spite of their age difference, Captain Roger was showing a strong personal interest in Kella. He took her to lunch one day from the office. They both sat on a banquette against the wall looking toward the center of the room. He sat close, closer than necessary, she thought. "I knew when I first met you that we were going to be friends," he said. "I love that you were born in North Africa. The Tuaregs, your people, have a great history. To say they were the lords of the desert is an understatement. You must be proud. I've worked on and in North Africa for a long time. I know that we're interested in many of the same things. I know the meaning of the tattoo on the back of your hand. I bet that not many people know that you are from noble lineage."

Not sure how to respond, she said, "Do you speak Tamasheq?"

"No, but my Arabic is not bad." He continued in Arabic. "I love your eyes. They are beautiful." Squeezing closer, he enumerated what he liked about her body, growing bolder. Over coffee, he put his hand on hers and suggested they go to a friend's apartment nearby to which he had the key. "I want to show you his collection of Tuareg art objects. I'm sure you've never seen anything like them. They are rare and valuable." He smiled.

"I don't think so. Not today, not ever," she said.

But he was not easily discouraged. She wanted to report him to somebody, but she knew that in this French military working milieu, she would only be hurting herself.

She also concluded that the captain's relationship with al

Khalil was not completely professional. She had noticed, for example, that Roger had a rather luxurious new Mercedes SL convertible, a car that a French army captain couldn't normally afford. She had also come across enough clues to conclude that the French oil company Total was paying bribes, or tribute, to the AQIM through Roger in order to be left alone in Algeria. Roger, with the acquiescence of Total, took 5 percent off the top. But she had nothing that would stand up in court and held off saying anything to the general.

Al Khalil was visiting Paris and they were at the Chernoviz safe apartment. The captain was finishing a glass of red wine, and al Khalil had a glass of lemonade in his hand. They were sitting back in easy chairs. The TV was on but the sound was turned low.

"My office is coming up in the world," Captain Roger said. "Somehow we were assigned an ENA graduate. Incredibly, she is knowledgeable about North Africa. In fact, she was born in Mali, around Timbuktu."

"I suppose you're lucky to get talented help. I wish I could say the same. But she doesn't sound French. Is she?"

Before answering, Roger stood up and went to the kitchen to pour himself another glass of wine. The weight of each step extracted a squeaking complaint from the prewar parquet floor. "That's an interesting question. I guess she could claim a Malian passport, a French passport and even an American passport." Roger explained his statement.

Al Khalil asked, "Doesn't the fact that her stepfather is an American diplomat give your security people a problem?"

"He's not only a diplomat. He's an ambassador. But on the other side of the scale, her grandfather is head of our organization."

Startled by Kella's background and credentials, al Khalil paid close attention now. This was information he could possibly use. "Really? And her father, or stepfather . . . Where is he an ambassador?"

"You won't believe this—in Israel."

Detecting that he was on the cusp of actionable information, Tariq asked, "When she goes to visit, I want to know." He was aware of his sudden authoritarian tone but didn't bother to disguise it, knowing he didn't need to.

A few days later in her DGSE office, Kella received a Cimeterre report, a transcript of a telephone conversation between al Khalil and Salim.

> AL KHALIL: I am proceeding successfully with our Gaza friends. We'll be on the ground in a week.

Using an Internet bulletin board on vegetarian cooking, as prearranged with Steve, she shared the information with him. Steve replied,

> As I told you last time we met, the enchilada wannabe wants to transfer his cooking to the east. If we're going to affect the outcome, we need to be in the same kitchen. Could you pay your parents a visit? The date for the ceremony to which I invited you is coming up and I'll be there as I hope you will also. We can discuss that on the phone.

CHAPTER THIRTY-NINE

Al Khalil confirmed with a glance that the two Egyptian police cars still sandwiched his bus. The Egyptians had insisted, explaining that it was a routine practice adopted following the killing of tourists near Luxor. He and his thirty men had left the fourteenth-century St. Catherine's Monastery in the southern Sinai that morning. They were heading north along the Red Sea coast toward Taba, a resort on the Egyptian side of the border with Israel.

Al Khalil looked at his men. Some were dozing. Some were praying, fingering their prayer beads. Except that as part of their disguise, al Khalil, under the Islamic concept of *taqiya*, concealing one's Muslim faith for self-protection, the prayer beads were rosaries and they were all in the garb of Cistercian monks. Al Khalil, who had spent much of his childhood in Belgium, where the Trappists had several monasteries, seized on the monk disguise because the Cistercians had split from the Benedictines in the belief that life in the abbeys was becoming too comfortable. They had formed a reformist Cistercian order, its vows including the observance of nearly complete silence. Another even stricter Cistercian order, the Order of Cistercians of the Strict Observance, was created later. To have his Salafists remain as silent as Cistercians suited al Khalil just fine. In his explanation to his men, the reason was that they could not be questioned individually at the border. But personally, he was just as happy that they remain quiet. Al Khalil, or Father Jerome Benoit, as his current passport read, was the only one in their group permitted to speak in order to facilitate the trip.

As part of their cover, many carried away souvenirs and religious trinkets from St. Catherine's. However, the Salafists had considered the visit well within the parameters of their religious beliefs. St. Catherine's Monastery was located at the base of Jebel Musa, or Mount Moses, a 14,800-foot peak where Moses, one of the prophets accepted by the Quran, was said to have received the Ten Commandments. The monastery was also built on the site where Moses was believed to have seen the burning bush. Also of interest to the jihadists was the mosque inside the walls of the monastery. Al Khalil had planned the visit as a means of strengthening their cover, and perhaps also as a reconnaissance of a Christian site to be soon reconquered.

While getting his men ready in the Malian desert camp for the coming operation against an Israeli nerve center, al Khalil had told them, quoting from an al Qaeda manual, "The confrontation that we are calling for does not know Socratic debates, Platonic ideals or Aristotelian diplomacy. But it knows the dialogues of assassination, bombing and destruction. Islamic governments have never and will never be established through peaceful solutions and cooperative councils. They are established as they always have been, by pen and gun, by word and bullet, by tongue and teeth." Al Khalil trusted that even if they couldn't understand the meaning of *Socratic debates*, they did understand the rest.

The convoy had had to stop for three roadblocks, and it was late in the day when they reached Taba, an Egyptian resort where his Hamas contact had told him the control checks were not always as thorough. Rather than try to face the Israeli security gauntlet that night, they stayed at a hotel. They left early the next day and walked across the border, vehicles not being allowed through.

Father Benoit said that they were on a pilgrimage to Jerusalem. He explained their vow of silence, and that they came from six monasteries in Belgium. "I come from the monastery at Orval. Maybe you've heard of it."

"Orval beer? How about St. Sixtus beer? Why is it so expensive?" the Israeli guard examining the pile of passports asked, smiling.

Surprised by the guard's question, al Khalil, whose research on his cover had not been sufficiently thorough, replied, "Our Trappist monasteries started selling beer in the nineteenth century. Since we don't eat meat, it's a welcome addition to our diet. In those days, it was much safer to drink beer than to drink water. We also make cheese. Beer and cheese give us the income we need to live and to maintain the monastery, a little bit like your kibbutzes, I imagine."

"What about St. Sixtus beer? Why so expensive?"

"I suppose the price is simply a reflection of the supply and demand."

The guard looked up at al Khalil speculatively. "I suppose. It's famous even here. I'm not a *kibbutzim*, but you're right. It sounds very similar. Are you visiting anyone in Israel? You're not importing any beer, are you?"

"No, we don't travel with beer bottles. We'll definitely stop to visit our Trappist brothers at Latrun. And, of course, Jerusalem. And if we have time, other sites with religious significance. But Jerusalem is our first priority, of course."

"I notice that your passports are not all Belgian or Dutch. Why?"

Al Khalil again was surprised. Though he did not easily become anxious, he felt a fresh prickle of sweat. This seemed an unusal depth for a screening. The questions, although not hostile, were precise and insistent under the cover of social chitchat. The guard was obviously trying to lull him into complacency, to lower his guard. But no Jew would ever be smart enough. He found the interrogation offensive, especially considering the source.

His body tightened. He fought to keep his composure. With exaggerated slowness, he said, "Right. The six Belgian and Dutch monasteries sponsoring this trip each has an exchange program with other monasteries all over the world, wherever we have brothers. As you can tell, we have nationals from South America and from Canada, Australia and so on." Tariq had carefully asked his Saudi contact to produce passports from non-Muslim countries in order to keep Israeli security concerns to a minimum.

The Israeli inspector was friendly enough but was obviously following a well-structured set of questions. Unfortunately, the guard knew more about Belgian beers than al Khalil had anticipated.

They were through in two hours, walked out and saw their Israeli transportation, another bus. This one driven by

Hussein, who had arrived earlier by himself through the Tel Aviv airport with an alias Sri Lankan passport. His cover was that of an agent providing transportation and hotel accommodations, and coordinating the group's travel and logistics. They were on the road for forty-five minutes when Hussein alerted Tariq that he thought a car was following them—at a discreet distance, but nevertheless following them. "If that car is still there before we make the next turn toward Ashdod, let's go toward Jerusalem instead. I don't want to have to abort this early in the game."

Tariq looked at his map and gave Hussein directions. "We don't have a choice until the main road turns west and becomes Route 25. If we still have a tail by then, continue to go straight north and stay on Route 90. That way, we also avoid going by Dimona. If they have suspicions now, driving by Dimona is not going to help. We'll go to Jerusalem, just as I told the border inspector was our intention. We can spend a day there. I'll have to change the timing with Hamas. They expect to transfer the weapons tonight at the Ashqelon Crusader castle, where they're hidden. It'll delay the final attack by twenty-four or forty-eight hours. You can tell Rashid and Karim in Gaza."

The Israeli follow-on car let them go after they passed the turnoff to Route 25. Al Khalil looked at the desolate landscape of the Dead Sea, a green-blue lake surrounded by tortured salt and limestone formations. The road went through washed-out yellowish rocky terrain. He looked to his left, to the west, and saw what must be Masada, now a four-hundred-meter-high publicity icon on which the myth of the Jewish nation had been founded. He turned away in disgust.

CHAPTER FORTY

"Can I use the car to go to Tel Aviv? I need to buy lighter clothes. It's hotter here than I'm used to in Paris. Besides, I should probably buy a new dress for the investiture in Jerusalem. What do you wear to a knighting?" Kella said.

Her stepmother, Alexandra, replied, "There are excellent shops on Dizengoff. But I do need the car this morning. Ezra is coming in about half an hour. He could drop you off in Tel Aviv and maybe we can meet for lunch on Dizengoff."

Kella agreed. She liked Ezra, her stepfather's driver. He had already shown her a photograph of his two daughters, eight and eleven, both dark haired with huge smiles. Ezra was an Iraqi Jew, born in Baghdad, who had made aliya—emigrated to Israel—with his parents when he was a young child. Kella had asked him, "Ezra, you would do me a favor if you spoke to me in Arabic. I don't want to forget it. Where does your name come from? Why do I think I heard it before?"

Ezra, in his forties with dark hair and always very correct, had said in Arabic, "Yes, miss. I am a Babylonian Jew. I was named after Ezra the Scribe, from the Torah. My father wanted me to be a rabbi."

Kella sat down to change her shoes. The TV was on and was giving the news in English. The broadcast had already started, and the reporter was saying, "—apparently for several years. It was transported by truck from Niger under an agreement reached by A. Q. Khan, the Pakistani scientist who has been under house arrest for several years. The camp belongs to an organization that calls itself IMRA, the

International Muslim Relief Agency, a social-welfare group with branches in several African countries bordering the Sahara. Still according to the *Times of India*, Malian authorities have refused to take its calls, while the IAEA has responded that it is looking into the story. Our TV station has done some independent research and determined that IMRA was founded by Tariq al Khalil, a Muslim academic who usually lives in Brussels. We have not yet been able to reach him for comment."

Kella jumped up with one shoe on and the other in her hand. She gave a barely suppressed "Yes!" pumping her fist at the same time. Her initiative had borne fruit. Her friend had been able to place the information that Coulibaly had passed on to her and Steve in the much-respected *Times of India*. She was very pleased.

Alexandra walked in and stared curiously at Kella. "What is going on? Something good on TV? The media only tells us about conquests, war, famine and death."

"Nothing really. Just before I left Paris, a friend told me that she was trying to place an article, and I just heard it on the news."

Kella was ready to go when Ezra arrived. "On second thought, I'll see you at twelve thirty not on Dizengoff—too crowded and touristy—but at the Haviage Restaurant. It's Yemenite. You'll like it, on Yermiyahu Street. I don't know the exact address. Taxi drivers will know."

"*Salaam aleikum.*" Ezra smiled when she got in the back of the black Lincoln Town Car.

"*Aleikum salaam,*" she responded.

The ambassador's residence was located in in a residential neighborhood on the northern side of Herzliya, ten miles north of Tel Aviv proper. Surrounded by a security wall, it backed onto a public beach and was less than a hundred yards from the sea. It was conveniently close to the Dan Accadia Hotel, also on the beach, where the ambassador played tennis on weekends, often with the Israeli prime minister. They occasionally included the CIA chief of station and Ben Gal, the Mossad director.

The car turned right and made its way toward National Road Number 2, which linked Israeli urban centers from Jaffa, just south of Tel Aviv, to Rosh Haniqra on the Lebanese border. Kella had visited Jaffa the day before. The visit had evoked a painting in the Louvre by the French painter Gros, titled *Napoleon Visiting the Plague Victims of Jaffa*. As she stood looking out to sea, Kella thought that Napoleon's lightning victory over Egyptian forces had opened a new chapter in world history. It brought home to the Arabs, or it should have, the power of European nations to invade their lands at will. She thought that the Muslim religion was still dealing with the trauma of their impotence following a period of imperial dominance. For centuries, Muslims had found external causes—the Mongol invasion, Western colonialism—to explain and rationalize their situation. In a weird way, she thought, the attempt to kill Steve in Morocco and the attack that had killed people she knew in Timbuktu were a result of Napoleon's victory over the Egyptians.

"You will be surprised to learn, I think," said Ezra, bringing Kella out of her musings, "that Tel Aviv has what you call a red-light district, and we're about to drive through it. It's called Tel Barbach." He chuckled.

Kella looked around, but they were still on the coast road.

"The girls hang around here by the side of the road and take their customers to the right, into the dunes." He was still grinning at Kella's surprised look in the rearview mirror. "That looks like one down there," he said, pointing straight ahead about a hundred yards down the road. "I rarely see any of them in the daytime."

Kella did not think the woman in front of them was acting like a prostitute. She limped and seemed to be crying. As they got closer, they could see her clothes were ripped. Her hair was in wild disarray, as if she had been in a fight. It was clear that she was motioning for help rather than for a paying client.

"I will call for help," Ezra said as he reached for his walkie-talkie radio. "Marine Guard Post One, this is Mobile One."

Kella leaned forward from the backseat and said, "Stop, Ezra, stop. She's hurt. We can't just drive by and leave her here. Put the radio down and stop."

They were now very close to the woman, who was standing her ground in the middle of the road, with one hand up imploring the black car to stop and the other hand on her leg, where she was apparently hurt. There was no other car in sight. Kella could see that Ezra was torn. He probably had been told never to stop, but the situation looked dire.

"Stop, look at her . . . We'll take her to a hospital." Kella felt sympathetic, given her own recent experiences.

Ezra stopped and Kella immediately got out and ran to the woman. Kella didn't speak Hebrew and called to Ezra, who was still in the car. "Come on, help me, she can hardly stand. Let's get her in the car."

Ezra took a quick scan of the surroundings before opening his door. He then stepped away from the car to help Kella. As soon as he was near her, two men stepped out from tall bushes on the side of the road pointing Uzis at Ezra's chest. They were still twenty feet away when Ezra wheeled around toward the car, at the same time reaching down for his ankle holster. He had his hand on his gun when the bullets hit him and knocked him to the ground. The killers were walking quickly toward him, and he tried again to reach his gun. But a second burst of machine-gun fire ripped into his chest, up his neck and into his face, blowing out the back of his skull.

Kella was struggling with the woman, who, now acting strong and healthy, had her arms around Kella and held her fast.

"No! No! Ezra!" she screamed, tears running down her

cheeks, as she saw Ezra's bloody corpse flung in the road. Less than a minute had elapsed from the time she had reached the woman and convinced Ezra to get out of the car. Two more men had appeared, also armed. They forced Kella toward a car hidden off the road, an old four-door Fiat. One man drove the Lincoln off the road into an area with bushes and palm trees. He covered it with a tarp and battened it down. Kella was pushed into the backseat of the Fiat and was surrounded by her captors—one on each side of her and two in the front.

CHAPTER FORTY-ONE

"Whether you believe or not," Steve said, "you feel in your bones that something important has happened here." He stood with other aspirants and knights of the Order of St. John of Jerusalem, Knights of Malta, all in tuxedos, on a small square in front of the Church of the Holy Sepulcher in Jerusalem. The knights wore red capes with the white Amalfi cross.

"I thought the church would be bigger. It's a tight squeeze, with all these other buildings," Steve said, sounding surprised. They were waiting for the investiture ceremony that would make Steve a knight of the Order. The Church of the Holy Sepulcher, the central shrine of Christendom, looked up at the minarets of the mosques on each side of it.

The church's reddish brown stone and brick facade rose from street level without the usual steps leading to a parvis to enhance the building's profile and status. Half of the double-arched entrance was walled in.

"Getting this ceremony approved by the church authorities has been a hassle, I'll tell you," Marshall said. "The church is managed by six warring orders, running from Franciscan Catholics to Copts, Ethiopians, Greek Orthodox, Armenians and Syrians. Each has jurisdiction over a specific part of the church. The Ethiopians, if I recall, own the roof." He smiled. "I'm not making this up. By the way, didn't you tell me that you had invited Kella? Isn't she visiting her parents in Tel Aviv?"

"Yes, I did. I thought she would be impressed, my becoming a knight and all. But she's not here yet. It's not like her to be late. I don't know what could have happened," Steve said.

As they were speaking, a patriarch of the Greek Orthodox Church walked by with full gray beard and tall black hat.

They had a few minutes before the ceremony, and Marshall brought Steve inside to descending stairs. "Look," he said, pointing to the left wall where scores of crosses had been crudely carved. "The Crusaders made those. Some of them were Hospitallers, which is what the Knights of St. John were originally called. In fact, what you see was rebuilt by the Crusaders after the Fatimids, the only Shiite caliphate, systematically destroyed the building."

A Franciscan initiated the investiture ceremony in the Franciscan church inside the northwest quadrant of the main church. Because of the many nationalities represented, national anthems were dispensed with, although the American, French, Russian, Canadian and British flags were displayed in honor of the countries of those present.

The grand commander, a Canadian, recounted the history of the Knights of Malta. As "Hospitallers," they began in 1099 to assist pilgrims to the Holy Land. Recognized by a papal bull in 1113, they quickly took the form of a military order of chivalry and left the Holy Land after fighting and losing the last Crusader foothold at Acre in 1291. They established themselves first in Cyprus, then for over two hundred years on the island of Rhodes, and finally on Malta. There they remained until Napoleon forced them out, and they split into several groups with bases in Russia, the Balkans, Northern Europe, Italy, the Americas and in Australia.

Then Steve's moment came. He stepped forward, kneeled and received the light touch of the sword on each shoulder as the grand commander said, "I hereby bestow on you, Stephen Church, the rank of knight in the Sovereign Order of St. John of Jerusalem, Knights of Malta."

Then the grand commander hung the white eight-pointed Amalfi cross around Steve's neck with a red ribbon, and an assistant placed the red cape with the white cross on his shoulders.

As they were standing outside after the ceremony, a knight who had introduced himself to Steve as Chevalier Desandre—"Antoine Desandre," he had specified—walked up to them. Chevalier Desandre was probably in his early fifties, and gregarious. His red cape came down almost to his ankles, making him appear shorter than he was. His fleshy face was topped by short russet hair. He said, "One other bit of history you Americans might like to know is that the French officers in Rochambeau's army at Yorktown were all Knights of Malta. There's a painting of the surrender ceremony that clearly shows that all of the French officers wore the Amalfi cross."

Steve was only half listening, searching for Kella.

As the group milled around in front of the church still dressed in their investiture regalia, a monk in a brown robe walked by. The monk was looking down in apparent prayer, but his glance strayed to the unusual sight of the knights. Steve glanced at him, and for a millisecond, their eyes met. Steve felt an instant flash of recognition, but dismissed it, his mind on Kella.

Later, in his room at the King David Hotel, Steve checked his e-mail messages and found one from Karim:

Arrived in Gaza with my UAV boss Rashid. The father
is supposed to arrive in Israel this week with a team
from the camp. They will be dressed as monks. I heard
that a meeting will take place in Ashqelon before final event.

Steve had given Karim his e-mail address, although at the
time, Karim didn't have his own laptop. *He's coming up in
the world,* thought Steve, pleased, but even his pleasure
with Karim could not push away his disappointment at not
hearing from Kella.

Steve had told Marshall that he had met Karim in Geneva
and that al Khalil was adjusting his sights from a long march
out of the Sahara to a more instantly gratifying operation
somewhere in the Middle East, probably Egypt or Israel. He
had not, however, told him that he had decided to go it
alone, without the stultifying oversight of the CIA.

He started to tell Marshall about Karim's latest information when Marshall put his finger to his lips, pulled
Steve into the spacious bathroom, turned on the shower
and said quietly, "The Israelis know of my CIA background . . . you never know," he said, pointing at the walls.
"Although I hope they've got more important ways to use
their time."

Steve said, "Al Khalil now has a couple of UAV people in
Gaza, and al Khalil's fighters and al Khalil himself are somewhere in Israel disguised as monks. I don't know what
they're cooking up, but it must be important for him to be
leading the charge. There's supposed to be a meeting in
Ashqelon before the actual operation."

Marshall continued, "Monks? UAVs? We can't go to the Israelis with this information. By itself it doesn't mean much.
Looks like we should go visit the sights in Ashqelon. We
need more information for it to become actionable."

Steve nodded. "This message reminds me of something.
Earlier today, I saw a monk walk by—when we were standing

outside the church. He looked familiar but I couldn't place him. Now I think it could have been Tariq al Khalil."

"That's his cover to get into the country—'cover for status' it's called. There are thousands of religious tourists in Israel every year, so hiding in plain sight is what he's doing," Marshall replied.

Before Steve and Marshall left, a special TV news bulletin announced that a suicide bomber had just blown himself up, killing twenty other people in a restaurant in Netanya, a resort town on the Mediterranean coast north of Tel Aviv. The TV station had live coverage of the tragedy. The area was cordoned off, but organized chaos reigned. Fire trucks, police vans, ambulances and uniformed men and women worked amid shocked, sobbing and wounded civilians, some lying in the street, some looking for friends and relatives.

Steve took a drink from a bottle of water on the table. "Another suicide bombing. I don't know how the jihadists convince these people to do it. I assume the seventy-two-virgins story is just a product of the Western media."

Marshall took his shirt from the closet and started to put it on. "Don't be so sure. More than one bomber who survived for whatever reason has talked about the seventy-two virgins as a bonus from God. For me, the greater puzzle is in the statements of support from parents. In my opinion, these young people are just handy weapons. They're being used by Hamas, these"—Marshall hesitated, searching for the right words—"demagogues of death, who don't volunteer their own bodies to be blown up. They manipulate these frequently impressionable, naïve youths."

Steve threw the empty bottle in the trash. "I wonder, is *suicide* the right word? Usually suicide is a very personal act. To me, suicide is the act of taking your life without being told or forced or convinced. Their society glorifies death. In their own way, they're all Manchurian candidates. This is a lot more about power than it is about religion."

"Yes. As others have done before, Hamas and the rest are

using religion as a front, as a cover for their own ends, to gain and exercise power." Marshall slipped his tuxedo jacket on and Velcroed the red ribbon holding his Amalfi cross near the top button of his shirt in back of his neck. "Well, let's go down to the dinner, the last official event in your investiture, and the last speeches. Maybe Kella is downstairs looking for you. We'll go to Ashqelon tomorrow and try to get a lead on al Khalil. If he's dressed as a monk and his team is using the same cover, they shouldn't be that hard to find."

As Marshall walked out, Steve said, "I called Kella earlier. I left a message. I'm beginning to worry. I'm going to call again now. Hopefully, she'll tell me she's waiting downstairs. I'll see you down there in a few minutes."

CHAPTER FORTY-TWO

The apartment windows were cloudy from the soft rain that had been intermittent over the previous few days. Brussels was dark and glistening. David Ben Tov, Salim's Mossad case officer, his *katsa*, had arrived at the safe apartment a half hour early to do a little housekeeping. David made a mental note to get operational funding for a maid.

The doorbell rang and David let Salim in. "We haven't heard very much from you lately. Is anything wrong, Salim?" David asked, after giving Salim a cup of coffee. "Where is al Khalil?"

"I told you about our conversation in Gao. He wanted to attack Israel. But I followed your suggestion and I convinced him to focus on Iran instead."

"And what is al Khalil doing now? Where is he?" asked David.

"I haven't been in touch with him recently—I don't know. I assume he's probably in Niger or Mali, back to the Sahelian project. I would know if he was in Europe to give a speech."

"Wasn't Israel his real target?" David asked. "Don't you think he's planning something against Israel?" He tried to look directly in Salim's eyes, but Salim looked at a watercolor on the wall with the hint of a grin.

He turned to David and felt the knot in his tie as if to make sure it was perfectly centered. "I don't know that."

"If he is, tell me. Another conflagration in the Middle East is not going to help anyone, least of all al Khalil and the Ikhwan."

After the meeting, David went his through his surveillance-detection route before returning to his Israeli Embassy office on avenue de l'Observatoire. There, he sent his report to Mossad headquarters in Tel Aviv:

Salim's evasive manner is troubling. The Gao meeting probably was a watershed. With a man of al Khalil's stature and vision, nothing is out of the question. In the absence of other information, it is best to assume the worst. While we have been fortunate to keep him away until now, his focus may have changed. We need to alert our sources within our borders.

CHAPTER FORTY-THREE

"Welcome," said Mahmoud Salah, the Hamas operations chief, to al Khalil and Hussein as they stepped into the apartment on El Wad Street, a curved main thoroughfare in the Muslim Quarter of Jerusalem. "I have occasion to think of you every time I come here by way of the Jaffa Gate. Did you know that its original name was Bab al Khalil? Some people still prefer to use that name."

They were in a well-furnished living room. The man who had opened the door was tall, physically young, but with old eyes that had seen more than their share of violence, injustice and suffering. Tariq and Hussein, who had changed from monks' robes to less-conspicuous slacks and shirt, sat down on a low and long banquette against the wall at Mahmoud's invitation.

"The time to bleed the invader, the occupier of Muslim lands, is here, *al hamdu Allah*. With your help, and with Allah's blessing, peace be on him, we are going to show the world the righteousness of our cause," al Khalil said.

"*Al hamdu Allah.* I trust your journey was pleasant and safe. We were expecting you earlier."

"Yes, the border control point took longer than I expected. Are you in touch with Rashid and Karim?"

"We have received their equipment. Getting it through the tunnels under the Egyptian border took a month. Your men needed more time to assemble the planes and the ground stations. They are ready now. My entire operation has been devoted to this project. We have been able to do nothing else. When you give the green light, we'll help your men to deploy them to the takeoff point. Our commitment is total. The risk is high. But I agree that the stakes are worth it," Mahmoud said.

"Yes. We couldn't do it without you. We are in your debt. But we all work for the same goals." Al Khalil paused and then asked, "What about our hostage?"

"My men captured the American ambassador's daughter. No problem. We can hand her over as planned."

Al Khalil stood up. "His daughter? Did your men know that the ambassador would not be in the car? Was the American flag on the car furled or unfurled? If there was no visible flag, then your men should have known that the ambassador was not in the car." Looking pointedly at Hussein, he continued, "Hussein, did you explain all this when you helped plan the kidnapping?" Al Khalil again looked at Hussein and shook his head, deflecting his dissatisfaction toward his own deputy, since he needed Mahmoud's assistance.

Mahmoud interrupted. "His daughter may be even better. An ambassador is in the government's service. There is little sympathy for a government employee, a functionary. He is supposed to take his chances. Besides, the American policy is to not negotiate for the safety of its own people. But a young dependent, that's something else. And a young woman, that's even better."

"Are the weapons ready and in place, as you and Hussein planned?" asked al Khalil.

"Yes, they're hidden in the Christian castle. A good idea. No one ever goes there except the occasional tourist. Using the remains of the Crusader occupation is clever. As is your cover, monks who make beer and cheese." Mahmoud laughed. "It's ironic. It's right. It's an inspiration from Allah, the Most Blessed, the Merciful." He grinned in appreciation.

"The Jews are not as smart as they think," replied al Khalil. "Tomorrow night, we'll pick up the weapons. We'll attack the next morning right after prayers. It will be dawn, enough light for Rashid and Karim to fly their pilotless planes before the roads get busy and before the workers show up at the facility. There will only be a night crew. Are your men ready, Mahmoud?"

"Yes, it will be a great victory to the glory of Allah, the Most Blessed, the Merciful."

As they were leaving, al Khalil looked at Mahmoud. "Islam has two sides. While we submit to Allah's law, we also have a duty to have others submit as well. And that makes Islam a warrior's faith. It is written, 'It is in the nature of Islam to dominate, not to be dominated, to impose its laws on all nations and to extend its power to the entire planet.' It's time for the world to see this other side, to feel the sword of our faith."

Hussein, who recognized the statement as one of Tariq's favorite exhortations to his men during training and indoctrination, nodded, and Mahmoud replied automatically, "*Al hamdu Allah.*"

CHAPTER FORTY-FOUR

Steve drove a rental car with his father toward Ashqelon on Route 35 after turning west at Hebron. "Any news from Kella?" asked Marshall.

"Her cell doesn't answer. I've left several messages. I also called her parents' house, the ambassador's residence, but I haven't been able to get through to whoever is answering the phone. Anyway, I left my name and number, but she hasn't returned my call. She can't be home. Otherwise, she would have called."

"Well, I'm sure she's OK. She may have been needed at some 'command performance' event, something important her father said she needed to attend. I knew an ambassador once whose daughter was the hostess for all of her father's official functions. The wife was not interested—too busy having an affair with the chauffeur, who was a major in that country's security service."

"You're probably right. But, after we're done in Ashqelon, I'd like to drive up to Tel Aviv and find out what's going on. So, what's the plan? What are we going to do in Ashqelon?" asked Steve.

"Here's the Israeli checkpoint to leave the West Bank into Israel. There's a line. Let's get the Ashqelon map out." He took it out of his bag on the floor between his feet. "I think we should split up. You keep the car and I'll find a taxi, pretend to be a tourist and have him drive me around. You focus on the old city and I'll focus on the new city." As he spoke, he pointed to the old and the new cities with his finger. "We'll divide up the town. You have the best chance of spotting al Khalil if he's given up his monk disguise. We'll meet at the bus terminal at five P.M. Here . . ." He again pointed. "If one of us gets lucky, he should call the other. We'll meet and sort out what we've got. We'll have to decide whether to get the information directly to the Israelis or to go through the ambassador or the local CIA chief of station," Marshall said.

On the way, Marshall told Steve, "Did you know that Ashqelon is one of the oldest urban settlements, about five thousand years old? It's where Samson and Delilah had their famous barbershop scene. During the Crusades, because the city was the gateway to Egypt to the southwest and to Jerusalem to the northeast, it was the scene of several key battles. It changed hands three or four times, was destroyed and rebuilt almost every time, once by Richard the Lionheart and another by Saladin, the Kurd who eventually defeated the Crusaders."

An Israeli soldier walked up to their car and motioned for them to lower the window. "Passports, please," he said, keeping his Galil rifle loosely pointed at them. He glanced at their American passports and then said, "That line on the left." He then moved on to the next car.

Steve pulled out of the line and got into a shorter one, where they were asked to get out and the car was thoroughly searched. Eventually, they were allowed through.

Steve said, "If you're a Palestinian, you could be here a long time. Working on one side of the line and living on the other must be difficult."

"It's impossible."

"Now that I'm a knight, I feel personally involved in the history of the place."

Marshall continued, "The Knights Hospitaller fought at Ashqelon, and you can still see the ruins of the Tower of Blood, also called Hospitaller Tower. Now the area around the Crusader castle is a national park. There are probably campers, young Western tourists, in the park. And there is a Club Méditerranée right next to the park by the northern wall, not far from the Jaffa Gate."

Once they reached the town and went over the map of the city again, they separated and began their search. Steve kept the car and drove south on Hatayasim past the Painted Tomb, made a left toward the town hall and parked near the Histadrut building in the old city. From there he started walking. He knew there was only a slim probability of finding al Khalil, but it was their only chance. While he was looking around, he thought about where Kella might be. Could she possibly still be in Paris, held up by work? But why wouldn't she have alerted him? If she was in Israel, she couldn't be that busy that she would have forgotten. Or maybe they had miscommunicated on the date? That also seemed improbable.

He walked past old buildings that contained restaurants, offices, small hotels, smaller apartments and town houses. As he was approaching the railroad station, he saw a van pull up to a two-story house. Two people came out to help the driver carry what appeared to be food, dishes and glasses for a lot of people. Steve assumed the van belonged to a caterer. However, the men who came from the building didn't seem to be dressed for a holiday or a celebration. They looked to be in their twenties, and fit. Steve noticed that they wore combat boots. But in a world where teenage girls often wore combat boots as a fashion statement, Steve didn't think twice about the caterer's van and kept walking.

About a half hour later, Steve was walking on a quiet street with no vehicular traffic and very few pedestrians. The van he had seen before stopped about ten feet in front of him, pulling up to the curb. He assumed that it was making another delivery, even though it wasn't parking in front of a doorway. Two men emerged from the back and two from the cab. As he drew abreast of the van, they seized him, and before he could even try to free himself, he was hustled into the back of the van, where his hands were tied with plastic handcuffs and he was blindfolded and gagged with duct tape. As the van started moving, the men threw a large duffel bag over him.

The van moved quickly. He felt they had gone only a short distance before stopping. Still in the duffel bag, he was carried out. When they extracted him, they tied him to a chair, still blindfolded. Steve assumed that although he was looking for al Khalil, clearly the man had found him first. He expected the worst. There was no reason he could think of why his life would be spared. Why hadn't they just killed him in the street? Perhaps his captors thought that their chances of getting away were greater if they killed him under more controlled circumstances? Suddenly he feared for his father. Would they track him down too? They might surveil the car to see who came back to it. He thought of the keys in his pocket, with a tag that provided the license-plate number of the rental car.

His more immediate thought was to escape. He wasn't sure if anyone was in the room with him, but he thought not. He stayed very still but could detect no movement, no breathing, no scraping of a shoe on the floor. By peering down, he had a minute window through which he could see his knees and, if he moved his head, a small patch of floor. He couldn't see his bonds. He tried to loosen his hands, which were tied behind his back, but only succeeded in cutting the skin to the point of bleeding. He tried to move his feet as well, but to no avail. Since he couldn't get away from his current situation, what could he say to improve his situation, assuming he had the opportunity to say anything? He would stick to his tourist cover. He had no brilliant idea. Talking was probably not in his captors' plan. He wondered if al Khalil would question him or if he would leave it to someone else. Would al Khalil know who he was? Or recognize him? Was this still about the Quranic document? After what seemed to Steve to be at least an hour but was probably much less, he heard someone come in the room and walk toward him. Then the tape was ripped off his mouth and the blindfold was removed. Tariq al Khalil stood before him and dismissed the two men who were with him.

Al Khalil seemed taller somehow. His gray eyes were laserlike. Steve now understood what Kella had meant about his eyes—like a snake hypnotizing its prey, she had said. He was about three feet from Steve, his arms crossed, dressed in black slacks and a dark blue long-sleeve shirt. Steve noticed that al Khalil's beard, shaved when dressed as a monk, was now starting to grow back. Steve understood only too well that this was a dangerous man.

"*Marhaba*," Tariq said mock-graciously. "I know you, Steve Church. Do you believe in fate? Is it fate that you keep popping into my life? Why are you here? I saw you in Jerusalem wearing a costume. Was that a Christian cross, a Crusader cross, perhaps? We know that you are all Crusaders, wanting to take our lands, you Americans and the Jews. You're the ones who want to go back in time, not us. Or are you still doing research to prove that the Quran is a false document?"

"I know you too. Tying me up like a sausage is a strange welcome. This isn't the Arab hospitality that I've heard about," replied Steve.

Al Khalil's lips compressed into a thin, unfriendly line. "This will add to your extensive experience with Arabs. I don't have a lot of time to spend on you. Tell me why you're in Ashqelon."

"Do I need a reason? I've never been to Israel before, and since I was here for a ceremony in Jerusalem, I'm trying to see some of the country."

Al Khalil waved his hand dismissively. "That's not good

enough. You seem to turn up wherever I go. I learned that you were in Timbuktu. What in the world does the CIA want in Timbuktu? Yes, I know you're with the CIA. You didn't take a lot of precautions to hide it when you were in Morocco."

Surprised at the accusation, Steve countered, "I recognize the symptom, common in the Third World. It's called CIA fixation—the CIA-is-everywhere-and-they're-after-me syndrome. But speaking of Jerusalem, wasn't that you dressed as a monk in front of the Church of the Holy Sepulcher? When did you convert to Christianity?"

"You must have been dreaming. Unlike your pope's declaration that Islam acts against reason and therefore against Allah, I'm trying to reason with you. Islam is not violent unless forced to be. Tell me what you're doing here."

Now that he could see, Steve reviewed what he knew about his captors. There were at least the four who had snatched him off the street, al Khalil, and a couple of other men he had heard when being brought up the stairs. Did they have weapons? Al Khalil appeared unarmed. Steve guessed that he was on the second floor. The bedroom had a window. He was thinking that he could probably overpower al Khalil and let himself out the window and down to the street. Whatever he did had to be quiet, though, and it had to be quick to succeed. However, nothing was possible until he was untied. "Why don't you untie me and show me that Islam is still the faith of the civilized, not of the barbarians."

Al Khalil moved to the back of his chair and undid the handcuffs, but Steve's legs were still tied to the chair. Al Khalil smirked and said, "Maybe you can talk better now that your hands are free. Why are you in Ashqelon? Why did the CIA send you here?"

Steve felt his best tactic was to throw al Khalil off the track. "And you're going to put me to the sword if my answer doesn't make you happy? The same way Islam spread the faith, by the force of arms—the bully of the Mediterranean world? Isn't your theological rationale for violence, your excuse, that Allah is beyond reason? That makes all thoughts of human restraint irrelevant. It gives your armies and thugs the right to do anything at all, including the use of suicide bombers and the mass killing of civilians, in order to bring the rest of us to submit to Islam."

At first al Khalil's smile had made an effort to resurface. He even appeared mildly amused that Steve would dare to go toe-to-toe with him on the subject of religion. He answered by walking up to him and slapping him with an open hand. "You, as an unbeliever, cannot use Allah's name without risking your life. You forget that Islam modernized the Western world. Our thinkers—Averroës, Avicenna, Ibn-Khaldūn—brought the Europeans out of their Dark Age. You're showing your ignorance by looking down on Islam."

Steve tested his ropes by trying to force his legs apart whenever he thought al Khalil was looking away, but had no luck. "All the men you named were rational, or rationalists, in spite of Islam. One was Persian and the other two, born in Andalusia, were a product of the mixed Arab-European culture. I wonder what any of them would say about today's Muslim violence and intolerance. When the West complains about Muslim violence and intolerance, what is the Muslim reaction? Its leaders send crowds into the street to destroy, and to kill, making the West's point. And if Islam has any intention of fitting into the current century, Muslim leaders need to understand that they have to recognize basic rights, such as practicing whatever religion you choose, or none at all."

Al Khalil now paced in front of Steve. He moved his hands from behind his back to point a finger at Steve each time he asked a question or rebutted a comment. "Hypocrite. You Christians murdered and pillaged our towns during the Crusades. Wasn't that violence? And what about the civilians you killed in Afghanistan, in Iraq?"

"You're right about the Crusades. But that was a thousand years ago. When you kill noncombatants it's by design. When we do, it's unavoidable, because your people have this habit of hiding your soldiers and your artillery in schools and hospitals and mosques."

Al Khalil sneered in fury. "There are no civilians, no noncombatants in the West. You are all guilty. Either you voted for the leaders who do war against us, or you are all in armed forces in one way or another or you pay taxes for your war machine."

Steve was pleased that al Khalil was no longer focused on the reason for his presence in Ashqelon. He continued, "We moved on; we progressed; we had a reformation. You didn't. Your theology and your way of life are still locked into the twelfth or thirteenth century. The Quran was probably useful and even progressive a thousand years ago. But it has forced Muslims to stay behind the rest of the world. Am I not right?"

At once, by the look of fury on al Khalil's face, Steve realized he'd gone too far.

"Blasphemer!" Al Khalil's voice was rich with fury. "To call the word of Allah, may he have mercy on us, 'useful'! Dog! If I didn't have a better use for you, you would be dead."

He went to the door and called out. The same men who had kidnapped Steve returned. At al Khalil orders, they put the handcuffs back on Steve's wrists, in front of him this time, cut his leg restraints and led him out of the room. Al Khalil personally replaced Steve's blindfold, tightly.

As they went down the stairs, a somewhat-calmer al Khalil said, "When these houses were built, they all had to include a bomb shelter. Most are made of reinforced concrete with no windows, always under the house. You can reflect in there. Oh, I almost forgot. You'll find someone you know in there as well."

Although he couldn't see him, Steve turned around

quickly toward al Khalil on the stairs above him, waiting for him to reveal the name of his other prisoner. Could it be possible that al Khalil had also captured his father? He didn't want to ask, afraid to give him more information than was wise.

That night, al Khalil sent Hussein and four of his men in two vans to the national park on the coast. In the dark, they entered through the central Jerusalem Gate, lifting the barrier to allow the vans through. They turned left at the main parking lot and right toward the water. Another left and they were in a small parking area on the south side near the ancient citadel, close to the beach. There they met two more of their comrades, whose cover was that of vacationers at the Club Méditerranée next door to the park. Hussein asked, "Izem, are all ten of you at the club?"

"Yes, *Al hamdu Allah*. We are ready. We had no trouble when we arrived at the airport. And the Club Méditerranée bus was there to meet us. *Taqiya* is good." He smiled suggesting that wine and women were sacrifices he was willing to make for Islam.

Hussein was not amused. He motioned toward the Club Med to the north. "Your men should all be here. We brought another van to bring them with us. Tariq wants us all together tonight so we don't waste time assembling in the morning. Go get them while we put the weapons in the van."

Mahmoud, the Hamas military chief, and several Hamas foot soldiers had been waiting for them in the parking lot. Mahmoud told Hussein, "The weapons cache is nearby. We have to walk toward the jetty, on the beach."

When Steve didn't show up at five, Marshall waited a half hour and then started walking east toward the old city. He was soon in front of the Histadrut building, where he found the rental car, parked and empty. Unfortunately, Steve had the key. He walked the old city for an hour before returning to the car. It was still there and still locked. He had seen no sign of Steve. He had tried to call him and left several messages. But Steve had not returned them. Knowing that Steve was anxious to get up to Tel Aviv to check on Kella, Marshall was surprised at his son's disappearance. Could he have been arrested? Hurt in an accident? He tried to find out about hospitals, but not enough people spoke English, and getting telephone information was impossible. He found a hotel and rented a room. It was clear they were there for the night.

After dinner, Marshall went out walking again. The car was still there. After about thirty minutes, he knew from the sound of the waves and the salt air that he was close to the sea. It was now dark, but he kept walking and looking. He made a left on Hatayasim and saw signs for the Club Méditerranée on the right. He continued past the "closed" sign at the Jaffa Gate entrance to the national park. He turned right into the main parking lot and went toward the beach.

Not knowing exactly what instinct was leading him, he turned left at the old rampart wall along the beach. As he walked he heard men talking in muted voices somewhere in front of him. The language sounded Arabic. He continued to walk toward the sound, but he moved more carefully. The voices came from a small parking lot. There were several vehicles, but none had its lights on. The sound of Arabic told him these were not tourists camping in the park, and he was puzzled that they were there at night. He stopped, and then retraced his steps to take the stone stairs down to the beach. He now could see the outlines of several men going down the steps to the beach toward what he remembered to be the southern limit of the park, where the ruins of the Hospitaller Tower were located. After the last man in the group had reached the beach and turned left, Marshall advanced, wary of being caught between the men and the steps from the parking lot in case there were more people coming.

It sounded to Marshall as if the group had stopped and that the men were digging. He started to get closer, but he could see no possible hiding places in case they turned around and came back. He stopped and listened. The men were still working. Then he heard them coming back toward him and he backed up. As he passed the steps, another group of men came down, and they called out to him in Arabic in low voice. He hurried away past the steps along the beach. The man who had called out to him from the steps stopped, once he reached the beach, and looked in Marshall's direction, hesitated, then walked away from Marshall toward the digging.

Marshall was trying to put some distance between himself and the voices. But before he reached the steps to the main parking lot, he heard running footsteps behind him. He ran up the steps and heard the footsteps getting closer. He decided that the legs chasing him were younger and faster than his, and he jumped off the stairway, listened and went back down toward the beach along the rampart. Supporting beams were jutting out of the old wall, and he lowered himself onto one, then another, and then dropped to the beach. He hoped his pursuers would continue into the parking lot and assume he had driven out. However, he realized that another person had stopped and was looking down in his direction. He froze at the base of the wall. He stayed there a minute without hearing any sounds above to indicate his pursuer's intention or direction. He moved to the right, away from the suspicious group, and heard one man calling the other above him. They were coming down to look for him. He first ran farther to the right but knew they would catch him in a footrace, so he headed for the water and entered the shockingly cold waters of the Mediterranean. He submerged himself completely and pulled himself along the bottom toward deeper water. He was about thirty yards out when he heard the popping sound of a small-caliber weapon outfitted with a silencer. He submerged completely and swam for his life toward deeper water. He hadn't heard the bullet's splash and wondered if the shot had been fired at random or at him when he surfaced. He changed direction and swam parallel to the beach before surfacing again. As soon as he came up, he felt the sting of a bullet hit him in the shoulder, above the left collarbone. He was running out of breath but submerged again and tried to swim a few yards before he was forced to come up for air. His left arm suddenly was useless. There was no more shooting. He looked toward the beach but could see nothing except the black outline of the ramparts. If his pursuer was on the beach, he couldn't see him. Perhaps he was kneeling. He tried to swim again, realized he was going against a light current and turned on his back. He floated with the current toward the area of the digging.

CHAPTER FORTY-FIVE

Rashid visited Karim in his make-do hangar, an old warehouse used by a grocery-store chain in the days when the Israeli border was open. They had been in Gaza several weeks, assembling the UAVs that Hamas had brought from Egypt through the tunnels. Rashid's message was simple: "Karim, I want the planes technically perfect by noon tomorrow and fueled by four. We'll be up most of tomorrow night, and the next morning it's showtime."

The next night, under orders from Hussein not to reveal the final details until the last possible moment, Rashid briefed Karim in the Gaza City apartment where they had been living. "We have two targets and we'll have separate takeoff points. The dispersal will increase our security.

Everything has to be ready by four A.M. tomorrow morning. This is what we've been working for all these months."

There was knock on the door, and a key turned in the lock. Mahmoud Salah walked in. He could see that Rashid had started to brief Karim and he said, "Go ahead, go on," as he pulled up a chair to the table Rashid and Karim were using. Papers and maps were on the table, as well as cups, a teapot and a plate of sugar-coated cookies.

Rashid continued, "My target is Palmachim Air Base near Yavne, just thirty-four kilometers away. It's a base for helicopters, UAVs and the Arrow antiballistic missile. Karim, my mission is to support your strike against the actual target, a secret defense installation south of Palmachim and close to the Nahal Soreq Nuclear Center. You will enable al Khalil's fighters to take the objective. They plan their assault as soon as possible after sunrise to give you enough light to see. Tomorrow, sunrise will be at 0620. I want you to be over your target as soon as possible after sunrise but no later than 0640. Mahmoud has a sketch of the place."

Mahmoud pulled a hand-drawn sketch from a manila envelope, when Karim interrupted him. "If you have the coordinates, why not look at the Google Earth satellite photo on the computer?"

Mahmoud turned abruptly toward Karim. "I have better information right here. You can look at your damn computer later. Besides, I bet that the Israelis wouldn't allow their sensitive locations to appear on a publicly available system. The official front, the cover, for the installation is that it's an experimental agricultural-development center. All this over here," he said, pointing with a pencil, "is fields. They're growing everything from giant watermelons to giant carrots. This is the main road, and this is the access road that goes directly to the gate and to the installation. Al Khalil's commando force will be here." He pointed again. "They're known to show the place to foreign visitors, mostly from Africa, but once they brought Indians from America, to

teach them about drip irrigation. Over here are the buildings for farm equipment. Don't waste time and ammunition
on them. Here is the main building. Pretty large. Looks like
a warehouse. Actually nothing happens here, above the
ground anyway. The real classified work takes place in
underground spaces. We don't know how many stories
there are down there. Tariq and Hussein are going to find
out tomorrow."

Turning toward Rashid, Karim asked, "What's your plan?
Where will your planes be when I come in from the sea?"

"I'll attack first, because we want the Issies' attention to
be elsewhere than at the main location. Also I won't need
as much light and I assume that Palmachim has security
responsibilities for your target. We want them to be very
busy when you attack the farm."

Mahmoud, holding a cookie in one hand, said, "At the
same time, I have three suicide bombers attacking Israeli
checkpoints, and two mortars will be set up to fire at Palmachim Air Base just before your attack. It will cause casualties and distract the Israeli response." He took a bite of the
cookie. Sugar stuck to the bottom of his mustache.

Karim picked up Mahmoud's pencil sketch and studied it.

The sun was threatening to appear on the horizon as Karim
prepared to taxi a RUAG Ranger UAV down a field outside
Jabaliya, in the Gaza Strip. It reminded him of Colonel
Spaceck's words during an early meeting in the El-Djazair
Hotel in Algiers: "The advantage of the Ranger over the Predator is first of all the price. Then, it's going to be easier to
transport. The Predator has a wingspan of fifty feet, as opposed to nineteen feet for the Ranger. Also the Predator is
sold as an entire system of four platforms with a large
ground command station. It has a crew of fifty people, more
than you can handle!"

Rashid had said, "What about armament? Missiles?"

"Yes, that's a problem. The Ranger's payload is fifty kilos, and one Hellfire weighs forty-five kilos."

They had eventually settled on the Ranger. Later, Rashid had customized the UAVs to allow them to carry Hellfire missiles and small bombs.

Karim soon had the Ranger in the air and turned it over to the other two men on his team. He instructed them to "Get it up to five hundred feet heading directly west, two hundred ninety degrees." Then he put two additional Rangers up and told their crews, "Fly them west at altitudes of four hundred and three hundred feet. One hundred feet of separation will give us an increased margin of safety when we maneuver them."

A few miles away, Rashid was going through a similar protocol from a beach between the Shati refugee camp and the border with Israel to the north.

CHAPTER FORTY-SIX

Hussein looked at his watch as their small convoy pulled off under trees on a side road. It was six fifteen A.M. They were less than ten minutes from their objective. Hussein thought it would give them at least five minutes more than they needed. His cell phone signaled that it was receiving a text message and he flipped it open: *Green*.

He said to al Khalil, "Rashid's UAVs are up. On time."

"Good."

He looked at the men in back of the covered delivery truck they were using and told them, "We have twenty-five minutes."

Hussein opened the window, still looking at his watch. He waited. He strained to hear. At six twenty-five A.M., the faint sound of an explosion came through, and then another. "The mortars," he said, looking at al Khalil.

"Yes and three *shahid* just reached paradise. I hope they took a lot of Jews with them."

Hussein noticed that cars were beginning to appear. He didn't want to stay parked any longer. He said to al Khalil, "We're right on time."

"Move, go," al Khalil commanded the driver.

The men in the back checked their weapons again.

Following his brief meeting with al Khalil, Steve had been taken to the bomb shelter of the house in Ashqelon. The room was pitch-dark. He knew very well, having gained insights into al Khalil's operation when he was running Karim, that al Khalil's men were killers. Whatever the purpose for keeping him alive, he doubted al Khalil had any intention to keep him alive longer than necessary.

Although his eyes became accustomed to the dark, Steve could still see nothing. He assumed there were no windows. His wrists were still bound but he could use his hands to explore by moving along a wall. A familiar female voice in the room said something in Arabic.

"Kella? Kella? Is that you?"

"Oh, my God! Steve!"

Steve moved toward the voice and he heard her move, apparently getting up.

They touched against each other in the dark. "What the hell is going on? How long have you been here? Are you OK?" he asked.

Kella sobbed briefly. In a quiet voice, she recounted her experience since her capture. She had spent one night in another location. She had not gone through any checkpoint and assumed that she had not left Israel. With one exception, no one had said much to her. She was just a tool, a commodity, to be minimally maintained until she could be used. "At first, I thought that as the American ambassador's daughter, they would try to exchange me for Palestinians being held by the Israelis. Now, I'm not so sure. Anyway, no one is saying anything to me or asking me anything. Someone gave me a lecture. I thought I recognized al Khalil's voice. He told me about the crimes that Americans were committing every day against Muslims. And about the Jewish occupation of Arab land, and that the Americans and the Jews were the real terrorists. But it wasn't a conversation. Al Khalil wasn't interested in a dialogue. How about you? How did you end up here?"

Fearing that whatever he said was being recorded or somehow being listened to, Steve stuck to the same story he had given al Khalil. He was careful not to mention that his father had come to Ashqelon with him.

They slept little, their handcuffs rubbing their wrists raw. At one point, when he determined Kella was still awake, he tried to raise her spirits. "Did I ever tell you about the first time I was kidnapped in Israel?"

"This has happened to you before?" she asked in amazement.

"Yeah. I was in high school when my older sister came to stay with us from college for the summer. A friend stayed at my house one night. Around midnight, my older sister woke us up. She had brought an Israeli girlfriend with her. They said that they were kidnapping us. I remember that the Israeli girl was doing her military service and hoped to go to some Florida college on a tennis scholarship. They snuck us out of the house—with no resistance from us, I should add—and drove us to an orange grove. For a couple of hours we just hung out and drank beer."

"Sounds like quite an adventure," Kella said, sounding a bit cheered. "Given your prior experience, I expect you to get us out of this mess."

In the middle of the night, Kella and Steve were walked out of the house and put into the trunk of a Renault. It was a tight fit. Steve protested, "We can't breathe in here. If you want to kill us, just do it. If you want us alive, you have to give us more room. Tell them, Kella."

Kella translated in Arabic and one of the men agreed. They left Steve in the trunk and moved Kella to the floor of the backseat, covered with a blanket. Other men talked quietly as they loaded into other vehicles. Steve could hear the occasional metallic sound of weapons hitting against each other, of magazines being loaded and of breeches chambering the first shell. Then they were moving for about forty minutes.

They stopped, apparently waiting for something.

As they were waiting, Abdul, the driver of their car, stepped out and called his wife. Kella could hear enough of Abdul's side of the conversation to make out that the driver seemed to be saying good-bye. "Tell my father that today I will serve Allah's cause well, that he will be proud of me. Tell our son when he grows up. They will be talking about me. I will be known in our history as one of Allah's warriors."

The trunk opened and Steve felt his blindfold being moved to his forehead. The driver leaned over him and showed him the ravaging effects of forty-five years without dental care. Steve recognized his cell phone in the driver's hand. It had been taken from him shortly after his capture. The driver talked to him in a low voice and held the phone open for Steve to see the text message that he had found. The text read, *31 degrees, 43 minutes N—34 degrees, 49 minutes E; 31-55-59N—34-42-26E. 0630 hours tomorrow.*

Steve felt confident that Karim's message meant nothing to the driver. The driver's gestures and body language indicated that he thought he was doing Steve a favor. Steve assumed that his Good Samaritan was putting some credits in the bank. If the operation failed, he would need a friend on the other side. It also occurred to Steve that he might have shown the text message to al Khalil first.

The blindfold was replaced and the trunk closed. They began to move again.

It was 0625 hours.

CHAPTER FORTY-SEVEN

At 0534, Lieutenant Schlomo Gazit scanned his screen. He had been on duty in the Palmachim Air Base SIGINT Center building near the beach for nine hours. He knew from the clock on the wall that he had one hour to go. His mind drifted to his young bride at home waiting for him. He would be with her in an hour and a half.

Lieutenant Gazit noted a call originating from outside Israel to a number not registered in Israel. The keyword that triggered the message to surface must have been the coordinates, he reasoned. He had hundreds of other messages to screen and had not time to research the location. He knew that the antenna field and the giant satellite dishes located on Palmachim Air Base collected millions of messages, most of which were irrelevant to Israel's security. He looked at the clock again, then at Sarah's photo on his desk. He went back to the message and the word *tomorrow* gave him a reason to put it in the queue rather than to forward it for action.

An hour later, as he was going off duty, Gazit's eye caught the text of an Arabic-language call from a number originating in Israel but from a phone not registered in Israel. The call was to a Gaza number. He left it for his relief to take appropriate action. Gazit walked out to his car and hurried home.

At the controls of his first UAV, Rashid looked at the smooth waters of the Mediterranean on his screen. He lowered the Ranger's altitude slightly to better evade detection by Israel's coastal radars. As he came over the beach of the Palmachim Air Base from the sea, he could see the space center to his left. He let it go. Rashid's targets were of a tactical nature—the helicopter fleet, the 200th UAV Squadron and any aircraft that could be called on to counter al Khalil's ground attack.

He headed straight for the two-thousand-meter runway. As he got closer, he could see hangars on the other side of the runway and several AH-64 helicopters parked close together. He knew that even if the rest of his mission failed and his UAVs were shot down or crashed, the cost of these three battlefield helicopters meant he was more than even. He fired. He circled back and dropped a bomb on another group of helicopters.

Rashid handed the controls of the first Ranger to someone else to bring back to base and he took command of the second Ranger closing in on the beach. He aimed at HH-65 Short Range Recovery helicopters parked near a hangar. All five machines were evidently ready to go, since their full fuel tanks exploded and became wicks for thirty-foot-high flames with a rising wall of black smoke.

He then focused on antiaircraft positions and devoted his last UAV against what looked like the base's headquarters building. He ran out of UAVs before he ran out of targets.

A few miles south, Karim brought his Ranger over the beach, and within seconds, he was looking at the experimental farm on his screen. He brought the UAV up a hundred feet for a quick look at the overall target, anxious not to hit the wrong building. He identified the access road and looked for the vans he expected to see there. However, he didn't see them and assumed that they were hidden by vegetation near the road. But he only spent a couple of seconds looking for al Khalil and his fighters. He could see the extent of the fields and quickly identified his target. With Mahmoud's sketch next to him, he identified the large parking lot to the side of the main building. He lowered the Ranger's altitude, swung it around to approach the building from the front, lined up the computer game–like aiming device on the front entrance and fired his first Hellfire missile. He saw it strike before he raised the nose of his UAV to fly over and to the right of the building. He circled until he was facing the front of the building again, but found that the dirt and smoke blinded his aim. Kicking himself for not having thought of this foreseeable problem, Karim flew to the left, came around to line up the sidewall of the building, aimed, and fired his second missile. It hit the ground about ten feet in front of the wall. The angle was so shallow that the missile didn't explode until its nose hit the wall. His bad aim turned out to be a lucky mistake. He then directed his Ranger directly south to get out of the way of the two other Rangers he knew were coming in behind him before heading back out to sea hugging the waves, hoping to make it more difficult for any Israeli pursuit.

As Karim's second missile exploded, al Khalil's four vehicles drove down the access road toward the gate of the compound. The first van drew near and slowed as a guard came out, appearing confused and looking over his shoulder toward the first explosion. As planned, the driver had his window open, and as he got closer to the guard who was holding his arm up, he shot him. He fired a burst at the guardhouse just as another guard came out. The driver crashed his vehicle through the bar across the road and headed for the main building. Al Khalil saw the second Ranger fire its missile against the roof of the main building and he shouted in anger. The missiles were supposed to be aiming for the walls to make entrance easier for his fighters. The third followed quickly but overflew the building. The driver of the van slowed down and stopped to stay out of collateral-damage range. The UAV swung around and came at the building low from the side. Instead of firing its missile, it crashed and exploded against the building.

People ran out of the building. Several fell, wounded or killed by the air strikes. Some of them were armed and uniformed. A tall man in front of them seemed to give them orders. He pointed at the approaching vans and spread his few men in defensive positions hastily. The first van came under fire. Hussein told the driver, "Pull over, quickly." He turned toward the back of the van and shouted, "Everybody out." He jumped out first and began firing at the Israeli security detail.

Hussein spread his men out and told them, "Move forward. Don't stop here."

Using the sparse cover, Hussein's men quickly dislodged the outnumbered defenders. They were soon at the front steps of the building. Tariq, Hussein and their men ran up the steps toward the front entrance. The Renault was following fifty feet behind the last van but was stopped just beyond the gate by a metal plate that had swung up out of the road, either automatically or activated by an alert guard.

Abdul and the other Hamas soldier jumped out of the Renault. One pushed Kella out and the other pulled Steve out of the trunk. With AK-47 muzzles prodding their backs, Kella and Steve, their blindfolds off but their hands still tied, ran toward the building.

It was 0640.

Rachid, Karim and their crews were busy flying their UAVs back to their Gaza bases when Mahmoud, who was with Karim to monitor the attack on the primary objective, said, "You have to ditch your drones at sea. You can't return them here. The Israeli Air Force will find them and destroy half of

Gaza. You should have used them kamikaze-style against the objectives. Call Rashid and tell him."

"We can't do that. We can use those UAVs again."

"Trust me. The Israelis are taking off right now and they're getting ready to retaliate. Don't worry. What you've done is worth a hundred of your drones. Call Rashid and tell him, now."

Karim motioned for one of his crew and turned away from the controls of the UAV he was flying south. "What if we land them in Egypt, on the sands of the Sinai. We just fly them a few kilometers farther, past Gaza into the Egyptian desert?"

Mahmoud smiled and said, "That's a political decision— above my head. But in the heat of combat, soldiers have to make difficult decisions. I think we can handle the results. The Egyptians won't be happy. They'll confiscate your planes, but it might save Gaza from the usual overreaction of the Jews."

"I'm calling Rashid," Karim said as he grabbed his phone.

Mahmoud stood in front of the crews and told them, "Land all your drones in Egypt."

Karim was pleased that Mahmoud had stopped using the word *toys* to describe his UAVs.

CHAPTER FORTY-EIGHT

The fires started by the first Hellfire missile spread quickly. Flames surrounded the front entrance, and smoke rose above the roofline. Al Khalil and his men reached the top of the concrete stairs leading from the parking lot to the entrance, but were stopped by the fire. Hussein yelled for his men to follow him toward the side of the building where the Rangers had created entry points. They jogged around the side of the building following Hussein and, with only light opposing gunfire from the few survivors of the initial skirmish, climbed into the building. They spread out into what seemed to be a warehouse with offices at one end. The walls were decorated with agricultural posters, and there were signs over office doors in Hebrew and in English. They split up and pushed farther into the building, peering around corridors and office cubicles. The two missile attacks against the roof had, against their initial expectations, caused considerable damage. They found bodies inside the building proper, apparently killed by falling chunks of the roof and outside walls.

An office door opened and two men ran out, drawing bursts of gunfire from Hussein and his men. One of the runners was wounded but kept moving across an open lobby toward a corridor. The Israelis stopped and fired a few shots toward the Salafists to keep them from rushing them. Al Khalil's men ran toward their position as soon as the firing stopped. The two men were running down the corridor, seeking the temporary safety of the next turn, but the Salafists won the footrace and gunned them down.

When the attackers reached them, one was already dead. The other had chest wounds and would not live long. Hussein told one of his men, "We're going to finish clearing this floor. You stay here and find out where the rest of them are. We're looking for a door that'll take us downstairs. Kill him after you're done."

Hussein first made sure there were no other live occupants on the ground floor and then told four of his men, "Go back to the front gate and hold off the first responders, whoever they are. They might be firemen or they might be assault troops. It's important that you slow them down. We need time to find out where everyone is, where the real work of this place is done. Then withdraw back here. You have your radio." Turning to another squad of men, he instructed, "Find defensive positions around the building. Keep me informed."

Hussein instructed the rest of them, "Go look for locked doors. The most secure-looking door is probably the one we want." They found two doors with numeric keypads. Al Khalil ordered the wounded man brought to the door and asked him, "Where does this go?"

The bloody employee mumbled, "It's just a closet. Nothing in there."

Al Khalil took the Beretta .38 from his holster and shot the man in the left foot. He asked, "I'll give you another chance. I don't have time for your heroics. Where is the entrance to the underground? Is there an elevator, stairs?"

The man implored, "The door is behind you and to the right. It's in the back of an office marked 'Director.'"

"Carry him," said al Khalil. "He's coming to the door with us."

They quickly found the director's office. Behind an imposing desk was a door leading to a small private bathroom. In the bathroom was another door with an electronic pad. "What's the combination?" asked Tariq.

"I don't know. I've never gone down there. I'm not authorized." The speaker was a middle-aged tanned man in overalls and ankle-high leather shoes. His fingers were short and thick, his fingernails stained by soil.

"You're staying alive as long as you're willing to help us," al Khalil said. "If that's all you have to say, you're on your way to your heathen hell." He raised his pistol.

"Wait! Yoram was allowed to go down there. But he's dead, and the combination won't work unless the thumbprint is first verified." He pointed to the pad, which had a two-by-four-inch black plastic screen beside the numeric box.

Tariq ordered, "Go look into Yoram's pockets. No, bring him here. We'll need his thumb."

In a few minutes, Yoram's body was on the director's desk, the blood from his shirt staining the wooden surface. Yoram had been a thin man, balding, in a white shirt. His dead eyes stared at his killers from under stylish rectangular glasses.

Tariq was handed an address book, which he looked through. On the last page were a series of prices in shekels. They were added, and the sum was a six-digit number.

Now they could all hear firing outside. Hussein guessed that the first counterforce had arrived and had tried to come down the main access road.

With the sound of machine-gun bursts in the background, al Khalil had one of his men stand the body up so that he could press the dead man's right thumb against the vertical screen. Then he punched the six numbers in the order of the sum derived from the address book. He tried the handle, but the door didn't open. He reapplied the corpse's thumb against the screen and tried the series of numbers backward. A green light went on. "Get the body out of the way, and get ready," Hussein ordered. He pulled on the handle and stepped back for two of his men to fire into the opening. He had the door open about three feet when a blast from the other side of the door blew it completely open, knocking two men off their feet feet and killing the man closest to the door.

Hussein said, "Booby-trapped. In case the combination was obtained under torture."

Hussein took charge and went through the doorway first and ran down the stairs on his left. His men followed. Looking for other booby traps, they reached the bottom, where Hussein saw another door in a narrow corridor. Hussein told one of his men to fire at the lock, which had little effect. Another one placed Semtex against the hinges and the lock below the handle, and blew the door. Hussein again rushed through the opening, staying low. His men followed on the run and, with guns raised, spread into the rooms on the right and left. They found twenty-two men and women lying face-down in a large room equipped with several rows of computer terminals that faced a twenty-by-thirty-foot electronic map of the Middle East. Tehran and several other locations in Iran, Mecca and Riyadh in Saudi Arabia, and Damascus in Syria were lit in red, with all the other capitals in green.

* * *

Last to go downstairs after the takeover of the building were Steve and Kella. They were marched first into the large general-purpose computer center, which reminded Steve of a visit to the Houston space center, and then into a small side room that contained the building's fuse boxes, spare computers and computer boards. Abdul, their driver and now their guard, who Steve could see wanted to get them out of the way where he could watch them easily, found this room and decided that it was the electronic equivalent of a broom and mop closet.

It was 0720 hours.

CHAPTER FORTY-NINE

At 0530 hours, Lieutenant Colonel Moshe Avidan and his fifty Shaldag troops began their day. They had just completed ten days of joint training with the British Special Air Service, the senior special-operations unit in the world. Avidan was pleased that the SAS had chosen to hone its desert fighting capabilities against his Shaldag troops. Each unit had learned from the other.

Avidan had begun the week with a briefing to the SAS in Building 12, the compound from which the Shaldag worked and trained.

"This base was named for the Palmach, the first Israeli special-operations unit. In 1974 Palestinian terrorists took over a school in northern Israel. During the rescue, twenty-one children and four adults died. As a result, the Israel Defense Forces reorganized the special units that had grown as a result of the many terrorist attacks.

"As a part of the reorganization, Sayeret Shaldag, also called Unit 5101 or Shaldag, was created and based at Palmachim under the air force and as part of the Southern Command headquartered at Beersheba. We are now the country's primary counterterrorist and hostage-rescue unit, and the only one with its own small helicopter fleet. Our workhorse helicopter is the AH-64, which also fires the Hellfire missile." Avidan kept to himself that his command was also responsible for long-range patrols outside of Israel, and for marking targets for fighter-bomber–launched laser-guided bombs. He also did not reveal that his troops had fought the Hezbollah in southern Lebanon.

Moshe Avidan wanted to pattern his career after former prime minister Ehud Barak, Israel's most highly decorated soldier, who famously had led the Sayeret Matkal, Israel's primary special-operations unit, during the 1970s.

That morning, Lieutenant Colonel Avidan was leading his men on their daily run. They reached the beach. He always led them where the sand was softer, which required more effort. Today they were running without their equipment, because they had been on maneuvers with the SAS until the middle of the preceding night.

Avidan loved this part of the day. He had learned from his girlfriend while at Stanford that the runner's high was not produced by an increased level of endorphins, a seventies idea, but because the body naturally produced a chemical similar to THC, the psychoactive component of marijuana. Whatever the cause, he always looked forward to prolonged physical exercise and imagined bliss-inducing chemicals flowing to his brain.

He and his Shaldag unit were several miles away from Building 12 when a UAV flew over their heads. Seconds later, they heard explosions. Avidan made an immediate U-turn on the beach and they started running back as fast as they could. At 0700 hours, Avidan called the operations center on his radio, but there was no connection.

He sent his second-in-command with his men back to Building 12 to get ready for action and he headed toward the Ops Center. He first saw the smoke before coming around a block of living quarters, and he realized that the building had been a target of the attack. A firefighting unit had just reached the building and was deploying its hoses. Other unit commanders were arriving at the same time, but no one had concrete information. The stories they exchanged ran the gamut, from a full attack on Israel by the surrounding Arab states, to one single coordinated attack against the primary air bases, to the assassination of the Israeli prime minister, to UAV attacks against the country's nuclear center at Dimona.

At 0740, Avidan and the other officers who had met outside the destroyed Ops Center learned that the base commander had died in the attack. They all made their way to a crisis center half a mile away. There, the ranking officer took charge. Through the communications at the center, they learned that Palmachim was the only base to have been attacked and that there was no general invasion. However, someone at the Soreq Nuclear Center near Yavne had received a phone call saying that a Rafael center had also been attacked.

Avidan was pulled aside by the acting commander, together with the base's air-police chief and the head of Unit 5707, who was Avidan's friend. Unit 5707 had been created in 1996 to obtain pre- and post-bombardment intelligence during the continuing war in southern Lebanon, a mission that Unit 5707 took from the Shaldag. Unit 5707 sometimes trained with the Shaldag, had similar armament, and could be used to supplement the Shaldag unit if necessary. The acting base commander, General Uri Shomron, said, "This attack seems to have come from Egypt. Our aircraft were able to shoot down two or three of the UAVs as they tried to get away, but the rest crossed into Egyptian air space. Our pilots asked for hot-pursuit authorization, but they didn't get it from the national command authority, so far. They are authorized to follow them but not to conduct aggressive operations over the Egyptian border."

A colonel brought him a message, which he read. He then looked at his men and said, "Jerusalem is getting in touch with Cairo and with the United Nations. A retaliatory attack against Egypt is not out of the question. Our aircraft are already in the air over international waters, waiting for a decision to attack. That's the big picture. Now here's your part."

He turned and looked at Avidan. "There is a hostage situation developing just south of here at the agricultural-experimentation center." He walked over to a map and pointed to the location.

Avidan, still in his running gear, had obtained a towel, which was slung around his neck. "Is that where I heard the other explosions when I was running on the beach? Is it part of the attack on the base?"

"It looks that way. It all took place at the same time. The ground attack was preceded by UAV strafing and bombing. There were also suicide bombings at the border checkpoints in Gaza. All within a few minutes of each other—well coordinated. As I told you before, we received a few mortar rounds on the base. They hit the runway and the canteen. Ten wounded, four killed. We're looking for the mortars. They were probably fired remotely. In any case, Moshe, I want your unit to get ready for a takedown operation against this location." He pointed to the agricultural station on the map.

He turned to the Unit 5707 commander. "Your unit will be in support. Go to your units, I'll get you maps as soon as I can. Now I'd like to see Colonel Avidan alone, please."

When they were alone, the general said, "You need to know that this is not exactly an agricultural station. It's really a Rafael installation. I don't know myself what they do there but it's related to national security. So you're probably not trying to save farming experts—the hostages are most probably scientists and the like. I know it makes no difference, but I thought that I'd tell you. I'll send the maps over."

"Not to worry, sir. We have maps of all government installations in Israel in Building 12."

"Right, I should have known." The general smiled and shook Moshe Avidan's hand. "Good luck, Moshe."

It was 0830 hours.

CHAPTER FIFTY

Al Khalil had expected to find a secret military project underground, and he was not disappointed; both his and Hamas's conclusions were confirmed. He understood that taking the building was one thing—it had been simpler than he had anticipated—but now came the hard part, making the most of what was only an intermediate success. First, he needed to know what this secret installation was, its importance and how he was going to use it to his advantage.

He was in a room off the main computer center with a large glass partition allowing him to see inside the computer control room. He called Habib, his Carnegie Mellon graduate, and told him, "I want you to start interrogating our prisoners one at a time to find out what this center is for. Start with that one over there. There's something about him that tells me he's different. He doesn't look scared, but I think you'll figure out a way to make him talk."

The prisoners sat on the ground with their hands tied in back. One man sat almost by himself on the side of the group, stolid and in his own world. The man combed his brown hair down the middle and wore a tie, unusual in itself.

"As you're doing that, have someone collect all the ID cards, everything that will tell us who they are, their ranks, whether any are related, who they work for, everything. In fact, just have them empty their pockets completely. It'll give us an insight into each and probably, from their notes and other pocket litter, what this place does. But be quick. There's a whole country out there that wants to take us down."

Al Khalil went upstairs to check on Hussein and the imminence of an Israeli attack.

In their electronic broom closet, Steve and Kella's wrists were still manacled. The room was narrow but deep and lit by a single overhead light. Another door in the back and on the left provided alternate access. Steve went to the door, turned his back to it in order for his hands to reach the handle, but it was locked, as he expected. He searched for some tool he could cut through the plastic with but saw nothing with a cutting edge, only electrical wires and related equipment. He was considering breaking a computer screen to use one of the sharp pieces, when the door opened and Izem came in, closing the door quickly and looking behind him. "So, you're the hostages! Abdul told me he was guarding a couple of Americans. His description fit you to a T," Izem said. "Why are you here?"

Steve was astonished. "The same question to you. Aren't you on the wrong side? Though I'm glad to see you. Can you help us get out of here? Are there other Tuaregs here with you?"

"Izem!" Kella cried. "I never thought I'd see a friendly face in this group of killers."

Izem gave Kella a respectful nod, acknowledging her and her tribal lineage. "I joined like many others, to make a living. After Steve left Mali, I couldn't just live with my brother.

I had to earn some money, and my military background was my only métier. Then, because I had joined, other Tuaregs followed me. Then it sort of got out of control. I couldn't leave. Unfortunately, my Tuareg brothers have become believers in al Khalil and his cause. I lost any control I had over them."

Steve asked, "And what about Karim, where is he?"

"Hussein sent a team to Gaza that includes Karim, Rashid and a few others. Karim controlled the planes that kicked off the attack. Now his job is done."

Kella turned around to show that her hands were tied. "Can you get us out of these?"

"I can, but this is not the time to get you out. There are still over thirty of us, and the Israelis are probably getting ready to attack. You don't want to get caught in the crossfire."

Izem quickly cut through both sets of handcuffs with a knife he took from its sheath on his belt. "You better look like you're still tied. Here, I'll put this wire around your wrists. You can get out of this with little effort, and it will be more comfortable." He substituted a short electrical cord for the handcuffs. "I better go."

Steve said, "There will never be a perfect time to break out of here. We can't wait for the Israelis to come in here. I'd rather take my chances shooting our way out than to get shot by Israeli commandos, or by al Khalil in a final act of revenge. The sooner the better. Get us weapons, Izem.

"Wait . . . ," he added, catching Izem before he left. Steve looked at Kella. "Kella wants you to rally your tribesmen. Tell him, Kella."

Kella spoke quickly. "Yes, tell them who I am, my ancestry and that I expect them to follow our customs. Tell them that to do otherwise will sully their family names. If they won't listen to you, bring them here to me."

Steve had never heard Kella exercise her tribal leadership before. In fact, she had always downplayed it. He saw by the look on Izem's face that she had struck a chord.

Izem said, "I will come back as soon as I can. Be ready."
Steve saw Abdul peer in suspiciously when Izem went out
the door.

Back in Building 12, a sergeant found Lieutenant Colonel
Avidan in his office putting his combat gear on, handling
the phone and reviewing maps. "Sir, our helicopters were
destroyed in the UAV attack. I'm trying to obtain replacement choppers, but there's a lot of confusion out there. No
one wants to make a decision, to sign off on an authorization."

Avidan looked up from the maps and shouted, "How is
that possible? Where the hell was our antiaircraft defense?
Our coastal radars? Was everyone sleeping? Were they on
leave? OK, get me Acting Commandant Shomron's office."

"His office was destroyed. I can't reach him."

Leaning forward with one hand on a map and the other
pulling a Sig Sauer pistol from a bag on the floor near his
desk, his voice a bit lower, he said, "Call the crisis center
then. And get me the squad leaders in here right away." Avidan laid out other weapons on his desk on top of the maps.

"Crisis center? Yes, sir."

It took Avidan another thirty minutes to obtain authorization to use replacement aircraft. His five squads of eight to
nine men quickly took their places on the helicopters. Avidan rode to battle with the first squad. As he looked down at
the damage, he felt that this was his moment. History would
remember his name. His men were divided into groups with
one of three primary skills: entry, rappelling and climbing,
and sniping. They were equipped with older but extremely
reliable M4A1 assault rifles with the M203 grenade launcher
attached. Their side arms were Sig Sauer .40-caliber pistols,
the long-awaited replacement for the 9-millimeter model.
The snipers used the Israeli-made Galil rifle, from the same
manufacturers that had created the Uzi.

After sending a reconnaissance UAV over the building to

determine the strength and disposition of his enemy, Avidan took his three helicopters at treetop level toward the objective. Flying at close to two hundred miles an hour, they were quickly on the target. As soon as they landed on a back parking lot, the Shaldag team found firing positions, which they had chosen from the real-time images provided by their reconnaissance UAV. Avidan got on his cell phone and said, "This is Gideon One. We just landed. Tell me how the TIBAM team is coming along. I need them here as soon as possible with their laptops and CD blueprints of this building, to include 3-D, if they have them."

Avidan could see several men in defensive positions around the building. They moved inside when the helicopters landed. He also noticed several armed men making their way toward the main building from the guard gate in order to avoid being cut off. He sent a squad after them. At first, the Salafists skirted the fence around the property until they realized that the Israeli helicopters covered the back of the complex. Then, using what sparse cover was available, they headed directly for the building. They almost made it. As they were moving toward the entrance point used by the first assault team, Israeli snipers hit two of them. The other two ran for their lives toward their point of access. Neither made it.

Down in the underground center, al Khalil, alerted to the arrival of the Israeli troops, grabbed a phone and dialed the American Embassy's number. When the receptionist answered, he said, "Give me the ambassador quickly. This is urgent."

"Who is calling please?" said the poised and friendly female voice.

"Tell the ambassador that I have news of his daughter. This is an urgent call. I repeat: this call is urgent. For her and for him. Now put him on the phone."

His call was transferred upstairs to the chancery and to

the ambassador's secretary, who also asked, "Who is calling please? The ambassador is in a meeting. Let me take a message and he'll get back to you."

"I told your other receptionist this call was urgent. It's about the ambassador's daughter."

The next voice, a male, said, "Hello, this is Ambassador Hastings. Who is this?"

"I have your daughter, Kella. If you want her back alive, get in touch with your Jew friends and tell them to stop the attack that is now under way against my position. I am in command of what the Jews call the Desert Agricultural Center near Palmachim Air Base. They will know exactly where, when you call them."

There was a moment of silence, and then Hastings said, "How do I know that you have her, that she is alive? Who are you? What do you want?"

"That's too many questions for now. If you don't tell the Jews to stop their attack, they will be responsible for killing your daughter. I'll call back after the attack has stopped. Oh, I almost forgot. I also have one of your CIA officers, Steve Church." Tariq al Khalil hung up.

While al Khalil was on the phone, Hussein had assembled his remaining fighters at defensive positions at the ground level. There they waited for the assault.

Downstairs, Habib tried to obtain information from the Israeli scientists. One of the men going through the Israelis' pocket litter had interrupted him. "Look, two of them have the same last name. They're probably married—Shoshanna and Aaron Amitai."

This gave Habib a plan. He would talk to them separately, first on a scientist-to-scientist basis, and then ratchet up the pressure and use violence if necessary. Shoshanna was a nuclear physicist and Aaron, who had a *PhD* after his name, was an expert on lasers. Scanning through the other IDs, Habib noticed that Amitai was the only one claiming a PhD, although he assumed that this might mean that Amitai was the only one flaunting his doctorate. Habib was starting to form an idea of what this center was for, but he couldn't believe the conclusion he had reached. He continued to question the Israeli scientists one by one, but focused most of his time on the Amitais. He spoke to them as their equal, which he was, in terms of education and knowledge, and they responded to him, but with very general statements that were not helpful.

Nevertheless, he started to put the pieces together. He knew that the laser, invented in the early 1960s, and at first considered to be a solution without a problem, had shown its military uses in "precision engagement" during the first Gulf War. He was also aware that laser weapons had become serious counterweapons to the ballistic-missile threat. The Airborne Laser Program had demonstrated that a missile could be shot down at a range of several hundred miles. On a smaller scale, the Zeus, a laser developed by the U.S. Army, was being used in battle to destroy mines from the air. Another laser weapon had destroyed artillery shells and mortar rounds seconds after they were fired during field trials. A laser beam, with its speed of light, lack of recoil and long range, was an attractive defensive technology, because ballistic missiles were constructed with lighter metals, as were aircrafts. They could take down a biological, chemical or nuclear missile before it left enemy territory.

Habib went to report to al Khalil. "I've obtained enough information from the scientists to conclude that we're dealing with some sort of laser gun. But I reached a dead end. They refuse to get into the details I need. If we had more time, I could probably get some of them to cooperate willingly. But since we need the information now, I think we have to use tactics your fighters are better at than I am."

"Right," replied al Khalil. "You should have told me earlier." He called one of his soldiers and told him to help Habib, who took him into what had become the interrogation room, furnished with computer stations and maps.

He had given orders to tie Shoshanna to an office chair before he left the room to seek al Khalil. This was the first signal that Habib was changing tactics. He now said, "OK, we tried it the easy way. Unless you start telling me about the specifications of the weapon, its capabilities and controls, we're going to bloody your neat uniform and your spick-and-span laser center."

She looked at him with wide, defiant eyes. "I knew it. I'm not afraid. My people have survived the Holocaust. You and your kind are doomed to fail, just like the Nazis."

"Well, we'll see how well you survive," Habib said, then motioned to the guard, who produced a bayonet. Under Habib's direction, he took one of Shoshanna's hands, pressed it on the computer table in front of her and made as if to apply the blade to the first phalange of her little finger. She pulled her hand from his grasp in fright. The soldier then forced her hand back to the table and, with a sudden and powerful thrust, plunged the bayonet through the back of her hand and into the wood of the desk. She screamed in shock and pain.

Habib was startled and somewhat unsettled, but he told himself that extreme measures were necessary. "Now, tell me about the controls. There must be some pretargeting already programmed. Tell me about that. Give me what I need on timing of the laser and on the power settings."

Her only response was to spit in his direction.

The guard said, "I will get her husband." Habib nodded and the guard came back with Aaron Amitai, who, upon seeing his wife's hand nailed to the table, ran to her and tried to pull the bayonet out. The guard hit him on the side of the head with the stock of his AK-47 and sent the Israeli scientist sprawling. His wife called out his name, but Amitai stayed on the floor for a few seconds, blood trickling down his face.

"Stand up." The guard prodded him, then tied him to another chair and, with a glance, handed control back to Habib.

"You can stop this," Habib told Amitai. "Your wife doesn't have to go through any more pain. But you must give me the information I want. We will get it, one way or another."

Amitai said, "You are a fascist devil. I don't care that you claim to pray to some god. It's not any god I've ever heard of. Stop what you're doing to my wife."

Habib motioned to the soldier, who pulled the bayonet out of Shoshana's hand—only a small whimper escaped her—and then walked her out of the room. Habib stayed alone with Amitai. He said, "Let's get serious. I graduated from Carnegie Mellon, physics and lasers. Don't think you can bullshit me. Now talk!"

"Who are you? What do you hope to gain? If you have the education you claim, then you know that this can only have one ending. Israel has been fighting back against people like you for a long time. You will not succeed. Give yourself up. Save your life."

Habib realized he was somehow losing control. How did his prisoner now have the initiative? He felt out of his element. He called the guard back into the room and said, "You can talk with me and provide answers to my questions, or I'll let you alone with him . . . or better, I'll bring your wife back and he can work on her. It's your choice."

Not getting any answer from the Israeli, Habib told the guard, "OK, bring her back."

Just before the guard reached the door, Amitai said, "Wait," in a resigned tone. He took a breath and said, "For us, this all started during Reagan's Space Defense Initiative project. But I took the Israeli part of the project in a different direction. The United States invited several countries to participate in the research-and-development phase, and Israel was one of them. Israeli scientists worked on the SDI R & D, both here in Israel and in the United States. The key obstacles, the real breakthroughs, took place right here." He stopped, looked at Habib and said, "I can't do this."

"Yes, you can. Here, have some water. I know that

Carnegie Mellon received federal funds related to SDI. Go on, but I don't need history so much as practical applications."

"I need to know that my wife is all right. I won't go on unless you release her."

"I promise we'll release her, but not before you answer my questions. Give me the information and I'll get her released. There's no way I can get her out beforehand. She's lucky that she's still alive."

Amitai collapsed in his chair. His shoulders slumped and he would have fallen out if he hadn't been tied to it. He made a slight gurgling sound and tears came down his cheeks. "Promise you will release her."

"I swear. May Allah cast me in hell if I don't."

Amitai sat up and continued after wiping tears from his face. "In any case, the idea was to find an effective way to counter the Soviet missile threat. We were looking at and experimenting with lasers powered by hydrogen fluoride. The American idea was either to have the laser in a 747 or to establish stations in space that, with the use of mirrors, could shoot a narrow laser beam to pierce the metal skin of the missile. Either the beam hits the fuel tank and the heat causes it to explode, or the beam burns through the electronics and causes a malfunction."

He paused as his eyes glanced at the bloodstains left by his wife's hand. "Although we were initially interested in SDI to destroy theater ballistic missiles before they leave enemy air space, we had a new weapon after we were able to harness the tremendous power we get from nuclear energy. We realized—actually, *I* realized—that we could now attack land targets, especially infantry. We were no longer limited to ballistic missiles."

"I can well understand how a laser beam could easily pierce the thin metal skin of a missile. But directing it at land targets is of a totally different magnitude, Doctor."

"Obviously. A beam still can't destroy a tank or a building, not yet anyway. However, anyone without protection is vulnerable. So the weapon has the potential to destroy armies out in the open and to keep the enemy's physical infrastructure fairly intact. We moved to deuterium fluoride, which has a longer wavelength and therefore allows easier transmission through the atmosphere. But it also requires larger mirrors."

Habib was extremely conscious of the time pressure. He wanted short answers, not lectures. "Yes, and where did all this take you? Where are you now? Is the beam operational or still in the research phase?"

"Well, eventually, in 1989 actually, after Reagan left the White House, the Cold War was officially over. Someone invented the term *peace dividend*, and money was no longer available for such martial enterprises. SDI research dried up. But we were very interested in continuing this research here in Israel. So that's what we're doing."

"I don't believe this is all research. Why, then, the maps on the wall? I can bring Shoshanna back in here if you want."

"Well, Shoshanna herself played a big role in thinking of nuclear power in new ways, in ways that the scientific world will one day recognize as historic watersheds. In the mid-nineties, our leadership, Rafael Industries, convinced Jerusalem to make a huge jump. We would power the lasers with nuclear energy. This would allow us to keep the laser gun here, on the ground, and only have to put the mirrors in space. With a lot of expensive and secret work."

Habib nodded, and said, "Did you say nuclear? That's impossible. Well, not impossible, but no one has harnessed lasers to nuclear power."

A smug grin crept onto Amitai's face. "Our Weizmann Institute has always been in the vanguard—not across the board, we're not a superpower. However, on certain technologies that touch on our survival, we've been on the cutting edge. We haven't publicized our advances, and for good reasons."

Although extremely aware of the need for quick, actionable information, the scientist in Habib couldn't help asking, "So tell me as a fellow scientist how you overcame the obstacles that no one else was able to conquer."

Habib read a mixture of despair and pride in Amitai's eyes, as if he knew viscerally that he was not likely to survive, but that that this was his only chance to get his story out. Was Amitai hoping for immortality? Was he dreaming of being mentioned in the annals of science that future generations would study?

Amitai said, "Have you ever heard of LAKAM, the scientific intelligence bureau of the IDF? Have you ever heard of Rafi Eban? He's a living legend in Israel. In 1960 he captured Adolph Eichmann, the Nazi, in Argentina. He's now an elected member of the Knesset, the Israeli parliament. Eban headed LAKAM when it recruited Pollard, the American spy who is still in a federal prison. LAKAM didn't go away when Eban went into politics. LAKAM was able to collect intelligence from the Russian, American, French and Japanese consortium committed to a nuclear-fusion reactor project in Cadarache, France, and from Livermore Laboratory in the United States. Being small has disadvantages— resources, for example—but advantages as well. We can quickly focus on important projects. Long story short, we set up a small experimental project. At first we used the deuterium-deuterium process to create helium three. However, we found that the intense heat and pressure necessary were containable only by using the tritium-deuterium method, creating helium four."

Despite the feeling that he was on the cusp of scientific discovery, Habib forced himself to move on. "That's impressive. But even if you use nuclear energy, you're still left with the distance from the space gun to the land target. So, I see two problems that you must have solved: one, the fact that the beam's energy dissipates with distance, and two, that the beam tends to be scattered by dust and particles in the atmosphere. Brute force can't be the only answer."

"You first test the scatter effect with a test beam, a smaller beam. Then you use the big laser to send a very specifically distorted beam that will be refocused by the dust and water in the air. But the key is the mirror. We needed bigger mirrors than had ever been used. The bigger the mirrors, the more complex they were. In order to distort the beam, we needed not hundreds but thousands of small actuators positioned behind the mirrors to alter the surface of the mirror to compensate, to 'predistort,' if you will."

"Yes, adaptive optics has been an essential part of the laser magic. But thousands of actuators? How big is the mirror?"

"I designed and built the biggest space-based mirror in the world. It's one hundred and eighty feet in diameter."

Habib paused before asking his most important question. "Then explain the control room. And how do you trigger the weapon? How do you target it? Is it now targeted against the red-light locations on the board?"

"The map, as you can see, is only of the Middle East, our 'near enemy.' We can target each city within a fraction of a second of each other. Would the entire city be destroyed? No. Very little of the city proper would be affected, unless the beam's heat starts fires. The beam would have to spread out to the size of the city. And the bigger the strike zone of the beam, the more the energy is dissipated. Further, destroying a brick-and-mortar building is different from piercing the thin metal skin of a missile that is built as lightly as possible. But anyone who was outside and unprotected within a small radius would probably be killed by the heat."

Habib said, "That's a fantastic achievement. I guess none of this is in the professional journals? Otherwise I would recognize your name."

"Aaron Amitai—Dr. Aaron Amitai. It will appear eventually, I'm sure."

Habib asked, "Have you actually field-tested it? Has the laser gun been activated?"

"We built an entire system one tenth the size of our current system, and the experiments were successful. We've never fired the actual laser gun, of course. It's our last defense. The United Nations and others can make their 'tut-tut' speeches. But we're the ones who will live or die. Anyway, we have to be ready, and we are. We should have fired it to show the world we had it. As a warning. Shoshanna made that recommendation. But she was ignored."

Habib still hadn't gotten the answer he sought. "I want to know how to target and fire the laser. Show me!" As a reminder of who was in control, Habib motioned the guard closer.

"My expertise was the space mirror. My wife Shoshanna is more knowledgeable on those details."

Habib felt that Amitai had manipulated him, to deflect his attention away from Shoshana, the one with the real answers. He felt vindictive but knew he had no choice.

He told the guard, "Bring his wife in here. And get him out. Don't let them see each other."

When she came in, Habib behaved as a more serious interrogator. "Dr. Amitai . . . ," he began. He wasn't sure that she had a PhD, but it wouldn't hurt to start with a show of respect for whatever academic credentials she had. It had worked with her husband. "Your achievements here are extremely impressive. Once this comes to the attention of the scientific community, you will take your place beside Newton and Einstein in science's hall of fame." He paused a second to judge her reaction, which, by the widening of her eyes, he assumed was surprise that one of the terrorists could speak with at least a veneer of education. Then a terse smile replaced her guarded demeanor, accompanied by silence.

Habib continued, "We are actually going to help make that happen. You're going to show the world your achievement by firing your creation. We're going to pick an uninhabited spot . . . in the Sinai, say. This will better show the world that Israel can and will defend itself. The current policy of keeping this weapon secret until after you're attacked makes no sense. Don't you agree that its main use is as a deterrent to war?"

"Why would you want to do something that would help Israel?" she asked in a tight voice.

"Because it will also help me. Think about it. We are against some of these Arab regimes, and against the Shiite resurgence flowing out of Iran, just as much as you are. I would like you to show me how your creation works. Your husband told me a great deal about the laser, and he said you would give me the rest, the operational directions."

She didn't respond, apparently mulling over an answer.

Habib continued, "The use of the weapon will strengthen Israel. And your name will become a household word in all of academia."

The guard came in holding something in his fingers. He showed it to the Israeli, and she gasped. Habib drew closer and saw that it was a finger, freshly cut and still bleeding.

"I knew it. You are butchers!" she cried.

"Be that as it may. That finger is simply a small example of the alternative to your becoming famous. Do we have a deal?"

She nodded solemnly. Her jaw muscles bulged out.

It was 0915 hours.

CHAPTER FIFTY-ONE

His arm still throbbing from being shot, Marshall had floated with the current, which had brought him to the jetty. He held on and, hiding behind a pylon, witnessed Hussein's men unload the cache at the foot of the tower of the Hospitallers. One man, apparently on a random basis, would open one of the boxes and take out a rifle or a rocket-propelled-grenade round and examine it briefly before replacing it and allowing the wooden crate to be carried away.

After the men left, Marshall pulled himself painfully toward the beach. His feet touched bottom and he stumbled out of the water. He followed the beach rather than returning through the parking lot, aware that some of the men might still be there. Eventually he reached his hotel room, took off his clothes to let them dry during the night, bound his wound—the bullet had passed through a muscle—and tried to get some sleep. The next day, after putting his arm in a sling, he rented another car and drove to Tel Aviv, to the American Embassy.

Following al Khalil's call, Ambassador Hastings immediately called his wife, Alexandra, to convey the news about Kella. He then asked his secretary to tell Jack Horton to meet him in the acoustic conference room.

Hastings had relatively little experience in the care and feeding of CIA station chiefs. His previous two postings had been as deputy chief of mission, and he therefore had not been in the loop, since station chiefs normally reported directly to the ambassador. He had heard horror stories of promising diplomatic careers broken by CIA "flaps," operations gone awry. There was a time, he knew, when, starting under President Kennedy, "treaties" were periodically negotiated between the State Department and the CIA. Nevertheless, most ambassadors felt vulnerable to the presence of a U.S. government agency in his domain whose role, by and large, was to carry out activities considered illegal by the host country.

Hastings and his COS, Jack Horton, had a good professional relationship. Horton briefed the ambassador once a week in the acoustic conference room—known informally as the ACR—the clear plastic room-within-a-room where all classified discussions were supposed to be held, country-team meetings in particular. Within the limits of "need to know," Ambassador Hastings was well-informed of the CIA station's activities. Horton had told Hastings that he would keep him informed at least to the extent of avoiding unpleasant surprises and to give the ambassador a heads-up prior to particularly risky activities with a high potential for political blowback.

Tall, with brown hair and rimless glasses, Jack Horton reached the ACR when Hastings's secretary was opening the door to the vault that enclosed it. He walked in and opened the lever that held the plastic door closed. A minute later, Hastings joined him.

Hastings asked, "Do you have an officer missing? Steve Church? Is there something I should know?"

"I have heard of *Marshall* Church. He was a senior clandestine service officer and one of my predecessors here. But as far as I know, he's retired. I don't know a Steve Church."

Hastings replied, "Steve is his son. You don't know anything about his visit to Israel? My daughter knows him. She told me he was here, or was coming. But that's what I wanted to talk to you about." Hastings proceeded to tell the COS about the phone call.

Horton asked, "Do you want me to talk to Shin Beth? Or are you going to have the regional security officer handle this?"

"You better handle it. If I thought it was simply a criminal issue, somebody trying to extort money, I'd give it to the security officer. But I'm sure that Kella's kidnapping is politically motivated. Kella would not have been kidnapped if she were not my daughter. She has become the shield against an Israeli takedown. But inform your Shin Beth contact quickly. The caller said there was an attack under way. The Israelis have to know immediately that my daughter is in the hands of the terrorists."

At that moment, the ambassador's secretary peered in and said, "Mr. Ambassador, there's a man named Marshall Church here to see you. He said it was important."

"Jack, you better get in touch with Shin Beth immediately. And then come back and join us in my office."

Marshall Church walked in just as Hastings was hanging up the phone after briefing the Israeli prime minister. Against all probability in this time of crisis, he had been able to get through.

Hastings offered his hand and said, "I have met your son. In fact your name just came up. Is Steve missing?"

Marshall Church grimaced and said, "Yes he is. We were in Ashqelon yesterday. We split up and he disappeared. He didn't come to our meeting point, and he didn't return to the rental car. Steve was expecting Kella to attend a ceremony in Jerusalem the day before yesterday, but she didn't come, and Steve couldn't reach her on the phone. Do you have any information?"

Hastings briefed Marshall on the phone call he had just received.

Marshall said, "That's Tariq al Khalil. Steve thought he recognized him in Jerusalem but wasn't sure. That's why we were in Ashqelon, hoping to spot al Khalil. And obviously, he has your daughter too."

Frowning, Hastings said, "You think that was a good idea, looking for al Khalil yourself?"

Marshall's lips compressed into a tight line. "You seriously think anyone, including you, would have taken us seriously? All we had at the time was a suspicion. I don't see the Israelis doing much based on what would have been unverified information."

The ambassador snapped back, "Why would al Khalil say your son is a CIA officer? Is he?"

"No, but he was mistaken for one in Morocco."

"I suggest that you stay here until the COS comes back. He's informing Shin Beth about the phone call. In the meantime, can I offer you some coffee? How about if the embassy nurse looks at that wound?"

It was 0930.

CHAPTER FIFTY-TWO

Avidan ordered, "I want covering fire directed at all windows and other possible firing points, now."

Then he told his intelligence team, "Go!"

Three men ran to the building. One deployed a light ladder, which he set up against the wall. The other two threw up grappling-hook rope ladders. After two tries, the hooks caught, and the two men climbed up to the roof. The ladder man first drilled several holes in the wall and then inserted listening devices equipped with microtransmitters. The two men on the roof set up heat-seeking sensors that could "see" through the roof and the walls. Avidan thought the takedown would be simple. The TIBAM plans revealed a one-floor interior with offices separated by drywall and cubicle separators, nothing that would provide safe harbor from the firepower of the Shaldag.

The Amitais gave Habib a quick tutorial on how to target the laser. The laser had several preset targeting options that included all of the Arab capitals of the Middle East, and Tehran. In the presence of the two Israeli scientists, Habib aimed the weapon to a deserted spot south of Cairo, ". . . to show everyone that Israel really has the capability to annihilate any of its enemies without using a nuclear weapon that, depending on the prevailing winds, could also wipe out part of the Israeli population." After getting the Amitais out of the room, he reset the laser to target the government centers of Tehran and of Algiers, per Tariq's orders. Tariq walked in to check up on his progress.

"Why not Cairo?" Habib asked.

"I will capture Egypt through the *threat* of destruction, not by actual destruction," said al Khalil. "Cairo is the most important center of influence for the Ikhwan brotherhood. The brothers will know what to do." Al Khalil gave only fleeting thought to his wife and daughter, Malika and Jamila, who were now living in Cairo. He wanted his daughter to grow up in a Muslim environment. In a sea of apostates, they were living in an island of Salafist purity with distant cousins. He had decided that their deaths, if necessary, were a small price, compared with his goals. However, for the moment, sparing Cairo made more sense from a political point of view.

Steve couldn't stop his mind from spinning. "Do you think Izem is on board? That he's trying to rally his guys to change sides? I don't know how long we should wait. Maybe he's not coming back. Maybe he's already been shot. But we need weapons."

Kella sat on the floor, her back against the wall, her features drawn and tired. She looked up at Steve. "I think so.

But that's easier said than done. What choice do we have?"

He pointed to the rear door. "Well, we have another door, if only we could open it. It's a long shot, but I wonder if we could pick the lock."

He walked back to the door and examined it. The pin-and-tumbler lock was about a foot higher than the lever handle, which itself had no lock. This was not a high-security area. The builders had placed their security focus on perimeter devices. Steve looked around for a thin piece of metal that he could insert in the lock, but saw nothing. There were several computer screens on the floor and an old desk against the back wall. It was dark in the back of their mini-bowling-alley prison, and Steve got down on his knees. He pulled the top drawer open. It was the main residence for a colony of insects. He looked inside a larger and lower drawer. He couldn't quite see anything distinctly, and he put his hand inside. He pulled out pliers, a hammer and wrenches in several sizes. But nothing thin enough to pick the lock.

Armed with a handful of tools, he sat on the floor and took the back off one of the computer screens. He pulled wires out where he could see them. Armed with a pair of cutting pliers, he detached a long wire, at the end of which was a stiff and thin piece of metal. He cut it off. He took a pair of long-nosed pliers and inserted one end into the bottom of the lock with one hand. With the other, he introduced the metallic pick in the lock and tried to feel the pins inside. He counted four.

Kella came up behind him. "Do you actually know what you're doing?"

"You pick up very peculiar pieces of trivia growing up in the house of an intelligence officer. So, yes. I'm trying to lift the pins out of the cylinder. The pressure I'm putting on the cylinder with the plier keeps the pins up after I lift them up. When all the pins are up, the cylinder should turn."

The long-nosed plier moved a bit and then all the way.

The lock had given up. He put his right hand up in a flourish. "Voilà." He then pushed the lever handle down slowly, and with Kella peering around him, he opened the door.

Immediately after leaving Habib, al Khalil went up to the ground floor to check up on their situation and see how close the Israeli commandos were to an assault.

Tariq al Khalil had also gone upstairs to call Salim on his satellite phone. He reached Salim in Cairo on his way to a meeting of the Brotherhood. Tariq gave him a short version of what was happening. "I want you to hold a press conference as soon as possible. You're on your way to Ikhwan headquarters? Great, schedule it there. But do it within the hour—within the half hour, if you can. Say that you have news of the takeover in Israel."

An angry Salim replied, "I'm surprised that you chose a target in the middle of Israel. I didn't know you to have a death wish, to want to die a martyr."

"This is the most important blow struck against the Zionists ever. This is historical." Al Khalil quickly brought him up-to-date on his takedown of the Israeli military installation masquerading as an agricultural-research center.

"Salim, this is your hour. Everything depends on our credibility. Alert the brothers to set up security around the press conference. The police may try to shut you down, or worse."

General Joulet was in his Paris office when an aide walked in with a message. "This is urgent, *mon général*." The message was an intercepted conversation from al Khalil's phone. He immediately called the Mossad representative in Paris and told him, "We have information concerning an ongoing hostage situation in Israel. Since one of the hostages is my adopted granddaughter, I have a personal interest. The leader of the group responsible is al Khalil. I'm sure you have as much information on him as we do. I don't understand this part about Israeli space lasers that your al Khalil now controls. I'd like you to ask your headquarters and get back to me. I need to brief the Elysée Palace quickly."

Joulet then called his daughter, Alexandra, wife of the American ambassador to Israel, angry that he had had to learn of Kella's kidnapping from intelligence sources. He then ordered that the entire Cimeterre case be reviewed by the inspector general's office, and that the responsible case officer, Captain Lucien Roger, be investigated and punished for incompetence or lack of integrity, or even treason.

It was 1030 hours.

CHAPTER FIFTY-THREE

Salim stood on a raised platform at one end of a large room lined with forty rows of chairs. The room was half-full but was filling quickly. He stood behind a podium with his notes in front of him. When the room was quiet enough for him to speak, he began.

"I bear witness that there is no God but Allah, and I bear witness that Muhammad is his slave and messenger. Muslim brothers of the world, peace be upon you and the mercy of Allah and his blessings. I bring you an important message from Tariq al Khalil."

After receiving his orders from al Khalil, Salim had tried to reach David Ben Tov but had not succeeded. He was holding his news conference in the Muslim Brotherhood center in Cairo. Not all of the city's media representatives were present; he had given them only forty-five minutes' warning. However, many Egyptian correspondents were present, especially those with a radical Muslim slant, who were more likely to respond to a call from the Brotherhood. Al Jazeera was there, he noted with satisfaction, and would spread Tariq's message worldwide.

"Today is a great day for Islam," Salim continued. "Thanks to the inspiration and guidance of Allah, the Beneficent, the Merciful, Islam has started to reconquer the lands of the Caliphate. Our son and the right hand of Allah on earth, Tariq al Khalil, may Allah continue to favor him, has taken by force of arms an important military center in the heart of Palestine. On his behalf, I address this message to the chiefs of state who have brought their countries back to the pagan era preceding Allah's revelation to the Prophet, may Allah favor him."

Salim picked up a sheet of paper from the podium. He moved to the forward edge of the platform and raised his voice to mitigate the absence of the microphone. "To you, false leaders, Tariq al Khalil says,

" 'Every day you are insulting Allah, the Merciful, the Almighty. You are blasphemers. You are worshippers of idols. You should be cleansed from the face of this earth. However, I, Tariq al Khalil, am offering you redemption. Instead of sacrificing you immediately on the altar to Allah, as I now have the power to do, thanks to Allah—exalted is he—I am giving you twenty-four hours. Twenty-four hours to hand over power to the Ikhwan, or to the Salafists in your countries.

" 'To my Ikhwan brothers, I say, this is the day when we begin the recreation of the Caliphate of old, when we establish Allah's law on earth, Sharia law, to replace the man-made substitutes. This is the day when we begin to retake our land, the Land of the Two Holy Places.

" 'Who shall rule? Those with the most votes? Those with the most effective and repressive control of the citizens? Or Sharia, divine law?

" 'I will not talk about the swift punishment that is to befall the enemies of our faith. I will soon exhibit a small sample of the punishment I will mete out to the infidel, corrupt, apostate rulers of our Caliphate lands, from Andalusia to Indonesia, unless they bow to the will of Allah, Lord of the Universe. In his service, my scimitar is sharp and ready for battle.

" 'To the brothers in Algeria who now call themselves "al Qaeda in the Islamic Maghreb," the guards of Islam's western garrison and to the other grandsons of Saladin, today we are restoring the glory of your forefathers.

" 'I repeat: twenty-four hours. Woe to those who don't take heed. The second strike will be geometrically more powerful. This is as the Battle of Badr was in predicting the success of the Prophet.

" 'May peace be upon you and the mercy of Allah and his blessings.' "

Steve and Kella stepped out of their cell into a dark space. They put their hands out and moved forward carefully. Steve realized that they were in another office in back of the large map of the Middle East. The door to their closet cell guarded by Abdul was on the back wall and to the right of the map. Steve determined that they were in an executive area from which the map could be activated and changed. There were two large desks and two doors. Still in the dark, Steve and Kella explored the corridor onto which the doors opened. To the left, they found stairs heading up to the right. At the top of the stairs was a vaulted door much like the one they had seen at the top of the other stairwell. They went back downstairs.

Steve said, "This must be another way to come down, and al Khalil must not have found it. Or he has a guard on the other side of the door."

They had been out about fifteen minutes when Kella said, "Don't you think we should go back, in case someone comes looking for us?"

Steve led the way. "I hope that the only one looking for us is Izem. We have a way out, but it's useless without weapons."

As Salim spoke to the media in Cairo, in Israel, al Khalil gave Habib his orders. "Can you operate this weapon without the Jew scientists? With or without them, you will target Tehran. I want to strike the buildings that house the Supreme Council and the office of the president, not the whole city. Then I want a similar strike on the Algerian government. Our Algerian brothers have been fighting and dying for many years. They've earned this help. Algiers and Tehran are lucky. They will receive only a warning shot. The laser should not be on full power this time. But next time, tomorrow, for the leaders who do not heed the warning, their populations will suffer grievously. We're not going to burn Tel Aviv yet. We want to lull them into inactivity. I want them to think that we're only interested in striking Iran and some Arab capitals. If they believe it's our plan, the Jews will leave us alone for a while. We're doing what they never had the guts to do. Plus, I'm sure the Americans are telling the Jews not to attack because of the two Americans we're holding. We want to delay an Israeli attack as long as possible so that we can finish our work here. We'll incinerate Tel Aviv later. Go do this now."

Izem tried to rally the small group of Tuaregs. There were seven left, not counting him. It was difficult to have private conversations with any of them. Some were upstairs guarding the entry points of the building. Others were downstairs guarding the prisoners, the Israeli scientists and the two Americans. He rounded up two from a Timbuktu tribe he knew well and brought them to the room where Steve and Kella were kept. "This is Kella, the ranking descendant of the leadership of our Udalan clan, one of the seven big Tuareg clans. We are all Udalans. We first fought the Arabs when they invaded and made us Muslims; we fought the French who tried to teach us that our ancestors were Gauls. Now we must fight these Salafists, the latest invaders. It is our duty to follow Kella. We owe her allegiance."

The two young Tuaregs looked at Kella and then at Izem with puzzled expressions. "This is just an American girl, an unbeliever. Al Khalil told us about Western girls, all prostitutes. Why do we owe her allegiance?" the taller one asked Izem in their native Tamasheq.

Kella spoke up, also in Tamasheq. "Because I am Tuareg, and this proves my authority," and she showed them the gold bracelet with the geometric-type Tamasheq script that had been in her family for generations as a symbol of tribal leadership.

Izem told them, "Look closer. See the Tuareg inscriptions?"

The two young fighters stepped closer, looking shocked that Kella had understood them and could speak their tribal language. One also attracted the other's attention to the four dots on the back of Kella's hand. By their hushed whispers and looks of awe, Izem could tell that the design had obvious significance to them.

The two young men inspected the bracelet as Kella extended her arm. They looked at each other in confusion and indecision. Then the shorter one inclined his head and in Tamasheq asked, "What is your order, *amenokal*?" The other soldier likewise looked down in submission.

Izem spoke up. "She wants to speak to all of the Tuaregs in here now. We want all of our tribesmen to act together."

Steve held Izem back as they left. "Izem, you can't keep going back and forth like this. Al Khalil is going to notice. We need weapons. Fast."

"You will have them."

As soon as Izem left, Steve went out the back door. "Stay here. I need to find out what's down the other side of that back corridor. Shouldn't take long."

"Be careful."

* * *

Steve could go faster this time, knowing that Hussein's men had not yet discovered the back corridor. Nevertheless, he assumed that they would find it in time. He made a right turn into the corridor, past the back wall of their cell, to another door about thirty feet down. In the dark, he felt another doorway and carefully groped for the handle. He turned the knob slowly and pushed the door open. He stepped into another dark space and closed the door behind him, then stood for a couple of seconds trying to sense his surroundings before stepping forward. He found a light switch and flicked it up to find himself faced with an emergency generator and, on the left side of the door, cases of water and canned food. The Israelis, he thought, were ready for a siege. But they had been overly reliant on cover and concealment. Why didn't they have a stronger armed-security group to defend their installation?

He turned the light off and went back to the corridor. He again turned to the right. Another twenty feet or so and he found a narrow corridor to the right. He followed it and reached the corridor that originally had led from the front stairwell to the large computer and map room. He turned left and reached another vault door with a pad for digital identification. A vault within a vault. What could be behind this barrier?

Steve turned around and made his way back to the supply room. He was loading a cardboard box when a tremendous explosion suddenly increased the air pressure against his eardrums severalfold. He was immobilized for a second and then grabbed his box, turned out the light and turned left into the corridor to get back to his cell. He heard footsteps and voices coming toward him in the dark and saw the beam of a flashlight at the far end of the corridor. His one chance was to go forward and slip into the room behind the map. He kept moving quickly in the dark toward the sounds. He entered the office in back of the large electronic wall map just as the light reached the bottom of the stairs. He closed the door behind him and found the back door to his cell.

Kella came up to him and put her arms around him. "What was that noise?"

Steve put the box down under the back desk. "I think they found the door to the back stairs and blew it open. There goes our escape route."

"Are you all right? What do you have in the box?" she said, and leaned down to look before Steve could reply. "Wow! Water! And Spam! Spam?"

"Yes. I found the crisis supply room. There was a kosher supply and a nonkosher supply. You're not Jewish are you? And a couple of flashlights."

Kella took a bottle of water out and gave Steve another one. "Look, Abdul brought these." Under the desk were two AK-47s.

Steve reached for one of the weapons. "Abdul?"

"Yes, Izem told him. Abdul has switched sides."

"Yes, or he's playing both sides."

The Shaldag team kept firing at the building's openings at random to keep the tension high and prevent the terrorists from getting any rest. While Avidan and his men had access to food and could rest on a rotating basis, Hussein's fighters had to be ready for an attack at any time. They had found fast-food and soda machines in the building and were not without sustenance. But they had had not slept the night before. They soon would be fighting their bodies to stay functional, alert and effective.

The TIBAM team delivered the classified plans of the building to Avidan, who became furious. Speaking to General Shomron on his cell network, he said, "General, you sent me on a mission with bad information. The plans the TIBAM gave me were false, showing a one-level interior. Now I have the classified blueprints showing me that the terrorists are in a subterranean complex with offices, labs and our country's secret weapon."

Shomron answered, "That's because your mission has changed, from liberating the hostages and killing the terrorists to disabling the laser."

"What's the difference? I have to go through the terrorists to get at the weapon, right?"

"No. Look at the TIBAM information. You'll see there's a sliding roof. For the weapon to become operational, the roof has to slide open. When it does, that's your chance to get into the installation. But keep in mind that when they open the roof, it means they're ready to fire. We have to hope that since it's their first time, there will be pauses as they try to figure out the next step."

Hussein was busy organizing his few fighters on the ground level and keeping an eye on the Israeli commandos surrounding the building. Not unexpectedly, they hadn't assaulted his positions yet. Obviously, the Israeli government put a high price on the value of the American hostages, especially the ambassador's daughter. But that didn't totally explain the Israeli force's relative lack of activity. He left his post to go speak with al Khalil.

They met near the top of the stairs. Al Khalil came up with an AK-47 in his hand. "Give me an update. How are the Israelis positioned?"

Hussein leaned on the railing, one hand holding the gun slung around his neck.

"They're firing to keep us busy, but they haven't attacked. I don't know what they're waiting for; it must be our hostages. Are you negotiating with them?"

"I'm keeping them at bay for the moment. Within hours, we'll have the entire Middle East in our hands." He told Hussein about the laser gun and his plan to fire it as a show of force against Algiers and Tehran.

Hussein let go of the railing and looked down at al Khalil,

a step below. "This is our chance to finally get rid of the Assad family. This is what I've been waiting for all this time, to revenge my family, my father."

Al Khalil took a step up. "Don't worry. Damascus will be in the second phase."

In an angry outburst, Hussein said, "Damascus! Damascus! That should be our first target. Kill the Assads. Kill those who killed my family."

"I will, we will. Be patient. Do we want an incinerated city? Or do we want the Syrian leaders to hand over the country to our Muslim brothers? Wouldn't that be a greater revenge?"

Hussein felt himself stiffen. "The Assad family is the greatest obstacle to an Islamic republic in Syria. The father, Hafez, and the son, Bashir, have killed thousands of our Muslim brothers. This is our chance. Don't wait. How long do you think the Zionists are going to wait before they attack us?"

"You're right about the Zionists. It's time to remind the American, Hastings, that we have his daughter here."

Steve picked up the AK-47 and a flashlight. "OK, I'm going to try to go out the back way. We can't just wait here for Izem. We don't know what he's doing."

Kella got up and retrieved the other AK-47. "Don't think you're leaving here without me."

"You'll be safer here. I'll come back to get you. Have you ever fired a gun, let alone an AK-47?"

"No, I haven't, so you better show me."

"Please. Stay here," Steve begged. He didn't want to worry about her.

Even in the dim light he could see the determination on her face. "Give up. I'm going with you."

Steve sighed, picked up the hammer that was with the other tools in the desk and nodded. "OK? Ready? First, about this gun. This is not an accurate weapon. It gets less accurate if you fire long bursts. Try to squeeze the trigger gently—don't jerk it—and then release it quickly. Also, it's going to kick and shoot up and to the right. You have to hold it. And don't point it at anything you don't intend to shoot dead. Ready? Wait for me by the door. Take a flashlight."

When Kella reached the door, Steve smashed all the circuit breakers. He then joined Kella at the door, and they went to the supply room. "I want to shut down the emergency generator in case it's programmed to go on if the circuit breakers fail." But the generator was quiet. Steve led Kella back down the corridor, now behind the beam of his flashlight. They turned right and took the first few steps, when a voice called out behind them, "Ahmed!"

Hastings's secretary put al Khalil through right away. Hastings was joined by Jack Horton, who listened on a second phone.

"Hastings," al Khalil said, "your Jewish friends are on the verge of attacking us. They've been shooting at us and your daughter is lucky to be alive."

Hastings stood up and said with force, "I want to know about my daughter. I understand that you also have another American hostage. How are they both?"

"Right now, they're fine. But if the Jews attack, either they will die from Jewish bullets, or from ours. I guarantee that they will not survive a Jewish attack. Talk to your Jew friends. I want their commandos to disappear. Then we can talk about your daughter."

"I heard about you when I was posted to France. Your status as the only intellectual that could establish a dialogue with the West is badly eroded." Hastings tried reasoning with him. "I can help you regain your standing if you stop what you're doing right now and let all your hostages go. Why are you doing this? I'm sure I could get you out of the country safely."

"Hastings, you're wasting my time with your demands. My next step will be to start killing the hostages. I haven't decided who will go first, the Jewish scientists or my American prisoners. Get those commandos to move back!"

Horton, the COS, wrote a quick note and handed it to the ambassador.

Looking at the note, Hastings said, "I want proof that my daughter is alive."

"You're hardly in a position to give me orders, Hastings. But right now, I can't bring her to the phone. She's in another part of the building. She is well."

Reading from another note, Hastings said, "I want you to take a photograph of her, and of Steve Church, with a cell phone, and I want you to e-mail it to me within the next few minutes. If that happens, I'll have the Israeli commandos back off. Keep in mind that my government is not in charge. Israel is a sovereign country." He gave al Khalil an e-mail address, which Tariq took grudgingly without agreeing to anything.

After al Khalil put him off by repeating, "Be patient," Hussein walked away, frustrated and angry. Al Khalil had put off Hussein for years. While his only reason to join Tariq in the first place had been to hit back at the Assad family, Hussein had never been successful in his attempts to influence Tariq into taking action against the Syrian rulers.

Al Khalil's last words to Hussein on the stairs were "According to the scientists, there is a sliding roof to allow the laser gun to shoot. Get some men up there."

Hussein went back upstairs and walked to a window opening being defended by one of his men. "Ayyub, take some men up to the roof. Part of it opens up. Find it and keep the Israelis off the roof."

Ayyub and three men went up through the damage done by the UAVs. Staying low to avoid being seen by the Israelis, they made their way to the wider part of the roof to the west. As they moved, Ayyub saw several black boxes on the roof. At first, he paid them no attention, not knowing if these boxes were part of the roof construction. He then stopped and lifted a box, revealing a wire going into the roof. He called one of the other men. They both examined the box. "I wonder if the Israelis put these up here to listen to us. What else could they be? Bombs? They look new, not weathered like the rest of the roof."

The second man was about to pull the wire, but Ayyub stopped him. "Not now. It'll show that we're up here," he said. They resumed their inspection of the western part of the roof.

At that moment a clinking noise was followed by a grappling hook on a nylon rope being pulled back toward the edge of the roof. Ayyub crawled closer to the edge, and the three others started looking across the roof for other places where the Israelis might be trying to climb. Ayyub and his men waited for the Israelis to show themselves above the edge of the roof. Another hook and then a third hit the roof. Three men were on their way up. One climber's head became visible, then the second and the third. It wasn't until the third appeared that Ayyub and his men fired, killing all three instantaneously, their bodies falling to the ground below. Ayyub threw a grenade to the base of the wall, assuming there were others down there waiting their turn to climb. He waited a second and then looked over the edge. He barely had time to note with satisfaction the Israeli bodies at the base of the wall before his head exploded from a dumdum bullet fired by a Shaldag sniper.

Meanwhile, al Khalil sent one of his men to send photos of the American hostages to the ambassador. He remembered that both Kella and Steve had cell phones that had been taken from them.

It was 1315 hours.

CHAPTER FIFTY-FOUR

Steve and Kella were on the second step of the unlit stairs, plastered against the wall at a right angle from the end of the corridor, listening to the footsteps coming toward them. The reflection from the beam of the man's light pointed at the floor in front of him was lighting the wall with increasing brightness. The voice shouted again: "Ahmed!"

Steve and Kella looked to their right up the dark stairs. Steve wondered why the voice thought Ahmed was somewhere in front of him. Or had he heard their footsteps and assumed that they were those of Ahmed? Steve's mind was racing, trying to decide how to deal with the company—whether to simply kill him as quietly as possible or to capture him and tie him up. He had concluded that they couldn't deal with a prisoner, when the man reached the end of the corridor and looked up the stairs.

Steve had the shoulder stock of his AK-47 cocked and ready to smash him when Kella stopped him. "Wait!" At the same time, she stepped forward and spoke Tamasheq rapidly, pointing her AK-47 at the man, whose face was hidden by a Tuareg *tagoulmoust*.

Steve had come within a millisecond of releasing his blow to the man's head. He could see the man's eyes widen with shock and surprise. Taking advantage of the element of surprise, Steve disarmed him and watched the dialogue, only guessing at what both were saying. After several exchanges, the man seemed to ask a question, to which Kella replied by showing him her bracelet and, a few seconds later, the tattooed design on her hand. The Tuareg paused a second and seemed swayed. Steve recognized Izem's name in Kella's next sentence, and she appeared to have closed the deal.

She turned to Steve and said, "He's with us, but he also wants confirmation from Izem."

"Tell him you want full allegiance now, or his family will never live down the shame."

Kella looked at Steve with surprise and translated. The Tuareg looked at both Steve and Kella in turn and replied in Tamasheq. Kella said, "That did it."

Steve said, "Well, I think I'll keep his weapon for now." He slung the Taureg's AK-47 over his shoulder. "Tell him we're going upstairs to save the rest of his Tuareg brothers from annihilation. Ask him how the Salafists are positioned upstairs."

Kella asked, and heard the Tuareg's reply. She told Steve, "He said there are about fifteen to twenty left, but some are downstairs, watching the prisoners. Upstairs, they're fighting from the windows, and he said there some are on the roof, but he doesn't know how many."

"Let's go." Steve moved up the stairs first. He stopped suddenly, turned around and asked, "What's his name?"

"Yubba," said the Tuareg.

Kella and Steve both looked at him in surprise, and Steve led them up the stairs again.

When they reached the door at the top of the stairs, the door was half-open and hanging on one hinge. The doorframe was a jagged hole. "Here we go. Ready?" He looked back at Kella.

She clutched her AK-47 more tightly to her side.

His AK-47 up to his shoulder and finger on the trigger, Steve slipped through the door without having to touch it. Shouting voices erupted in what sounded to Steve like a loud conversation. He motioned Kella to his side. "What are they saying?"

"They want the lights back on."

Although it was midday, light from the outside didn't penetrate very far beyond the few windows. The three of them had emerged in another office. Yubba motioned them to follow him. He opened the door slowly to reveal an external wall on the left. One of Hussein's men was standing on a desk he apparently had placed there and was pointing his gun out a window that was about ten feet off the floor. While his gun still pointed toward possible targets outside, his eyes followed the door's movement on his left. He quickly tried to move his gun into firing position when he saw Steve appear behind Yubba. But Steve already had his AK-47 pointed toward him. He fired and four 7.62-millimeter bullets penetrated the Salafist's chest. The almost simultaneous blows hammered him against the wall. He slid down the wall until he fell off the desk to the floor.

Steve's mind registered that he had killed another human being. But his dominant feeling was that of great danger. The man he had killed could easily have killed them both. He pulled Kella after him, moving to the right, paralleling the side toward which the Salafist had been pointing his gun. Now the other gunmen were alerted. They would assume a breach by the Israelis. "Hurry," he said. They moved out quickly and kneeled at an intersection of two corridors formed by seven-foot-high dividers. He told Kella, "Call to the Tuaregs in Tamasheq. Tell them who we are."

In Tamasheq, Kella shouted, "Izem and all of you other Udalan fighters. Now is the time to revolt against the Arab master, the poisoners of wells. Kill them now. Don't die for somebody else's cause. Stay with the Arabs and die. Join me and choose freedom. I will get you out of here alive."

They waited in silence. Steve said, "Repeat your message, and then let's move quickly."

Before she could say anything, Yubba shouted out.

When he heard footsteps and voices in front of them, Steve pulled Kella into the first office cubicle, where they kneeled awkwardly behind a desk. The footsteps drew closer. They saw Izem go past their hiding place running in a crouch. In a loud whisper, Kella called out in Tamasheq, "Izem, in here." In a few seconds Izem joined them.

Suddenly a loud Arab voice from farther down the corridor shouted, "This is Majid. The hostages escaped. Al Khalil is insane with rage. The hostages are our ticket out of here. They must be up here. Boulos! Gamal! Join me at the top of the stairs and help me find them!"

Izem said, "Now I know where they are. Stay here. The stairs are very close," and he pointed with the muzzle of his gun. He took Yubba's AK-47 from Steve and gave it back to him. He and Yubba headed in Majid's direction.

Steve heard voices and footsteps. Then gunfire erupted, stopped for a fraction of a second and erupted again. The sound was badly absorbed, and resounded throughout the warehouse building. It also sounded extremely close. Kella looked at Steve. He stood up in a crouch and moved out of the cubicle with his AK-47 out front.

Al Khalil was downstairs in his de facto office. He held Abdul, who was kneeling in front of him, by the hair. "How long have you been a CIA spy?"

"Never, never! May Allah curse me if I lie! Izem came to help the hostages. It's the Tuaregs. They are all spies. They are all infidels. They only made believe that they are Muslim warriors. Izem liberated the Americans, not me. I could do nothing."

Al Khalil pointed a pistol at Abdul's face. "You lie. You and Izem worked together, didn't you?"

Abdul held his hands up palms toward al Khalil. "No, no."

Still holding Abdul by the hair, al Khalil moved the muzzle of the pistol closer and closer to Abdul's right eye, his finger tightening on the trigger. In desperation, Abdul grabbed the gun with his hands. The gun went off as Abdul tried to push it aside. The bullet punched him in the neck. Al Khalil released his hair and Abdul fell forward. Al Khalil looked at him a second before firing another shot into the back of his head.

Izem and Yubba appeared in front of Steve. Izem said, "Majid, Boulos and Gamal are gone to their paradise." Then he called his Tuareg brethren in Tamasheq. Within five minutes, after some gunfire, during which Kella kept a firm hold on Steve's arm, three men appeared. They spoke with Izem. "We just lost one of ours. Hussein and several men are on the roof, and there are the men guarding the scientists, and al Khalil's guards—about fifteen to twenty fighters."

There was another conversation among the Tuaregs, which Kella translated for Steve. "The Israelis have a secret weapon downstairs. With it, al Khalil is going to first threaten the Muslim world with a warning shot against two cities, and then, unless all submit, he plans to obliterate the population of some Arab capitals."

Steve took a deep, steadying breath. "Let's go downstairs. We have to stop him."

As the Shaldag and Hussein's men battled for control of the roof on the western side of the building, Habib and the Amitais switched the nuclear power, piped in from the Soreq Nuclear Center, from the commercial grid providing electricity to surrounding towns, to exclusive military use of the center. The energy coursed to three lasers hooked up in series, using a triple-lens system. The system was designed to produce a laser beam with the effective power of a fifty-four-megawatt beam.

The roof was open less than a minute when Habib sent the beam to the satellite. It was received by one giant mirror, fed into the satellite and shot out through another mirror toward Algiers.

During a full minute, the beam bathed the area from the Place du Gouvernement and its complex of ministry offices on rue Docteur Cherif Saadane, past the railroad line along the coast, to the docks and overlapping onto the sea. Electric power in that part of the city came to a stop. All communications shut down. The explosions of war were absent. People on the street became instantly aware of increased heat on their exposed skin. Those wearing long sleeves or *jellabas* felt the sensation on their faces and hands. They searched for a cause but saw nothing to explain their quickly rising body temperature. They initially assumed that the heat was the prologue to the sirocco, the wind from the desert. But in seconds they dismissed natural causes. Their skin quickly turned pink and then red. Blisters followed, and the temperature of their blood and other bodily fluids began to climb to dangerous levels.

The lobby of the Es Safir Hotel, located between Place du Gouvernement and the sea, as well as most public buildings in the area, quickly filled up with people looking for air-conditioning. The instinct to move inside saved many lives. Some who lived or worked in apartments or offices on the top floors of buildings died from the superheated air. Fires erupted spontaneously. Any easily combustible material within the half-mile diameter of the laser burst into flames. Some drivers lost control of their vehicles and crashed. In three minutes, within the fifth-of-a-square-mile area, all was quiet. Later, fire trucks from other parts of the city started their sirens and headed for the blighted zone.

Within an hour, a French correspondent in Algiers called his report into his Paris office. "At 1430 today, the threat of al Khalil, the Salafist leader whose spokesman in Cairo delivered an ultimatum to the Muslim world to submit to Sharia law, materialized as a death beam from space. Casualties were minimal, considering the apparent potential of the weapon. Officials initially estimated one hundred people, but a check of hospitals reveals a somewhat lower number. But as a military strike intended to annihilate the enemy's physical infrastructure, al Khalil's attack was a failure. Physical damage was minimal. We are waiting for an official statement from the Algerian government. However, judging from the population's reaction, and placed in the context of al Khalil's threat communicated at the press conference in Cairo, the death beam has had a psychologically devastating effect. Waiting for the promised 'second strike,' which al Khalil said would be much more lethal, I am Jean Pierre Lemoine reporting from Algiers."

Habib switched the aim of the space mirrors to Tehran and fired. It was 1438 hours.

Hussein rolled over on his back. He had joined his men on the roof, knowing that the entire operation now depended on keeping the roof open so that Habib could fire the laser. He reached for his walkie-talkie. As his eyes registered the blue sky, still clouded by the smoke rising from the UAV attack, it occurred to him that his life was probably about to end. What had the years brought him? He felt angry and resentful and ashamed that he had not lived up to his commitment. He had bet on the wrong horse. Al Khalil had always had his own agenda and never intended to include Hussein's.

He looked away from the sky and focused on his tactical situation. He reached for his short-range radio. "Tariq, we can't hold out for your twenty-four-hour ultimatum. I could have told you, if I had known what you were planning. I expect the Issies to send another helicopter up. One or two missiles and we're finished. We were lucky to shoot down one of their helicopters. He made a mistake and got too close. This time they'll stay out of our range. Ask Salim to correct the time. Make it an hour, two hours max. Any longer and this operation is over and so are we. Send me more men up to the roof. This is the key point now."

In Tehran, the head of intelligence, Gholam Hussein Ejei, called Major General Yahya Rahim Safavi from his home in

Niavaran, a residential district of choice for the wealthy during the Shah's time. While about a third of its inhabitants had left the country since the 1978–79 revolution, a new class that thrived in the theocracy of the ayatollahs had replaced them. Ejei shooed away a servant who was offering tea on a silver platter. Safavi acted as though he were taking over the government following the deaths of both the chairman of the ruling council and of the president. Ejei knew he had to act quickly to support the new power center to survive the inevitable "night of the long knives," a cleaning out of officials with uncertain loyalties. "General, you must order immediate retaliation against Israel. We have the rockets. We have the aircraft. This is the time. Our population will applaud your courage. You will become the father of the entire Muslim world. They will follow your example and erase Israel from the face of the earth. Everyone will admire you. Now is the time to act."

"I have called for a meeting of our top military and al Quds commanders. I want you to be there—in two hours, at my house in Niavaran."

In Algiers, fighting broke out. The AQIM, led by Ibrahim el Maghrebi, which had never dared attack the government in Algiers proper, took the radio station and broadcast appeals for the army to join the new Islamic Republic of Algeria in response to al Khalil's message from Cairo.

Al Khalil was in front of a TV in what had become his headquarters, the office with the large window overlooking the computer room with the wall map of the Middle East. The TV was reporting on the reactions to his ultimatum. The CNN reporter said, "Arab governments are speaking out against the jihadist who allegedly captured the Israeli space laser weapon that caused casualties in both Algiers and Tehran. Tariq al Khalil, through his spokesman in Cairo, has threatened noncompliant countries with devastation from the la-

ser unless they submit to Sharia law. The threatened
governments are calling for all-out war against Israel, the
source of the death ray. Other Islamists claim that the Israelis are using al Khalil's name as a blind, as cover to attack its
Arab neighbors, that al Khalil is not in Israel and that he has
been seen in Yemen.

"Saudi Arabia has condemned the loss of life, without
criticizing al Khalil directly. The Wahhabist leaders of the
kingdom are supporting al Khalil's fervor and, according to
reports, are in negotiations with the royal family to take
over several ministries to strengthen the enforcement of
Sharia law and to allocate more funds to spread the faith
globally. Secular countries such as Egypt, Jordan, Tunisia
and Syria are the most strident in their demands for the
Arab League, the United Nations and the United States to
take action against Israel, the real culprit. A more militant
message is dominating the unofficial media, chat rooms,
blogs and YouTube. Tariq al Khalil's prior speeches and presentations are being quoted. 'It is time,' he is quoted as saying, 'for the Muslim world to go back to its roots.'

"Local radical Muslim groups have been emboldened by
al Khalil's words and actions. They are attacking police stations and more symbolic but undefended representatives of
secular power, such as ministry buildings. Imams and mul-
lahs have taken over churches and other non-Muslim religious edifices. The secretary general of the United Nations
has expressed his hope for more dialogue."

Al Khalil sat back. This was the Western media, which he
knew to be prejudiced. The real situation must be worse for
the Arab powers than he had just heard. CNN was, after all,
another arm of the American government. He searched for
the al Jazeera channel.

In Cairo, Salim, prohibited from holding another news conference, called correspondents. "Tariq al Khalil has short-
ened his deadline. You have seen what defying him means.

As of this moment, any government in the Middle East that refuses to hand over power to the Muslim Brothers or to Salafist groups will suffer a much more serious fate than Tehran or Algiers. This ultimatum is effective immediately."

Jack Horton, the Tel Aviv CIA chief of station, sat in the acoustic conference room with Ambassador Hastings. Horton said, "Any news about your daughter?"

"No. I asked al Khalil for a photo, which he could easily have sent by e-mail, but I have had no contacts with him since then. I don't even know if Kella is alive. What is the CIA reporting on this situation?"

"Since the second release to the press by al Khalil's spokesman, fighting broke out in Damascus and Jakarta. In Cairo itself, the outlawed Muslim Brotherhood activated their penetrations of the army and security services. Several Egyptian army units have made statements in support of an Islamic government. Muslim Brotherhood members are claiming majority power in the Egyptian parliament. Under free elections, they claim, they would have a democratic majority. I need to ask you a question. What is your plan in terms of getting our dependents out of here? It's only a matter of time before al Khalil hits Tel Aviv with that laser."

"We can't evacuate our people. It would show a lack of faith, a lack of support for the Israeli government during a crisis."

Horton's voice rose. "You're talking about perceptions. I'm talking about the lives of our families."

Hastings sat more erect. "I'm not approving an evacuation. I don't want to send the signal that the U.S. thinks the Israeli government can't handle this situation. Just think of the implications about the bigger issues."

"Well, with all due respect, sir, I'm going to tell my people that those who want to send their families out can. We'll figure out whether they're reimbursed later."

"It may already be too late for Kella," Hastings said. "I'm going to call the prime minister and tell her to start talking with the terrorists. We still don't know what the hell they want. I wonder if their plan went any further than the capture of this laser gun."

"Probably not. As long as they own it, they rule the world."

Hastings hastily got up to leave the ACR. "That's it! The Israelis have to find a way to destroy the gun. I'm calling the prime minister. You contact Israeli intelligence."

Horton left the ACR to inform his staff to evacuate their families, in view of the looming threat of a laser attack. Before they assembled in his office, he was thinking that perhaps the more timely survival action would be to leave Tel Aviv—there might not be time to get on a flight out of the country.

It was 1545 hours.

In the Israeli laser center, Habib was getting ready to fire the laser for the second strike.

Al Khalil walked past the well-armed squad of men that he had posted at the entrance of the laser center following Steve and Kella's escape. He took a quick look at the tubes, wires and machinery that populated the large underground room. "I was afraid you didn't have power. We lost all our power on the other side. That devil dog Church destroyed the circuit breakers?" He glanced around.

Habib pointed toward a corner of the well-lit space. "The laser has its own emergency generator for lights and air-conditioning—which is crucial, because this thing really heats up. But we're hooked up to the Nahal Soreq Nuclear Center to power the actual laser. I'll be ready to fire again in about thirty minutes. What are the targets?" Habib led al Khalil toward a control panel.

Al Khalil stopped, and Habib turned around to face him. With even more gravity and determination on his face than

usual, al Khalil put his hand on Habib's shoulder, and looking up over Habib's shoulder, visualizing the electronic
map, he said, "Riyadh, Tehran and Tel Aviv. This time, I
want full power."

Habib appeared surprised. "We just hit Tehran."

Al Khalil dropped his hand, but his eyes maintained their
intensity. "Iran and Saudi Arabia are the regional centers of
power. When both are weak and under my governments,
my Caliphate will rule supreme from Cairo. I will replace
the al Saud dynasty with my men, people loyal to me and to
the true version of our faith, people who will not invite foreign infidels to solve problems." Al Khalil paused and stroked
his black beard, now starting to grow out. "With a strong
power center in Cairo, I will establish a borderless region
covering the entire Middle East. I will also change that
name. *Middle East* is European terminology. Typical infidel
arrogance labelled each region according to its distance
from Europe."

It was 1549 hours.

Before Steve went down the dark stairs, he asked Izem,
"Can you collect any more of your Tuaregs?"

"There might be one other downstairs guarding the
scientists—that's all."

"Let's go, then. Do you know where this secret weapon is
exactly?"

When Izem shook his head, Steve said, "We better first
liberate the scientists. They can help."

When they reached the door to the large computer room
where the prisoners were being held, Steve held up his hand.
"Izem, go in by yourself first. Tell the guards that Hussein
wants them upstairs immediately. We'll deal with them
when they come out. Say that Hussein wants just one guard
for the prisoners and for the rest to come and help him. And
the one who's going to stay to watch the prisoners should
be your Tuareg brother."

Izem went in. Steve and Kella positioned themselves on each side of the door, and Steve told the two Tuareg fighters to step back and face the door. "Kella, tell them that the idea is to capture them, and not to shoot unless we have to."

The door opened, and the sound of footsteps signaled people coming through. Steve turned his light on one of Hussein's fighters. Almost as soon, a Tuareg plunged a knife into the man's throat and pulled him to the side. Steve was shocked by the unexpected violence but had no time to philosophize about it. More men were coming through the door into the darkness of the corridor, where the Tuaregs knifed and clubbed them into submission. An AK-47 went off as the finger of a dying man tightened on the trigger, causing an indiscriminate spray of bullets to hit walls, ceilings and bodies.

The light was knocked out of Steve's hand during the general free-for-all. He tried to use the stock of his weapon as a club, but bodies were too close together and arms soon grabbed him. He found himself on the ground with his hand closing around a knife and then around his opponent's wrist. Blood made his grip slippery, and he felt rather than saw the knife coming closer to his face. Suddenly, a flashlight came on, a shot rang out and his opponent went limp.

Kella pulled him up. "Are you all right?" she asked.

The surprise of the assault in the dark gave the victory to Steve, Izem and the Tuaregs. The AK-47 bullets had killed one Tuareg; otherwise they escaped with minor wounds. Steve wrapped a shirtsleeve around his hand after Kella, using a borrowed knife, cut the sleeve off.

The small space was filled with the smell of gunpowder and of sweating bodies. Steve's eardrums were still ringing from the painful blow of close-range gunshots. He found his flashlight and gave it to Izem, then motioned toward the computer room. "Bring them all back in here and tie them up, quickly."

"Kella, untie the prisoners." He pointed to the Israelis lying on the floor.

At the same time, as his ears still subdued the sounds around him, including his own voice, he said, "Listen up! This is almost over. Almost! The terrorists have discovered your secret laser weapon and are about to fire it, maybe at Tel Aviv. I need your help to prevent that from happening. Who's going to help save your country from this weapon?"

"We will," a woman said, and she and a man came forward. "I can show you." The man's hair was parted down the middle. Unusually, he wore a tie. The woman was in a white lab coat.

Steve said, "Izem, have two men guard them," pointing to the Salafists. "Bring the rest of your men. This is going to be the final test."

Before he left the computer room, he addressed the freed Israeli hostages. "If any of you have a way to call outside, tell them what's going on. In the meantime, it's best for you to stay here, help guard the prisoners. There's more fighting to come. Kella, how about staying here?"

Kella glanced at Izem, Steve and their small band. "OK, I'll try to find a working phone and call my father at the embassy. The Israelis can try to connect with their government."

Five Israelis came up to him and one said, "We're reservists. If you have guns, we can help."

"There are guns on the floor outside this room. Let's go."

Steve and the two scientists, with Izem, his Tuaregs and the five army reservists, turned left into the corridor, away from the stairs. The beam from Steve's flashlight cut into the darkness.

As they moved, the woman said, "The laser is at the end of this corridor. It's behind a vaulted door and a digital pad. But I can get in."

"Izem, how many fighters do you think are guarding the laser? How many are left?"

"I think five or six. Hussein is still on the roof with maybe five men. So Habib, al Khalil's Tunisian scientist, and probably al Khalil himself, plus five or six fighters."

They soon reached the vaulted door. Steve recognized it from his prior exploration.

"Is this the only entrance?" he asked the woman.

"There is a door in the back, for deliveries of equipment. But I've never been there and I don't have the combination."

Steve told Izem, "When she gets the door open, I'm sure the Salafists are going to make this a killing zone. Anyone who steps through that door is dead." He asked the other Israelis, "Anyone know how to open the door in the back?"

One of the reservists stepped forward. "Yes, it's in back of the cargo platform."

"OK, come and show me. Izem, once this door is open, keep the guys inside busy but don't try to go through. We'll attack from the rear."

Steve took the five Israeli reservists with him and they went to the left using a corridor that Steve had come through. Instead of making a second left toward the back stairs, they made a right toward the back of the building and turned right again at the end of the corridor. They were on a wide wooden platform the height of a truck bed and the length of the building's width. The platform was separated from the outside by two wide sliding metal shutters. There were two doors that led inside from the platform. One was the width of a three-car garage; the other was another vault door.

The reservist pointed to the large door and said, "That one opens from the inside only. This smaller door opens with a number combination and a thumbprint."

Then they heard the noise of machinery, of gears working and of metal grinding against inadequately lubricated metal. The reservist said, "That's the roof opening. That means they're close to firing the laser gun."

Steve pulled him to the vault door. "Go ahead, we have to get in there to stop them."

The reservist slung his weapon over his shoulder and set to work under Steve's flashlight.

Inside, al Kahlil said, "Habib, I don't know what's taking you so long. But that's probably all right. It's giving our brothers in Cairo and Damascus time to either force or negotiate their way into power. I'm going to talk to Salim. Be ready to fire in a few minutes."

He reached Salim almost right away. "Salim, what is the reaction to our second ultimatum? We're getting ready to fire again."

"Algeria is won. El Maghrebi was on TV a few minutes ago. He announced the new Islamic Republic of Algeria. There is fighting in a number of other countries."

"What about Saudi Arabia?"

"The al Saud family is negotiating to hang onto power, but the Wahhabists seem to have the upper hand. It's not a done deal. The royal family is buying them off. No need to laser Cairo. I'm in talks with the president. He has agreed to speak with you directly."

"Have him step down first, in favor of the Ikhwan. You can be the temporary leader until I arrive. Contact the army and prepare an immediate invasion of Israel after I laser Tel Aviv, which will be any minute now."

Steve and his squad were inside. They carried flashlights that revealed the space to be an office on the side of the spacious high-ceilinged portion of the warehouse occupied by the laser. Steve still heard firing at the other end of the warehouse. It had to be Izem keeping al Khalil's shooters at the other end of the laser center. The reservist motioned to their right as they came out of the office. "The control room for the laser is three doors down from here," he said.

The sound from the roof stopped.

As Steve and his men emerged, a fighter in front of the

door identified by the reservist shouted and shouldered his assault rifle immediately. He went down as two of Steve's men fired at him. Steve ran forward with Izem and the others behind him. He reached the door in back of the dead guard, opened it with one hand with his rifle shouldered. Al Khalil and Steve's eyes locked for an instant. Steve stepped inside, firing.

Al Khalil and Steve fired at the same time. Al Khalil's first bullet, fired with the AK-47 held at hip level, crashed into Steve's right side, and the rest of al Khalil's burst went off to Steve's right and up. Steve's short burst punched al Khalil back, stitching him from the groin to the chest. Al Khalil fell against a chair, which toppled over as his body fell to the floor. Habib had his hands raised in the air from the moment that Steve rushed into the control room.

Holding his side, Steve moved toward Habib, his AK-47 still leveled at him. "Close the roof. Shut off the laser."

Steve leaned against a desk in excruciating pain.

It wasn't until he heard the roof move back that he realized that al Khalil's dream of a new Caliphate was over, and that the Salafists' goal of imposing their harsh version of God's law on mankind was also over, for now.

He blacked out.

It was 1603 hours.

CHAPTER FIFTY-FIVE

Marshall had accepted Ambassador Hastings's invitation to stay at his residence until Steve's medical status became clearer. It was Sunday. Hastings, his wife, Alexandra, and Marshall were finishing their lunch at a large dining table.

Alexandra Joulet-Hastings took a sip of her Dutcher Crossing cabernet and said, "I am so relieved this turned out as well as it did. We were so afraid for Kella, and for Steve."

They moved to the living room. Large windows overlooked a patio, a pool, and down below, the beach and the Mediterranean. The inside walls offered a neutral cream backdrop for paintings on loan from the State Department's American Art in Embassies program. Alexandra had chosen a large painting by Bruce Marden, colorful lines on a white background; several smaller works by Marsden Hartley, including one called *Blue Hills*; and another modern work by Joan Mitchell.

Marshall put his glass down. "What's the reporting from Damascus, Jack?"

"The events triggered by al Khalil have given a young set of leaders the momentum to pressure Bashir Assad either to step down or to clean house. We know little about the impact in Iran, since we have no embassy in Tehran. In any case, the gains of the Muslim Brotherhood of the last couple of days have been turned around. But the previous governments are not back in charge either. New leadership seems to be emerging."

Marshall, who had earlier told Hastings that he occasionally did work for the Agency and therefore still had his clearances, said, "An Iranian counterattack was imminent. The Islamic Revolutionary Guard Corps took over after the attack killed Iran's top leadership. General Safavi was on the verge of launching his Shahab-3 missiles against Israel—after all, if the attack came from Israel, it was evident to the Iranians that the Israelis were only using al Khalil's name as a cover for their attack on Tehran. That was the Iranian thinking, anyway. But cooler heads prevailed."

Marshall adjusted his sling and moved his left arm into a more comfortable position. "There's more. The Iranian president was killed in the laser attack. He was in an open-top limousine coming back to his office from some sort of public event, a parade, I think, when the laser struck Tehran. Apparently the heat of the laser made the car's gas tank explode, probably more due to something about the car than due to the strength of the laser, I'm guessing. Couldn't have happened to a nicer guy."

A maid brought coffee. As she poured, Jack Horton, the CIA station chief, was let in by a security guard. "I just had a meeting with Israeli intelligence, and I thought you'd want to hear this, Mr. Ambassador." Hastings invited him to come in and asked Marshall to stay. Alexandra left the room.

"The Israelis have debriefed the Rafael employees and interrogated the terrorists. Each side states that the laser attacks could have caused many more casualties. But both the terrorists and the Israeli scientists seem to want credit for the moderation. Habib, al Khalil's PhD—he was educated in the U.S., by the way—is the one who figured out the weapon and fired it. He claims that he thought that al Khalil's orders were too inhumane, that he, Habib, had never signed on to commit mass murder. So, although he had no choice but to do as he was told, he said, he dragged his feet to delay the second strike. Eventually, as we know, Steve made his escape and stopped the second strike from taking place. We get a similar but different story from the debriefing of the Israeli scientists. One couple in particular, they're husband and wife, said that when they were forced to tell this fellow Habib how the weapon functioned, they intentionally misinformed him on the power settings."

"I'm not surprised," Marshall said. "Human nature at work. Al Khalil's attack has changed the politics of the entire Middle East. We'll be sorting out the positive from the negative for a long time."

Hastings stirred his coffee. "You're right. This provides a window of opportunity that we need to exploit quickly.

Governments from Marrakech to Bangladesh must give their people the hope they now get only from the extremists. Then the Salafists' base, their recruitment pool, will disappear."

Marshall turned toward Hastings. "You're being an optimist. That is not going to be their first priority; short-term survival, clinging to power, is going to trump your program. The first step the Arab governments will take is to try to do away with the Israeli weapon. They can't do it by force of arms, so they'll want to neutralize it through some sort of international weapons disarmament, or try to make it an illegal weapon, like the use of gas warfare after World War I." He added, "This is a wake-up call. I hope that al Khalil's attack will have convinced the world that the Salafists are serious and are playing for keeps. These are not people who want to negotiate."

Alexandra came back into the living room and sat down. "Kella has been through a terrible nightmare. She needs to stay here and decompress for a while. What about Steve—what are his plans?"

Marshall shrugged and said, "I suppose he'll go back to work, but we haven't had a chance to talk yet. I honestly don't know."

Kella stepped into Steve's room at the Ichilov Hospital of the Tel Aviv Medical Center, and before she could speak, Steve said, "Hey, listen to this. They're talking about my departed schoolmate." The TV hung suspended over the bed.

The speaker was a historian from the Jaffee Center for Strategic Studies. "The history of warfare has progressed via a series of epoch-defining developments in weaponry and technology. The stirrup, probably developed by the Chinese sometime during the first few centuries AD, gave mounted horsemen the stability to wield weapons with longer reach and range, using the horse as the first true 'weapons platform.' Later, the hand crossbow was so lethal that

Pope Innocent II forbade its use in 1139 as a machine 'hateful to God and unfit for Christians.'"

Kella sat at the one chair beside the bed. She turned from the TV to Steve and almost said something, but Steve looked at her and put his index finger up to his lips. She sat back and waited for the end of the presentation. Her eyes wandered over the medical equipment beside the bed, which among other things kept tabs on his heartbeat—which was normal, thank God, she thought.

The historian continued about the history of weaponry, some of which Kella found dull until he moved up to weapons she was familiar with. "In the hands of the Japanese in December 1941, the airplane, which had seen only fledgling service in World War I, shifted the balance of naval power across the Pacific in a single week. The submarine, which had first appeared in the last quarter of the eighteenth century, came into its own as a terribly effective weapon of war in World War II. 'Little Boy' and 'Fat Boy,' the first atomic weapons dropped at Hiroshima and Nagasaki in 1945, led to the surrender of the Japanese Empire and the dawn of the nuclear age.

"Military technology stepped into space the day that al Khalil used the Israeli laser against his apostate foes."

Kella smoothed the hair away from Steve's forehead. "How does it feel to have a place in history, to be the guy who stopped al Khalil from sacrificing thousands of people to his ego?"

Steve just shrugged. She imagined it was too much to take in yet.

"The full story hasn't leaked out yet, how close al Khalil came to firing that second strike. But that's not why I'm here. How are you feeling? Ready to go home?"

"As soon as they let me out. Are you coming with me? To Virginia, I mean."

"Do I look like a nurse? Only when you're fully rehabilitated."

"Well, everything works just fine right now. Lock the door and I'll give you a test run."

She pouted. "If everything 'worked' "—she placed quotations marks in the air in front of her—"your heartbeat should be much faster when I'm in the room."

He laughed and immediately winced, placing his hand against the left side of his chest. "Come here," he said, and tugged her in for a kiss.

"You are lucky to be alive. I just spoke to the doctor. He said that the bullet hit a rib and was diverted, or it could have hit your heart. I brought you some newspapers, by the way."

Steve picked one up and scanned the front page. "Listen to this. An influential moderate imam is calling for a joint international fatwa against the radicals. He said that Islam is a great religion and must not fear the twenty-first century, and also that a good Muslim need not revert to practices that made sense a thousand years ago."

Kella took the paper and glanced at it. "Well, it's a start. The Muslim moderates have been the silent majority. If they take charge of their future, the radicals are history." She paused a second and, with a gleam in her eyes and a smile, said, "Did you ask me about travel plans? I have some loose ends to take care of in Paris, and then I'm on my way to Virginia, ready or not."